Soulbound

SOULBOUND (The Republic 4)
By Archer Kay Leah

Published by Ashborne Stardust Press

Second edition, August 2019
First published by Less Than Three Press, 2018

Cover designed by Natasha Snow Designs; www.natashasnowdesigns.com

Map designed by Raelynn Marie

Print ISBN 978-0-9958275-8-5

Content Notes, Warnings, and Disclaimers

Soulbound contains some explicit content, all of which is meant for adult readers. While the main relationship is MM, there is an MMF relationship that overlaps with it.

This story touches on several matters related to mental health and depictions of emotional and physical situations that could bother some readers. This includes references to and depictions of self-harm, suicide, and mentions of suicide-related behavior and intent. There are also depictions of depression, PTSS/PTSD and complex PTSS/PTSD (post-traumatic stress syndrome/disorder), survivor's guilt, and complications with pregnancy.

The story also contains instances of graphic violence, references to rape and domestic abuse, mentions of human trafficking, references to torture in a character's past, and an attack using explosive devices, as well as descriptions of the aftermath.

Finally, this story includes brief references to transphobia in a character's past.

Please note the story uses the gender-neutral pronouns *ce* and *cir* for one of the characters. These are not mistakes: they are the chosen pronouns of that character.

To Chester Bennington, with my love to Linkin Park, their families, friends, and fans.

Thank you for the music and words that have helped so many of us cope. Thank you for the inspiration and your wealth of creativity. Thank you for sharing your gifts with the world.

Gone, but not forgotten.

And for anyone who's stared into that dark abyss, looking at the end. You're never truly alone. Keep fighting, the best you can. Keep trying. You're needed and wanted, even if you don't know it yet.

Acknowledgements

This story met several challenges during its crafting, and it couldn't have gotten this far without help. My deepest, heartfelt thanks to Hudson Lin for braving the manuscript as a beta reader and offering pointers on where it needed more attention, and to Victoria Miles for the never-ending support as a friend, fan, and for being part of the family in this household.

Warm thanks, also, to A.M. Valenza for the help when I freaked out during my edits so close to the holidays. Thanks for being so patient, generous, and for the advice!

And finally, but never least, thank you to Sam Derr, Megan Derr, and Sasha Miller for all of their support and for giving this book (and me) its original literary home at Less Than Three Press, where I didn't have to hold back or restrain the muses. Thanks for a place where we could belong and for giving the entire series the wings to fly. None of these books would've happened without you! <3

Soulbound

THE REPUBLIC BOOK 4

ARCHER KAY LEAH

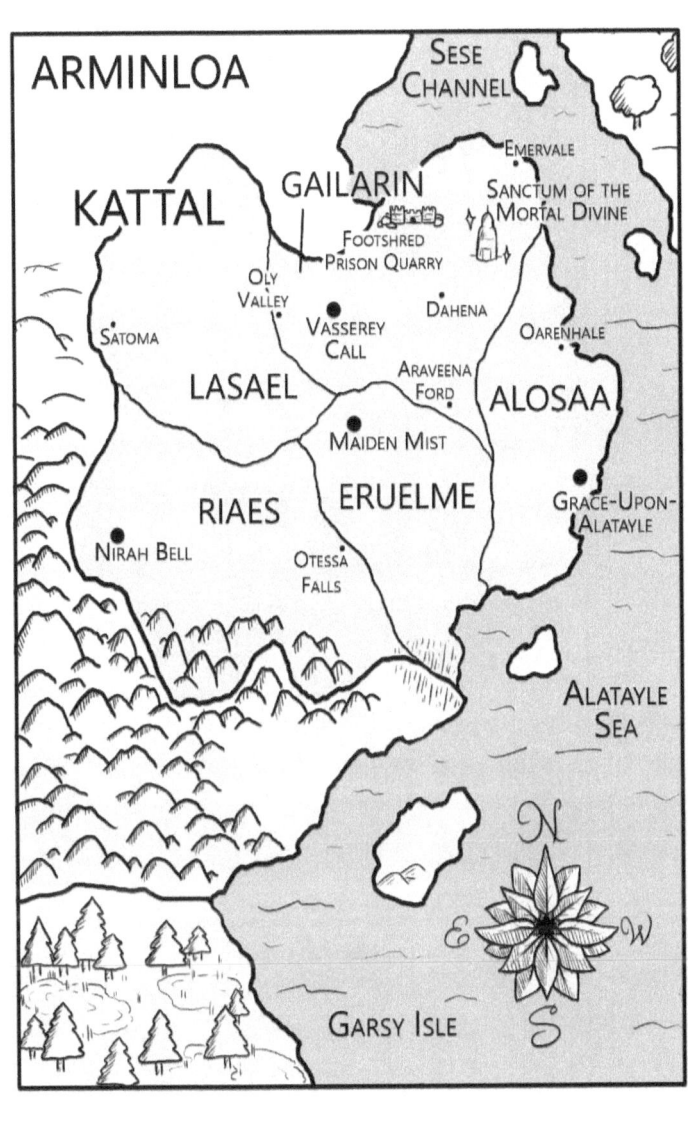

ARMINLOA

SESE
CHANNEL

EMERVALE

GAILARIN

KATTAL

SANCTUM OF THE
MORTAL DIVINE

FOOTSHRED
PRISON QUARRY

OLY
VALLEY

DAHENA

SATOMA

VASSEREY
CALL

OARENHALE

LASAEL

ARAVEENA
FORD

ALOSAA

MAIDEN MIST

ERUELME

RIAES

GRACE-UPON-
ALATAYLE

NIRAH BELL

OTESSA
FALLS

ALATAYLE
SEA

N

E

W

GARSY ISLE

S

Chapter One

"Are we done dying yet? *Please* tell me we're done and dead."

Mayr snorted at Aeley Dahe's question as she crossed the study and threw herself into the chair behind her desk. She yanked a thick red and yellow-striped blanket over herself and hid beneath it, dark blonde hair and all. Only her elbow peeked out from beneath to lean against the arm of her chair, the deep brown and green fabric of her tunic sombre compared to the bright blanket and dark red walls of the study. The rest of her black and brown travel attire was strewn across the golden-brown rugs that covered the floor, haphazard piles of soggy fabric abandoned between him and the fire in the hearth.

"If I say yes, does that mean you'll spend the rest of this afterlife nattering my ear off? Or can I get a nap first?" Mayr retorted before he launched into a fit of sneezes. Rogue strands of his long black hair caught on the bronze clasps of his heavy black cloak. Drops of melted snow fell around him, adding to the mess on the already slick floor. Somehow he managed to unlace his cloak and toss it into the chair beside the stained-glass window to his right. He fumbled as he unbuckled the belt strapped across his chest, happy to have the weight of his sword off his back. His hands were painfully numb and red as he laid his sword over his cloak. "Next time, when you think it's a great idea to visit a prison, *don't go when it's snowing*."

"And don't take you," Aeley added, turning her head. Even with her face covered, he knew she was making a face at him, tongue out, eyes crossed. If only the weather had frozen *that*. She may have been Tract Steward, but he would pay handsomely to see her stuck like that for a day. As her best friend and head of her family guard, it was only fair.

"Yeah, take Pellon," he said, flexing his fingers. "He likes freezing his balls. He loves warming them up afterwards even more."

Aeley snorted a laugh, followed by a groan. "Why didn't we bring *blankets*?" She whimpered and dropped her head back.

"Don't look at me. I don't do weather."

"No, you just do your guy. Hard." Aeley peeled back the corner of the blanket to reveal one of her brown eyes. "You'll break his back one of these days, you and your hips of thrusting greatness."

Mayr tore off his black scarf and tossed it at her, hissing as his fingers tingled and protested. The scarf landed on the floor in front of her desk in a limp pile. She *had* to remind him of Tash right then. *Just when I'd forgotten about what I promised…*

He wanted to be back out in the cold, cramped inside a freezing carriage. Or at Footshred prison, interrogating prisoners and rubbing their faces in the freedom they would never have. Or wasting time with Severn, the one councilman on High Council who hated him most in all the republic and wanted his head for a paperweight.

Anywhere else but home.

No, anywhere else but near *Tash*, the one person Mayr wanted to press up against and lose himself in for the rest of the day, wrapped up in warmth and desire and need.

And he has so much need.

"So are you going to tell him?"

Mayr blinked at the question, the words lost to him.

"Let's try that again," Aeley said slowly, flicking back the blanket until it settled in her lap. "Are you going to tell Tash everything about today?" She tugged up the sleeves of her tunic and lifted her legs onto the desk before crossing them at the ankles. Her muddy brown boots hung over the corner as she folded her arms and leaned back. "After all, it's the two of you I have to thank for these lovely talks with a gang family and chatting up Severn for crime numbers."

"We had help," Mayr mumbled. He stared at the fire, chewing on the inside of his cheek as unwelcome memories crashed through his unthawed thoughts.

"Mm, I remember. All the more reason to tell him everything. Him, Ress, Adren—they know how nasty the Shar-denn is. They're going to be running from it for the rest of their lives, I imagine."

"Yeah, I know." Mayr sighed and pinched the bridge of his nose. His headache was back. Then again, anything to do with the Shar-denn brought on any number of headaches, particularly when he considered the events that had led them to this point.

One event stood out from the rest, its three-week-old images on a continual loop inside his mind: a fight he should have seen coming, sprawled out inside Ress's house in Araveena Ford, the town where Tash and Ress had grown up as best friends and family. More than that, they had also been brothers in the Shar-denn, a brutal gang that continued to plague their republic of Kattal from one generation to the next. A gang they had both betrayed in their own ways.

Adren had planned to kill Ress on behalf of the Shar-denn, determined to punish him for his part in the arrest of Adren's family, but nothing had played out as expected. Although Adren started with the intention to avenge cir family, ce changed cir mind. After that, everything fell apart: Adren and Ress forged a romantic connection and decided to run from the gang, inspired by Tash's successful defection. When

Ress had called upon Tash to help them leave, Tash agreed and asked Mayr to do the same.

Their agreement came with a price: a brawl with members of the Shar-denn that injured not only Ress, but Tash, Mayr, and the others they had enlisted to help.

Just when Mayr had hoped the Shar-denn would never harm Tash again, they charged in with a wallop.

And now I hate myself because of what we have to do—what he *has to do. If he's ever going to stand a chance at protecting Adren from whatever comes for cir, he's going to have to fight back.* Him, *a priest, a speaker of peace, a soother of soul-sucking ailments—and* I *have to train him. Today. Now.*

He wanted to hide in Aeley's study forever.

As if she read his mind, she stared at him and wagged her finger at the door. Mayr let out a defeated sigh. They both had things to do.

"Sorry," Aeley said, swinging down her legs. "I'm sure you'd *love* to sit here and watch me read, but I need to concentrate." She smiled and tossed her long hair over her shoulder. "I'll see you at dinner, though."

"Of course." Mayr spun on his heel and crossed the room to the door. "If I see your wife, I'll let her know you're stealing her job and assaulting another quill."

Aeley laughed and waved him from the study. He obeyed without another word, knowing how much work she had, as if it ever ended. Although it was true: her work never *would* end as long as she was Tract Steward of Gailarin, their sizeable region in the republic for which she was responsible. Under the High Council's watchful authority, she managed everything that pertained specifically to Gailarin, from its citizens and finances to its resources and political games. There were always documents, always meetings, always someone in need of something. Gailarin did not run itself.

His thoughts, on the other hand, ran wide and far without any assistance from him. They whirled with possibility, every one of them a fleeting item on a subconscious list meant to tease and distract. If anything, they were delusions of urgency that ranted and railed against each other, flinging their heres and theres in a melee for attention. *Yes, no, to the left, to the right, check the guards, take a nap, make for the kitchen, run for dear life, let it all out…*

One thought. He needed to grasp onto one single thought.

Mayr stepped into the chilly hallway, hesitant as he closed the door to the study. With a hard yank on the gold handle, he waited for the latch to click before he let go, satisfied the dark red door would not creak open and bother Aeley. She needed to relax after their trip, not battle unwelcome gusts thanks to a door that begged to be replaced.

I'd tell her someone should replace it, but that

someone would probably be me, and I'm not allowed near hammers. Cupping both hands around his mouth, he breathed out and rubbed his bare hands together, willing the heat to remain in them. The study was warm thanks to the housekeepers, but the rest of the Dahe estate felt as though an ice spirit had moved in and built itself a palace.

All right, slight *exaggeration. It might have more to do with traveling in the storm after the frigid hospitality of my favourite politician. Here's to hoping I thaw out soon—Tash won't let me touch him like this.*

Mayr stilled, hands clasped in the air. Even when his thoughts trounced every bit of reason, his mind returned to Tash, his constant, his grounding point. The bit of rational thought that was so irrational he felt as if he stood in the eye of the hottest, wildest storm. Wrapped in the safety of the calm, he could watch the turmoil and destruction of the outside world as time crawled by.

And he had promised to throw punches at his one constant, making the effort to challenge him until one of them cried for mercy.

"I'll cry it now. Save us both the trouble," Mayr muttered, shoving his hands into the deep pockets of his black leather long coat. Its wet hem dragged along the floor as he shuffled up the hallway to his right. As he passed the empty meeting rooms, he stared at the grey and black stone floor, noting the cracks in the masonry and the unevenness in the spiraled patterns. Absentminded and desperate to hold something, he played with the damp gloves in his pockets, their tight-knit wool exteriors and thick leather interiors black like the rest of his clothes.

A shiver raced through him, roused by fears of what awaited in the training room downstairs. While his job as Head of the Guard was to secure the safety of everyone in the Dahe household and family, there were times he wished he could trade places with someone who did not love the people he did—someone who had no qualms with fighting with them for their own good, teaching them defensive strikes and offensive strategy. Although Pellon was a trustworthy second-in-command and close friend who would happily take Mayr's place in training, the responsibility was too heavy to shrug off. Love was even heavier.

I have to put them into the position to get hurt so they can be protected. That's the saddest, most backwards catch I've ever heard. Who came up with that bright idea? He stopped halfway through the corridor to peer out the windows looking onto the courtyard. Frost clouded the edges of the red windowpanes, framing the blustery, sunlit image of snow and harsh wind with a crystalline glint. The naked, heavy branches of the red trees swayed, staking claim as the only sign of life in the yard. Every few moments, the broken end of one branch tapped the windows in an erratic rhythm. The storm was surprisingly violent for the first snowfall of the year.

Grateful to have arrived home before the worst of it, Mayr flicked his glance to the seat below the windows. Set against the wall and built to accommodate two people, the dark red seat was cushioned with bright green and deep purple pillows. Someone had draped a grey and green quilt across one corner and a brown wool blanket across the other. The sight was tempting, inviting him to sit and think about something else other than Tash or meetings.

"No time to sit. Day's too long to even think about it." He pulled the tangled tail of his black hair over his shoulder and dragged his fingers through, yanking on the tats. Dignitaries from three villages in the south would arrive before nightfall for dinner with Aeley and a discussion about commerce, meaning he would have to look polished. That required more than a simple brush and change of clothes. Maybe he could entice Tash into a bath after they trained…

Mayr scrunched his nose. He enjoyed the sweat and heat of training, but the thought of harming Tash knotted his stomach. Since his adolescence, he had enjoyed the physicality of sparring, appreciating its challenges and the way it worked off emotions.

This was different. His desire salivated at the chance to try it with Tash. He wanted to watch

Tash go through the motions, to taste the power and strength in Tash and sense the danger. To be at Tash's mercy in the ring the same as he was when Tash made love to him.

None of it chased his anxiety away. Twice before, he had found Tash bruised and battered. Just as many times, Tash had almost died in front of him. Even though Tash was neither fragile nor incapable, a too-hard grip or wayward hit could ruin his life.

Still, he wanted Tash to prove his skills and show his harder side. He had missed seeing that roughness when they were in Araveena Ford, fighting to save Ress from being killed by the Shar-denn.

It was that same side of Tash that forced Mayr to work harder to protect Tash from himself. While he had not witnessed Tash deal blows during the confrontation, he was familiar with the consequences, having seethed over Tash's injuries for days. Dark bruises had marred Tash's skin for two weeks, and his knuckles had bled from scrapes and cuts. If Tash had not slept alone at the temple instead of the estate, Mayr would have raged over the wounds worse than he had.

Which is why we're training, my sappy, smitten self. This whole thing with Ress and Adren and keeping their asses alive is all the reason I need. It's the joy of contradiction wrapped up in the pretty trappings of love. Mayr sighed, drawing both hands down his face. The events in Araveena Ford were more of a turning point than he could admit to anyone. Although he had gone to the village on Tash's request, unable to refuse Tash's plea to help Ress, he returned with more than criminals and a reason for the High Council to punish him. Regret haunted him, its ghost screeching obscenities between his thoughts. He could have lost Tash that night. A punch to the head, a knife to the throat, a broken neck—one wrong move could have torn them apart. Given Tash's stubbornness and near-limitless sense of duty, violence and death could still separate them.

The fight was not all that bothered him. Since then, his head had been a mess and his heart even messier. Everything inside was rattled, his decisions pulled in all directions. His wants and hopes and needs knotted together until they were indistinguishable. Instinct demanded he do everything to make Tash happy, no matter the cost. No matter what had to be surrendered.

Yet fear commanded he do nothing at all. Fear that he would hurt Tash, breaking him in ways Mayr swore he never would. Fear of being hurt *by* Tash, his heart smashed by the one lover who took Mayr for who he was.

Fear that everything they wanted would never be.

Metal clinked, ripping Mayr from his worry. He peered up the corridor to the hallway at the end, first skimming the stairwell in the right corner, then the rest of the hall to the left.

Squeaky footfalls sounded, followed by quiet whistling. Both became distant as someone walked the north hall, away from where Mayr was in the east hall.

Nothing like the sound of someone on patrol, Mayr mused with a smirk. In the last day, he had doubled patrols and swapped schedules, pairing specific guards in teams and moving others to new locations and times. The changes were necessary, since Ress now lived at the estate along with Adren, who had also become Tash's charge due to cir magic and special lineage. Like Tash, both Ress and Adren had worked for the gang most of their lives. They knew too much, making them too valuable to lose. Given the Shar-denn's temper and their promise to kill members who defected, Mayr had increased security around them and the estate in hopes it kept the gang away. The Shar-denn would never take Tash again or anyone he loved—a promise Mayr would die to keep.

Mayr's lingering headache flared. Palms pressed to his temples, he squeezed his eyes shut against the list of things to do by day's end. He needed to amend the roster of guards. The recent changes were not good enough.

"One of those days, is it?" a voice asked from behind him, the feminine tone edged with amusement. "Maybe I'll go find you something that doesn't taste like rotten eggs to chase the feeling away."

An effortless smile spread across Mayr's lips. "Depends," he said, turning towards Lira Dahe. His glance flitted over her white shawl and rich mauve gown, its subtle red tinge visible where the dim sunlight hit. "If Cook's made some of those mincemeat tarts she was threatening to throw at me, the day might just clear up fine." He winked at her. "Keep me well fed, don't forget my sweet tooth, and I'll be the happiest fool walking."

"I'm sure—walking yourself straight into death by food." Lira clasped a brown leather-bound book to her chest and shook her head. Strands of her dark brown hair slipped from the jeweled combs keeping the loose curls out of her face. "I'd say someone should starve you, but I'm sure a certain priest would disagree. I suppose you're *his* sweet tooth?"

"Maybe. Tash *does* like to—"

Lira raised her hand. The layered mauve cuffs of her heavy gown fell back, exposing pale tan skin. As usual, black ink stained her fingers. "Wait, don't answer. I hear enough from your room when he's home."

Home. The word twisted Mayr's gut and stabbed his lacking resolve. It sounded normal coming from her, as though Tash lived with them instead of splitting his time between the estate and the temple at the edge of the village. One day, maybe Tash would consider the estate home. Maybe he would consider Mayr's bed his own and agree to live together permanently. *Assuming*

I ever find the courage to ask him.

Mayr stared at Lira, wanting to tell her everything. If only he could say the words. Aeley hated when he kept his thoughts to himself, and Lira was no more tolerant. While Aeley had every reason to berate him, having known him since they were eleven years old, Lira was a new friend with equal sway on his decisions. Lira had earned his trust after she married Aeley and supported her during the rough start of Aeley's term as Tract Steward. They were his sisters by choice rather than by blood, and he served them the best he could.

Still, he could not tell her what weighed on him when he should have been worrying about that night's dinner plans.

"Good to know we have an audience." Mayr swallowed the bile of his cowardice and grinned. "I'll make sure we scream extra loud tonight. Have to keep our admirers happy."

Lips pursed, Lira cast him a skeptical glance. "Entertained, maybe. *Maybe.*" She stepped past him and sank onto the window seat. As she fussed with her gown and shawl, the multiple skirts beneath her dress peeked out from under the hem, each layer a different shade of mauve. Born to the Derossa family, one of the influential Grand Families in Kattal, Lira's prim appearance marked her as a member of the higher caste. She always looked proper, always played her part, even if only in presentation. Unlike the rest of the

Derossas, she was disinterested in power and wealth. Content to work as Aeley's scribe, Lira asked for little.

Meanwhile, Aeley gave her everything. Despite the challenges Aeley's position threw at them, their marriage did not suffer. They worked together, often deriving solutions to fix Gailarin's problems through their unified partnership. Gailarin had thrived under the control of Aeley's father, Korre, the previous Tract Steward. Since his death, the region continued to prosper under Aeley's governance. With time and encouragement, Aeley was becoming the leader Mayr had always expected her to be. She stood strong for the nation of Kattal, no matter what.

And I'll be here as long as she is.

He never wanted to be anywhere else. His place was with Aeley, protecting her and those she guarded. A piece of him had always known his family's farm would never be his life's work. Just as his heart belonged to matters of defence, he would die with a weapon in his hand and fight in his spirit.

Let the Shar suck on that. If they want Tash, Ress, or Adren, they'll have to work for it so hard their ancestors will cry for mercy.

"You've got that face on," Lira said softly, laying her book on the pillow beside her. She drew the grey quilt around her shoulders and curled up on the cushions. "Was the meeting with Severn that bad? Or was it the prison? Did

Adren's family say anything useful?"

Mayr snorted. "I don't think nasty names and 'get out of my face' counts as useful."

"So nothing about what the Shar-denn will do now, I take it?"

"No, things about them were brought up in our meetings, just not what we expected." Mayr sighed, long and deep, then crossed his arms and rolled his shoulders to stretch his back. "It's been a long couple of days, that's all. More than a couple, considering the Feast of Taleyra was a few days ago. I still haven't recovered from that whole thing. Dancing diplomats, whimsical worshippers, merry musicians—too much happy for the first day of winter. Not to mention someone was sick all over my favourite staircase *twice*. I had to *clean it*." He stuck out his tongue. "I'm only thirty-one, Li. I'm too young to feel this bloody old. Tell me I'm not going grey already," he whined with a pitiful whimper, grappling at his hair.

Lira laughed, the light sound echoing in the hallway. "Better you than me. At least you'll look dashing. I'll just look a mess."

"Yeah, but you'll be a pretty mess. *Pretty* beats dashing."

"Says…?"

"Aeley."

"Ah. Guess that's settled."

"Hey, not my rules." Mayr raised both hands. "I say what I know and do what I'm told."

"Like make Councilman Severn so angry she wants your head for a mantelpiece?"

Mayr's lips formed a silent *oh*. His relationship with Severn, the councilman in charge of Kattal's public safety, had not improved since Ress and Adren's liberation from the Shar-denn. The tone he took at Ress and Adren's first hearing had yet to be forgotten, especially by Severn. She had requested that Aeley formerly reprimand him in front of the entire Dahe guard and the High Council—a request Aeley had denied.

"About that..." Mayr scratched the back of his neck, cold nails digging lightly into the black tattoos around his neck. "I may have apologized again today. Severn may or may not have heard it. At least she let me into her office this time. I was even served water. In a goblet. That was clean."

"Well, there's progress." Lira tilted her head. "Seriously, are you all right? Do we have to be worried?"

"Not about that," Mayr answered quietly. Arms folded, he leaned against the wall. "I'm just being difficult for the sake of being a pain. I blame the weather." He nodded at the windows. "It was clear when we left for the prison before dawn. Then this mess started around noon on our way home from High Council Hall. Don't know if this'll change our dinner plans, but Ae's more concerned about getting the paperwork done—something about villages in the east needing to sort costs for rebuilding."

"And?"

"*And* maybe I'm still getting used to our new arrivals."

"Ress and Adren?"

"I know we moved them in yesterday, but it'll take me time to get used to it." Mayr stepped closer to Lira, his voice lowered as he leaned forward, leaving little space between them. "It was one thing when they lived at the temple, but now… It feels like I have to be everywhere at once, doing my job four times over. I *know* they're safer here, but it makes me anxious, and I can't tell him," he whispered. "I can't tell Tash how on edge I am. It'll break his heart if we don't keep them safe. He loves Ress like a brother."

"I know. I have my reservations, too." Lira caressed his shaven cheek. "We'll get through it. In this house, we keep stubbornness and hope in abundance. How about you tell me how the meetings went? I'll let you rant about Severn and frustrating prisoners if it makes you feel better."

Mayr chuckled as he pulled away. "Tempting." He shrugged. "The meeting with the prison warden was a friendly chat over breakfast. The meeting with Adren's father and mother was grimy but not productive. They're set on taking the Shar's secrets to their deaths. The meeting with Adren's brothers—that was lively, but they didn't say one thing we could use. No names, no directions, no locations. Nothing."

"So if they aren't talking to Council or to you and Aeley, what happens to them?"

"Their trials continue and Council will likely vote to execute them for treason, slavery, murder, and every possible crime there is against Kattal. I don't know what else they'll do, other than send in Adren to ask questions."

"Throw Adren into a cell with the family ce's betrayed and watch them tear cir apart?" Lira scowled and crossed her arms. "That sounds damaging. Adren's already having enough trouble getting over abandoning cir family. I don't think that's going to be helpful."

"It could be. If they're enraged enough, they'll slip. If they drop the name of even one gang member, I'll take it. We need to round up these vile chunks of filth. They can't keep hurting people, stealing stuff, and breaking laws." Mayr scraped his boot heel across the floor and frowned at the wet streak it left. "We might as well do it now while the gang's gone quiet."

"'Gone quiet'? So Aeley's observations were right?"

"There's the interesting part." Mayr let out a loud breath, frustrated as he played with his gloves. The news should have made him happy, not spun his suspicions around a spool of doubt. "Ae's not the only one who's noticed a lull in the Shar's activity. Severn said she's noticed crime rates have gone *down* since we saved Ress and Adren, not up like we expected. Rathen and Kirra said they and the rest of the bounty hunters are seeing the same thing. They aren't bringing in so many criminals, and citizens aren't reporting as many incidents. It's just... quiet."

"That's *great* news." Lira smiled, though her glance questioned him. "Wouldn't it mean that everything the Council's done is working? That all the information Tash, Ress, and Adren gave them is doing what it should and the hunters are good at their job?"

"Maybe."

"Maybe?"

"It's hard to tell."

"Apparently it's just as difficult to smile about it."

"I'd smile if I weren't so confused." Mayr drew his fingers over one of the knives on the belt around his waist, comforted by the feel of a weapon. It was bad enough he had forgotten his sword and cloak in Aeley's study. "It's been three weeks since Ress and Adren defected. We should've seen retaliation by now—riots and raids, death threats, ransoms. *Something*." He squeezed the hilt of his knife. "The child of a faction boss doesn't run off without someone coming for them. By all rights, Adren and Ress should be dead."

"So this means what?"

"I don't know. I thought maybe Aeley was only seeing things in the numbers, but maybe the gang's taking a break. Or maybe we really have scared them. Maybe it's because Adren's family isn't in charge of their faction anymore—I don't know."

"Somewhere in there is a 'but.'"

Mayr twisted his lips. She knew him too well. "It'll pick up again soon. This break won't last. Maybe there's no reason—maybe things are just off. I'm still stuck on why they haven't attacked Araveena. They *love* intimidating the village, or so Ress says."

"You sent half a dozen of our guards to Araveena, and Severn is rotating them with republic soldiers," Lira said, one of her dark brows arched. "You told them to protect Tash and Ress's families and *be visible*. I'd think that has something to do with it."

"I didn't expect it to work *this* well," Mayr mumbled. He had expected a backlash similar to those Ress witnessed after Tash left the Shardenn: assaulted citizens, threats sent to Araveena Ford's magistrate, and any manner of revenge. Yet no one had been harmed. Was it the increased presence of soldiers, or had the Shar-denn decided attacking the village was useless? He prayed it was the latter.

Lira crooked her finger, beckoning him to her. "I'm not good at this business," she said as he leaned down to look her in the eye, "so maybe your instincts are right. What I *do* know is you can't live today if you're paralyzed by tomorrow." She tapped the tip of his nose. "We're alive, all of us, and a delightful priest is waiting for you downstairs. Deal with the Shar-denn later. For now, take the good you have and find peace. You need it."

As Lira drew away, Mayr nodded. Despite his doubts, he heard her, and for all of his stubbornness, he could not disagree. Tash's safety could not wait, nor could Mayr's need to calm the turmoil inside. Changes were coming—and maybe the changes started with them.

Mayr stuck to the doorframe as though his bones were nailed to the wood. He leaned harder against the frame, his folded arms tightening the longer he watched the scene before him.

In the centre of the bright, lantern-lit training room, Tash moved steadily through a series of stances and restrained strikes. His breaths were as even and controlled as the gentle glide of his arms and slow steps away from the door. Focused on the furthest wall, Tash remained inside the small white circle painted on the floor, the smallest ring inside the set of six concentric white, yellow, and red rings used for training. Barefoot and stripped to the waist, Tash wore only skin-coloured bracers and the loose, dark red pants of his religious vestments. The fabric was the brightest, most delicate thing in the room compared to the grey stone walls, the dull sets of metal and leather armour on upright wooden forms, and the metallic gleam of the weapons on the racks hanging on each wall.

Nothing compared to how beautiful Tash looked lost in the concentration of a warrior's meditation. Sections of his wavy hair were pulled back, the shoulder-length brown locks and blond streaks tied with a coiled and knotted black ribbon, a hand's length of which was left trailing. Not as brawny as Mayr, Tash's light tan skin strained while his muscles worked. The tattoo of a bird spanned his entire back, wings outstretched over his broad shoulders. The twisted body followed his spine and its outspread talons appeared to dig into his lower back. A crown of feathers cascaded across his right shoulder blade, as elegant as the tail that meandered around both of his hips. Meticulously detailed and shaded with black ink, the feathers appeared real.

Mayr needed little creativity to imagine how Tash used to look as a guard for a gang boss. With even less effort, he could guess at what sparring might do to Tash's physique now.

Not that I haven't nipped and licked and sucked every bit of him. Recalling the sensation of Tash's stomach tightening under his tongue, Mayr bit back a groan. After the talk with Lira, he had dragged himself downstairs and forced himself into a professional mindset.

One glimpse of Tash made keeping that

mindset impossible. *Goddesses know I could take him right now. One touch, one kiss—*

Mayr shuffled his feet and peered into the dimly lit hallway, wishing that alone could alleviate the twisting in his groin. There was a time for play, but this was duty and a chance to put his love to work. It was not enough to profess his feelings; he needed to show them. He wanted to make the last year and a half with Tash mean more than passing time and trading affection. While he treasured those moments, he yearned to give everything and hold back nothing. If anything, he wanted them to give up their solitary paths and build a life together.

Except I had that kind of life with Betta and it completely fell apart. I didn't even know what was going on. If it happens again, it'll be so much worse. If he leaves…

They could lose everything.

How is settling for having nothing any better? It's not fair to Tash when all he's done is give a damn. Disgusted, Mayr pushed off the doorframe and entered the room.

"Mind if I join? I hear it's more exciting with two people." Mayr crossed the room to the four chairs lined up at the end of the wall to his left. A pile of red robes lay over the back of one of the chairs. On the chair beside it was Tash's veil, the glimmering red fabric carefully arranged to avoid touching the floor.

Tash spun around and grinned as he lowered

his arms. "You finally got tired of watching. I was wondering what I'd have to do to entice you."

"You've done more than enough, thanks," Mayr muttered. He shrugged off his long coat and tossed it over one of the empty chairs. "I already need a cold bath."

"Pitching you into the snow naked should be sufficient."

Tempted by a dozen inappropriate answers, Mayr expected his mouth to ramble off words that sounded smart.

He stared at Tash instead, every coherent word lost. Bright blue eyes gazed back, intense and breathtaking. Mayr's fingers twitched, driven by his yearning to caress the curves of Tash's face. His skin screamed to feel Tash's lips, to be teased by his close-cropped beard. He wanted to feel Tash in all the right ways. *For a moment, maybe two. Just three measly moments —*

"You need to continue undressing," Tash said softly. "If we don't do this now, you won't want to later."

"How's that so bad?" Mayr unbuckled both of his belts. He slung the belt with four knives over the back of a chair, followed by his second, unarmed belt. With slow fingers, he unlaced his thick vest and stripped it off, then discarded it over the last chair. Just as slowly, he removed his long-sleeved tunic and dropped it on top of the vest. "We could just say we did it, right?"

"Mayr."

In playful retribution for Tash's not-so-playful scolding tone, Mayr stuck out his tongue.

Tash smirked. "Don't put it out if you're not putting it to use. I might just take this body home."

Mayr shrank back with a scowl. "Stop spending time with Aeley. You're starting to sound like her." To the sound of Tash's throaty laugh, Mayr yanked his lightweight shirt over his head and threw it down, adding to the pile of black fabric. Cool air danced over his naked chest, raising small bumps along his arms to his bracers. Shivers rushed through him as he unlaced his black, shin-high boots without withdrawing the knives from the sheaths sewn inside. "Yeah, sure, laugh," he said, pulling off one boot and stocking. "Next thing you know, you'll be moving in and going around like you own the place."

He froze, his bare foot in the air, the boot clenched in his hand. That was *not* what he had meant to say.

"Maybe one day I will," Tash murmured as he turned away.

Good job, self. Mayr dropped his boot and jerked off the other, the stocking coming off with it. *Next time, I should try asking him to marry me. He'll probably think I'm joking—again. Because every time I go to say it, some pathetic comment comes out. Meanwhile, all I want to do is tell him he means everything.*

Mayr kicked his boots against the wall,

tempted to slap the wall for good measure. He was a fool, but he knew why.

Giving into habit, he toyed with the locket and thread ring on the gold chain around his neck. He had been a husband once, his heart given to Betta for her safe keeping. Enamoured by her cheerful, addictive personality, he had loved her deeply, his head spinning with fanciful notions of a future together. They married when he was twenty, and she gave birth to their daughter, Iliane, months later, filling him with a joy that had no equal. Their family was worth everything he had to do to keep them happy. He gave them all he could, including his devotion and trust.

In return, Betta smashed, burned, and then crushed his heart into tiny flakes of hurt.

One year after their wedding, he was less than divorced: he was told they had never been legally married to begin with. Their private marriage ceremony in the forest had meant nothing. The priest that presided over the ceremony had been a fake. Their relationship had been a sham, and Betta had sent Iliane away before running away herself. On top of it all, there was the sad truth that Iliane was not his child by blood, but the daughter of Betta's lover.

For all his commitment and honesty, Betta had never given him the same, not until recently.

Betta may have apologized for everything, but it doesn't make it unhappen. It doesn't make me trust people any easier. Mayr slipped the chain over his head and cupped the gold locket in his palm. The only good thing to have come from their fake marriage was Iliane, the sweetest lie he had ever been told. When Betta had sent her away for reasons that still made no sense to him, he had never expected to see Iliane again.

Tash's gentle intervention had changed their fate. Without spite, without shaming, Tash had reunited them, a family broken by misguided youth. Betta was married and happy, steadfast in motherhood. Iliane was safe and loved, thriving with the attention and joy that were rightfully hers. Now twelve years old, Iliane had a heart large enough to love everyone and lived each day as though it would never end. Mayr was part of her life once more, welcome to love her as though he were still her father. *Despite the fact she'll never consider herself my daughter.*

He hung the chain on one of the pegs screwed into the wall meant to keep jewelry safe whenever guards trained. Of all the things he owned, the locket and ring were the most invaluable. Betta had given him the locket with Iliane's image inside, a gift meant to convey apology more than words could.

The ring, on the other hand, was innocence knotted into colourful bands. The purple, red, and gold threads were a token of Iliane's inner beauty and kindness. The circumstances in which she had given it to him still brought tears to his eyes. Not only had he done nothing to earn it, he had been a stranger to her.

You're so much better than me, Ili. Don't ever lose that. Mayr kissed his fingertips and pressed them to the ring. He would see her again in a week, a promise Betta had kindly made.

Right now, I need to keep my promise. After a slight twist on his black leather bracers and the tightening of his hair tie, Mayr spun on his heel and approached Tash. If Tash was going to fulfill his oath to protect Adren, they needed to ensure Tash was skilled enough. Tash may have held his own in the fight in Araveena Ford, but Mayr had to see it for himself.

Stopped before him, Mayr cupped Tash's jaw and stroked his cheek with his thumb. His heart raced as Tash leaned into the touch with a sigh. He hated the idea of Tash fighting. Priesthood aside, Tash had worked hard to build a peaceful life after years of anger and harm. Returning to what he used to be was wrong, regardless of Tash's adamant decision to serve as Adren's guardian. Tash wanted a tranquil existence, a choice Mayr fully supported.

I just want to take care of you. Mayr pressed flush against Tash, trapping the heat of their skin between them. *I don't trust Ress or Adren. I definitely can't trust either of them to save you when you need it, but I can't force you to stay away from them. This is the only alternative I can think of that doesn't end up in you hating me.*

Gliding his hand through Tash's hair, Mayr

drew Tash's lips to his and moaned at the familiar touch. The words he needed to say were impossible to voice. Even after what they had been through, he held back, wishing he could say everything with his body instead of words that could be thrown away. Tash was easy to kiss: his lips took and gave all at once, his tongue tasting without apology or demand. He read Mayr without words, replacing doubt with surety.

Which is why I can't lose you—I can't go back to being used and thrown away. Mayr wrapped his arm around Tash's back and stole a second, quicker kiss. Close together, his skin was a darker tan than Tash's, and almost as scarred. Where Mayr's scars were from training and fighting, the burns and knife marks on Tash's chest were reminders of the Shar-denn, incurred during punishment for not upholding his duties.

As Mayr's fingertips traveled over the old injuries, Tash curled his arm around Mayr's hip. The leather of Tash's bracer grazed Mayr's back, another foul reminder of the secrets Tash kept.

You can't go back to how things were, either. Never again, Mayr promised, burying his face in Tash's neck. He wanted to be the peace to Tash's wounded past. They needed to make new memories together and forge a happier future.

Fingers danced up Mayr's spine as he nuzzled Tash's scruffy cheek, breathing in the scent of fire smoke and woodsy, resinous incense. He loved how the warm, earthy aroma was confused between spicy and sweet, clinging to Tash's skin and hair and lips. When that scent graced his bed, he savoured how his pillows and sheets smelled of ash and trees laced with sweat and sex. But when his bed lost those scents and all that remained was musty fabric, he loathed their absence. It reminded him of being alone.

"You've been tending the sacred fire in the temple again," Mayr murmured.

Tash's lips glided over the tattoos on Mayr's throat. His bottom lip trailed as he worked up Mayr's cheek and settled under his eye with a whisper of a kiss. "Someone has to make sure the flames stay lit."

"And you're so good at that, keeping fires burning."

"Especially in you."

Mayr groaned. *No, no, no. We can't do this right now. Someone has to be the grown-up here.*

In a cruel betrayal of his raging erection and Tash's noticeable arousal, Mayr nipped Tash's jaw. "Shove me."

"What?"

"Shove me. Punch me. *Something*. Otherwise this won't go anywhere but down to the floor with something that isn't training."

"Something, hmm?" Tash grinned and stepped back. "We know how softly we love, soldier—" His features darkened with a sneer and growl. He gripped Mayr's cock and balls with a rough hand, squeezing until Mayr yelped and writhed. "Now show me how hard we fight." With both hands, he shoved Mayr.

Stumbling back, Mayr cupped his hands over his aching groin. "That's *not* what I had in mind!"

"Next time, be more specific." Tash raised his hands, beckoning Mayr to attack. "Now fight for it. Unless you want me to do it again—"

Mayr charged forward and threw the first punch, his right fist aimed for Tash's jaw. The instant Tash blocked the strike with his forearm, pushing Mayr's arm outwards and grabbing his right shoulder, Mayr jerked his left knee up, expecting to connect with the fleshy area near Tash's groin. *Payback's a—*

Tash pivoted and yanked Mayr's thigh. Fingers dug into Mayr's shoulder as Tash sent him to the floor.

"A little distracted?" A smug smile teased Tash's lips, his hair cascading around his face as he peered down.

"Try testing your reflexes, ball breaker." Mayr snorted and stood. He cracked his neck and knuckles as though he had meant to be taken down. "Next time you grab me like that, it'd better be followed by sucking me off." Fists raised, he assumed a prepared stance, one foot on the thick white line of the innermost training ring. "Let's do this. I'm aching to smack that arrogance out of you."

With a smirk, Tash mirrored Mayr's stance. "It took me a good smacking to get this arrogance to begin with." He crept around the white circle, hands raised. Mayr moved with him, watching for signs of his intention. "It's all the pretentiousness I've ever needed, courtesy of the Shar. Such a shame you don't appreciate it."

Tash's right fist came for Mayr, aimed at his throat.

Mayr slapped the punch away and rammed his left palm against Tash's chin. He held on, craning Tash's neck and forcing him back, his grip hard enough to make a point but light enough to avoid leaving bruises. "I wouldn't know why." He released Tash, only to elbow him in the stomach before shoving him with his shoulder. "You *know* they turn my cranks." As Tash stumbled back, Mayr readied himself for the next strike, one foot on the white ring. "Come on, show me how they like it."

A frown was Tash's answer as he regained his posture. "Hard in the ring, hard in bed—that's how." Tash faked a punch with his right hand then slapped Mayr in the head with his left. "So hard you're bruised no matter whether you're coming or going." He spun away, his right arm ramming Mayr's ribs.

Grunting at the contact, Mayr grabbed Tash's outstretched arm at the elbow and squeezed. He kneed Tash in the back and kicked him forward. Tash recovered quickly and charged at him. After ducking to avoid Mayr's slap, he stood and struck his forearm against Mayr's neck.

Mayr choked and staggered as he rubbed his throat. The strike would leave a mark, he was certain. Tash had applied more force than he expected.

"You're better than this," he thought he heard Tash say, the words muffled by Mayr's heavy breaths.

When he blinked and realized Tash was coming for him, Mayr stepped back to receive the punch. He snatched Tash's wrists and pushed, spinning Tash around and kicking him away.

Tash teetered, his hands out to catch himself. Once steady, he stood with his back to Mayr. "It's true, then: you're holding out," he said, almost too quiet to hear. He faced Mayr, his gaze heavy as he snickered. "The Shar's nowhere near as nice as you. It's a wonder your guards are any good. You're practically a den mother." Arms down, Tash strode towards Mayr, his curled lip making his derisive tone nastier. "So nice, so soft, so disgustingly pathetic, holding them close and petting them like precious little kittens—"

Mayr crouched and hugged Tash around the knees. As he stood up, he yanked hard and flipped Tash onto his back. Tash yelped, his head narrowly missing the floor.

Before he fell over, Mayr scrambled over Tash. He dropped onto Tash's hips, knees slammed to the floor. Sharp pain burst through his knees, but Mayr ignored it, too focused on ramming Tash's wrists to the ground on either side of his head.

"'Den mother' this," Mayr hissed, grinding into Tash. The more Tash struggled, the harder Mayr pinned him. He stole a suffocating kiss, thrusting deep as Tash moaned and returned the assault. Mouths crushed together, he sucked and toyed with Tash's tongue to silence the rest of the foul words in Tash's mouth. He would rob Tash of breath and offer his in its stead, claiming Tash and cleansing him of the Shar-denn's malice.

They writhed together, fighting to breathe, until Mayr ended the torture, unable to withstand the gnawing in his lungs. He shuffled back to sit on Tash's thighs, avoiding contact with Tash's hardened cock. "Go ahead and den mother my ass, you haughty bastard."

"Your beautiful ass," Tash murmured. "I'll do whatever you want to it."

Mayr leaned over until his mouth hovered over Tash's. "Take all the hate they taught you and roll it into a ball," he said, his bottom lip grazing Tash's. "Then pound into me so hard you forget all of it. Everything they taught you, whatever they wanted you to be. Make love to me and forget them." He slid his lips over Tash's in a softer kiss. "They had your past, but give me your future. Be *my* future."

Tash pressed his forehead to Mayr's. "I'm not going anywhere. I'm here to stay, mind, body, and soul."

The words stabbed Mayr's heart and slashed open his conscience, inviting self-deprecating insults to fling themselves about. How easy the sentiment seemed to be for Tash. No hesitation, no uncertainty, nothing to suggest he was not serious.

It would be so easy to ask him... so easy to give him a ring. Mayr drew his splayed hands down Tash's chest, his skin moistened with a light sweat. The longer he stared into Tash's eyes, the deeper he felt his future. Possibility whispered in the back of his mind, telling him to surrender his own past. He needed to run into Tash's arms, not stumble. He needed to believe Tash would never let him go.

"Mayr," Tash admonished gently, "I trust you, but I need you to trust yourself and *me*."

"I do."

"No, you don't. You're relying on soft defence instead of challenging me with brutality." Tash's fingers slipped down Mayr's jaw. "You're merciless in training with experienced guards— I'm asking for the same. I won't break, I promise. I wasn't a weak fighter." A faint smile passed over his lips. "If I was, they'd never have let me protect a faction boss. They would've assigned me to a cache house or made me protect dead bodies. I proved myself in those days—this isn't any different."

"You'll crack your head open." Mayr motioned angrily at the floor. "Or dislocate—"

Tash caught Mayr's wrists. "Stop." He clutched Mayr's hands to his chest. "I know the risks. I've had my share of injuries. But I need this, and I need your help." Freeing one of Mayr's hands, he brushed a kiss over Mayr's knuckles. "I give you permission to go full strength. That's how I learned in the Shar-denn: they threw me into the ring and watched the blood fly. I had to learn how to smash down my opponent before they broke me. It's a part of me now."

Mayr sucked in a breath. He whimpered his annoyance as Tash cupped his cheeks.

"I need you to challenge me, not teach me," Tash said. "I need to fight your experience and sharpen my skills. Give yourself the permission to be you."

It isn't an identity problem—it's me keeping you safe. It's me being the one you're safe with.

Given all the people and things that could hurt Tash, Mayr wanted to protect the time they had together, safeguarding it from everything that could break them. He hated that Tash had to leave the village and travel to other places to fulfill his oaths as a priest. He despised every time they said goodbye, always afraid it would be for the last time.

The fear and desperation were strongest when Tash attended a meeting of the Sacred Assembly or visited another village without Mayr. Although he did his best to accompany Tash on his journeys, Mayr still served Aeley first. There were times he could not trade one love and duty for the other, but he never let Tash go alone. On the trips Mayr missed, he sent at least four guards in his stead.

It's not enough. Even when I'm with you, it's not adequate. Mayr traced his fingertip along Tash's hairline, captivated as Tash closed his eyes and settled his hands on Mayr's hips. They were both servants to duty, unable to let people down. They could not stay by each other's side every moment of every day. Just as Mayr had sworn to take care of Aeley, Tash had sworn to serve the people of Kattal. They led separate lives with responsibilities that originated from opposite directions.

Then you come home and everything's all right. You fall asleep in my arms, and the world doesn't bother me as much. That's the real reason I agreed to Ress and Adren moving into the estate. It wasn't because I'm selfless or because of logic. It's because I wanted you back.

Mayr frowned and stared at the floor past Tash's shoulder. For three weeks, Tash had stayed in the temple, insisting Mayr remain at the estate. They had spent little time together while Ress and Adren attended hearings before the High Council and began community service to fulfill the stipulations of amnesty. Tash had stayed in the temple to protect Adren; Mayr had stayed at the estate to protect Aeley and Lira.

The time apart hurt Mayr more than the fight in Araveena Ford, particularly whenever he saw Tash's bruised face. Not being able to hold Tash had killed his patience.

Though it's been dead for a while, let's be honest. This occasionally sleeping in separate beds and thinking of the temple as Tash's home isn't doing it for me. There's too much space between us. With Adren and Ress here...

He could have a home with Tash.

If I try harder, show him I'm serious. No more jokes. No more lies messing with my head. The past can't have us.

"I'm giving myself the permission to be me," Mayr whispered. Fears were meant to be overcome. The past was meant to be conquered. To rise above them once and for all, he would prove Tash was worth the rest of his life.

One week, he promised, getting up and helping Tash stand. *I'll make your Uldana anniversary unforgettable if you give me one week. I'll prove I'll do anything for you... even if it means punching you in the face just to keep you safe.*

"We're clear, then?" One of Tash's brows arched. "No more holding back?"

"Real clear." Mayr grinned and assumed a proper stance on the white ring before he punched the air. "Bring it, ball breaker. No more holding back."

Chapter Two

With every congratulatory word and sincere embrace, Tash's guilt tore into his conscience.

It wasn't supposed to be like this. Today was supposed to be better. Tash swallowed back a scowl and picked up a silver platter of cheese from the table in front of him. He was where he wanted to be, surrounded by people he cared for, and he spent his days as a high-ranking priest in the Temple of the Four. It was the life he had fought for during his spiritual trials more than a year ago, wanting it bad enough to have given up almost everything. He should have felt nothing but joy and offered easy smiles, losing himself in the kind of laughter that pained his bruised ribs worse than Mayr's punches.

Instead, he was a mess. Every smile was a challenge, every laugh halfhearted. What had been the warmth of pride filling him at dawn had twisted and withered, diving towards shame by dinner. All that remained was the ugly side of his humanity and a false happiness he was an expert at faking.

Another lie meant to make everyone feel better. Meanwhile, all I want to do is to hide and yell and tear into my heart until it bleeds. Tash passed the platter to his left, letting go only when Aeley tugged on it. She returned his forced smile with a wink, the corners of her brown eyes crinkled as she grinned and fidgeted in her seat at the head of the table. Given the special occasion, she was dressed in finery befitting her roles as Tract Steward and hostess of the feast. Rather than her customary choice of pants and tunic, she had opted for a red and white gown with long sleeves, a low neckline, and a tight, white bodice laced up both sides. Someone had swept back her dark blonde hair with strands of white pearls on delicate gold chains, taming the long mass except for where it tumbled down her back.

Aeley's effort to make Tash feel welcome was not lost on him or his humility. Despite his request not to trouble herself or anyone else, Aeley had insisted they have the dinner. *"We Dahes celebrate victories and blessings,"* she had said. *"Your priesthood is all of that, so we'll drink and dine and serenade you with terrible stories and too much fuss. That's what happens when you're family."*

Her kindness alone should have kept his melancholy at bay, at least for the time it took to eat. The staff of the Dahe estate had set up several dining tables in the ballroom, arranged end to end, and covered them with pristine white tablecloths as though Tash were a dignified guest. Twenty-six wooden chairs with deep red cushions sat around the tables, each occupied by someone important to him.

The sentiment of the celebration was appreciated, but the thought of Aeley considering him family grounded him in reality. He never wanted to come between Mayr and Aeley or tempt Aeley's anger. Her acceptance of him spurred his hope and a hundred wishes he ached to fulfill.

Those small joys failed to dispel the deeper truths. The dinner honoured his ability to pass the Uldana Trials and obtain the highest status of priesthood, but doubt and shame kicked up every memory and torment. His past would never stop haunting him. The ghosts would never settle.

"Here," Mayr said from Tash's right, handing him a glass bowl of diced vegetables and potent herbs in a thin cream sauce. "Looks like Cook's in the spoiling mood. She's made all your favourite things." He grinned and swept his hand over the table, careful not to hit any of the elegant platters set among the white tapered candles and gold goblets. "We must've caught her on one of her good days—unless you've been kissing up to her, using your charms."

Tash blinked back the conflict between what had been and what was, seeing only Mayr. Their fingers brushed as he took the bowl, the touch igniting better memories. Along with them, he caught the wafting scent of roasted meats in savoury gravy, spice tarts topped with mounds of caramelized winter fruits and sprigs of frozen herbs, freshly baked bread slathered in honeyed butter and blackenfroste berries, and heated balenut pudding on biscuits glazed with mead icing. Voices collided around him, the various tones weaving in and out of loud and soft as he caught snippets of conversation.

Time had slipped by again. Stuck in his head, he had removed himself from the comforts of life and missed precious moments.

But no matter where I go, Mayr, you find me and bring me home.

"The only one I kiss up to is you," Tash murmured, leaning into Mayr. His lips grazed Mayr's earlobe before settling on his smooth cheek. He breathed in the faint, spicy perfume on Mayr's neck, tempted to nip the skin around the unadorned collar of Mayr's black tunic. "You're my most favourite thing, something she can't offer."

"Good to know." Mayr's hand crept beneath Tash's red veil. His calloused fingertips slid under Tash's hair to caress his neck in slow circles.

Tash shivered as Mayr teased his spine above the collars of his robes. Compared to their first training session a week ago, the touch was a seductive whisper. His back, ribs, and limbs were still bruised and tender from sparring, though he was not as damaged as Mayr feared.

You went too easy on me, but we'll work on it. Tash drew back from Mayr to add spoonfuls of the vegetable mixture to his already full plate.

Regardless of what Mayr thought, Tash enjoyed the physical training. While he could do without the pain and the reason to fight, he missed the exertion and discipline. *At least now I'm doing it for the right reason, and it's something we can do together. It's another chance to feel you close.* He held the bowl tight in both hands. *Because there you were, being careful like no one else has. You have no idea what it's like being in love with you... It's like curling up in a warm haven and getting lost in blissful daydreams.*

Stifling a sigh, he stared at the colourless glass bowl. Etiquette told him he needed to pass the bowl to Aeley.

Frustration commanded he throw it to the floor just to watch it shatter.

He needed the glass to burst into scathing shards the way his inner peace did. He wanted to point at the mess and yell "That's me!" because he was sputtering on words to describe how he felt and the strength to share them.

His will used to be stronger. *He* used to be stronger, drifting through the days alone, confiding in priests who offered kindness without fully understanding his pain. With their help, he had worked towards an inner calm. The Uldana Trials had been his greatest effort to earn absolution from the Goddesses and set himself free.

Life had not worked out as he anticipated. The Trials had taught him absolution was more than a word or action from the Goddesses: it was a matter of forgiving himself and surrendering to love. The Trials also brought him an abundance of family he could not disappoint. Not only did he worry about the priests, he had reunited with his parents and sister, none of whom he wanted to abandon again. Then there was Ress and his cousins, Mayr and his family, and Adren, a lost soul who needed protection from a world that believed cir kind were myths.

For a spiritual journey that was meant to help him, the Trials had skipped around freedom to run straight into chaos, complicating his life more than the Shar-denn had.

"Here, let me," Mayr whispered, taking the bowl from Tash. He offered it across the table to Lira, who sat at Aeley's left, opposite Tash.

Another lapse—and I look like a fool.

"Sorry." Tash's face warmed. He stared at his hands, hoping no one noticed the tremble in his fingers. The tremor decreased the harder he pressed his wrists against the edge of the table, the dark brown leather of his bracers biting into his scarred forearms.

Mayr clutched Tash's hand. "Don't be. You've had a lot on your mind." When he squeezed Tash's fingers, Tash's hands steadied. "Tell me about it later. Maybe I can help?"

He sounded so hopeful, a part of Tash splintered.

I want to tell you everything, but I can't keep

showing you how miserable and paranoid I am. How many times can you go through the same things without getting tired of it? You're already restless, pulling away from me with your own secrets. I feel it. I see it. These last few weeks have changed us, but I'll fight to keep you, even if it means battling anguish on my own.

"Thank you." Tash drew the back of his hand down Mayr's cheek, fighting the urge to kiss him. Although their guests would have expected it, he wanted to avoid the attention. His sister, Allaysia, sat on the other side of Mayr, waiting for a reason to tease them. She was not the only one who would find a kiss fodder for playful embarrassment: Mayr's sister and brother, Estara and Loftin, and Ress's cousins, Bremary and Covran, were trouble in their own rights.

That's without considering the children. We should set an example if we're ever going to have one...

Gripping his fork, Tash poked at his food and mixed the piles together, channeling regret into the assault. He and Mayr were not ready to discuss children, apparent from Mayr's reactions since Tash first made the suggestion. Mayr had said they would discuss it after Tash had been an Uldana-level priest for a year. *Now that day's here, and he's not any more interested than he was three months ago. With Ress and Adren here, I don't see him agreeing at all. There are too many dangers, too many distractions. Our attention is too divided to make it work, especially if he's changing his mind about us. If we're already starting to slip, a child won't bring us together; they'll tear us apart. Sometimes the best course of action is inaction.*

Tash cast his gaze down the tables, past the candlelight and gleaming silver and gold dinnerware to the rest of the ballroom, with its grey walls of wide coarse stones and silver gilding. A fire blazed in the large hearth in the wall to his right. Torchlight illuminated the silver and black tapestries depicting winter scenes in forests and ice-breaking ships on the seas. Between the tapestries hung large snowflake-shaped decorations, crafted from silver-streaked parchment with a blue tinge and white lace that glimmered with jewels. Each snowflake was the size of a shield used in battle and fastened to a lattice of white gold. The decorations had been up since the Feast of Taleyra the Righteous, the holy observance to celebrate the beloved consort of Navara, the Goddess of Justice and the winter season.

The clink of metal tore his attention back to Aeley. She rose from the table, goblet in hand, and everyone fell silent. Lira stood beside her, dressed in a modest white gown. The dress hid everything except her hands and boasted the latest fashion of tiered lace cuffs with small white bows at the seams. Her dark hair was curled tight, swept up by white ribbons and narrow strands of silver.

"Before things get too serious and we lose some of you to the brew, I'd like to interrupt everyone—mostly because I can," Aeley announced.

"At least you're honest," Loftin responded from five seats down on Tash's right, his voice deep like Mayr's. "We've always known you're an attention whor—" He caught himself, choking on the last word. Several snickers floated through the air. "Sorry, I'll shut up now. I'm getting Tara's glare of personalized doom."

Soft laughter followed from the rest of their guests. Leaning back, Tash glimpsed Estara flicking her fingers at her brother and uttering what he supposed was a threat.

"One of these days, Loftin, she's going to stuff you—and I'm going to help." Aeley grinned and tipped her goblet at him. "That's tomorrow's fun. For now, Lira and I want to say a few words." She flicked her glance to Tash. "We've had the pleasure of knowing Tash for the last year, and I truly mean it's a pleasure. He's the kind of person that doesn't remain a stranger for long. He's easily found a place in our lives and settled in."

"Which is why hosting this dinner required no second thought," Lira said. "As dear as he is to Mayr, he's also endeared himself to us. We can't help but want to celebrate with him." She raised her goblet towards Tash. "This toast is for you, from your family and friends—a thank you for touching our lives. To your happiness."

"To your happiness," voices echoed, followed by whistles and cheers for good fortune. Goblets raised in Tash's direction. His family beamed their encouragement. Mayr's hand clasped his.

Tash's stomach churned. He forced a smile until his face strained too much to continue. "Thank you," he managed, lifting his goblet of wine.

While everyone else drank in his honour, he battled the excruciating need to be sick.

Beside him, Mayr joked with Allaysia, the sound of her giggles warming Tash's heart. During the eleven years he had avoided his family, he had missed his sister's dulcet tones and youthfulness. Whenever he looked at Allaysia, he saw parts of himself mirrored back: light tan skin, brown hair with blond strands, and blue eyes inherited from their mother, Parase. Their resemblance to their father, Kilienn, could not be denied. Nor could the fact their emotions tended to eat at them, often tumbling out in an embarrassing display.

Despite everything, she still believed in Tash. For all the distress he had put her and their parents through, she still loved him, even when it hurt.

To think I'd convinced myself I was too old to need Ally's advice and help. Tash snorted and picked at his dinner with small bites. *I still need her to be my big sister, especially when I'm too stubborn to see what's good for me.*

If he focused hard enough, he could remember the frivolous games they played as children, often revising the rules until they learned to best each other with ludicrous strategy. Or the pranks they pulled, taunting each other until they erupted in a fit of angry shouts and thrown sticks that gave way to playful slaps and belly-aching laughter. With seven years between them, Tash had been at Allaysia's mercy, several steps behind her. He had always fumbled to find himself, always wanted to be her shadow.

Those childhood joys and woes defined his existence until the Shar-denn claimed him, murdering his innocence when he was thirteen years old. After that, he had struggled to be half a dozen steps ahead of Allaysia to protect her from the gang. She was a seamstress like their mother, not a trained fighter. Her life revolved around their family, their family's tailoring shop, and her friends. Without Tash's determination and strength as a guard, the Shar-denn would have tortured her with their lust for violence and control.

He had done what he could for Allaysia, no different than what Ress had done for his own family. Where Tash had severed ties with his family, telling himself they were dead until he believed it, Ress had chased his family out of Araveena Ford—except for Bremary and Covran, two maternal cousins who refused to leave.

Those same cousins sat on the other side of

Allaysia. Just as Tash loved Ress like a brother, he considered Bremary and Covran extended family. He had spent time with them as a child, wanting to be their friend, but worried they might not accept him because Allaysia was everyone's favourite. They resembled Ress more than their own brother and sister, favouring the same dark eyes and hair, tan complexions, slender forms, and similar height. Like Ress, they were in the metalsmith business and managed the shop in Araveena Ford their great-grandparents had started.

A shop Ress had abandoned to save Adren, who fidgeted at the table as though ce wanted to escape.

Seated across from Allaysia, Adren spoke quietly to Ress on cir left and leaned close to him, seeking comfort. Adren spared the occasional word to Pellon at cir right, though Tash suspected it was only out of politeness—Adren still seemed wary of Pellon's intimidating demeanor and large build. Dressed in a white gown with black ribbons under a black leather long coat, Adren had tied cir long red hair back into a loose tail. Visibly awkward with a nervous smile, Adren flicked cir gaze around the room. Ce kept one slender hand under the table, near the knife strapped to cir thigh.

Tash sympathized with Adren's need for precaution: having lived in the estate for only a week, Adren had yet to trust anyone or anything, least of all strangers and small spaces. Guards followed cir everywhere. It was also no accident that Adren sat between Pellon and Ress, or that Pellon occupied the chair between Adren and Lira. As the second-in-command for Aeley's guard, Pellon protected the Dahe family first and kept an eye on everyone else, particularly when they came from a family under investigation for every crime imaginable.

Yet Adren's move to the estate had changed more than security—it changed how Adren saw cirself. Life in the Shar-denn had ingrained expectations and perspectives in Adren that took time to undo. Even worse was the fact that Adren was unlike everyone else except for cir own kind, the Goddess-touched—a race no one knew how to find. Although ce seemed as human as anyone else, there was a touch of sacred blood in cir veins. Like all Goddess-touched, ce was a descendant of their goddesses, blessed with magic and a deeper, innate connection to the divine. Most had disappeared, but Adren's existence proved some still lived. More than that, they may have chosen to hide in plain sight, though it did nothing to help Adren. Tash did his best to guide Adren through the challenge of trading a criminal past for a law-abiding future, but his help was limited. He had no answers for how a Goddess-touched made it through while dealing with their magic and the call of the divine.

It's almost as frustrating as not knowing what bloodline ce's from. He feared it would take years to find the answers about Adren's origins. That would not stop him from trying, however, even if he had to spend fifty years buried beneath a mountain range of books. The more he learned about Adren, the more he found significance in the things that even ce shrugged off. Adren shared more in common with the goddess Navara than ce realized, right down to the duality in their balanced natures. Adren's soul flourished within two beautiful sides of self that flowed from one to the other, their fluid movement as elegant as the words ce used to name cirself, capturing the essence of that soul with intent.

Ce was more than masculine or feminine, more than hard or soft, more than anything that defined cir: ce was a whole of many, where the lines between were so fine they disappeared completely. From light and airy to dark and braced, Adren's dichotomies bled into one another, instantaneously shifting from cir quiet and uncertain nature to the louder, determined part of cir that burned as hot as cir magic. Adren reminded him of the human form of Navara that occasionally slipped through the realms to change the world from within the mess people had made rather than work around them.

And what a mess we've made.

Tash slouched as he slid his gaze towards Ress. He eyed the scar that marred Ress's right jaw, a crude mark inflicted after Tash had left the Shar-denn without telling anyone. Though Ress did not hide it, preferring to wear his brown-black hair short around his worn, lean features, the scar bothered Ress as much as his injured knee. They were permanent wounds, like the gashes Tash had stabbed in Ress's trust.

Trust I'm never going to have in full again. He's right: when I destroy lives, I really commit. Even my good intentions are a straight path to death.

Fork steadied in his hand, his dinner barely consumed, Tash stared at the silver ring on his right hand. The ring embraced his middle finger like a talon. Long and curved from knuckle to fingertip, the ring was ribbed and detailed like a bird's claw. From the base, a chain extended across the back of his hand to a metal link on his bracer. A gift from Ress for Tash's eighteenth birthday, the piece represented the claw of Halataldris, the legendary bird that kept company with Emeraliss, the Goddess of Love. Not only had Tash been named after that bird, its image adorned his back.

A piece of my flesh I gave to the Shar. I surrendered to them that easily. I let them violate me. Disgusted, he laid down his fork and snatched his goblet. With each sip of wine, he swallowed back the bile and sickness fighting their way up. *I took the sacredness of the Father of All Birds and soiled it. I abused Mother's beautiful memory. How can I be fit to be named after a messenger of love when I spent so much time playing with hate?*

Because he knew better now, Tash reminded himself. He had stolen his soul back and offered it to the Four, believing in the compassion of the Goddesses.

It's the only thing keeping me together. Glance flitting upwards, he caught Ress's gaze and small smile. To his relief, they had patched several holes in their relationship. Tension still haunted them, but they could live under the same roof without tearing each other apart. *It doesn't hurt that I'm protecting Adren. Taking care of who he loves is the least I can do for everything he's done for my family.*

They would be dead if not for Ress.

Tash slid his attention to his mother and father. Parase and Kilienn sat to Ress's left, laughing and conversing with everyone around them, including Mayr's parents. Time slowed as Tash stared at his mother, unable to look away from the soft curves of her face. To see joy dance across her features lit the fire of determination in him. He yearned to see her rosy-cheeked and glowing more often. She was stunning, her dark hair plaited and pinned with jeweled combs that matched her fine blue gown with its expensive lace and pearled ribbons.

Beside her, his father appeared prim and composed like always. Kilienn wore his shoulder-length hair tied back with white ribbon, drawing out the grey streaks in his brown locks. Dressed to match Parase, he wore an embroidered blue tunic and long, black vest fastened with thick clasps of black pearls. His deep blue coat hung to his knees, hiding little of his black breeches and boots.

Life had not been as cruel to Tash's parents as he had feared. Despite the rough years, Parase's blue eyes gleamed as though she kept a hundred comical secrets. His father was no less jovial. From where he sat, Tash overheard fragments of the stories Kilienn told. It seemed his name came up every few words.

A heated blush crept up Tash's neck. There was no escaping his family now. Given all the years they had worried over his demise, it was only fair they torture him with embarrassing childhood tales and youthful indiscretions. If his father wanted to share stories about Tash running around without clothes on to test a poor theory of invisibility, Tash owed him as much. If his mother wanted to share her version of the first time he kissed a boy—then promptly slipped and tumbled into the pond, picking up leeches along the way—he would not stop her, especially since the story made Mayr smile.

"Really?" Mayr laughed and curled his arm around the back of Tash's chair. His glance swept over Tash's still-full plate, though he seemed to ignore it. "The kiss was *that* good?"

"It certainly was for the other boy." Kilienn grinned and wagged a piece of bread at Tash. "He went in headfirst trying to pull our boy out and got fishes down his shirt for the trouble. I've never heard so much fuss over trying to get out of the water. All that splashing and shouting for dear life."

"I was *eleven*. I couldn't help it." Tash stifled a frown. "We were a bit stunned, that's all. He didn't expect it."

"Especially when you kissed my cousin first, right in front of him," Ress added. He smirked and arched one of his brows. "Comparing, I think you said?"

"Wait, *what?*" Bremary dropped her knife, her eyes wide. "Which cousin?"

"Raeda," Tash mumbled.

"My *sister?*" Bremary squealed. "How did I not know about this?" She swatted Covran's shoulder. "Did *you* know?" When Covran shook his head, she jabbed her fork at Ress. "You slimy little eel! No one told me he went on with her."

Tash rolled his eyes. "I didn't. It was just the once. She ran off while I was drowning and decided that was it."

"Something about hating water," Ress muttered, holding his goblet to his lips. "That girl could drown in a puddle." He gestured to Bremary with his other hand. "Don't you go throwing that knife at me, saying I'm making fun of her. Raeda only yelps at the sight of fish and cringes whenever you mention rain."

Covran snorted and nodded his agreement.

Beside him, Loftin guffawed and elbowed Covran. Almost on cue and perfectly in synch, Bremary and Estara flicked their fingers at their brothers.

"If you want to rethink our families being in the same room, now's a good time," Mayr murmured, brushing his lips over Tash's cheek. "Their combined absurdity is starting to look normal. We could leave now and be ridiculously naked in no time."

Tash laughed. "Because being simply naked won't do."

Mayr grinned and sat back, sliding his empty plate away from him. "Not when I know what's underneath those robes." Slowly he drew his hair over his shoulder and let it tumble over his well-fitted tunic. He wore his hair loose, the way Tash enjoyed it most. As Mayr coiled several strands around one finger, he teased Tash's sensibilities. "Everything simple is worth doing extravagantly with you."

"Mayr," Tash whispered. He sucked in a breath, denying the part of him that wanted to make love to Mayr's mouth. His appetite for food lacked, but his need was famished, desperate for comfort and tender touches—anything to remind him he was alive.

They needed to finish dinner first. *Considering what everyone had to go through to be here...* Tash cast his gaze over the last half of the dining placements, most of them occupied by Mayr's family. Malary and Renett, Mayr's father and mother, sat to the left of Kilienn, dressed in simple, modest clothes meant for a winter day in a village rather than a party at a fancy estate. After them were Estara and her family: Dayla and Efae, her nine-year-old daughter and six-year-old son, and her husband, Teneth, who sat at the corner at the end of the table. Loftin and his wife, Orlee, sat on the other side of the table. Their eight-year-old son, Alith, sat between them, his patience strained from trying to behave.

From the first day Tash had visited Malary and Renett's farm, their family had welcomed him. Their generosity struck him deeply, almost bringing him to tears the first time he dined with them. They were a family of strength, steadfast in morals and hope.

Everything he found in Mayr.

There was more than a touch of Renett's gentle spirit in Mayr. Renett lived each day with stubborn honesty and tended to her family with fervor, undaunted by her inability to walk after an accident with a horse and cart that left her paralyzed from the waist down. Her spirit was bright and loud, intense like a flame. With long black hair curled around a softly rounded face and pale blue eyes that stared deeply into the souls of others, Renett was mother to Mayr as much as she mothered everyone else.

By the Four's sweetest graces, you've married someone just as kind. It's not hard to see where Mayr gets it from—a blessing I can never thank you for enough. Malary's love for Renett was undeniable. It was his sarcasm and gruff tone Tash often heard from Mayr; it was his grey eyes Mayr had inherited. A farmer all his life, Malary was fit with short, shaggy hair that was equally grey as it was dark. Although he had said little to Tash the first time they met, Malary's attitude changed after Tash asked to stay in Mayr's life permanently. They had spoken dozens of times since, discussing a wide range of matters.

More than once, Malary had cautioned Tash and told him to take care of Mayr. The glint in Malary's eyes had dared Tash to beg for forgiveness before he even committed a transgression.

Estara and Loftin were just as protective of their brother. Four years younger than Mayr, Estara and Loftin were twins, resembling one another in most ways. Estara appeared nearly identical to their mother, with black hair and blue-grey eyes. Loftin shared the same features except for his grey eyes and short hair. Both were playful and mischievous, unable to remain still, their bold personalities displayed openly. No one could predict what they would say.

The rest of their family was a mixture of similarity and difference, though all three children were dark-haired bundles of curiosity and wonder, carefree even when they got lost in trying to be grown-ups before their time.

You shouldn't worry about growing up so fast, Tash wanted to tell the children. They needed to revel in their childhood, to run into the chaos and spin colour in the hearts of their parents.

No different than what Iliane's doing with Mayr. He leaned back to glimpse Iliane near the end of the table on his side, seated between her parents. The thick ringlets of her dark brown hair bobbed on her shoulders as she nodded and gestured excitedly to Efae. She was a younger version of her mother, with the same hair, large brown eyes, and round face. Her stepfather, Barin, towered over both her and Betta with ruddy blond hair and bright green eyes.

The effect Iliane had on Mayr stole Tash's breath. Ever so sweetly, she tapped into a part of Mayr no one else did.

Finding her was one decision I'll never regret, even if it meant keeping secrets. Tash's gaze drifted to the floor. He had gone behind Mayr's back and poked into his business without his consent. *I had to try. You suffered with me during my Trials. You kept me alive when others wanted me dead. The least I could do was restore the piece of your heart that went with Iliane. Aeley didn't think I would, but all it took was a little hope.*

The reward for his efforts had been Mayr's reaction when he saw Iliane for the first time since her infancy. Ten years of loss had collapsed in a single moment, accompanied by a look of endless love and silent tears.

Now Iliane was a fixed part of Mayr's life. Even Aeley welcomed her, despite the tension that remained between Aeley and Betta. Estara and Loftin's distrust of Betta was equally noticeable. For those reasons alone, Betta sat close to the furthest end of the table with several people between her and those who would not forgive her past choices.

To provide extra protection, two priests sat near Betta: Armamae and Kee, who had assumed her place at the end of the table, facing Aeley. In their presence, no one would dare harm Betta, even with words.

Tash snickered at the thought. Kee was used to reining people in, given her position as Overseer of the Temple of the Four on the outskirts of Dahena, the village in which the Dahe estate resided. Her calm, composed demeanor was no match for her rigid determination. When Kee committed to something, she did not stop until the deed was thoroughly achieved.

Kee caught Tash's glance and smiled, raising her goblet towards him. Like Tash, she wore the glimmering red robes of an Uldana priest. A red veil covered her long black hair except for the handful of strands around her shoulders, framing her tan face and dark eyes.

Once more he was struck by how much she reminded him of Hastal, one of their beloved goddesses. Both were known for their regal bearings, unshakeable devotion, and pasts that had required battling expectations forced upon them. Those pasts had shaped their strength and desire to protect others, their journeys accompanied by painful years when others had shackled them to the identity of men regardless of their innate need to be recognized as women. Where Hastal had been criticized by ancient gods and worshippers, Kee came from an island community of the Temple of the Pure Triad, an exiled sect that rejected the teachings of the Temple of the Four. Emeraliss, Laytia, and Navara were their only goddesses, and they denounced Hastal as a trickster false god who led people astray from their true selves.

Unable to endure the Pure Triad's intolerance and be the boy they wanted, Kee fled the island when she was sixteen. After stealing a boat in the middle of the night, she paddled across the Sese Channel and ran to the nearest Temple of the Four. Upon discovery by their Overseer, who found her weeping at the altar, Kee begged them not to throw her out.

The Overseer had offered Kee refuge and kindness, no different than what Kee gave to those in need. Even when members of the Pure Triad arrived to take her back, the priestesses of Hastal had formed a line and stood against them, staves and shields in hand, intimidating and determined.

That same afternoon, Kee was both exiled and given a new home. Just as the other goddesses had stood by Hastal's side and demanded She be recognized as one of them, Kee had found her way with the help of priestesses she admired. All else was her calling, Kee said, a new life with a lighter spirit. Since then, she had a soft spot for those who needed protection and second chances, including Tash, Adren, and Ress. Moreover, she recognized something of herself in Adren, their plights similar despite their circumstances.

As always, Kee appeared the consummate priest as much as Armamae did, though his veil hid his grey hair. Shorter and quieter than Kee, Armamae had been blessed with a kinder past and family he rarely spoke of. He had also survived the plague that ravaged the older generations of Kattal forty years ago. The same illness had robbed both Tash and Mayr of their grandparents and great-grandparents, a fate they shared with at least half the families in the republic.

Yet Armamae was more than one of the oldest priests in the Dahena temple: he was Tash's mentor and close friend, one to whom Tash owed a debt greater than he could ever pay. Without Armamae, Tash would not have Mayr.

Without any of his family and friends, he would not have a life to want as badly as he did. Just looking at them gifted him with fondness and hope, even though he said little to them as they ate, afraid that his darker thoughts would burst forth and ruin their dinner. Being with them in the here and now, surrounded by their love and good will despite all of his faults, he was a part of the world in ways he could never completely describe. This life, these hearts—he had bled for them, wept for them, begged to be wrapped in their safety and feel like he belonged. Whatever his loved ones were to him, he wanted to be for them, shielding them from the harshness of the world. He yearned to be soft and gentle and kind like they were, holding onto the life they offered as if he had done something to deserve it.

Except wanting this life and deserving it are different things, especially when the price is taken from the living.

There were two loved ones missing from the feast, men he considered brothers.

And I killed them.

Teeth clenched, Tash blinked back tears and gripped his dining knife. He rubbed the metal with his thumb as he fisted his other hand in his lap. Everyone was present except for Varen and Nimae. They should have been beside Ress, laughing and telling crude jokes. They should have recounted the past with everyone else, kissed until Ress slapped them both, and mocked Tash for loving an agent of the law. *I stole that from them. In trying to save them, I killed them.*

When he listened hard enough to the silence, he swore he heard Varen's ghost.

I can't stay here. I can't do this.

He dropped his knife and pushed away from

the table.

Mayr clasped Tash's knee. "What's wrong?"

"I need to clear my head," Tash said softly.

"But are you all right?" Mayr glanced at Tash's plate then at the knife lying haphazard on the table. "If it's your nerves, I'll get you a bit of spiced cider or warm up some milk and honey."

"What if it's not?"

"I hear I'm a good listener." Sadness clouded Mayr's gaze. "Tell me to come with you. Don't deal with the ghosts alone."

Tash's reply came as a kiss, hard and needy, desperate to swallow Mayr's words and breathe his compassion. Pulling Mayr close, he drank in the taste of mincemeat laced with icesworn mead and rich syrup, wishing he could stay. He had no right to drag Mayr from the feast. The burdens were his alone.

"Just a few moments," Tash whispered, noting the stares pinned on them. "These thoughts don't want company, but if people ask…"

"I'll handle it." Mayr cupped his cheek. "If you need me, say it. Signal. Do something."

Before Mayr could say anything more, Tash kissed his cheek and strode across the ballroom, escaping into the empty hallway. His robes trailed along the floor as he wandered the corridors. His boots made soft noise with his rushed paces. The weight of his long veil tugged on the simple comb in his hair that kept the veil in place, a reminder of the heaviness of his oaths.

Nothing was as heavy as regret.

I shouldn't be getting this attention. I survived the Trials, but my reasons were selfish. I'm a priest because I want to help people and do good, but for their benefit or mine?

Tash sighed and turned up another corridor, his paces slower. He had not wanted the feast. The only reason he had agreed was because it was important to his family, Mayr, and their friends. *Meanwhile I can't bear to look at them for more than a moment. I can't love without reservation anymore. Not because I can't love them unconditionally, but because I can't love myself unconditionally.*

Most days, he could peer into a mirror, listen to his own voice, feel his own skin, and like what he saw. Some days he loved himself as much as he loved others. Other days, he loathed everything about the tamed brute within.

I can't stop feeling like I shouldn't be here.

Every time he looked at Ress, he saw Varen and Nimae. The four of them had made a pact to be friends for all of their lives. They had loved each other fiercely, enduring the Shar-denn together when there was no way out. Their oath had protected them from brutality by other gang members. While Ress had worked as a metalsmith and coordinator of trafficked and stolen goods, Tash had become a guard for the faction bosses and their families, warding off assassins, law enforcers, and attacks from other factions. Varen and Nimae had settled for defending faction members on campaigns and raids. Their duty had been to protect thieves and slavers against other criminals, bounty hunters, and anyone who got in the way.

Once Varen and Nimae told their families they were lovers, there was no getting between them. Ress and Tash had protected Varen and Nimae's relationship without hesitation, determined to keep the Shar-denn from using them against each other. When Nimae had purchased a house in the woods for him and Varen, Tash and Ress told no one, safeguarding their privacy.

Everything changed the moment Tash fled the Shar-denn, leaving them all behind. Even worse changes ensued after he gave a list of names of gang members to the High Council.

Ress, Varen, and Nimae had been on that list.

Tash had begged the High Council to save them, to grant them mercy. They were good men—they only needed to be freed to show it. In return for leniency, Tash had given the High Council everything he knew about the Shar-denn, down to the smallest detail about the houses of the faction bosses. Every training method, every cache house he knew of, all the names he remembered. The information crammed in his memories had filled a dozen stacks of paper and consumed several wells of ink. His fingers had cramped from writing it all out, requiring warm wraps and massage afterwards.

On his knees, he had thrown his humility at the twelve councilmen, convinced it was the only way to save his brothers.

It didn't save them, though. They turned Ress into an informant and ruined his life. They killed Varen. Now Nimae's disappeared. If he's out there, he's not all right, but if he's dead...

After the night Ress had thrown the truth in his face, Tash found the courage to ask Councilman Severn and the bounty hunters what had happened to Varen in their custody.

The truth made him sick.

You killed yourself, Varen. You. *Always so hopeful and full of life—you kept us going even when we were covered in blood and complaining about the stench. You were our beating heart, and you slit your throat faster than the hunters could slam you down.*

For days after learning the truth, Tash's stomach had refused to settle, losing everything he ate. Locked in an altar room in the temple for two days, he had prayed and cried until his eyes swelled and no tears remained. No one successfully persuaded him to leave the room until Mayr intervened. With little force, Mayr had dragged Tash to the estate, made him drink broth, and enticed him to sleep.

Tash stopped in the middle of the corridor. "Mayr," he whispered, clinging to its safety like a prayer. He needed something to hold onto before he lost himself. He needed his warm shadow.

Turning back towards the ballroom, Tash

shuffled over the spiral pattern in the floor, his thoughts focused on Mayr. *When darkness takes me, you remind me who I am. I try to give you better, but sometimes it's hard not to beat myself down. I don't want to be a burden, just the strength you need. I want to leave the past behind completely and be your future.*

Except the past ignored the boundaries he set. Tash could not lock up his rage over Varen, Nimae, and Ress. Every time he saw Councilman Severn and Councilman Cota, he wished justice upon them. The High Council had not been honest. They had never informed Tash they had Varen in custody, nor had they disclosed his suicide. From the accounts of the guards in charge of Varen, Tash surmised they had purposely led Varen to believe he and Nimae would be executed or receive severe punishment if they failed to cooperate.

It took everything Tash had to empathize with the High Council. The guard in him wanted to rip bloody, gaping holes into the councilmen in revenge; the priest in him imagined how they felt and justified their decisions. Neither he nor the councilmen were morally superior. He tried to remain patient with them, showing who he really was.

Tash rounded the last corner and crept towards the ballroom. Stopped on the furthest side of the entrance, he haunted the doorway while kitchen staff cleared away the food. Guests mingled around the table, but his gaze stayed on Mayr.

In an instant, Tash's heavy emotions tangled into a chaotic ball and bounced away, replaced by an unrestrained lightness. Even dressed in black and armed with knives, Mayr was a brighter presence than all others. He had been since the first time they met. Brought together by a mutual lover, Sarene, Mayr and Tash had been strangers in a busy tavern, anticipating one night of delights followed by an amicable parting. Tash had never expected to forge a connection that went deeper than pleasure, weighted with familiarity and spiritual desperation.

Soulbound, that's what the priests say we are. Spirits bound through memory and fate, transcending time and the voids between life and death—and we found each other. I finally got to say the words my soul needed to get out, like I'd been keeping them silent forever. Then there you were, vulnerable and broken like me, needing to hear those very words. Being with you feels like releasing a breath I never realized I was holding.

Arms crossed, Tash leaned against the doorframe, a smile teasing his lips. The first time they met, he had wanted to forgo words and surrender himself. Sarene may have looked pretty, but it was Mayr who stole Tash's attention. With his hair out, his grey eyes focused and clear, Mayr had been devastatingly gorgeous, far too much for Tash to deny.

Tash held back a giddy laugh. After their first kiss, he had been lost to Mayr. Their souls had recognized each other as crucial parts of themselves, drawing them into a dance with hope.

He savoured that hope every moment they had together. Mayr's need to love and be loved emanated from him like an aura, haunted by a carefully guarded vulnerability Tash wanted to keep safe. He understood what most never stopped to consider: Mayr's jokes were defensive jabs; his harsh tone and toughness were warnings to ward off those who would harm him, because beneath was a tender soul that needed someone to care.

And I do. I want us to have a life together, full and happy like you are with Iliane right now. I'd give anything to have that every day.

Tash laughed as Mayr and Iliane stood at the end of the table and slapped each other's hands, giggling while they played. When the slaps stopped, Mayr held out his hands, palms down. Iliane raised hers beneath his, her palms upwards without touching his. They traded long, determined stares. Too fast to predict, Iliane tried to slap Mayr's fingers before he moved away. She succeeded every two or three attempts, smacking him hard.

Tash suspected Mayr let her win those rounds, as intentional as Mayr's inability to catch Iliane's hands after they reversed positions. Competitive as Mayr could be, his only goals where Iliane was concerned were to make her laugh, ensure she felt loved, and keep her safe.

The sight enthralled Tash. He had never wanted children, but seeing Mayr with Iliane changed him. Goddesses willing, they could have a family of their own.

Assuming I don't run him off because I'm asking for too much. Tash backed away from the door and leaned against the wall. *There's something coming—something that'll change what we have. Mayr's so quiet. He's trying not to say what's wrong, but he may as well be screaming it. Ever since Araveena he's avoided telling me the truth. It's only worsened in the last week. That day we sparred, there was something in his eyes... a choice I'll need to make.*

He wanted to stop worrying, but he had been fooled more than once, believing his relationships were solid until they became nightmares. Like the others Tash loved, Mayr would leave by his own volition or be repelled by Tash's constant meddling, especially if the Shar-denn intervened.

It doesn't help I've pulled him into this business with Ress and Adren. Now he's got Council's target on his back. I never should've gotten him involved...

If Tash's carelessness continued, he would lose everything.

His heart meant well, but he still made all the wrong decisions. Matters were no better when he considered the days he struggled to balance his religious responsibilities with loving someone he was terrified to lose. Could they withstand his dedication being split down the middle? Mayr's attention was equally divided, caught between dealing with Tash while taking care of Aeley, Lira, and the other guards.

It's not fair to expect him to keep living this way. He'll want out eventually. Soulbound or not, we might just be doomed.

Tash bit down hard and glowered at the doorframe. *No*, he would *not* damn them that easily. Forget his self-pity and derision—he could not let them sully everything that made life worth living. Even a fraction of love was worth clawing the soul apart to get at the worthy bits hidden inside. Doubts were a powerful force, but so was determination. If doom wanted them, it would have to destroy the Realm of the Dead first.

Chapter Three

For better or for worse, Mayr would stick to his plan, no matter Tash's mood.

Mayr slid his glance to Tash as they walked the dimly lit corridor. Once more, Tash's head was lowered, his gaze skimming the pattern of black stones among the grey. He said little, though the creases in his forehead worried Mayr more. Tash had been secretive and withdrawn all day, unwilling to discuss his Uldana anniversary. Dinner with their families had only made things worse.

Misery was far from what Mayr had anticipated. He had relied on Tash being lighthearted and open to the rest of the night. Soured thoughts could ruin everything.

That'd be unfortunate, considering. Mayr let out a slow breath. *It'd also be heartbreaking and awful because I'm tripping all over myself to be what he needs.*

While he lacked the specifics about what was wrong, the list of possibilities was short, particularly given Tash's pained expression whenever he peered at his family or Ress. Since Ress and Adren had entered their lives, Tash fell into dark moods more and more. For Tash's sake, Mayr wished Tash would distance himself from them and anyone else who dredged up the past.

All the more reason for us to be together—I can balance all of that. No ifs, no maybes, no I-could-tries. Nothing less than the commitment to take care of you, whatever it takes. Drifting towards Tash until their arms brushed, Mayr grasped Tash's hand and intertwined their fingers.

Startled, Tash flashed Mayr a small smile, his eyes gleaming. At least Mayr had that much. A smile hinted at hope he could use.

They turned down another hallway, their strides synced. Surrounded by the familiar silence of the estate at night while everyone was in bed save the night watch, Mayr's curiosity itched to hear Tash's voice. He wanted Tash to dump all of his pain and embrace a new word for what he was to Mayr—a single word that would change everything.

Maybe I shouldn't do this now. Maybe I should get him to talk first. Mayr frowned at the conservatory doors at the end of the long hallway. The white glass in the two red wood doors was too opaque to see through, though a soft yellow glow emanated from the other side.

He could stop them there, midway in the hall, or he could carry on. They could talk about Tash's misery or explore joy.

You need this as much as you need that, he reasoned, glimpsing Tash's sagged shoulders. *You need something good to hold onto. At least I hope it's good. Please tell me you've meant everything you've said. Let all those promises be real. The thought of any other possibility…*

He was caught between wanting to be sick and running away, and he really wanted to avoid both of them.

"You look like you're on a mission. Dare I ask where we're going?" Tash teased as he caressed Mayr's hand with his thumb. "Or is this last house check meant to lull me into submission before I'm devoured?"

"Depends on how you feel about being devoured." Mayr grinned. "I like having something to swallow. Thick, hard, wet—it works for me."

Tash's breath hitched, a faint blush creeping up his cheeks, only to be followed by a fit of coughs. "Slow or fast?" he asked huskily.

"*S-l-ow*." Mayr stopped to sweep back Tash's veil, unable to resist trailing his lips over Tash's ear. "By morning, every part of you will have felt these lips," he murmured before sucking on Tash's earlobe. "Every moan, every whisper returned with tongue, teeth, and touch. All that'll be left is come and your exhausted remains."

Breaths ragged, Tash clutched the back of Mayr's neck and groaned against his throat. "Take me away from all this," he whispered. "Make me forget."

That was all the permission he needed. Mayr

snapped up Tash's chin and claimed his mouth, crushing their lips in a kiss he felt all the way to his toes. His body raged like a fire, burning away doubt as he traded moans with Tash, the eager sounds echoed by greedy touches.

They needed to ravish each other and hold more than the fabric tightened between them. They needed to be skin on skin, sweat-slicked and gliding over each other, sliding in and out of their heat until they were spent.

Hands cupped around Tash's face, Mayr kissed Tash with every bit of ardor he could muster. Everything was in place. Everyone with a role in his plan had played their part. Even he had managed to slip away and tend to necessary details without Tash asking questions, including why Mayr smelled of soap and savoury oil.

He needed to make his move.

"Come on." Mayr spun on his heel and led Tash through the hall by the wrist. Stopping at the conservatory, he reached for the gold door handles.

"Wait, what are you doing?" Tash eyed Mayr with a dazed look. "It's freezing in there."

"It's been a mild day."

"It's still winter. Cold, icy."

"I have every confidence you'll keep me warm." Mayr turned the handle slowly, testing how long he could prolong Tash's horrified expression. Silent laughter toyed with his memories of their first time together in the conservatory, their hideaway to touch and worship among fragrant scents and the inspiration of life. No season would keep them from it.

"Have you lost your mind?" Tash stepped back as Mayr pushed on the door. "It's been locked since the Feast of Taleyra."

"Yes, and now it's not."

"The gardener's the only one that goes in."

"Not tonight." Mayr held out his hand. "Come in with me, even if it's just for a moment."

The uncertainty on Tash's face deepened before he clasped Mayr's hand. "A moment."

Mayr slipped inside and coaxed Tash with a gentle tug. A wall of warmth hit him, the air thick with a myriad of aromas, blending sweet flowers and woody leaves with scented wax. Quiet pops and hisses sounded from around the room. Before him, the white marble path and its silvery-blue veins appeared golden in the candlelight.

Tash's grip tightened as he stopped. His shaky breaths cut through Mayr with all the sharpness of a scream.

"I don't understand," Tash whispered. "How?" He glanced over the room. When he looked back, tears glistened in his eyes. "Why?"

Mayr closed the door and wrapped his arm around Tash's waist. "Magic," he said against Tash's jaw, "for you."

Moving behind Tash to embrace him, Mayr rested his chin on Tash's shoulder to survey the transformed room. In the spring and summer, the conservatory boasted flowers of various colours and glossy leaves with a multitude of hues, but in the winter, the garden beds were home to plants that thrived in the cold. Prickly bushes of rich purple branches and brown, tear-shaped nuts stood strong among the red-black shrubs of hard, coarse leaves striped with yellow. They towered over hardy flowers with ice-blue petals, black leaves speckled with silver spots, and dusky blue tendrils that crept onto the marble path. Winter vines coiled around anything they found, their deep blue limbs and rugged, mauve leaves anchored to the remnants of summer vines and thick, yellow stalks of plants that would bloom again in the spring. Where the gardens ended at the edges of the glass walls, vines grew upwards in tangles on wood lattices. White leaves lay scattered over the soil and paths.

Unlike other days, the conservatory looked ethereal. Bushes that normally glistened with ice glimmered with drops of water from an imposed thaw. The colourless glass walls were not opaque due to snow and frost but from steam and heat. Throughout the room, white candles flickered, joined by small brass lanterns that hung on the bushes on either side of the marble pathway. Around them, crystalline glass balls and silver ribbons hung from shrubs and vines staked upright. Strands of shimmering glass beads looped and twisted around the stalks and limbs, accompanied by chains of bright blue jewels that dangled from leaves and mimicked the creeping vines. A light layer of silver dust gave the soil a metallic sheen like delicate snowflakes.

Even the pool of water in the centre of the room was adorned. The round enclosure of white and silver stones stood to Mayr's knees, filled with water warmed by Adren's magic. Candles floated on the surface amidst silver petals. Beside the pool lay a pile of thick blankets and colourful silk pillows. Gold, purple, and red fabrics beckoned, offering a comfortable space to love and be loved.

Tash latched onto Mayr with trembling hands as if he never wanted to let go.

Not bad for a week of conspiring, Mayr mused, smiling into Tash's shoulder. The ornaments had been the easiest to arrange, most of them from the collection used for the Feast of Taleyra. Each year for the feast, the conservatory was decorated and opened to guests as a reprieve from the festivities in the ballroom. Afterwards, the baubles were removed and the room left unlocked but closed tight to keep the cold air from the rest of the house. Sometimes Aeley or Lira visited the conservatory, bundled up in winter attire while they contemplated. Other than them and the occasional guard, only the gardener, Noa, entered in order to tend the plants and check for drafts and damage. There was no reliable and efficient heat source, particularly given the large space and extensive glass encasement. While other Grand Families experimented with ways to warm their conservatories, Aeley preferred to keep the winter garden as it was.

Except for one night. Mayr buried his face in Tash's neck and breathed him in. *For tonight it's warm, beautiful, and ours.*

"Ecstasy in glass," Tash whispered. "How?" He held out his hand and glanced upwards as though he expected rain to fall from the fogged ceiling.

Slow and steady, Mayr glided his fingers down Tash's extended arm, lingering in the crook of Tash's arm with circling caresses before continuing over his bracer and into Tash's palm with a feather-light touch.

"If you look hard enough, you'll see," Mayr answered.

As Tash shivered and drew his arm back, Mayr laughed softly and twined their fingers. He lifted Tash's arm towards the wall to their right, gesturing to one of the water barrels. Inside the perimeter of the garden beds were water-filled troughs and buckets, all strategically placed.

Mayr folded Tash's arm across his chest. "Adren tried all week to come up with something. Then ce came up with this, all elegant and perfect." He slid both of his hands up Tash's chest, over his shoulders, and stopped at Tash's neck. "Inside the barrels and troughs are rocks infused with Adren's magic. They're so hot they boil the water and let off steam," he murmured against the sensitive skin behind Tash's ear. "Even the pool has them. We're fine as long as we don't touch them." Brushing Tash's veil and hair aside, Mayr licked Tash's nape. "It won't last long. Adren says it takes less than half a day until everything goes cold. We should—"

Tash was a blur as he turned and kissed Mayr with so much fervour it hurt, both hands gripping Mayr's neck, keeping him there for the devouring.

Mayr surrendered with a choked cry. He met each thrust of Tash's tongue with his own, their lips attempting to meld and move as one. Arms around Tash's waist, Mayr held tight and ground against Tash. Fingers raked down his back, Tash's desire staking its claim without restraint.

In an instant, his weapons belt was unbuckled and in Tash's hands.

"We don't have much time then," Tash said, tossing the belt aside and seizing Mayr's second belt. Tash's face flushed as he fumbled with the buckle. "We need to make the best of this." He flung the second belt behind him. The leather and metal skidded across the floor into a shrub.

Not a breath later, his palms clamped around Mayr's cheeks. In a heated frenzy, he jerked Mayr in for another kiss, almost toppling them both.

Mayr groaned, gripping Tash by the elbows to steady himself. He fended off Tash's impatient grabs for the hem of his tunic. "I have to... Stay still, you."

Caught in a daze, he clutched Tash's arm to ensure they both remained upright. In slow movements, Mayr grasped the comb on the underside of Tash's veil and drew the headdress away, careful not to tear the fabric, despite Tash's fidgeting. Gingerly he folded the veil and placed in on the floor behind them, away from the plants and soil.

The next moment, Mayr took to Tash's mouth with a loud moan that died on their lips. His fists crushed the front of Tash's robes as he yanked Tash against him. Fingers quested over his waist and dipped into sensitive crevices. A tantalizing pressure traced the outline of his cock then continued downwards between his legs.

The growl that rumbled deep in his throat forced their lips apart. Hands on Tash's hips, Mayr scrunched Tash's robes upwards, only for the three layers to gather quickly in his fists until he could hold no more. Slipping his hands beneath the layers, Mayr worked his touch over Tash's chest until he grazed his hardened nipples. To the sounds of Tash's murmurs of approval, Mayr pinched and played, circling his fingertips around the nubs.

When Tash craned his head back and tugged Mayr's hair, Mayr's patience burned out. Agitated by the barriers between them, he scrambled to rid Tash of the robes. Together they struggled to remove the crumpled fabric, fingers stumbling over closures until they gave up. Mayr pulled the robes over Tash's head with little care, then balled them up and threw them over his shoulder. The bundle hit the doors before Tash made fast work of Mayr's tunic and discarded it in the same direction as the robes.

Mayr's naked skin welcomed the steamy air as Tash's hands traveled across his shoulder blades, gripping and stretching on their journey down his back. Pressed against Tash's bared flesh, Mayr kissed him with agonizing tenderness to temper the frenzy they had started. Time was important but not enough to rush through what he needed to do.

Instead, he sucked on Tash's bottom lip until Tash whimpered and attempted to take control. Mayr leisurely denied his efforts and worshipped Tash's upper lip with the same attention. Only when Tash's lips felt lavished to exhaustion did he offer a kiss that was all softness. His body had made its desire known through fire and desperation, but this kiss came from his soul. Emotions poured from him like water and turned to honey in their mouths, sweetening the kiss until it became the slightest touch of skin on skin, one breath away from chaste.

Silent, Mayr unclasped the chain to the talon ring from Tash's bracer before removing the ring and chain. There would be time for pain in their pleasure but not then. With the same amount of care, he drew his chain with the locket and Iliane's ring over his head.

Jewelry clutched in one fist, Mayr wrapped his other hand around Tash's and led him towards the pool. Small bubbles from the heated rocks at the bottom broke the water's surface while white candles small enough to fit in his palm floated on top, silver petals stuck to several of them. Beside the pool lay a brown wood bowl no larger than his hand. He laid the ring and necklace in the bowl and moved it away from the blankets and pillows to keep their treasures safe.

The removal of their boots and stockings was not as cautious, followed by the careless tossing of the items to either side of the marble path. Reminded of their first time in the conservatory, Mayr stepped onto the blankets and sank down into the pillows. He leaned back against the side of the warm pool and offered his hand to Tash.

A dreamy smile was his reward as Tash accepted and kneeled on the blankets. Once he took his place between Mayr's raised knees, he eased back into Mayr's arms. A contented sigh slipped from him as he cuddled close, his back sliding along Mayr's chest. He curled one arm around Mayr's neck and nuzzled his chin.

"I love you," Tash whispered, threading his fingers through Mayr's hair. "With my life, my breath, and every piece of my soul, I love you."

Mayr squeezed his eyes shut. He needed to remember the words he wanted to say, questions he had practiced a hundred times in the last week. No matter how terrifying the answers might be, he had to ask.

Please don't let this hurt.

Licking his lips, Mayr let his hands roam over Tash. If he distracted himself, maybe the words would simply tumble out. He followed the tightened muscles of Tash's chest to his stomach and further below, snaking beneath the tied waist of Tash's red pants. Encouraged by Tash's moan, Mayr stroked his shaft, the flared head already wet with pre-release.

His cock twitched its approval as Tash drew up his knees. Mayr's fingers continued through the hot crevices and around Tash's balls. He cupped the tightened sacs then fluttered his fingertips over the entrance behind them.

Tash's back arched. A strangled whimper cut through his ragged breaths. He clenched Mayr's knees tight enough to scrape skin through Mayr's pants.

"I love you, too," Mayr mumbled, cowardice washing over him. Those words were easy to say, but he hid behind them. Convenience was not the same as doing what was right.

It was time to move on. He had to leave Betta and her betrayal behind. The past only clouded the issue, as did the memories of his other failed relationships. Rejection could not dictate his life any longer. There was no debate, no delay, and no excuse. There was only the need to make Tash his completely.

I still don't know how we're going to work it all

out, but I have to stop worrying about every detail. I'm so scared that I'm throwing myself into pointless logistics and pretending I don't know why.

Logistics they could work out, but rejection was a soulful ache he could not withstand, especially if Tash dealt the blow. He knew how deep the hurt could go, having been rejected once by Tash only to watch him court death.

Mayr would do anything to keep it from happening again. Tash was worth the agony, and so was the clarity that came with his love. It had taken Mayr their entire relationship to finally understand the truth of his failed romances: he could waste a lifetime blaming others, but he had done it to himself. In a twisted state of self-sabotage, he had purposely chosen the wrong lovers just so they *would* leave.

His avoidance of men had been equally damaging, limiting his chances of finding someone he could settle down with. None of it was by accident or coincidence but a way to ensure he was never happy.

He had always been too afraid to meet the right person.

After Betta, he was terrified to commit his love to someone else. To protect him, his subconscious had played games to keep him miserable.

Then you appeared. Mayr leaned his forehead against Tash's temple. *I convinced myself you were safe because we were in it for the sex, but the joke couldn't have been more on me. You're the missing piece.*

There was only one way to find out what their future would be.

Settling his hands on Tash's waist, Mayr pressed his lips to Tash's ear. "So... how many children do we want?"

Tash startled. He leaned aside to look at Mayr, eyes wide. His lips moved but no words came. A blush spread across his cheeks before he licked his lips and turned away. "One," he said, laying his hands over Mayr's. "Maybe two."

"Two sounds like a good number." Mayr hummed behind his smile. "I'd be willing to try for three."

With a shaky breath, Tash all but melted into Mayr's embrace. "And this... you... This is real?"

"I promised we'd talk about it."

"Yes, but after *at least* a year. I thought..."

"Hey." Mayr tilted Tash's face towards him. "You remember what you asked me, right? That if I was with the right person—"

"—If you'd try being a father again. I remember."

"Good, because it's all you," Mayr whispered. "So let's do it. As long as you're with me, the number doesn't matter."

Tash scrambled from his cozy place and turned around, pushing Mayr's legs down and straddling his lap. He pinned Mayr against the pool, arms around Mayr's neck. The pink blush of his cheeks flushed red, as intense and bright as his eyes. "You have me," Tash said. "I'm with you every step."

The last words came out in a whisper, overpowered by a soundless kiss so full of intent and promise it left Mayr dizzy.

As Tash drew away, Mayr chased his mouth and reclaimed it with a groan. Tash's hold around his neck tightened, his body pressed close. He forced Mayr against the pool until his back scraped the stone. Barely feeling the twinges of pain, Mayr stretched his arms out along the edge of the pool. While Tash attacked his throat with an onslaught of sloppy kisses, Mayr let his head fall back in mindless surrender.

Hard found hard as Tash ground into him. More than once, Tash slid over the swollen tip of Mayr's cock, eliciting fiery aches and protests at the fabric between them. Unbearable as the burn was, Mayr wanted more.

Clenching the inside of the pool, his hands submersed in the hot water, Mayr lifted to rub against Tash. Pull matched push in a frantic rhythm. Tension coiled and pummeled Mayr's muscles, squeezing his insides. The low hum of Tash's throaty moans tumbled over his, converging in a rush of vibrations that surged through Mayr. Shivers wreaked havoc on his control and nothing could stop him from bucking his hips. He was ready to burst. The only thing stopping him was a question, one he needed an answer for before he screamed Tash's name.

Mayr choked back a moan and plunged one hand into Tash's hair, spraying water over them both. Although his intention had been to enjoy the conservatory until dawn and ask the most important question afterwards, his decisions were breaking apart and crafting a new design. Waiting took too long. He wanted to watch the sun rise knowing Tash's answer.

"Upstairs," he managed hoarsely, pushing Tash back.

There was no argument as Tash stood and helped Mayr up, then moved to retrieve his boots. Mayr grabbed his hand and tugged. "Leave them."

They hurried from the room and through the corridors, half-naked and needy. Mayr ignored the guards they passed. Time was the only one he could not reason with, the one thing he feared at that moment, even if it teased him as brazenly as the guards would later.

Still holding Tash's hand, Mayr rushed into the darkness of the foyer inside the main entrance and turned to the staircase to his right. The wide steps were barely visible in the thin moonlight from a window at the top of the stairs. Not trusting himself to take more than one step at a time, he gripped the vine-decorated banister while they climbed the stairs.

The scorching sensation of Tash's lips on his was fading. He missed the throb of his heart whenever Tash spoiled him with adoration and pleas for more.

Mayr stopped halfway up the staircase, his feet planted firmly on the landing. He cupped Tash's face in both hands and kissed him hard. Tash backed him against the banister, keeping Mayr in place while their lips and tongues played without mercy.

Guiding Tash by the shoulders, their mouths never parting, Mayr turned and continued up the stairs backwards. For every step Mayr took, Tash followed, his hands wrapped around Mayr's neck. The kiss deepened with the laborious trek, persisting even while they maneuvered through the hallway between the bedrooms. Eyes closed, Mayr led as much as he obeyed Tash's gentle push.

When Tash slammed him against a door, Mayr ripped his lips away in surprise.

Palms slapped the door on either side of Mayr's head. Arms locked him in. Tash pinned Mayr with his body, the hunger on his face apparent even in the thin light.

They had reached his room, Mayr realized. At the other end of the corridor, the jangle of keys and quiet footfalls accompanied the lingering shadows of the night watchmen.

Chest heaving, Tash nipped another kiss and palmed Mayr's cock through his pants. If he knew the guards were watching, he made no indication. His hand delved under the ties and fabric and roamed over Mayr's thigh to fondle him from behind.

Whatever sounds or movements the guards may have made, Mayr heard nothing past his groan of approval. His fingers fumbled over the doorknob grazing his ribs. One awkward turn and the door opened. They stumbled inside before Tash kicked the door closed.

"Wait." Mayr swept his glance over the darkened room. Warmth lingered from the hearth more than thirty paces to his right, the scent of smoke and burnt wood remnants of the fire he had put out earlier, convinced they would not be in the room until later. The bed was against the wall to his left, dressed neatly with layers of soft sheets, wool blankets, and a thick blue and black quilt his mother had sewn. Earlier that day, he had thrown every pillow he owned onto the bed and arranged them along the headboard. His favourite mauve pillows, usually kept in the two black chairs beside the window with matching mauve curtains, stood among six white pillows in attempts to look orderly and possibly romantic.

Tempting as it was, they could not tear the bed apart yet. He focused on the window instead, the open curtains forcing his attention to the moonlight. Rays of light passed through the stained-glass window, tinged a faint blue-green. The floor near the window seemed to glow, bathed in the most intense stream of blue light. Around it, thinner bands of green and blue-green ebbed outwards to the rest of the room.

The light reminded Mayr of the four white feathers in the glass keepsake box on his armoire, a sign from the Goddess of Love the first time he had made love to Tash. They, too, had glowed and stolen his breath.

There was no better sign than that. Hand in hand, Mayr led Tash across the room and guided him into place on one side of the pool of light.

"Stay." Mayr raised one hand. "Don't move. Just… right there."

He barely heard Tash's agreement as he dashed to the bed. Kneeling on the side nearest the door, he reached beneath the bed frame and patted the floor. Nestled against the wall was the small wooden box he needed, one that fit in his palm and weighed next to nothing. Inside, it contained a whole life with a thousand hopes and promises.

His return to the window was more controlled than the giddiness trapped inside him. He wanted to say everything all at once, not one syllable wasted.

"Now that we're talking about kids," Mayr said, standing in front of Tash, both of them partially in the light, "we can move on to the next matter. Because what you said before—that our children will need protection and have what's rightfully theirs—you're right." He opened the box and held it between them where the light was brightest.

Tash's ragged breath could have knocked

them both over.

Perfectly illuminated inside the box was a pure white metal ring that glistened blue. Nested in the thick band were four bright blue diamonds, all of them round and polished. Two silver feathers curved around the stones, one above and one below, each etched with minute detail.

Eyes glistening with sudden tears, Tash raised his hand, hesitant to touch. "Say... Tell me..." His voice cracked, hushed to a whisper. "*Please.* I need you to..."

In three steps, Mayr pressed himself to Tash's side. His free hand rested on Tash's hip as he leaned his forehead against Tash's. "Marry me."

A rogue tear slipped from Tash's eye, only for Mayr to catch it with the back of his finger before it reached Tash's cheek.

"Yes," Tash said softly, shaking as he wove his fingers through Mayr's hair. "An eternity of yes."

"Then you get the pretty." Mayr grinned, snatched the ring from the box, and placed the box on the windowsill. Resisting the urge to laugh at how quickly relief coursed through him, he focused on sliding the ring onto the middle finger of Tash's left hand. The band fit well, snug and beautiful as he expected. In the stillness, he nuzzled Tash's cheek. "Now I can make you come."

A passionate kiss silenced his laughter completely. In a flurry of motion, crumpled fabric, and tossed bracers, they ended up naked and on the bed.

Mayr crawled up the mattress towards the small table left of the bed. On his hands and knees, reaching for the vial of oil on the bedside table, he spread his legs further to display his naked rear and garner attention. For extra measure, he wiggled and bowed down from the waist, the glass vial in his fist.

A nip on his right buttock made him groan. His back seized. The sensation of teeth and short hairs as they grazed both of his rear cheeks locked him in place, his bottom exposed and vulnerable in the air. The nips grew into bites, followed by kneading and lapping.

As Tash's tongue slipped into his cleft, Mayr buried his face in the blankets and pushed back, offering to take everything Tash wanted to give. He loved when Tash lingered, when his mouth demanded more.

Tash's mouth took what it wanted with the added pleasure of his fingers. The tip of his tongue passed over Mayr's tight entrance, first to tease then to prod and seek entry. One finger pushed in slightly before Tash licked a path from Mayr's sac up to his lower back.

Hard, wet strokes caught Mayr in all the right ways. He rocked gently, holding his breath as Tash sucked around his hole and moaned.

"You did something—added something," Tash said, his voice low and husky. Fingertips crept over Mayr while Tash devoured him, his tongue thrusting inside.

Mayr laughed into the bed, but cut it off with a throaty hum as Tash slipped his finger into him. He had hoped the savoury flavour of the new oil would please Tash. It was meant to be tasted not merely used and wiped away. "I may have come up here after dinner and washed up. Maybe rubbed in whatever you think is there." With both arms folded under his head, the vial still in his hand, Mayr peered behind him. "Good or bad?"

The answer was a moan and a muffled, "Good," followed by the familiar burn of Tash's finger twisting inside. Another finger traveled downwards to caress Mayr's balls, and Mayr cursed his agreement. He wanted to feel Tash in him, to surrender to the breach as Tash filled him.

Tash's hand snaked up Mayr's thigh and over his ribs, until Mayr slipped the vial into Tash's hand. The blankets pulled taut with Tash's shifted weight as he sat back to work with the oil and toss the vial aside. A moment later, his tender touch returned, comforting as he slid two slicked fingers into Mayr.

Mayr mumbled his appreciation. The blankets pooled beneath his head the more he clutched them and drew inwards. He swayed with the rhythm set by Tash and sighed with contentment. This was how they liked it best: slow and drawn out, with Mayr at Tash's creative mercy and controlled wickedness. On occasion, they switched to fierce, blinding sex or Mayr drove into Tash until he tore into Mayr's back, but this was different. This was them; their bliss, their equilibrium. Vulnerability and safety wrapped up in affectionate leisure—

Mayr shouted into the mattress. Tash's fingers were *there* again, stroking the sensitive spot inside that always made Mayr lose his mind. Warm pre-release trickled onto the bed and wet Mayr's stomach, leaving his cock aching for more.

From behind, Tash laughed softly. "Come." He stroked Mayr's hip. "Enough play. Come to me." Tash helped Mayr to his knees, his hands slathered in sweet-scented oil. Carefully he sat on his heels and guided Mayr back, his knees closed between Mayr's parted thighs.

Before he fell into Tash's lap, Mayr reached between them to grip Tash and rub pre-release over his oil-slicked tip. Tash breathed sharply and rolled his hips. His cock pulsed in Mayr's grasp, tight and hot, strained to the point of desperate need.

Time for a new game, Mayr decided, aligning Tash's cock to his entrance. All at once, he pushed down while Tash lifted up. They groaned in unison, Mayr taking Tash to the hilt. Grinning as he leaned forward, Mayr rose until the head of Tash's cock teased the inside of his opening. The next instant, he fell back, taking Tash fully once more, accompanied by another of Tash's delectable moans.

Tash's response was quick: pushing Mayr's

thighs further apart with his knees, he clutched Mayr's hips tight and thrust deep. They rose and fell together, again and again. Tension chased anticipation, the beast of intensity unfurling between them. Every rise was like a breath in, moist and open, the wet sounds of skin sliding over well-oiled skin filling the gaps between needy pants. Every fall felt as if they set that breath on fire and demolished emptiness. Grounded in moments meant only for them, their gasps were as deafening as the cries that screamed love.

They rocked vigorously, the bed creaking in protest. Tash laced the fingers of his right hand through Mayr's then shifted to pound anew. His left hand stroked Mayr's cock, the smooth marriage ring gliding over him.

The sight of his ring on Tash's finger cast Mayr into a dizzying haze. The diamonds glittered in the wash of moonlight that reached the bed, brilliant and stunning even under a glistening coat of oil and pre-release.

This was their life. Not Mayr's alone but *theirs*. Come what may, Tash had said yes.

An eternity of yes — a forever of being yours.

Mayr slammed down, throwing them both off their rhythm. He clenched his muscles to clamp tight around Tash's cock, and as he pulled off with tortuous slowness, he arched into Tash without releasing the strength of his hold. At the tip, he repeated the process, his back straining.

Once, twice, three more times.

Tash growled and yanked on a fistful of Mayr's hair. His tightened grip jerked Mayr's shaft. Almost on his knees, Tash lifted Mayr higher, one thrust after another. Shallow, stunted breaths filled the air amidst the whimpers and grunts that heralded the end.

"Mayr," Tash warned, driving his fingers between Mayr's legs. A sensual caress flitted over Mayr's tightened sac, too light to ignore.

Tash may as well have kicked him.

Mayr whined and snapped forward, clawing at the bed as he came. "Halataldris," he rasped. His head throbbed with the sound of his own heartbeat.

Behind him, Tash shuddered and cried out. A whimper escaped Mayr as he rode Tash's release. He bit down hard enough to taste blood on his bottom lip. The moment Tash finished, Mayr collapsed onto the bed, ensuring he took Tash with him.

"Wait, let me—" Tash withdrew and fell onto his side, sweat glistening on his forehead. Through his gasps, he smiled wearily. "Good?"

"Mmm." Mayr hid his face against Tash's damp shoulder. The scent of sex and oil wafted around them. Sticky release smeared his skin. Deep breaths were impossible, forcing him to pant into Tash's neck. "Perfect."

Tash's throaty laugh turned into a light snort. He squeezed Mayr's hip before standing and padding across the room for a wet cloth. On his return, Mayr spread his legs and lay still while Tash wiped him down, then himself. Not long after, Tash took the cloth back to the table.

Mayr slid from the bed, yanked off the top blanket, and tossed it into the corner. By the time Tash returned, he had flipped back the blankets, thrown both mauve pillows to the floor, and repositioned the white pillows across the headboard so he could lie back on the middle two.

Tash crawled into the bed from the right side. Cuddled against him, Tash buried his face in Mayr's neck, one arm curled over Mayr's waist. They lay in a long silence, finding the calm together. A peace settled inside Mayr, deeper than satisfaction, more intense than joy. He could lie there forever, wanting for nothing but more time.

"Guess what?" Mayr whispered.

"Hmm?"

"We're getting married," Mayr sang quietly.

Tash lifted his head. "And it's what you want? I didn't rush—"

Mayr pressed his fingers to Tash's lips. "Don't, Halataldris. This—us—I'm not doing anything I don't want to do. I trust we'll make a marriage work. I trust that if we have a family, you won't take our child away or force me out of their life."

The kiss Tash brushed across his mouth stopped him from saying more.

"Thank you," Tash murmured. "I know it's not easy for you to give out trust. I'll cherish it always." His fingertips crept across Mayr's lips. "I'll strive to stay worthy of it."

"You don't have to strive. Just be you." Mayr caught Tash's fingers and held them. "You turned down being an Uldana priest for me. I still don't know how to respond to that except to give you my trust and heart and anything else you want." He planted tiny kisses across Tash's knuckles. "I needed time to get myself together, but I've been losing my mind from knowing what I really want. I had to wait for the ring to get finished first."

"A beautiful ring."

"Ress did well."

"Ress?"

"Well, yeah." Mayr snorted. "He would've whacked me with his cane had I not asked. So we came to an agreement: he got a space to work in and all the shiny materials, and I paid for everything. After Araveena, I wasn't going to let you go without some sort of—" He clamped his mouth shut. Did he need to spoil the mood by mentioning *that* night?

Tash propped himself up on his elbow. "No, don't stop. Without what?"

"A commitment." Mayr let out a defeated breath. "I told our families getting married changed nothing. I reduced it to an excuse of inheritance. But it *does* change things. It's more than names on a piece of paper and an argument about birthright and final wishes." He rolled onto his side to face Tash. "I could've lost you. So while I'm terrified of getting married again, I need you to know how I feel, that you mean more to me than my fears."

"Mayr..." Whatever his unspoken words, the tears in Tash's awestruck gaze said everything.

"I'm offering you my life, Halataldris," Mayr said softly. "It's what I want, and I want you to feel it, too."

"I do," Tash whispered, "more than you know."

"Then it's settled." Mayr grinned and swept Tash's hair over his shoulder. "You'll be mine, I'll be yours, and we can still enjoy the conservatory before it goes cold."

Tash's eyes widened. "Naked and slow?"

A mischievous laugh bubbled up from Mayr's core in answer. On the list of things he planned to do by morning, naked and slow was only the start.

Chapter Four

Someone loved him enough to tie their life to his.

Tash blinked awake. Sunlight greeted him, accompanied by the quiet crackles of fire between steady snores. Lying on his right side, facing the grey stone of the bedroom's outer wall, he sensed the weight of Mayr slumbering behind him on the mussed bed. If his memories could be believed, they had made love in the conservatory until dawn and witnessed the first rays of dim, pink light before they stumbled back to bed.

Words pounded in his head, shepherding his thoughts along whimsical paths of insatiable desire. With the slow lick of his lips, he tasted Mayr's countless kisses and musky essence, comforted by the familiarity of his lover.

No, not just my lover... Tash snaked his left hand out from beneath the covers. The marriage ring glinted white and blue on his middle finger, its details exquisite and real. *He's my betrothed.*

Tears threatened to overtake him. He curled his fingers into his chest and gripped his pillow with his other hand. His emotions refused to grant him a reprieve, no matter how hard he wished them away. Since the proposal, he had nearly wept each time Mayr did anything sweet or thoughtful, which leaned on the side of every other moment. His unbidden tears had earned him endless starry-eyed smiles and tender touches, whispers of soul that assured him he was where he ought to be.

Someone had found him worthy. Someone wanted him just as he was.

No words could express how high and fast his spirit wanted to fly through the ether of the universe, announcing the news. If he could have traded places with the divine bird Halataldris, Tash would have soared through the heavens and brought back a piece of a star to adorn Mayr's hand as a token of his love.

How wrong he had been; how poorly he had assumed. His fear of Mayr's secretiveness led him to believe the worst.

You weren't pulling away from me—you were trying to get closer. Tash clenched his jaws and squeezed his eyes shut. He had spent the day before lamenting the dead and casting shadows of expectation onto Mayr. All the while, Mayr had intended to offer light to the gloom. His affection lifted Tash from the abyss and set him on a peak, then they had greeted the new day with laughter and caresses that still burned in Tash's memories.

Tash opened his eyes and unfurled his fist. He wiggled his fingers to watch the diamonds in his ring catch the light, awed by their very existence.

For someone to call him husband... It was unexpected, given his rotten luck with romance. Hope followed him into every dedicated relationship, but disgust always chased him out of them. Inesta, his first love, had trapped him in an ultimatum and loathed his decision to save her life. His second love, Naliss, had tired of Tash's need for seclusion and walked away. The third, Erithe, had killed herself, leaving Tash convinced he had pushed her too far.

His choices had never been acceptable, his fears never tolerable. Those he gave his heart to had rejected him, frustrated with his inability to be more even after he tried to be whatever they wanted him to be.

Then there's you. Tash smiled at the soft snorts and smacking of lips as Mayr rolled onto his back. *You'd hunt my other loves down and bury them in guilt if you could, if I'd let you.*

As it was, Mayr showed care for Inesta's safety, ensuring she was protected while she pursued her new life in Alosaa, the neighbouring tract east of Gailarin. Mayr disliked Inesta, yet he had asked Rosayra, the wife and Head of the Guard for the Tract Steward in charge of Alosaa, to look out for her. Without Tash's knowledge or plea, Mayr had made a personal request of another Head Guard and been granted a favour usually reserved for those of Mayr's blood. Instead of leaving Inesta to fend for herself, Mayr acknowledged Tash's love for her and offered what Tash could not: a happy life where no one could hurt her, not even Tash.

You didn't deserve any of this, Ines. I know you'll only ever see me as the monster that ruined your life instead of the coward that couldn't stand losing you. I understand why you left, and I can't blame you — I would've left me, too.

"I'm sorry," Tash whispered, fighting the urge to glance at his scarred forearms, one of his most shameful secrets. Although the Shar-denn had permanently marked him, carving the flesh of his thighs and calves with blunt knives and thin strands of barbed metal, his self-inflicted wounds were the ones he always hid.

Ugly as they were, he could withstand the scars from the Shar-denn. The meaning inherent in their existence painted his character in a way other markings never would. They were a sign of overdue rebellion, a symbol of reclaimed morality. After Tash refused to murder innocents, his Shar-denn brethren had beaten him until he bled from every orifice. His chest and legs were covered in hideous burns from punishment, scarred tissue filling the holes where flames and heated stakes had been shoved inside his injuries. Guards he had called friends had tortured him until his throat was stripped raw from screaming, all because he would not execute the children and grandchildren of a man his faction's boss considered a rival.

Still, the only wounds that drove him away

from his own reflection were the ones from his own knife. They were the story of his wounded heart, written in skin. Not only were they reminders of loss, they were souvenirs of his journey from monster to man.

Grateful as he was to have Mayr, he owed just as great a debt to Inesta for shoving him onto the path he had traveled to get there. Inesta had demanded he choose between her and the Shar-denn to test his love. She diminished herself to what she considered a simple choice, as if the options were not intertwined by a complicated web.

The ultimatum had tested his love, that much was true, but the way Inesta misinterpreted his choice was even worse. What she saw as him ending their relationship because he cared too little could not have been further from the truth. Walking away from her, listening to her wail and scream obscenities at him while he fled her parents' home, had left Tash in agony. Her screams had twisted his courage until he drowned his emotions in several bottles of fulore, the strongest alcohol he had kept in his private collection in a Shar-denn cache house.

Unable to face his family and peers, Tash had hidden in Nimae and Varen's home while they were on a week-long raid and drunk himself useless, his eyes swollen shut by tears. Alone at the house in the secluded woods, he had screamed at the night. Barely upright in the middle of the glen behind the back shed, he threw anything he could find at the trees. When he tried to throw an empty bottle of fulore, the bottle shattered in his grip. Angry that even the drink punished him, he had thrown a handful of shards, yelling at the pain he should have felt from the glass embedded in his hand.

Afterwards, he had picked the glass out of his wound, calm as he focused on healing himself. Sometime after midnight, he had passed out on the floor in front of the cold hearth, covered in bloodstains and soot.

Fresh pain had awoken him at noon, a brutal reminder of what he had given up. Inesta believed his choice reflected his true desires, that he wanted to steal, kill, and maim rather than marry her and raise the family she had begged him for.

None of it was true. He *had* chosen her, protecting her from retribution. Had he left the Shar-denn, the gang would have killed them both. They would have sold Inesta over and over again, exploiting her to death. Though he told her as much and swore he loved her more than life itself, she had thrown a mirror at him. He could still remember the noise of the frame splintering and the shattered glass.

The day after their parting had burned as viciously as the night before. The venom in her tone had scorched his love. His heart had tried to beat true, though it floundered with the memories of how much she wished he would die. His knives had never looked more like a saving grace as they did the second night without her. Like the broken bottle, he had needed a distraction. A problem he could solve. A pain he could soothe.

The first time he slit his wrists, he had been completely sober. His hand shook the whole time. No tears had fallen, just blood all over the kitchen table. In the moments afterwards, Inesta's name had not been on his tongue. He had put her aside to tend to himself, driven by the need to clean and bandage the jagged wound. Strangely satisfied, he had sat on the back step with another bottle of fulore and recounted the sensation of ripping himself apart simply to put himself back together.

When he did it again two nights later, and the dozens of times after that, the calm it brought became an addiction—enough that after Naliss and Erithe left him, Tash added more slashes to his arms. His forearms were permanently numb in a way his heart never would be.

With Naliss, the scars reminded Tash he could not think only of himself. He had to be strong and give everything his lover wanted and needed, even if it meant putting himself in harm's way. No one wanted to help bear his problems. No one would stand by him while he hid from the Shardenn. Love could not exist in the shadows: it was only worthy in the open.

Unlike Inesta, Naliss had not challenged

Tash's love. Instead, Naliss had packed everything he kept in the small house the priests had provided Tash and kept his departure blunt. It had taken mere moments to end a relationship crafted in little less than a year, unceremonious as Naliss stood in the front doorway and announced he was leaving. After a bitter rant full of disgust and exasperation over Tash's paranoia and emotional shortcomings, Naliss had turned and left Tash to stare at the slamming door.

Erithe never gave Tash that much. She simply approached him in the village market, told him they were over because he rushed her with unbearable expectations, and walked away.

Tash had hurried after her and grasped her hand, desperate to save their gentle, often complicated love, but Erithe had yelped and jerked away. *"Leave me alone! You're smothering me,"* she had cried, catching the attention of all the villagers around them. Never had he felt so small.

He offered to do anything to make her happy, pledging to turn himself inside out to love her better, however she needed. In response, Erithe had stumbled away, gaping as if he had threatened to kill her. She ran before he could say anything more.

A week later, part of him withered while he mourned her death, her life lost to the river. Her sister had railed on him and thrust her fist in his face with a farewell note from Erithe, demanding

Tash tell her what he had done to make Erithe kill herself. Although Erithe had struggled for years with an ever-growing sadness that attacked her in fierce waves, tearing her away from the joys in life and leaving her in anguish, she had never mentioned the intention to take her own life. Mostly she had spoken of feeling worthless and uncertain, and Tash had done everything he could to assure her she was wanted. Despite the thousands of times he told himself Erithe had been too miserable to carry on, Tash still believed he could have stopped her had he paid closer attention.

Swallowing back his regret, Tash wiped his wet eyes with his pillowcase. He could not change the past. Had he not yearned for companionship and physical touch, he would have sworn love off altogether after Erithe. Instead, he had gone from one casual lover to the next, content to leave the bed of someone he never intended to continue seeing. Unconditional love always passed him by.

Until now.

Mayr stayed even when it was better to leave.

I may never deserve you, but I can't let you go. I tried and it hurt worse than all the other times. Tash curled into the mattress, wishing he could forget. *I tried to cut you out, to carve you into me, but it didn't work. The pain kept flowing and I couldn't stop—I didn't want to. I sobbed while I did it, crying your name, but I'll never tell you that. I'll never tell you I dug harder every time I whispered I loved you. I'll give you my heart but not my shame. I can't bear seeing the horror in your eyes.*

He would protect Mayr as much as Mayr protected him.

Tash's family had never seen his marred arms, and he would never tell them, knowing how they would react. But Mayr knew the why and how of each scar. Rarely did Mayr speak of the marks, but he did not ignore them. His touch was always soft; his lips tender as they kissed the various lines. By those efforts alone he lessened the sting of what they meant.

Despite his shame, his scars were more than reminders of what he should not do: they were a record of how he had found himself by Mayr's side, with a life worth having instead of wasting away in misery. They were explanations for who he was, reasons why fear drove him to such despair and joy lifted him higher than wings ever could. They symbolized what it meant to truly live and learn how to love himself, bringing him that much closer to Emeraliss.

Past loves, past hurts... They were a glimmer of memory compared to his present, a beautiful dream that transformed his waking hours into the stuff of fanciful ballads.

Tash smiled at his ring before shifting backwards until he nudged Mayr's hip. The quiet snores stopped, punctuated by grunts as Mayr turned onto his side and draped his arm around

Tash's waist. The snores resumed a moment later, and breaths danced over Tash's neck as Mayr's hold tightened, drawing Tash closer.

While the embrace felt good, the heat of Mayr's skin on his was even better, particularly where Mayr's half-hardened shaft pressed into his cleft. With the leisurely roll of his hips, Tash rubbed against Mayr, encouraging Mayr's cock to tease his opening—a reminder of Mayr's merciless thrusts earlier that morning, which had left Tash raw and hoarse.

Mayr stirred, his moan overtaken by a hum. He wrapped himself around Tash and rocked into the seduction. "Morning," he murmured, brushing a lazy kiss across Tash's shoulder. "How'd you sleep?"

Twisting, Tash curled his arm behind Mayr's neck and wove his fingers through Mayr's tangled hair. "Like your husband."

"Mmm, I like that." Mayr lavished Tash's neck with open-mouthed kisses and the scrape of morning stubble. "We'll have to make sure it never stops."

"Keep loving me like this and it won't," Tash said, craning his head back. "Goddesses know what it'll take to pry me away from you."

"A clumsy clan of three-eyed ogres with mortifying disgruntlement issues and stinky jelly feet?"

Tash laughed until Mayr nipped his throat. He groaned, unable to do anything else. "I was thinking something *slightly* less legendary."

"All out fiery brawl in a sinking mud pit—" More kisses continued along Tash's collarbone. "—with a hundred ass-for-brains that can't be broken."

"Bigger than that."

Mayr pulled away, his grey eyes bright despite his solemn expression. "War. Massive and bloody, where the only end is death—that's what it'd take to drag me away from you. Even then, I'd tell death to take its ugly ass home. I'd take on the Goddesses themselves just to stay by your side."

In a hard kiss ripe with intention, Mayr robbed Tash of words and blew apart any semblance of a reply. Tash twisted in Mayr's embrace as their tongues traded one taste for another. He would do anything to wake the same way every morning for the rest of their lives.

"I think you need to turn over," Tash muttered against Mayr's lips.

A moan answered him, followed by a kiss that sucked the air from his lungs until he gasped.

"No, you *really* need to turn over," Tash insisted, unprepared for the tight grip that seized his hardened cock. He choked. Fingertips caressed his tip, circling with a feather-light touch that dared him to scream.

"If you say so," Mayr whispered, drawing one finger along the underside of Tash's shaft. He slid his fingers through the patch of dark curls around the base and tugged, grinning while Tash hissed and arched into the touch.

Tash nudged him back, a growl lodged in his throat. Giggles tumbled from Mayr as he rolled onto his stomach and hugged his pile of pillows.

Once Tash spread Mayr's legs and kneeled between them, the laughter stopped. When Tash splayed his hands over Mayr's back, Mayr flexed and shifted into Tash's touch. Unable to tear his gaze from the tight, tan skin adorned with black and red tattoos, Tash glided his palms up Mayr's spine. A shiver wracked Mayr's body, small bumps rising along his neck and shoulders.

To behold the beauty before him was one thing, but to touch was altogether divine. He cherished the scent of sweat and perfume that wafted around them. Even more, he took immense pleasure in curling the ends of Mayr's hair around his fingers.

Leaning back, he released the coils, delighted as Mayr's hair pooled in an ebony cascade between his shoulders. Tash pulled gently on the soft tresses, straightening them to their full length past the midpoint of Mayr's back. The faint aroma of soap clung to his hands, the scent of dew and raw honey reminding him of dawn on a mid-spring morning. Fresh, enticing, addicting... He hummed while he combed Mayr's hair with his fingers.

Mayr sighed into his pillow. "You're playing again." He peered over his shoulder, one brow arched. "Will you *ever* tell me what my hair did to get this kind of attention, or is that the best kept secret on this side of Dahena?"

A smile crept over Tash's lips. "No secret, just a private moment."

"Ss. Moments. You realize I'm growing it longer for you, right? You and your private, secret-keeping self. I think that deserves a—"

Mayr groaned from the kiss Tash planted at the centre of his back, in the dip around his spine. "And I thank you for it," Tash whispered over Mayr's skin, "but it's still not a secret. It's a memory wrapped around a memory, a vision of beauty on beauty. A reminder of when I was a child, easily distracted by lovely things."

Tash laced the black tresses around his fingers. "I was in the back of my parents' shop, practicing my terrible writing skills. In all of the ungainliness of a frustrated seven-year-old, I knocked over the ink well—straight onto the fabric leaning against the table. It hit the floor before I could do anything, ebony-black ink all over snow-white silk." He shook his head, fighting a smirk. "It was terrifying, knowing the cost of that bolt; knowing how angry my parents would be. But when I scrambled to sop up the ink, sunlight hit it and bits of silver glimmered in the silk. It was the black of night cuddled up to a blanket of untouched snow. From the right angle, it looked like the stars had been plucked from the night sky and planted in the snow like glass flowers—breathtaking and awful in all meanings of the word.

"You, however, are awful in only the one sense," Tash said, leaning over Mayr to kiss his neck. "You inspire much more than desire in me. I feel such awe for you my heart aches."

Mayr whimpered as Tash slid his splayed hands down Mayr's back. He paused on each tattoo then followed their lines with a steady caress. On Mayr's left shoulder blade was a pair of black songbirds. Entwined by their feet with their wings unfurled, they carried a crown of red, bell-shaped flowers between their beaks. On his right shoulder blade, twin bearcat cubs joined at the hip, with identical snarls and small tails up in the air. The birds represented Mayr's parents, the cubs his brother and sister.

Towards the middle of his back, on his left side near his ribs, was a detailed arawolfe on the prowl in honour of Aeley. Ears up, black snout down, and long, thick fangs bared, the wolfe looked menacing... until one's gaze drifted to the right, onto the image that represented Lira: a second wolfe, dressed in the furs of a red doe, sitting on its haunches with one paw up to tap the first wolfe on the nose.

Tash held back a laugh. When Mayr had suggested he would add the tattoo in all its humour, Lira doubted his sincerity. She had been equally horrified and honoured to see the completed design.

His hands continued downwards to the vine that meandered over Mayr's right hip. The vine was as long and wide as his hand with slender leaves and four red buds—a mark to remember Betta and Iliane by. Mayr had wanted the rest of the vine to go over his ribs and up his chest with flowers that progressed to full bloom as Iliane grew up. The last flower would have been tattooed over his heart, a symbol of Iliane's eighteenth birthday. After Betta left him, however, those plans had been thrown away and the permanent image left behind.

As permanent as the bird that occupied the bottom half of Mayr's back.

Tash held his breath. The ink was still dark, only weeks old. The painstakingly detailed work resembled the image on Tash's back, merely a smaller version. The mark had not been there before his previous meeting with the Sacred Assembly. It was only after—on the night he returned to Dahena—that he discovered what Mayr had done in the four days Tash was away. His place in Mayr's life had been staked, his significance etched into Mayr's skin.

He showered the tattoo with kisses, lingering longer the harder Mayr moaned and ground into the mattress. A steady lick from Mayr's buttocks to the small of his back gained loud mewls for more.

Tongue questing further, Tash worked his fingers into Mayr's cleft to stroke his opening.

Mayr was a study in taste and memory: the sweet oil they usually used mingled with the savoury oil Mayr had added, their combined flavour pleasurable on the tongue. Together with the musky residue of release, the scents roused memories of the quick, hard slap of skin and the mind-numbing throes of ecstasy.

"Slow, my love," Tash murmured, gliding his hand over Mayr's hip. "Let me—"

A knock on the door startled them both. Mayr's hips jerked, his backside catching Tash in the chin.

Mayr rammed his face into his pillow and grumbled a string of muffled expletives.

Tash sighed then rested his forehead on Mayr. "The guards noticed you're late for work. Remind me to haul Pellon out for a beating—sorry, *training*. Your second-in-command should know better."

Snorting as he sat up, Mayr struggled to yank a thin white sheet from the pile on the bed. "You're cute when you're annoyed." He drew his thumb along Tash's bottom lip. "And when you pout, I'm totally undone."

Another knock sounded. Mayr untangled himself from the rest of the blankets and hobbled from the bed, wrapping the white sheet around his waist. Fabric trailed behind him while he answered the door.

Tash rolled onto his back and flipped the blankets over his bared erection. He scowled at the ceiling, unable to make out what Mayr said to the visitor. *Maybe I'll be lucky—maybe he can get out of whatever they're fetching him for.*

As the door closed, Tash waited for Mayr to get dressed.

The clink of glass confused him.

"What—?" Tash stared at the tray in Mayr's hands. The aroma of pastries, spicy fried meat, and seasoned eggs filled the air. Two glass goblets were filled with pink juice and decorated with coils of black kimmer fruit that hung from their rims. "Breakfast?"

Mayr flashed a boyish grin. "I wasn't going to let the morning go *that* easily." His hips snapped playfully from side to side on his way across the room to the table and chairs near the furthest wall.

When my boy schemes, he schemes hard. Tash's stomach growled as he eyed the food, desperate for a taste. "How many other things do you have planned?"

"There might be a couple."

The moment Mayr placed the tray on the table, another knock rapped the door.

Now what? Tash waited as Mayr sauntered to the door to greet the second visitor with little more than cheerful thanks.

The door closed a second time, revealing a glass vase in Mayr's hands. White flowers streaked with bright purple and gold lines flowed over the rim, the tri-layered starburst petals in full bloom around vivid gold centres. Branches of lustrous silverwood completed the arrangement with stalks of thick, blood-red leaves.

Speechless, Tash pushed up from the bed and followed Mayr, scooping up his red pants from the floor along the way. By the time he reached Mayr's side, the vase sat at the centre of the table. Tash stroked one flower, the head of petals as large as his hand.

"My favourite," Tash whispered. "How did you—?" From what he knew, the flower was grown only in specific gardens in the Alosaa tract. It was not native to Kattal, having been brought from lands in the south by Tract Steward Oaren's family and tended in expensive warm houses that kept summer plants all year. He last saw the flowers during a visit at the Oaren estate with Mayr and Aeley. Previous to that, he had seen them only when he had taken refuge in a temple in Alosaa.

"I know someone." Mayr pursed his lips and snapped his fingers, his gaze on the armoire against the wall to Tash's left. Before Tash could ask what trouble he intended to get into, Mayr retrieved a small wood box from the armoire. Returning to the table, he cracked open the box and set it beside the tray. A white metal ring glinted inside the rich purple lining, the single blue diamond within the band flat and oval. Two detailed feathers curved around the stone, etched into the metal instead of sitting on the band like

Tash's ring.

"*Now* we can have breakfast." Mayr cast Tash a scolding frown. "Especially since you didn't eat much last night."

And we'll discuss it later, Tash finished, the unspoken words hanging in the air. He reached for the ring but did not touch, yearning to see it where it belonged. "May I...?"

"That's why it's there." Mayr's eyes gleamed as he pulled out a chair and fell into it.

Pants discarded over the chair beside Mayr, Tash snatched the ring from its box and sank to the floor, kneeling between Mayr's legs. His hand trembled as he slid the ring onto Mayr's middle finger. "I wasn't sure this would ever happen. I didn't think you'd want to marry anyone again."

"You're not *anyone*." Mayr tilted Tash's head back, one finger crooked beneath Tash's chin. "You're my earthbound Halataldris," he whispered, "as sacred and beautiful as your namesake. That's why I tattooed his image on me—I want you on me, in me, always with me."

A kiss brushed over Tash's lips, gliding across his skin like the purest silk. The whispered sentiments echoed in his thoughts, melting his emotions into a warm, sticky puddle. Whenever Mayr called him by his full name, Tash's knees weakened and his heart kicked. Every syllable was a tug on the invisible thread that bound them, freezing time for an instant—long enough for him to fall in love all over again.

Once Mayr drew back, Tash's breath went with him, his lungs aching until he remembered he needed to inhale.

"You need to eat." Mayr tucked Tash's hair behind his ear. "Because I don't care *what* you say, come is *not* a suitable replacement."

Tash laughed and fumbled his way into the chair next to Mayr, slipping on his pants before settling. He would yield to Mayr's sensibilities, unable to deny how delectable the jam and cream pastries looked beneath dollops of orange preserves and slivers of mixed nuts.

While Mayr arranged the goblets and brown clay plates on the table, Tash swept his glance through the room. Like the other bedrooms in the estate, Mayr's room was large, with a high red ceiling and dark red wood panels where there was not expensive grey stone. Yet unlike the other bedrooms, Mayr's room was modestly decorated. The large table in front of them was simple and round, fashioned from black wood without carvings or engravings. The table legs curved gently like the legs and arms of the matching chairs, four of which surrounded the table, though it could accommodate eight. On the other side of the table sat a pile of folded, cream-coloured linens and a metal washbowl filled with water.

In the centre of the wall behind the table was the small hearth with its dying fire, a bucket of fresh water beside it. Above the hearth, small treasures were displayed on the stone mantel. They were trinkets from Mayr's family, including four small, wood statues of the Goddesses with red veils pinned to their heads and a white candle that had never been lit. The fact that the statues of Navara, Goddess of Justice, and Hastal, Goddess of Protection, were on the inside did not escape Tash. Nor did he miss the closeness of Emeraliss's statue to Hastal's, the Goddess of Love no less worthy of Mayr's devotion than Hastal's protectiveness.

Next to the statues lay Mayr's first dagger from Korre Dahe, a gift from when he was eleven, crafted from black metal with alternating thin red and gold bands around the hilt. On the left side of the mantel rested a crown of dried pink flowers and white ribbons from Estara's wedding, where Mayr had stood as a witness. On the right side was a crown of purple flowers and yellow ribbons from Loftin's wedding. In the direct centre between them lay a third crown, the gold and pink flowers with coiled black ribbons a reminder of Aeley and Lira's wedding.

Alongside the crowns stood a handful of yellow, woody grass with hollow stems and dried green buds in a red clay cup. Tied around the stems was a bright yellow ribbon signed by every member of Mayr's family—a keepsake from his parents' farm, taken from the harvest the year he left home to live at the Dahe estate. Beside it, a lock of Aeley's blonde hair lay in a blue glass bowl tied with a narrow black ribbon, a souvenir from the first time Mayr had bested Aeley in the training ring.

A red and black shield hung above the mantel, divided into quarters. Two gold bearcats stood rampant in the middle, and the Dahe motto was engraved around the gold edges: *"Time dares us all, but forever does not yield; as the heart of Kattal beats, so do we."*

The wall to Tash's right was devoid of decoration except for the stained-glass window, its blue and green panes arranged in the image of a tree. With the mauve curtains still open, light spilled over the two black chairs beside the window and the grey blankets draped over their curved backs and thick arms. The wall behind him was equally unadorned, save for the bed and two black bedside tables. A worn black chest sat at the foot of the bed, emptied of the blankets and linens it contained during the warmer months.

The rest of the furniture in the room consisted of what stood against the wall to his left: a black chest of drawers that contained formal attire, a metal chest of weapons, and a wide armoire crafted from red wood darker than the colour of blood—a gift from Mayr's parents when he became Head of the Guard. The armoire's gold handles were exquisitely engraved with vines, and carved into the bottom of its doors were stalks and flowers with a bear cub sleeping among them, a look of contentment on its face.

Tash could not help but smile. As hard as Mayr wanted to seem, his family would never stop seeing the softness in him. It was no different than the spiritual reverence Mayr rarely showed, except for the items on top of the armoire in their makeshift altar. Four gold statutes in the likeness of the Goddesses stood on either side of the glass keepsake box containing feathers Tash was certain came from Halataldris, the Father of All Birds. Around them were four thick white candles, a bowl of water next to a bowl of red earth, a crown of white flowers and white ribbons, a silver goblet and bowl for offerings, a silver matchbox, and incense in a clay bowl.

Although Mayr said the altar was for Tash, he sensed there was more to it: a need for Mayr to connect to the Four on his own terms, without anyone to tell him how to show veneration. He never saw Mayr use the altar, yet the candles burned down whenever Tash traveled without Mayr, suggesting Mayr used the altar in secret. Perhaps he wanted to reconcile what Tash brought into their lives. Mayr had always doubted the Four's existence, but had come to realize the Goddesses were more than alive—They saw Mayr as much as They saw Tash.

Tash shivered and turned back to his breakfast. His Uldana Trials had made it clear he was being watched. Emeraliss had stood at his side between the worlds of the dead and the living, giving him permission to abandon the

139

strict rules of the priesthood. Not only had Emeraliss understood his struggles and gifted him with guiltless clarity, She had anointed him as a servant. His soul was bound to Emeraliss as much as it was to Mayr.

Assuming that's true, what we are. Tash glanced at Mayr while they ate, debating the theory that they were soulbound. Deep down he wanted to believe they were more than two people who had stumbled across one another, taken by appearances and whatever drove them to love. He wanted to believe they were meant to be, regardless of the barriers posed by time and death. Such barriers had always been suspect to him, never endless, never absolute.

"You're thinking again," Mayr said softly, tapping Tash's knuckles.

"Just reflecting on what we have." Tash nibbled a flaky pastry and licked his lips as seductively as he could. "What about you? You're quiet." He leaned forward to suck glossy drops of bright red jam from Mayr's lips.

Mayr blushed. "Thinking about what we want."

"We?"

The blush deepened. "What I want. For us."

Tash scooted closer. Perched on the edge of his chair, he trapped Mayr's knees between his. "Which is?"

Mayr caressed Tash's lips. "I know there are children who need homes—orphans we could take in—but is it wrong to want a child of our own, from us? Would it be terrible if we put off adopting for a little while and try something else? Am I really that insensitive?" He drew his fingertips along Tash's jaw, his brow furrowed. "Is it strange to want to raise a child of your bloodline above all others, even my own? To see a bit of you in their eyes whenever they look at me? How self-absorbed is that?"

"You are not self-absorbed." Tash forced himself to breathe as he kissed the back of Mayr's hands. "Nor are you insensitive. You love deeply. It is not a violation of morality or a crime. I would beg Emeraliss for a chance to hold a child of yours in my arms and never let them go. I'd do anything to have it."

Mayr's face brightened. "Yeah?"

Tash leaned his forehead against Mayr's. "Yeah." He exhaled slowly and considered his next words. It was their only alternative, even if it unsettled him. "There's another option, one you mentioned after I first suggested having children, though perhaps only in jest."

"Maybe." Mayr nuzzled Tash's cheek. "Or maybe I was hoping you'd see value in it."

"I wouldn't put it past you." Tash leaned into Mayr's touch. "You and I... we feel something when a woman strikes our fancy, no different than men." He steadied Mayr's chin with one hand to look him in the eye. "So maybe that's our second option. Maybe our experience with Sarene was a way to open our hearts to something new. For others in our position, adoption is the only choice, but we could... if we could find someone... if someone were willing to be ours..."

Mayr sighed and kissed Tash. "*Ours*," he echoed. "I wouldn't want to do it any other way."

"And I wouldn't mind seeing you happy," Tash said, pulling Mayr into his arms. "You didn't have a fair chance with Iliane, not like what I want to give you."

"Is it what we want, though? Can we share our bed for this? Share each other? Because I might get jealous, I'll be honest. If you start to prefer them over..." Mayr hugged Tash tight. "If we do this, we're in it together. Promise me that."

"I'll swear to it however you need. No one can take me away from you, no matter what's between their legs."

Laughing quietly, Mayr kissed Tash's throat. "I love when you talk crude."

"Just as I love when you fight for me."

"So we'll do it? Not that we need to rush." Mayr lifted his head, his nose scrunched, tongue out. "I'm all for someone who's *not* Sarene. Someone we actually *li*—"

Tash drowned the rest of Mayr's words with a kiss, hard and wet, weighted with moans. As Mayr sank into his embrace, Tash felt Mayr's annoyance bleed away between them, back into the past where it belonged.

"We should finish eating," Tash said against

Mayr's lips. "We're needed elsewhere."

"Can't I just drag you back to bed and pretend no one else exists?"

"If you want Pellon and Aeley to annoy you for the rest of the week, go right ahead."

Mayr huffed. "I *suppose* you have a point." He pouted and dug into his food, stealing glances at Tash.

Tash chuckled and worked through the rest of his meal, unable to forget the seriousness of their agreement. They would commit to a family, a shared life, a home. Everything he had given up had come back around.

This time, there would be no running away.

Chapter Five

"What did you do?"

Mayr grinned at Tash's question as they entered the ballroom. "Told you I had more plans."

"Here I thought everyone had gone home." Tash peered around his veil, eyes narrowed. "What else don't I know?"

"I can't tell you that." Mayr laced their fingers together and continued towards the elegantly dressed tables. All day he had let Tash think dinner would be a small affair with Tash's family. In truth, the number of guests had increased from the previous night's celebration of Tash's Uldana anniversary. "I figured they need to eat, so why not?"

Tash's amused gaze suggested he believed nothing about Mayr's flimsy reasoning. As they neared the tables, all attention turned onto them. Almost everyone sat in their places from the previous night. The only differences were the switch in Mayr and Tash's placements and the additional guests.

"Sure, *now* you grace us with your presence." Loftin twisted in his seat, throwing his arm over the curved back. His lips contorted as he scrunched his nose. "Figures. Whenever *you* plan these things, you starve everyone to tears first."

Mayr led Tash to his seat and veered towards Loftin. "Only you, bane of all existence. Someone's got to torment you." He folded his arms, settling back on one heel behind Covran's chair. "Orlee won't let me test you in the ring, so I need to get my kicks somehow—older brother's prerogative and all."

Estara jumped out of her seat and hurried around the furthest end of the table. The hem of her heavy teal gown swished along the floor, the toes of her scuffed black boots peeking out from beneath. "Oh, Loftin," she called, slowing on her approach. "Look at me for a moment."

Loftin tensed and turned slowly. "What?"

"Nothing much, just—" Estara's blue-grey eyes widened as she jammed a candied orange fruit the size of her fist into his mouth. "—there, you're fed. Dinner's done. See you tomorrow." She patted his cheek and ran away before he could grab her, giggling on the way back to her seat.

"Mama!" Dayla and Efae shouted in unison, their jaws dropped while Alith and Iliane howled with laughter.

Chuckles and snorts sounded from the adults, save for Malary, who bowed his forehead into his palm and shook his head. Bremary threw up her arms in agreement and signaled her appreciation to Estara in a flurry of motions. Even Orlee's eyes were bright as she giggled behind her hand.

Loftin blinked, the fruit clenched between his teeth. Arching one brow, he tilted his head and gazed around the table. "Wha?" he asked, drawing fresh laughter.

Aeley grinned, her goblet tipped towards Loftin. "Never a dull bunch, I'll give you that." Beside her, Lira struggled to remain composed, her cheeks red, glance aglow with disbelief.

Mayr gripped Loftin's neck and kissed the top of his head. "Love you, kid. You're *such* a good brother." After ruffling Loftin's black hair, he headed for his place between Aeley and Tash.

The laughter quieted. Loftin removed the fruit from his mouth before sputtering and licking his lips. "Thanks. Love the hospitality here." He frowned at Aeley. "Weren't you supposed to save me? Something about protecting citizens from *displays of public embarrassment*?"

Aeley shrugged. "Let me know if it stops being justifiable retribution and I'll think about it."

Loftin huffed and stuck out his tongue. The next moment, he raised his goblet in her direction. "Here's to you knowing exactly what to say." When Aeley winked and nodded, he sipped his drink and flicked his fingers at Estara.

A cleared throat silenced the room. "Perhaps it would be best to say the blessing now," Priestess Kee announced, pushing up from her seat, drink in hand.

Murmurs of agreement followed. All except Renett stood, goblets held towards the food on the table, the thick aroma of herbs, butter, and smoked vegetable glazes filling the air.

"To the Four Goddesses of life, being, and divine understanding," Kee started, loud and clear, "I ask for blessing upon this feast…"

The rest of Kee's blessing was a dull mumble behind Mayr's thoughts. He clasped Tash's hand, his gaze falling to Tash's fingers. The marriage ring looked perfect on Tash's hand, as if it was always meant to be. There would be no doubt Tash was his, not anymore.

"… Blessed be the Four," Kee finished.

"Blessed be the Four," everyone else intoned before drinking and taking their seats.

Excited chatter spread through the room. Food was passed around the table, but Mayr remained standing. Aeley's shrill whistle brought movement to a standstill.

"Thanks." Mayr cleared his throat, daring to meet the curious stares. The wide smiles of Ress, Pellon, Aeley, Kee, and Armamae betrayed the secret they already knew, but the joy in Iliane's eyes reeled him in. Perhaps she would appreciate the changes to come—maybe even enjoy the idea of being a sort-of sister.

Reminded of the silence, he gripped his goblet of mead. "A few of you know why we're all here, and it's not only because we wanted to spend more time." Mayr flushed. "Not that we don't, it's just we—I—there's been a slight... change in plans." Silently cursing his nervousness, he held his goblet towards Tash. "So here it is: we're getting married in the spring, and we'd like all of you to be there."

The responding cheers and whistles echoed through the room, goblets hoisted in the air to the shouts of congratulations. Tash beamed before Mayr kissed him, the sweet gaffa nectar on his tongue a delectable complement to Mayr's bittersweet mead. Allaysia squeaked with amusement just before her arm crept around Tash's waist to give him a squeeze.

Mayr fell into his seat and leaned into Tash. "Love you."

"And I you, troublemaker," Tash whispered, stealing another kiss.

"But we love you both, all of us," Allaysia said.

Tash and Mayr parted to look at her. She rested her chin on Tash's shoulder, her lightly painted face framed by soft brown and blonde curls. "This is the greatest news, and we've really needed it. After everything our family's been through..." Allaysia hugged Tash, her lips grazing his cheek. "It's good to see you so happy, Little Bird. Little Bear will love you real good."

"Little Bear?" Mayr asked.

Allaysia shrugged. "You've got the snarly defensiveness of a big, nasty bear but all the play of a cub. That's who you are to me, to us," she said. "I'd wager that's who you are to everyone."

She had no idea how accurate she was. The image of a bear cub had been engraved in his furniture since childhood thanks to his mother's ability to read her children deeply. His heart warmed to hear Allaysia gift him with a nickname—her way of saying he was family. "Thanks, Ally." Mayr kissed her cheek.

Allaysia's face lit up. "You're welcome." She straightened in her chair and accepted a bowl from Bremary. Quick words passed between them, accompanied by glances at Mayr and Tash for whatever reason.

Mayr let out a long breath and sat back. His plans had fallen into place with less difficulty than anticipated. With his fear tamed, he worked mindlessly through the motions of accepting dishes from Tash, adding food to his plate, and passing the dishes to Aeley. His thoughts were scrambled, unable to remain still, no different than his body. Try as he may, he could not stop fidgeting.

Once his plate was filled, he commanded himself to calm down. He picked through his dinner, snatching pieces of conversation. To his relief, Tash ate at a steady pace and conversed with a light, playful tone. Whatever ghosts silenced Tash the previous night had retreated.

A quiet sigh slipped from Mayr as he studied the others at the end of the table. Betta's attention was on Iliane, but he suspected she was pleased by the news. Finally, both he and Betta could be happy, moving forward in their lives with Iliane kept safe and cared for, one of the few lasting connections between them that truly mattered.

Content to hold on to the relief of seeing Iliane laugh with her mother, he swept his focus towards the four new guests. Beside his mother sat Orae, the woman Mayr considered a second mother. When his parents had moved to Dahena to claim the land Malary inherited from his uncle, Orae had befriended them and welcomed them into the community. Since the accident that left Renett paralyzed, Orae visited the farm weekly to ensure Renett felt included in the bustle and blunders of society, a kindness for which Orae was aptly suited. She had owned a tavern in the village for as long as Mayr could remember, the business passed down from her mother as was the tradition set by the generations of foremothers before her.

Age had caught up to Orae, yet she remained the headstrong woman who had helped instill confidence in Mayr. Her long, white hair hung in narrow plaits with orange ribbons and gold beads woven throughout. The skin around her dark brown eyes was wrinkled, but her gaze was youthful as she grinned, listening to tales she would no doubt tease Mayr with later. Tiny in stature and frail only in appearance, her memory was long and sharp like her wit.

Across the table from Orae were her youngest son, Liele, and his nine-year-old daughter,

Girana. Given the amount of time Mayr had spent in the tavern over the years, Liele had become a good friend, mostly with the tavern bar and empty tankards between them.

Yet it was the woman beside Orae that steadied Mayr's attention for countless moments: Arieve, Orae's granddaughter from her first marriage. Except for the shapely figure that teased Mayr's imagination and golden-brown skin that became richer over time, Arieve resembled her father, complete with the same gently lilted speech and feminine grace. Thick black-brown hair tumbled down her back in a mass of tamed curls and thin plaits, the blonde streaks throughout almost as white as the tablecloths. Long lashes framed her hazel eyes, their irises more green than brown, particularly around the middle. The outer rings of her eyes were a lush green like a field at the end of spring, fresh and alive. Warm. Deep enough to sink hearts, Mayr's included.

Heat raced across Mayr's cheeks. He stared at his plate, unable to meet Arieve's gaze. Although she worked in the kitchen at the Dahe estate in the afternoons and evenings, then spent her nights managing Orae's tavern, he rarely saw Arieve as much as he wanted.

A blessing in disguise, he reasoned, downing a hasty mouthful of mead. Arieve was a past of longing wrapped in the beauty of the present, a delicate fragment of temptation from his youth.

She was a hope he had never shaken off, only hidden under layers of justification and doubt. Part of him would always be drawn to her, his feelings nestled in his jaded core. No one knew the truth, not even Tash.

He might never know. I can't talk about it, let alone tell him. Mayr's blush continued to spread, its warmth creeping down his neck. Several times in his life, he had considered courting Arieve. Each time, he shied away and chose other women. Eventually he had stopped thinking about wooing her altogether.

Still, he remembered being sixteen and fumbling his way into infatuation. Arieve's beaming smile and bright laugh had haunted him as much as her expressive eyes that suggested she saw leagues-deep into a person's spirit. By the time he was seventeen, he had fallen hard for her but reeled away, desperate to stop what could not begin. Only fourteen, Arieve had been too young, four years short of lawful marriageable age. Had he tried to court her, their parents would have intervened. Rather than part from her completely, he had offered her small gifts, long walks, and a horrible attempt at poetry to express what feelings he could.

Once he met Betta, however, he had forfeited the chance to be with Arieve. In Mayr's eyes, Betta had been the most beautiful woman in Dahena, his lust lured in by her big, brown eyes, wavy brown hair, and undeniable charm.

Convinced that Betta was the one he was meant to be with, he pushed aside his feelings for Arieve and told himself they were nothing but youthful fantasy. He had remained faithful to Betta, unwilling to betray her.

All of it fell apart when Betta left him. Every emotion he had raged forth, including his feelings for Arieve. Mayr had mourned the loss of Betta and Iliane, caught between cursing Betta's existence and pining for what he mistook as truth. His grief attracted not only Aeley's vengeance and his family's disgust, but Arieve had offered unwavering kindness that broke him further. Her thoughtfulness had stung; her sweetness had tasted bitter to his soul. She had been so sympathetic it burned, and he had beaten himself with sad laughter to think she was on the pained side of his false marriage instead of that which made her his wife.

Alone and afraid of betrayal, he had seen a second chance with Arieve present itself and wither. For all his affection, he refused to take advantage of her. At the time, he had not been fit to be anyone's lover. It would have been unfair to shove his unhappiness onto her. In a final decision that still rattled his nerves, he had promised he would not reduce her to being the girl who cleaned up the mess he made.

There was also the fact she referred to him as family. *Like a brother, a cousin—something equally as close while being so distant.*

After Betta disappeared, he had allowed Arieve to console him, but only as family rather than a potential lover. To keep his distance, he had sought women who were nothing like Arieve—women who ended up breaking his heart.

But whenever those women left, Arieve tried to make him feel better. Not only did he like the attention, he liked *her* attention…

Realization smacked him hard.

Mayr resisted jamming his fork angrily into the gravy-drowned vegetables on his plate. Was Arieve another reason he had purposely fallen for those women? Had he used them to gain her affections without stepping over the boundaries? Was he *that* desperate? Goddesses knew how cunning his subconscious was. Arieve always comforted him. He had let her see the wounds bleeding him dry when he was too scared to show Aeley. Arieve had the smooth touch of water, while Aeley had enough mettle to be a battering ram.

There had always been barriers between them. If not age, circumstance, or perception of familial ties, it was a matter of their relationships. He had always been with someone else, as had she. Arieve had gone through a number of lovers, though she had been with her girlfriend, Coye, the longest. Their on-and-off relationship claimed the better of six years.

Regardless, he pined for her from across the

furthering distance. Despite his love for Tash—insatiable and consuming as it was—one look at Arieve made him giddy like a little kid. Hundreds of memories danced in the air between them, playing a tune on his wishes with the truth of what could never be.

The warmth drained from Mayr's face as he glimpsed Tash's smile and felt his playful nudge. Tash had already spent a great deal of empathy on Mayr's emotional downfalls from Betta. Would Tash be as understanding if he knew about Arieve?

Never had he been so embarrassed to care about her.

No, not embarrassed—ashamed. Mayr slipped his restless fingers into Tash's hand and squeezed. *Because you're sitting here, ready to marry me, and I'm seeing the shadows of what could've been. All I want is to fall at your feet and beg forgiveness.*

As Tash kissed his cheek, Mayr sucked in a breath. "I love you," Tash whispered.

The words destroyed every reply Mayr yearned to give. He never should have invited Arieve to dinner. With her and Tash at the same table, Mayr's skin crawled under the grimy silence of a liar. Although he loathed keeping secrets from Tash, some things were difficult to share.

Their conversation at breakfast made things worse. If he could have spat out the words instead of gagging on them, he would have suggested Arieve be the one they asked to share their bed—if only she liked him that way.

I'll forever be an ass. I'll just go drown my bad ideas now.

"Hey." Aeley poked his elbow. "Still with us?"

Mayr blinked. "Yeah, I'm just—"

"—Working?" Aeley smirked. "Or is the excuse closer to home?" Her glance flickered towards his lap.

"Ae." Mayr pursed his lips. "Not exactly dinner-appropriate."

"When are we ever? Have you *seen* your guests? Why be on our best behaviour when they're perfectly candid?" Aeley shrugged and sipped her drink. The flared sleeve of her white tunic pooled around her elbow, revealing tan skin lightly marred with scars from fights. "It's refreshing, being ourselves with people who don't want any less. Formal banter is boring."

"Speaking of being ourselves…" Lips twisted as he shifted his thoughts, Mayr drew his thumb around the rim of his goblet. "I need to ask you a serious something."

"And I need to give a serious answer?"

"Preferably." Mayr cleared his throat and leaned close to Aeley, his voice lowered. "Tash and I talked about things going forward, except *I* need to know if you and Lira will support our decision. We'd like to have a family, but this is your home." He avoided Lira's curious expression. "If you don't want kids around, I understand. If you want us to leave, I'll get us a home that's just ours. I did it with Betta, and I can do it again."

Aeley stared at him, merely blinking as the silence between them warped into a tense discomfort the longer she said nothing.

Her cheeks flushed as her stunned gaze darkened into a glare. Aeley slammed her goblet down. Gaffa nectar splashed over the rim, staining the tablecloth with violet drops. "You unimaginably filthy hole of a horse's ass!"

The shout stilled movement around the table. All banter died. Lira glowered at Aeley before casting Mayr an apologetic grimace.

Mayr shrank back. Aeley's anger crept through his skin and bore a hole into his confusion. Even worse, he hated being watched during a harsh reprimand. "What? What did I say?"

"Don't you dare," Aeley answered, jabbing the table on each word. "Just because Lira and I don't want children doesn't mean we hate them. *Don't* take away our chance to be aunts and spoil whatever brood you have until they're good and rotten."

"Ae..." Mayr coughed into his fist and looked down the table, eyes narrowed as he challenged the surprised glances.

Estara was the first to catch on. "Back to the futility of taxes," she announced, her sharp gaze pinned on Loftin. She rolled her wrist, gesturing to the rest of the table.

"And the joys of human sacrifice," Loftin added, mimicking his sister's motions with emphasis, "because that's what I'm here for. Plus the food. Always the food."

Snorts and laughter sounded, followed by resumed chatter.

Mayr breathed out, only mildly comforted by Tash's grasp on his knee. "Thanks, Ae, because that's *definitely* the reason I was practically *whispering it to you*."

"If you wanted it to be private, you should've waited." Aeley folded her arms and leaned back. "What's done is done, so here's what you wanted to know: stay, raise a family. It might be our home, but it's yours, too. We won't kick you out, ankle-biting offspring or no."

Lira reached across the table, her hand falling short of Mayr's. "And if you need help, say so. We'd be happy to assist, any way you need."

"Yeah, don't be stubborn." Aeley grunted and shuffled in her chair until she leaned closer to Lira. "Set a good example."

The blatant scolding on Lira's face while she scowled at Aeley made Mayr laugh. Lira was one of the only people who could chastise Aeley without suffering refusal, backlash, or harsh words. Certainly Lira was the only person Aeley willingly fell to her knees for.

The conversation was far from over, even as the rest of dinner passed with quiet conversation.

What focus Mayr managed to keep was spent on his food and the sound of Tash's voice. The biggest distraction was Tash's hand kneading the inside of his thigh, his arousal and Tash's fingers hidden by the tablecloth. Every time he considered brushing Tash's intimate touch aside, he recalled the previous night. This was the Tash he preferred: happy and playful, needing to touch, even if etiquette raged over it.

The touch grounded Mayr. His nerves calmed. Steady desire soothed his restless thoughts, tethering his need for comfort to Tash's discreet, perceptive ways.

When dinner ended, so did his patience. Once the kitchen staff whisked away the last of the plates, Mayr caught Aeley's gaze and nodded towards the hall.

Aeley dipped her head in agreement. After a kiss to the back of Lira's hand, she followed Mayr from the room. They said nothing on the way to Aeley's study, giving Mayr time to sort his words.

The door clicked shut behind Aeley as she followed him into the study. "I'm sorry," she said, leaning against the door. "I didn't mean to embarrass you in front of everyone. I should've waited, but the whole thing threw me. I thought you considered *this* your home, completely. Then you were talking like it wasn't and I just... froze, I guess."

"Overreacted, more like," Mayr muttered, glancing at the fire already lit in the small hearth.

He crossed the room to Aeley's desk and sat on the edge, gripping the wood in tight fists. If his question at dinner stunned her, she was going to hate what else he needed to say.

"Yes, fine, *overreacted*. But it was a slap in the face." Aeley sighed and joined him on the desk, perched on the edge beside him. The desk creaked in protest but held them both. "You're the only family I have left. Everyone else is dead or gone." She flicked one of the scrolls lying to her right, her voice quiet. "So when my truest brother starts talking like he wants to leave, I can't help but feel abandoned." With more flicks, the scroll fell to the floor. Aeley shrugged and stared at it. "I've got Lira, but I need a little more, you know? If that means having you *and* a mob of tiny little droolers, I'll take it."

Mayr sighed, letting his gaze wander over the study. The room had changed little since Aeley's father, Korre, died three and a half years ago. Except for the vibrant portrait of Korre above the door, most of the study remained as Korre had left it. The room was a memorial enclosed in red wood and stained glass, both practical in its use and a way to keep Korre close. Hints of Aeley showed throughout: a smooth, black wood box on her desk containing three of the black quills she favoured; a blue glass bowl with her favourite brittle spiced nut bark in the top drawer of the desk; and worn copies of the books Korre had read to her as a child tucked in the back of the locked bookcase in the corner to his left.

The most obvious sign of Aeley's use was the hole-riddled target painted on the beige wood planks on the wall to Mayr's right. They had assailed the target countless times since Mayr nailed it to the wall with her help, smashing his thumb and fingers with a hammer more times than he could count. Just thinking about it made his fingertips hurt, accompanied by the memory of Aeley's laughter while he had danced around, cursing every nail in existence. By that point, Korre had taken to his sickbed, leaving his Tract Steward work to Aeley. The target had been Aeley's way to work off frustration whenever her duties became too much.

When Korre's sickbed became his deathbed, however, the target had been assaulted by the rage of heartbreak. The night Korre died, both Mayr and Aeley went round after round on the target, throwing knives until their shoulders ached and tears blurred their vision too much to continue. Since then, the red, white, and yellow circles offered a whisper of comfort at stressful times.

Memories. Comfort. Home. The small room gave Mayr more than he could bear to part with.

He let out a slow breath. "It's not just about children, Ae. Our whole lives will be affected. Some things will *have* to change."

"Like...?"

"We'll have to rely on Pellon *a lot* more." Mayr

crossed his arms and stared at the floor. "I can't be everywhere at once, so if I stop living up to what you want, I'll understand. If you want someone whose attentions aren't this divided, I'll step down," he said, barely able to stop his voice from wavering. He curled his fingers into the crooks of his arms, clenching them tighter the more his stomach churned. "I'll give up Head of the Guard and let Pellon take over. He loves you like I do, and he'll give his life for yours and Lira's."

A raging flush coloured Aeley's cheeks. In a flurry, she grabbed the brown book on her desk and beat his arm. "You stubborn, over-considerate ass! Stop being so damn selfless! That's not *at all* what I want, and you know it!"

The corner of the hard cover scratched Mayr as he leaned away, hands raised in defence.

Aeley tossed the book to the floor, disgust on her face. "You need to have your own life, your own family. So you'll probably end up with a couple of little torments that'll eat up all your time. That's *life*. Some people even call that *normal*." She folded her arms and huffed. "And guess what? I'm a big girl now. We can work around these things."

"Aeley, lis—"

Aeley shoved her palm into his face, narrowly missing Mayr's nose. "No, *you* listen. Have I complained about you and Tash? No, and I don't see any reason to." Frowning, she cupped his cheek. "I don't feel like second best. You need to stop assuming I do."

Mayr bit the inside of his cheek, overwhelmed by a deluge of emotions as if a trap door had bottomed out in his heart. "If you say so," he whispered.

"Why are you being so...?" Aeley withdrew her hand. "You love being Head Guard. Why even suggest giving it up?"

"I'm not used to having everything I want," Mayr mumbled. "I'm waiting for something to happen—for all of it to be taken away. Everything will go wrong and it'll be so bad I can't fix it." He wiped his eyes with the sleeve of his black shirt, drying the few tears that surfaced without warning. "I'm afraid I'll wake up one day and find out I can't have it all. Someone's out there, dying to make me choose, I know it. They're waiting for me to mess it all up so they can make it worse."

"Well it won't be your boy that does it," Aeley argued, "and it certainly won't be me or Lira or your family. We're too stubborn." As Mayr laughed, she wrapped her arms around his shoulders. "You're stuck with us for the rest of your life. Certainly Tash isn't headed for the door—he's itching to crawl inside you and stay there forever. Not many people would go looking for your former wife so you could have closure. Fewer still would encourage you to get along with her so you could see Iliane."

"He even managed to get you to talk about Betta. You actually told him where you found her."

"Yeah, well, he makes compelling arguments." She tapped his forehead. "My point? Don't worry. He's not going anywhere and we're not kicking you out. I won't ever make you choose between us."

Warm as her words were, a malignant shadow toyed with his doubts. "It's not just that," Mayr murmured, his glance falling to her black pants. "It's everything I can't stop. All the people… the hate… There's a death sentence on his head. Now there's Adren and Ress's mess. What do we do when the peace runs out? What happens if the Shar finds him and comes to *collect*?" He gagged on the last word as if it were tar.

"The best we can do is move on, be vigilant, and protect those we love. Tash will get the same treatment as Lira. They're family, and you and me, we take care of family. *As the heart of Kattal beats, so do we.*"

In a trick of memory, Mayr swore he heard Korre in Aeley's voice.

He hugged her tight enough to make her gasp and hiccup. "Your father would be proud." Mayr laughed as Aeley flushed and covered her mouth with the back of her hand. "Think he'd approve of my marriage?"

Aeley cleared her throat. "He'd run the committee we're forming to plan the wedding."

"Ha, ha. Funny."

The instant he caught Aeley's droll stare, he

knew better. A committee would be the least to form.

"At least he wouldn't have to go through the 'what are your intentions' bit," Mayr said, picking at an imaginary piece of something on his shirt. "We're too old for that."

"Don't count on it. He'd have done it all for you. Besides, I did it already."

Mayr froze. "Wait, *what*?"

"Oh, yeah, a while back. Tash took it rather well. He and Lira could write my speeches."

Jaw dropped, Mayr studied Aeley's smirk, waiting for her to say it was a joke. When she shrugged, he closed his mouth.

"To be perfectly honest, I'm thinking of asking Tash to be my official primary advisor," Aeley said. Ankles crossed, she swung her feet, the heels of her boots tapping the desk. "I'm tired of relying on Father's contingent. I'd like someone I can turn to whenever I want, and I could certainly do without the headaches of too many opinions." A scowl tightened her lips. "Assuming I could steal him away. I know he's committed to doing something about Adren, plus the monthly Sacred Assembly meetings and the rites and all the things. There's not much time for anything else."

Mayr blinked, lost for words. That evening was one surprise after another. "You could still ask. I'm sure he'd appreciate it."

"You think? It's not too taking-him-away-from-you?" Aeley leaned back onto her elbows, squashing scrolls beneath her as the desk groaned. "He's thoughtful, not afraid of the ugly side of strategy. Then again, he's been on that side, unlike my advisors. They've always played nice, and they're trained to give the right answers. I'd prefer someone who's lived it. He wasn't raised by tutors and wealthy families. He's seen the lower, middle, and upper classes and whatever's lacking in between."

"Not to mention the dirty work."

Aeley sat up. "He knows the reality, not only the sap-coated truths. I can visit villages and talk to magistrates all I want, but I don't hear everything. Tash knows the truth better than I do." She tilted her head, her expression inscrutable. "He has ideas, new options for old problems. Plus he'll argue with me. He honestly cares about people and doesn't have a private agenda. I could use someone like him. Someone I can trust like you and Lira and Pellon."

Mayr narrowed his eyes. "Stop sounding like you could fall in love with him. He's still mine."

"Oh, I know, but I get it." Aeley grinned and patted his cheek. "He's had it rough, but I trust him with you. Otherwise I'd have gutted him senseless, ripped off his goods, and sent the rest to the Shar for tough eatin's."

"*Poisoned* eatin's," Mayr corrected before arching one brow. "You've been spending too much time around Ress and Adren. Keep this up and you'll horrify the rest of the aristocracy. I think they'll fall down dead with a single dose of gutter slang."

"Please. Try four doses and a batch of *actual* poison."

Mayr surrendered to a body-shaking laugh before he kissed Aeley's cheek. "Thanks."

"Of course. One request?"

"Ask and I'll do it."

"Let Lira and I be family. We'll do anything, whether it's watching over children, indulging childhood hobbies, or whatever else." Aeley clutched his hand. "I'll adopt your kids into the Dahe line as wards or something. I'm sure we can come up with the right term or make up a whole new one. Lira's talented and creative—you should see the poetry she's written for me and painted all over my…" She blushed pink. "Forget I said that. Just know we could find something no councilman or Steward could contest. Then no one could take anything away from your kids *ever*."

"Sweet as you are, Ae, I can't let you go *that* far," Mayr argued, "but it's nice to hear."

Aeley smiled slyly. "So how do you intend to go about it? Want me to look into orphans? I can send out letters and have names for you within the week. Babies? Toddlers? Schooling age?"

And there it is. Mayr's face warmed. The desk felt like a bed of hot coals, and he fidgeted until he fumbled off the edge altogether. "We were thinking of something… else. A little more work and a lot of intimacy and… Dammit." Mayr rubbed the back of his neck and focused on the floor. "Us and a girl, that's it."

"A surrogate mother," Aeley suggested. "That's what you want?"

"I guess? Or is it something else? Someone we could trust. Someone we could enjoy time with outside of sharing a child." Mayr sighed and shuffled to the door. Muted clicks seemed to answer his steps from the corridor on the other side—the sound of someone passing through the hall.

Mayr waited for the clicks to disappear before he continued, thankful whoever it was had rushed by. "Honestly? I don't know how we'll do it. There's no tact to going up to someone and asking if they'll have our kid. That's *not* who we are. That's creepy." He spun on his heel to face Aeley. "I'm *very* aware of the interest in bedding us, so finding a lover won't be the problem, but having a child? It's not a small favour."

"Still, it's not unheard of. Give it time? Hard effort?" Aeley struggled to hold back a laugh. "Just try, but not too hard?" She groaned and bashed her forehead into her palm. "Sorry. My mouth isn't all sorts of sex right now, honest."

"Oh, it is, but only for Lira." Mayr smirked and leaned against the door.

Quiet rattles sounded in the hallway, startling him.

"You're right, though," he said, pushing away

from the door. If someone waited on the other side, he needed the conversation to end. No one else needed to know. "We're not rushing into it. We're letting it happen, however it does, if it does."

"I'll support whatever you decide. If I get a smart idea, I'll let you know."

"Thanks."

Silence fell, deep with meaning conveyed by long gazes and soft smiles. Why had he expected Aeley to say anything different?

Three loud knocks rapped the door, scaring them both. Cursing under his breath, Mayr opened the door.

Arieve.

Every foul word tumbled back down Mayr's throat. "Hey." He leaned against the door, one arm sliding up the side.

In an instant, he tripped on his own feet and stumbled into the door, swinging it open further.

"You can't possibly be drunk already." The corners of Arieve's eyes crinkled with her smile, her glossed lips painted pink like her cheeks. Dark curls and plaits cascaded over her shoulders, the firelight lending a golden hue to the white-blonde streaks in the fringe of hair across her forehead. She held a silver tray, presenting two glass goblets filled with a bluish-purple drink and fragments of gold leaf sprinkled on top. "Otherwise, this might be a bad idea."

"What's a bad idea?" Mayr grimaced, his

mouth suddenly dry as if filled with pillow stuffing. Quick to recover, he smoothed his shirt, resettled his belts, and slicked back his hair, pretending he meant to be clumsy.

"Your after-dinner drinks. Lira was going to bring them, but I thought I'd save her the trip. She's having fun trading stories with your mother." Arieve cleared her throat. "I didn't want to interrupt your conversation."

The tray rattled in her hand, the drinks threatening to slosh over the rims.

Mayr steadied the tray. "Thanks for that. This. These." He offered her an awkward smile and took the goblets. "I'll let you get back." *So you won't see me kick my own ass for being completely inappropriate.*

"Thanks, Arieve," Aeley called from her desk.

"You're welcome." Arieve hesitated as she lowered the tray. She swayed gently, the rich green layers of her tiered, ruffled skirts moving with her. "I'll let you finish."

Before Mayr could say anything else, Arieve hurried down the hall and around the corner.

"I wonder what the mix is this time." Aeley snatched one goblet to sniff it. "Hint of gaffa nectar, soured pamolea extract, and a bite of fulore. Plus maybe, probably—" Another sniff. "—syrup from the Sailor's Sweetheart bush." She took a sip and nodded. Flakes of gold leaf clung to her top lip. "Not as fun as last night's concoction, but I could get used to it."

"That's what you always say." Mayr brushed the flakes from Aeley's lips with his thumb.

Aeley wiped her mouth on her sleeve. "Not always, just a lot. Cook knows her stuff. To be fair, she's known me since I was three, getting into her puddings and tarts anytime she turned around. I trust that when she serves up a hodgeypodgey drink, it's got personality." She tapped her goblet against his. "I'm heading back to our guests. You should, too, considering it's *your* party. We can resume this conversation later."

After a kiss to his cheek, Aeley flounced out the door and through the corridor, humming to herself.

Mayr stared into his goblet, watching the gold swirl in an abstract pattern. *My stomach. My head. I can't even…*

He set the goblet on Aeley's desk. He needed Tash's forgiveness more than he deserved a fancy drink.

As he exited the room, questions assaulted him hard enough to drown the sound of the door latch as it caught. One question practically shouted above all the others: how much had Arieve heard of his conversation with Aeley?

His heartbeat faltered. He was mortified. The door was not impervious to sound. What would Arieve think of him had she heard…

Hey, self, shut up! It doesn't matter. Mayr grumbled and hooked his thumbs around the back of his belts. *It still comes out to you're taken and happy, so you* really *need to shut up now.* Dragging his heels, he wandered through the corridor and turned into the next, towards the ballroom.

Around the corner, Arieve leaned against the wall, head bowed, her face hidden by her hair. She twined the trailing black laces of her bright green tunic around her fingers and pulled taut, then released them only to repeat the process. The empty tray rested beside her, abandoned against the wall.

"Hey." Mayr stopped, careful to leave two foot lengths between them. "I thought you went back?" He toyed with his marriage ring, twisting the band nervously. Memories of Tash surged forward, the airy weight of his kisses almost real enough to feel.

"I wanted to wait for you." Arieve raised her head and offered a tender smile. "I probably won't get a word in the rest of the night given the company, so I thought…"

She was in his arms before he could reply. Her hug stole his surprise, shredding it until all that remained was stunned.

"Congratulations," she murmured, her forehead tucked beneath his chin. "He's got a good heart, solid. You've found your match. If the Four could grant me one wish tonight, it'd be for you two to have everything you desire."

Mayr hesitated, his hands hovering over

Arieve's back. Touching was a bad idea, especially while he kept Tash from the truth. "Thank you." Quick as he could, he embraced Arieve and pushed her away, feeling worse than the coward he was. "Let's go back. I need to stop my mother from revealing every baby story she has, or everyone's going to hear about my naked backside and trailing diaper crowns."

Arieve picked up the tray and started up the hall. "I'm sure Tash is soaking them up as we speak." She laughed, the joyous sound digging up a dozen memories.

Memories he needed to lock up and burn down.

He followed Arieve and cast his gaze to the ceiling. *Please, Reverent Goddesses, get me through tonight. Then let's talk about strength of will, because one of these days I'm going to have to confess everything, and it'll hurt more than scorching my pride.*

Chapter Six

If he could have scripted their fate, Mayr would have opted for kissing Tash until the end of his days. Long and easy, with Tash's name on the tip of his tongue. Every moment felt like floating on a raft of feathers and fragrant wood on a lulled blue sea, basking in adoration.

Mayr glided his arm over the back of Tash's chair and tilted his head towards the wall behind him, shifting the slant of their mouths. Returning Tash's drawn-out moan with his own, Mayr smiled against Tash's lips, content to leave words for another day. Tash edged closer, eager and relentless. His legs slid along Mayr's as he caressed a path over Mayr's jaw and down the back of his neck, keeping Mayr close. Their last uninterrupted breaths had been some time back, forgettable and irrelevant. Had Mayr tried to count the moments since their kiss began, he would have run out of fingers and toes half a dozen times over.

Seated in the corner of Orae's tavern, they stole what intimacy they could. Light touched nearly every corner of the dining area, but Mayr had blown out the candle in the lantern on their table. The little shadow they gained only served their mouth play, allowing them to cuddle together at the furthest end of the tavern, in between two curtain-covered windows. Outside, the village was cold and dark except for a faint glow from other buildings. The silhouettes of the pottery, weaver's workshop, and typographer's office across the road were barely visible through the foggy windowpanes.

Inside, Mayr and Tash were warm enough for a light layer of sweat to dampen their skin. After leisurely enjoying their dinner, the slow transition to an unyielding kiss had been simple. Around them, raucous voices filled the tavern. Patrons occupied almost every measure of space, putting each of the tables to full use. People shouted, jeered, and roared their amusement, throwing coins at each other and playing with painted discs. A crowd surrounded the bar, drinking and laughing. Among them were guards from the Dahe estate, as well as villagers and travelers who had purchased accommodations for the night. The dining room smelled more like ale and beer than food from the kitchen, though the heavy scent of spiced meat pies lingered. The muffled pitch of a fanciful tune flitted around the disconnected noise, played on a hardy guitar by a young musician. More than one person had been inspired to dance and flail their arms, keeping time with the melody while they kicked their heels and scuffed the floorboards.

ARCHER KAY LEAH

There was only quiet in Mayr and Tash's corner. Lost to the warm touch kneading him, Mayr intended to leave the corner with new memories. They had sat at the same table the first time they met, chosen by Tash for its observational advantage. Sarene had been with them that night, oblivious to the silent bond they forged.

Now it was just the two of them. While far from a paradise, it was still a comfortable place to escape. Two weeks had passed since Mayr proposed to Tash, and their dinner out was meant to be a reprieve from the routine they had adopted—an effort to retain spontaneity and liveliness. He never wanted their marriage to become a chore. A schedule. A drill.

Tash nipped Mayr's lips. "I think I may have finally kissed you enough to touch the threads that craft your soul." Slipping his hands through Mayr's loose hair, he guided Mayr's head back and kissed the hollow of Mayr's throat. "The fire in me hates to let you go."

"Thankfully you don't have to, not permanently." Mayr curled his arm around Tash's neck and pressed their foreheads together. He drew back the delicate veil to expose Tash's unshaven jaw, his fingertips gliding over Tash's cheekbone. "I'll always come back to you, no matter where we are." His caress ventured over the thin folds of Tash's ear and down his nape. "Those threads you talk about keep me in knots

176

for you, and you're the only one who can unravel them."

Tash hummed and nuzzled Mayr's cheek. "Perhaps we're soulbound by fire and thread."

"I'm good with that," Mayr murmured, catching Tash's lips once more. He cradled Tash's head against his shoulder with the crook of his arm.

A cleared throat brought their mouths to a stop, raiding the peace between kiss and contented moan.

Mayr swung his attention towards the figures that stood beside their table: a man and woman, both fidgeting nervously. They appeared no older than eighteen, their rustic traveling clothes heavy and worn, drenched from the falling snow. Both flushed beneath their flickering stares. "Yes?"

The man cleared his throat again. He removed his flattened brown cap and ruffled his shaggy dark hair. His partially gloved fingers worked his cap in circles. "I—we, I mean—we're here to—that is, we'd like—" The man shot a glimpse to the woman at his side, her arm looped around his. "We've just gotten married. We've come from the temple to..." His flush deepened. "We saw you sitting here, kind priest, and thought you might be able to bless our bed?"

"You don't have to," the woman added, her free hand shoved into the pocket of her green, knee-length coat. Curls of bright red hair dangled from beneath her pale yellow knit hat. "We can see you're busy." She tugged on her husband. "I told you this was a bad idea. Let's leave them alone."

Every bit of Mayr wanted to agree.

"I would be pleased to bless your wedding night." Tash stood, offering them a kind smile. He squeezed between Mayr and the table to join the couple, his robes falling around him in graceful folds. "You have a room upstairs?"

Both the man and woman nodded.

"Very well, if you allow me to get the items I need, I'll follow you to your room." Tash tilted his head and regarded them with an expectant expression. The couple returned his stare until he swept his hand towards them. "Perhaps our magnanimous Goddesses would like to celebrate your names first?"

The woman grimaced. "Sorry. I'm Nelda and this is Daury, my boyfr… my husband."

"Well met, Nelda, Daury. You may call me Tash." He reached for a serving woman as she wove through the crowd and beckoned her close.

A new member of the tavern staff, Mayr realized. One he did not know, save for her name: Elarel. She crept between bodies towards Tash, an empty tray in one hand and a metal pitcher in the other.

"What can I get you, your priestliness?" Elarel stopped between Tash and Mayr, the layers of her bright yellow, orange, and red skirts pinned back by shiny silver brooches. She flashed Tash a grin before eyeing Mayr. "Now that you've sucked his face clear off, shall I get you more to drink? I think there's cake in the back with your name practically iced on it."

"Tempted as I am, it'll have to wait." Tash motioned to Nelda and Daury. "I need you to fetch me some things and take them upstairs, if it isn't a bother?"

"For you? Never. What things?"

"A bowl of water, a goblet of the lightest tasting drink you have, salt, four white candles, a bowl of strong herbs, and a stick of incense—the sweet kind Orae keeps for romantic evenings."

Elarel beamed. "I'll be up shortly." Without another word, she turned and pushed through the crowd.

"I'll meet you up there," Tash told Nelda and Daury. As they shuffled away, his attention returned to Mayr. "I'll be back soon, kindest of loves." He brushed a kiss across Mayr's mouth. "Keep your desires kindled for me."

A moment later, Tash was a blur of vivid red fabric disappearing into the expanse of earthy browns and greens accompanied by blacks and greys.

Mayr sighed and stretched out his legs, his fingers interlaced behind his head as he leaned back. His long coat and cloak pulled under him, their bottoms still wet from where they had trailed over snow. The hilt of a knife dug into his back, protesting his choice of angle, while the heels of his boots slipped through the puddle of melted snow that had formed while he ate.

Annoyance jabbed him, his impatience wishing for Tash's swift return. Mayr straightened and tugged on his tight black pants and fitted black shirt, both of which clung to him in all the ways Tash enjoyed. He had put them on specifically so that Tash would tear them off, but now he was too warm to be dressed and tempted to rent a room just to bed Tash sooner rather than later.

Tavern patrons glanced in his direction, enough to take in his face but not long enough to engage in anything that would cost them. Mayr cast his gaze from one person to another, searching for weapons, foul play, or anything that would keep him occupied.

The well-behaved, rule-abiding patrons were boring, he decided. Slumping back, he draped his arm over Tash's chair, pinning Tash's red long coat with his equally vibrant red cloak and wool short coat. He tapped his fingertips in time to the lively tune playing through the tavern.

The moment Arieve entered his sight, he froze.

Not now.

Not ever.

She spotted him from the other end of the tavern, her stare locked to his. Stopped in front of the tavern entrance, Arieve hesitated, turning as though deciding in which direction to flee.

When she moved towards him, her steps were slow, the time between them forced into a painful crawl. Dressed in long, dark skirts and a frumpy, grey wool sweater, Arieve was an image of comfort on the cold night.

Meanwhile, his comfort was upstairs, abiding by duty and leaving him to weather things on his own.

He had avoided Arieve since the engagement dinner. For years he had taught his instincts to regard her as a friend only, untouchable in all ways. Now *he* was untouchable, in wish and doubt and second chances. His conscious self needed to learn that, even if it required staying clear of her completely.

I'll never be ready for it, but I can damn well try. Mayr offered a strained smile as Arieve stopped at his table, a leather-bound ledger in her hands. *It might be the best wedding gift I can give Tash, even if he never realizes it. I still haven't told him...*

"Hey, stranger," Arieve greeted, her tone too warm to ignore. "I heard you were here." She eyed the chair beside him. "Where'd he go?"

"Upstairs, doing his priestly thing."

"Oh." Arieve's disappointed gaze fell, restless as she drew her fingertips along the table's edge. "So, umm... How many days till the wedding?"

Mayr snorted. "I'm not keeping count."

Arieve smirked, one of her delicate brows arched. "Right. I know you, remember?"

Her burning stare obliterated his lie. "One

hundred and twenty days," Mayr answered quietly, his confidence drifting away in defeat.

"Once a romantic, always bound by romance." Arieve tapped the table, the rhythm erratic as she pulled her bottom lip between her teeth. "And you're serious about it? *Really* serious?" She blushed and tugged on the collar of her sweater. "Never mind, ignore me. I'm full of terrible questions."

Given her frazzled state, ignoring her was difficult. In the awkward silence between them, the essence of whatever bothered her hollered louder than any patron.

They were saved by Tash, his return marked by mutual sighs of relief.

Mayr all but jumped up. "All done?"

"Yes." Tash stepped around Arieve to kiss Mayr, his eyes gleaming with laughter. "Everything's been cleansed and blessed. Whatever happens now is between them, Emeraliss, and anyone beside their room."

"Behave," Mayr muttered, flicking his glance to Arieve.

Tash spun towards Arieve. "Once more we're graced with your presence. It's always a joy."

The hug Arieve gave him was timid and stiff. "Congratulations, again, both of you."

"Thank you." Tash withdrew, his brow furrowed. "What's wrong?"

"I'm… It's… fine. I'm fine."

"You're not," Tash argued. He cast Mayr a

doubtful look. "Neither of you hide your worries well. Please, Arieve, what do you need?"

Fright danced over Arieve's features before hiding behind uncertainty. "It's complicated… and horrifyingly simple. It's so simple it's almost too complicated."

Alarm lashed at Mayr with frightening thoughts. Had something happened to her, Orae, or another member of her family? "What's going on? Do I need to settle a score with someone? Fetch the best healer?"

"What? No!" Arieve peered over her shoulder. "Follow me. Just… follow."

With their winter clothes in their arms, Mayr and Tash stayed close to Arieve on their way through the crowd to the office in the back of the tavern. Small with bookshelves from floor to ceiling, the brightly lit office was tidy and smelled faintly of smoke from a pipe. A desk sat to the left of the room across from three chairs to the right. The window on the opposite wall was latched shut, the curtains drawn back to reveal the half-foot of snow on the windowsill.

As Arieve closed the door, Mayr tossed his coat and cloak onto one chair then draped Tash's coats over them. When he turned towards the desk, Arieve was already laying down the ledger.

"I guess it's no secret that Coye and me split again," she said, leaning against the desk. "I'm losing count of how many times that makes. We're never perfectly on-point. I always want more than I can have, or she wants less than I need to give." Her nonchalant shrug did nothing to ease her sorrowful expression. "It's not a lack of love. I feel it—I feel *her*—but there's always something keeping her back. Now I want to move on. I need to stop stalling my life because she can't trust me or her or make up her mind."

Tash stepped forward. "There's nothing wrong with that," he said softly. "Sometimes it takes embracing the wrong things to recognize what's right."

"Or what's never going to be there." Arieve swept aside the fringe of hair across her forehead. "Meanwhile, you've got yourselves figured out." A wistful smile curved her painted lips. "It took a while to find your match, Mayr. Now I'm hearing how far you intend to go. Grandmother was talking to your mother, teasing out the wedding details and your plans to start a family." A blush coloured her cheeks. "I also overheard your talk with Aeley the night of the proposal. I didn't mean to—it just happened."

Mayr felt the blood drain from his face. "Arieve, what you heard—what I said—I didn't—"

"What? Mean it?" Arieve bowed her head. "Don't tell me you didn't."

"Well, no, I did. It's just..." Mayr looked to Tash, desperate for help. He was going to say all the wrong words, he knew it. "I don't know how much you heard, but it probably sounded odd, insensitive. Not even close to being socially correct."

"A child that's yours is how I understood it. It couldn't get much more socially correct." Arieve gazed at the rugs beneath their feet as she fingered the worn edge of the desk. "Were you serious about it? You're sure you don't want to adopt?"

"Yes," Tash answered, stepping towards Mayr.

"If you can't have what you want, will you take that other option to feel fulfilled?"

"Yes." Mayr drew close to Tash, the backs of their hands brushing. He needed the comfort of touch, to let Tash's essence ground him. There were too many silent questions screaming for an answer. "Though it might be the *only* option, because who would want to have a child with us?"

Arieve's stare captured his. "I would."

In two words, she slew his heart.

In an instant, she changed the world.

Tash gripped Mayr's wrist, hard enough to hurt. Out of shock, Mayr suspected, but perhaps it was to keep Mayr from running out the door.

He needed to flee. He needed to hide. He needed something safer than standing in the same room with his other half and the woman he had given up on.

This was not right. It made no sense.

And he was cold, so cold. Lost, spinning out of calm thought and drowning in the realization that she was sincere. Arieve's features were drawn, pinched as she looked away. This was not a joke at his expense. This was the truth, simple and liable to tear into their friendship.

Mayr snatched Tash's hand in both of his faster than he could understand what was happening.

"You're not the only ones who want kids," Arieve said quietly, circling the toe of her boot over the floor. "I have for years, but Coye doesn't. Since I never wanted to give her up, it's always been a choice, and I've always chosen her. Now I'd rather choose me than a relationship that keeps failing. I'd drop everything to have a child with you than have none at all." Her next smile was lopsided. "Considering I've crushed madly on you forever, I'd love to finally work out all these feelings I have. If you'd ever let me in that much."

Mayr choked on breath alone. He sputtered and stumbled, fragments of words tumbling out in a mess of noise. "Arieve," was the only thing he said with certainty.

Tash's arms wrapped around him, pulling him close before his knees could buckle.

"Breathe," Tash whispered against his temple. "Hold onto me and breathe."

Arieve pushed off the desk and rushed forward, reaching for Mayr. "I'm sorry. I didn't mean to startle you this bad." She recoiled and drew into herself. "I don't know how to say any of this. I never have."

Clamping Tash's arm with both hands, Mayr was at war with himself. Emotions and rational thought clashed in a painful raid. "What you're saying… I've got to be hearing it wrong. You and me, we've only ever been… and you called me family. We've always been separate, always at the wrong time—"

"I know." Arieve worried her bottom lip. "There's been a lot of dancing around the truth. We're never quite right at the best times, but so perfect at the worst. You've always been my look-but-don't-touch. Mine to fix when you were hurt, and mine to lose when the world offered you better. Now I feel bad for even looking." She motioned to Tash. "Of all the men you could've had, the one you chose does all the right things…" Arieve cleared her throat and backed towards the desk. "Let's just say I'd be happy to help."

"While that's flattering," Tash said, "I'm trying to understand what I'm missing." He pressed his forehead to Mayr's temple. "I feel like I'm standing in a private moment that's not mine to have."

Mayr stilled, alternating between focused and unfocused. His gaze clung to the paintings on the wall behind the desk: happy portraits of Arieve's family, including one of Orae's first husband and their two children beside the portrait of her second husband and all of Orae's six children. Each of Arieve's five aunts, four uncles, and twenty cousins appeared at least once in the paintings, most of them family portraits. Few members of their family remained in Dahena. Of those still alive, the majority chose to live in other villages in Gailarin, leaving Orae, Liele, Arieve, two of her aunts, and a hand count's worth of cousins to manage their family's property. Arieve's mother and father, Vilady and Elamare, owned a house near Dahena, but they were usually elsewhere. Both were tax collectors, though Elamare was also known as a purveyor of relics. They traveled as their jobs required and visited Dahena at least once a month, often after a visit to the tax clerks in High Council Hall.

A glimpse at the painting of Vilady and Elamare only proved how much Arieve was like them. Elamare's hazel eyes were as green as Arieve's, and his long, black-brown hair tumbled over his shoulders in tight curls and braids, decorated with yellow beads and orange ribbons that appeared all the brighter against his lovely black skin. Both Elamare and Arieve were bright souls with a sparkle in their spirit as if they were living stars or jewels. On top of it all, Arieve was blessed with her mother's tender perceptiveness, proud bearing, and golden-brown complexion.

Mayr's attention skipped over the other paintings to the top left corner. There hung his favourite portrait on the wall: the image of a young Arieve, no older than sixteen, with a smile that could light someone's entire world for all of their life. A life he had been certain they would never share. A life he had committed to someone else—one that could spiral into misery quicker than he could collapse.

"I'm sorry," he whispered, clutching Tash tighter. "So sorry."

Tash's breath skipped across Mayr's cheek. "For what?"

"For not telling you everything," Mayr mumbled, "for never losing these feelings. I owe you better, and I've been a complete ass." He flushed beneath Tash's scrutiny. "I can't even say it *now*, even though *you're* here and *she's* here and this would be a great time to stop being foolish."

Silent moments passed, weighted with his struggle to string words together as Tash's eyelashes fluttered against his skin.

"Mayr," Tash murmured, "say it."

"I don't—"

"Let go. If you can tell yourself what this actually is, you can tell me." Tash's fingertips glided down the back of Mayr's neck. "Say you have feelings for her and set yourself free."

A chill raced down Mayr's spine, small bumps rising along his skin where Tash touched. Words tumbled from his lips, slow and stiff. "I've had a... thing for her since we were kids, but we've never done anything." He turned his head, catching Tash's lips on his. "There was a line—a *really good* one—and—"

A kiss silenced him, soft and smooth, without

tongue, without command. A gentle kiss he would never tire of receiving, full of compassion and hope with all the warmth of a loving embrace.

"Thank you," Tash whispered. "You can stop fretting now. You don't need to apologize." He cupped Mayr's cheek. "You needn't hide. I've got you."

"But—"

"You'd challenge a servant of Emeraliss?" Tash arched one brow. "I'm the last one to scold the inconvenience of love, which is exactly what this sounds like." He glanced at Arieve.

Arieve hunched her shoulders. "Since I was sixteen, I figured if I committed myself to any man they'd have to be like Mayr. Then he married Betta..." She let out a long sigh. "I was so disappointed, enough that when she left him, I was pleased. *Pleased*, like I was full of myself and happy to be cruel. Then I found out why she'd left and I wanted to rip her apart. I wanted to tell him what I felt, but I didn't have the courage to even *flirt* with him, let alone confess."

"And I put it out of my thoughts." Mayr leaned into Tash. "I hurt too much to do anything after Betta. It wasn't worth ruining our friendship."

"Yet it's come back around," Tash said. "Maybe that's the whole point."

More silence, almost deafening in what it did not say.

Arieve approached but stopped two paces away. "As much as I'd like to continue this—as long as I've waited to *hear* it—I have to get back to work. I just needed to tell you we all want the same thing. Instead of waiting for someone to fill the gap, we could try having it together." Hesitant, she reached for Mayr and Tash, finally settling one hand on each of them. "I'm not involved with anyone. I *want* to get pregnant and wouldn't mind the fooling around it takes to get there. It wouldn't have to be permanent. I'm *not* looking to destroy your marriage. Consider it friends helping one another, and we'll leave your marriage intact. We'll protect it."

Before Mayr could answer, she withdrew her hand. "It's ideal, too. Since I work at the estate, you'll be around for the pregnancy, and after, I'll be around to parent. It's better than consigning ourselves to what we don't want."

"Why us?" Mayr asked, his mouth dry. "Why not someone else?"

"Other than the fact I've always dreamed of kissing you?" Arieve drew her fingertips across her lips. "I trust you. I don't want to be with someone who'll resent having a family or use a child against me. I don't mind being a single mother, but I also don't want to use a guy to have a baby without their agreement." She tapped Mayr's shaking hand. "I've adored you for years. I'm not asking to get married, I'm not demanding anything, but I can't ignore this. It's like fate's stepped in and hijacked opportunity."

With a gentle smile, she moved to the door. "The two of you can think about it. Whenever you have your answer, whatever it is, you know where to find me."

In Mayr's mind, the quiet sound of the door closing behind her was as jarring as a hammer striking the wall. He blinked, unable to focus on anything but the floor. How could he even begin to fathom what had just happened?

"We should go," Tash suggested, tugging Mayr's hand until he reluctantly agreed to follow. Without words, they dressed in their coats and cloaks, the brown-black fur capelet of Mayr's cloak still damp. Donning their scarves and gloves, they left the office and wove their way through the tavern to the front door.

Cold, dry gusts greeted them outside. The snow had not let up since their arrival, descending upon the village in large flakes. A group of youths shuffled past the bakery on the other side of the road, singing wintertide carols off-tune and trudging through the foot of snow. They tossed snowballs through the air, resulting in pelted victims and peals of laughter.

Meanwhile, Mayr's world had flung itself into a stop.

In-step with Tash as they trod the flattened path left by the wheels of a wagon, Mayr dug his hands into his pockets. Snow crunched beneath their boots, echoing his grinding thoughts.

After all the years, after all the doubt, he could have told Arieve he loved her and that would have been enough.

I really know how to ruin things. Mayr glimpsed Tash from the corner of his eye, barely seeing Tash's face around the red hood of Tash's cloak. *Why do I always sabotage the things I have?*

"I can read your worries from here," Tash said, moving closer to grasp Mayr's hand. "Talk to me."

"This is where you're supposed to be angry," Mayr mumbled. "You should be disgusted, unsettled, lecturing me on disrespect." He glanced at their clasped hands. "Not being so perfect and loving and *nice*."

"Hey." Tash pulled Mayr to a stop and faced him, his brow furrowed. "What have I ever done to make you think I'd react otherwise?"

Mayr shrank back, huddling into the warmth of his coat. "I wasn't honest with you. Of all things, you prefer honesty. I let you down. I wanted to tell you how I feel about her, but I couldn't. Then you found out like *that*..." His gaze dropped to the hand with his marriage ring. "The timing couldn't be worse."

Tash gripped Mayr's arms. "Mayr, I encourage honesty in all things, but I don't demand it. Everyone has secrets—from themselves, from their loves, from the world. It's in our nature, how we were put together. Sometimes the truth is so far we can't grasp it. You know love is sneaky," he said softly. "It seeps into our hearts and sets things into motion without our command. We can deny it and lock it away, but it yells and fights and bangs on the walls until it wins. Even if chance and circumstance get in the way, love eventually comes to light."

"But—"

Tash's cold hands cupped Mayr's cheeks. "You did nothing wrong. I have not been slighted. I don't feel any less loved." A smile softened his features, his eyes gleaming in the faint moonlight. "Truth be told, I feel *more* loved." He took Mayr's hand in both of his and kissed the back of Mayr's fingers. "You could have sought her. You could have turned me away, but you didn't. For that I am yours, come all complications and embarrassing moments that make you stammer and struggle."

Heat swept through Mayr's cheeks. "Now you're just making fun of me."

The grin Tash gave in reply twisted knots in Mayr's gut. "It makes me laugh, I'll admit." Tash brushed snow from the tip of Mayr's nose. "You're unspeakably ravishing when you're flustered. When your emotions get too far ahead of your words and you can't catch up." His fingertips settled on Mayr's lips. "It's like falling in love with you all over again."

Mayr swallowed hard, painfully aware of the effect Tash's touch had on him. Perhaps he could salvage the night after all. "Yeah?"

"Yes. Besides, she's cute. Your taste in women

isn't entirely different from my own."

"Sounds like you're trying to say something."

"That I understand, for one. How you can care for someone and be afraid to admit it. I can't fault you for that, especially when what *we* have fell prey to the same thing," Tash said quietly. "I don't have a need to be angry, or the right. You're so patient with my love for Inesta, and I won't complain about your feelings for Betta or Arieve. You're allowed to feel *something*. I never demanded you give that up."

"I still feel like I should."

"And miss the opportunity thrown at us?" Tash clasped Mayr's hands and swung them gently. "We're incredibly blessed, sweet love. It's an unexpected gift. However it's come to us, whatever the path, it's a chance to have everything we want. No one has to get hurt along the way. No one needs to be ashamed or uncomfortable."

Mayr held his breath, waiting for Tash to add a caveat. When none came, he breathed out, long and slow. Tash's optimism and reason forged ahead faster than Mayr's thoughts. He still could not make sense of why he was not standing alone at the side of the road, watching Tash walk away in anger. His heart had been sold on a hard fight, armed to his frozen back teeth with apologies and gifts to prove his love.

Instead, Tash bounced on his toes in boyish glee, blowing away any hint of jealousy or disapproval Mayr had anticipated.

"You'd be willing to go through with it?" The question tumbled out of Mayr's mouth, difficult and dry.

"The better question would be are *we* willing to."

Unable to remain still, Mayr walked up the wagon tracks. Tash followed, his stride matching Mayr's. "Maybe," Mayr said at last, shoving his chilled hands into his pockets. He wanted to be at home, warm in his bed, away from the cold and his shock.

"Perhaps this is better answered in a different way." Tash hummed and eyed the road ahead. "Are we opposed to having a threesome? Would it be so horrible to have three sweat-slicked bodies smelling of sex in the same bed and enjoying it?"

"*What?*"

"You heard me. Would it be terrible to have one hand around my cock and the other inside her, both of us coming for you?"

Mayr choked and coughed. His mind screeched to a halt, stuck on the image of all three of them tangled up in sheets. "No...? I guess... no? Just strange?"

"You enjoyed yourself when we were with Sarene, and look what came of that." Tash clutched Mayr's hand. "I would've done anything for you that night. You were beautiful, coming undone in my hands, letting me see *you*. Your trust sustained it, not my desire. I suppose the question is if you trust me now?" he asked. "Can you trust in us? Arieve's attractive, playful, and kind. If you love her..." He exhaled, his breath drifting in the air like white smoke. "It'll be easier for you. If it's easier for you, it'll be easier for me."

Tash stopped and slipped his fingers beneath Mayr's chin, turning Mayr's face towards him. "I love watching you, when you sleep, when you laugh, when you're in the throes of release. Watching you and her is something I'm willing to try, if for no other reason than to have a family. I'll do it to have the chance to see you with our child, playing and learning and being the father I know you are. I value our future too much to surrender to jealousy."

The husky tone of the last words sent a shiver through Mayr. "How can you be so sure?"

"I'm not completely certain, but it's worth an attempt." Tash smiled wistfully. "We didn't approach her; *she* offered it to *us*. She wants to be a mother, something I welcome happily."

"How do we raise a kid together, though?" Mayr argued. "There's when and where and how, not to mention providing and sharing responsibilities. It could take *months* to sort, and we might not agree."

"We *have* months, Mayr. Besides, you know her. You know her family, her values. We're likely to agree on a great many things simply by our natures. The rest we can find a solution for. We can make this work."

"You're not going to give this up, are you?"

"Not when you're being too stubborn to see the answer right in front of you."

Tash's hopeful look struck Mayr harder than an axe at the knees. Agony hacked Mayr apart, ripping back his wants and needs from what was right. While Tash tried to grasp their happiness before it floated away, Mayr was too occupied with finding reasons to run.

Not even finding—making up. Here he is showing me what it means to be loved and I'm fighting like I don't want it. But I do. I want us to have the family of our ridiculous dreams. Arieve... she came to us, and he's not punishing me. How can any of that be wrong when it sounds so right?

Growling, Mayr pulled Tash off the road towards the cobbler's shop. Beneath the eaves where the snow was shallow, Mayr pushed Tash up against the black wood wall and slipped his knee between Tash's legs, pinning him in place. Persuaded by thoughts of possible futures, he claimed Tash's lips with a hard kiss that deepened quickly, guided by Mayr's desperation to taste Tash's love and hope rather than just hearing them. Words were easy—he needed actions. He needed to see what they could have, to feel what they would become. If he wanted to have it all, he needed to be open to it.

When he drew back, they both struggled to breathe. Mayr held Tash close, groaning as their chests rose and fell together at the same strong pace. Snowflakes clung to Tash's eyelashes. His nose and cheeks were red in the dim light, but his blue eyes had lost none of their sheen. Cold as his skin was, Tash's mouth was warm, the taste of him both savoury and sweet in a burst of peace and pleasure. To all of Mayr's senses, he was irresistible.

He would follow Tash anywhere, into anything, whatever his heart desired.

"I'm yours," Mayr whispered. Slowly he raised one of Tash's hands with his own and pressed it to the wall, palm to palm as he interlaced their fingers. "If we go into this together, we'll get through it together." He lifted Tash's other hand like the first, their gloved fingers interlocked tight against the wall. "If one of us changes our mind — if one of us wants out — say it and we'll stop. Both of us go in, both of us come out. That's the only way this is going to work. I won't leave you behind. If we're setting rules, that's my first and only. The only answer I need."

Chapter Seven

Yes. We're going to tell her yes… assuming either of us has the courage to say it.

Tash opened his eyes, disappointed to find the bedroom dark. The fire was out and little light slipped between the curtains, suggesting dawn was still on its way.

Meanwhile, I can't go back to sleep, even if I wanted to. With a stifled sigh of surrender, Tash untangled himself from the skewed blankets. Mayr remained where he lay on his stomach, face turned towards the door, both legs and one arm sprawled while his other arm hugged his pillow.

Tempted to embrace Mayr's warmth and escape the chilly air, Tash forced himself from the bed and into his sandals. He had a long day ahead. In addition to training two new Metah priests and cleansing the altar rooms dedicated to Emeraliss, he was to be the officiant at both a child's blessing in the morning and a marriage rite that evening.

If I'm going to be distracted, best do it now. The last thing I need is to get the words wrong and bless the infant with all the grace of a wobbly old goat. Tash crept towards the wall across from him, stopping at the armoire Mayr had given him three days after their engagement. The armoire bore the strong scent of the hard, red-black wood it was crafted from, as if the trees had been felled only days before. Etched into each corner of the armoire were bouquets of flowers, fern leaves, and feathers, identical to those of the chests on either side of the armoire.

The armoire and chests belonged to Tash, Mayr had made that clear. Mayr had also insisted he would share the mantel above the fireplace and add a set of shelves for Tash's personal items, which were few but welcome nonetheless.

He's really trying. From the armoire, Tash withdrew a pair of his red pants and breathed in the woody scent that clung to the fabric, unable to stop his smile. *We're actually going through with all of it. Him and me, bound in vows and law and love.*

Love that would include someone else.

His delight sobered. He donned the pants, tying them loosely before he crossed the room to the makeshift altar on Mayr's armoire. A week had passed since Arieve's proposal. Since then, he had discussed the issue at length with Mayr to pick apart the merits and faults. The decision could not be made lightly, nor could they let it pass by. *Now we have to make our decision worth something.*

He flipped open the matchbox on the left side of the altar and fingered the long matches before drawing one. Mayr insisted on purchasing the matchsticks rather than allow Tash to rely on the Temple's supply. They were a luxury, affordable to those who could spare the funds. The Temple received chests of matches from wealthy benefactors, including the man responsible for their production, but Mayr spared a portion of his wages to maintain a collection for Tash, separate from the estate's stores.

Even in something so trivial, Mayr's care was limitless.

Which is why this family will probably work, assuming we have Emeraliss's blessing. Tash struck the match and lit the four white candles and incense. *No matter his love for Arieve, however deep it runs, I have faith in him. None of this would be happening if his love for me weren't real. Despite my carelessness, despite what he's gone through, he's taking me as a husband. Moving on hasn't been easy for either of us, but still. Still.*

Tash waved his hand over the bowl of floral-scented incense, sweeping the ribbon of smoke over the altar as he focused on the four gold statues.

"In those I trust," he recited, whispering the words he spoke every morning. "With heart invested in all things beloved by the divine, I bid the Sacred Four fair morning. Emeraliss, Lady of Love's Light, I recommit my soul to share in the might of Your graces." Tash dipped his fingers into the bowl of lukewarm water and flicked drops across the altar from left to right. "Such is the depth of my servitude. Grant me the kindness that comes with love and the wisdom therein."

He backed away and kneeled in front of the armoire. Head bowed, he sat back on his heels and held out his hands, open palms turned upwards. *In all things, I am this, blood and bone searching for the truth. Reverent Ones, guide my spirit. I am willing and ready...*

Eyes closed, he let the familiar words of prayer take over. His mind filled with the images of the Goddesses as he saw them during his last Uldana trial. Statues, tapestries, and paintings could not compete with such ethereal beauty. Just as the universe could not be captured in a jam jar, the essence of the Four could not be accurately portrayed. No physical tool would capture the light that radiated from within; no brush or chisel could recreate the shifting threads of their being. The Goddesses were as stars, their brilliance best seen from the darkest depths.

Between life and death, Tash had appeared before the Four and wept for want of a life with Mayr. On his knees, under the burden of apology, Tash had stolen a glimpse of Emeraliss. Her long hair shone like the sun, bright yellow and white and grey, hanging in tiny plaits, thick curls, and cascades of jeweled strands. As Emeraliss had grasped his shoulders, he realized her skin shifted in waves from warm bronze to deep umber to black as the night sky, each angle revealing a different hue. The gauzy, glittering layer of

Emeraliss's slashed white gown had been soft and cool, sliding over him like her gentle gaze.

She forgave him that day, accepting his faults and pardoning the lie he had led himself to believe. Instead of punishment, he had incurred the rawness of love, its words and expectations stripped away. Witnessed by the other goddesses, Emeraliss had bound Tash to Her by word and tether. The chilling sensation of the chain formed from woven light and silken ribbons still played across his right wrist, its glowing white and blue jewels burned into his memory. Emeraliss had bid him to stay with Mayr, mortal rules be damned.

He intended to do so, even if Arieve possessed part of Mayr's desire.

Tash frowned and stuttered over his prayer. He had promised Mayr he would let Arieve in, not only into their bed but also his trust. His heart was not on the table for the taking, but he would not close off his emotions. More than once he had dallied in a relationship that included two others, though he had never invested deeply in them. Convinced he was better committed to a single person or no one at all, he had taken only sexual gratification from those encounters.

I didn't love any of them, and that's the difference. He fidgeted, forcing his position despite his restless fingers. There were multiple forms of love, he reminded himself, and he was capable of many of them if he let it happen.

Just as Mayr trusted him, Tash needed to trust

what they had.

For everything there is a price, a trade. Tash stared at the candles. *For the life we seek, I must trade a piece of him — a piece of myself. For a child that is ours, we must pay in love. Yet that love will become part of our child, returned in full several times over.*

His glance fell to the bear cub carved into the armoire. *I cannot enslave him to my doubt, nor do I have to turn away, hide, or watch bitterly as someone leads him to his happiness. I can go with him, be by his side. That which is the most meaningful often requires a fight. Yet when the fight is unnecessary, when the hurt need not be dealt, we can choose to surrender or persevere in peace. We can love our way through it.*

He wanted peace rather than despair. Above everything, his hope chewed on the edges of possibility, giggling at what could be.

Yet deep beyond his wishes, reason toiled with fear. Mayr was precious. He alone could shatter Tash. If Arieve took Mayr away…

Tash squeezed his eyes shut and bit down hard. He had promised Mayr he could give Arieve a fair chance. Likewise, Mayr had promised if either of them hated the arrangement, one word would release them. Only one word and they would walk away together:

Stop.

With a sigh, Tash returned to his prayer. When that failed, his words mangled by the rest of his thoughts, he leaned forward to touch his forehead to the floor. The cold stone was a welcome comfort on his flushed skin. *Emeraliss, give me strength. Grant me the courage to try and the faith to hold on. Bless us with the joy of a child's smiles and laughter and the innocence we lost. Give us serenity where we see only challenge.*

Tash pushed up from the floor and shuffled to the table across the room to wash and groom. Once finished, he returned to his armoire and pulled on his bracers. After multiple tugs on the bracer laces, he drew out a fresh set of robes. The lightest went on first, a single piece of unadorned fabric that hung loose and lacked closures. The next robe was the heaviest, made from thicker fabric in the winter than in the summer. He laced it closed with long red cord, through the two sets of grommets aligned from his collarbone to his hip. The last robe slid on with the most ease and could be closed with four gold clasps. He left the clasps alone, preferring to let the robe flow around him. Of them all, the third robe was his favourite, the brush of its flared sleeves and wide cuffs soft on his knuckles.

His veil was the final piece of his vestments, its comb easily slipped into his hair. A glance at his bedside table reminded him of his talon ring, a piece he avoided whenever he needed to appear the perfect priest. Guilt hit him every time he chose not to wear it, but he could not allow tokens of his past to bring bad energy into the formal spiritual space of others.

On his return to Mayr's armoire, he glimpsed

the bed. Mayr still slept, flat on his back, one arm curled above his head while the other dangled over the edge of the mattress.

Tash blew out the candles and left the room, closing the door quietly. He would let Mayr sleep for a while longer. A cup of steeped herbs was his first concern. *Something strong. Anything to shake these nerves.*

The dimly lit hall was empty, though he recognized the sound of the night watch in the distance.

The silence was more informative. For those who knew Mayr, one needed to note where there were no audible footsteps. That was where the guards truly were, hidden in the shadows. They were never far, always a dozen steps away from Aeley, Lira, or Mayr. Now that group included Tash, Adren, and Ress.

True to expectation, a guard slipped out from around a corner before Tash stepped onto the main staircase.

"Morning, Priest Tash," Gorgan greeted. His wide grin and blue-green gaze were friendly, but they did nothing to hide his visible fatigue, even with the loose curls of his dark blond hair dangling into his eyes. Like the other guards, he wore dark clothes, his heavy brown shirt laced all the way up his neck beneath a black leather vest. His black pants appeared immaculate, tucked into shin-high boots with black fur trim. As prescribed by Mayr's rules, he carried at least four knives:

two strapped to his thighs and two in his boots. He kept one hand on the hilt of the short sword at his waist, his posture at ease. "Did you sleep well?"

Not older than twenty, Gorgan was still in the basic training Mayr put all guards through. From what Tash knew, Gorgan would be subjected to another two years of that training before he was considered a full guard. The corner in the hallway was the second trial post Mayr had ever assigned him; the first was the perimeter of the stables.

"Morning, Gorgan. I slept, so I suppose you could call that well. Just as quiet as your shift, I think."

Gorgan nodded, a faint blush spreading across his cheeks. "I shouldn't complain. Could be worse, I guess."

"Indeed. There's nothing like guarding the outer doors and secret passageways and freezing the whole time." Tash descended the staircase, offering a smile as Gorgan joined him. Being followed as soon as he left the bedroom was a constant practice as of late, due to Ress and Adren's tenancy. While he had not laid into Mayr about the increased security, he wished the shadows would scamper off. The only one he trusted to remain that close for that long was Mayr, perhaps even Aeley.

Aeley had her own reasons for guards accompanying her, however. Those reasons may have led to her most recent proposal to Tash: the position of advisor.

Primary advisor, at that. On the last step, Tash turned right and rounded the base of the staircase, headed for the kitchen. Gorgan trailed behind him by three paces.

Tash ignored Gorgan, his brow furrowed while he considered Aeley's offer. She had asked him two days ago. At first he was pleased, but once the surprise wore off, uncertainty remained. He had no right to accept, even if it fell within his capabilities as an Uldana priest.

Still, he had promised to consider it, the least he could do to return her compassion for the circumstances in which he, Ress, and Adren had placed themselves. Aeley had stressed his experience in both the Shar-denn and the Temple made his opinions invaluable.

Tash wondered if she was prepared for the problems inherent in putting that much faith in him. Although he would never betray her, she needed someone savvy in politics and free of questionable affiliations. He was neither.

That's another problem for another day. Have to wake up first. At the end of the corridor, Tash pushed open one of the two vine-engraved wooden doors that led into the kitchen and hurried inside.

He stopped cold.

Arieve stood at one of the three grey stone tables in the centre of the room, tying on a long, light-coloured apron over her dusky green tunic and black pants. The two hearths to her right blazed with fire. The stone ovens in the wall behind her had also been lit.

Gorgan bumped into the doorframe behind Tash and cursed. Tash winced as Arieve startled with their arrival, a smile quick to brighten her features.

"Arieve," Tash said, clearing his throat. "You're here early." He shoved Gorgan into the hall gently, his other hand lifted to ask for privacy. To his relief, Gorgan nodded and disappeared further down the corridor.

"Cook's not feeling well." Arieve rolled up her sleeves. "She asked me to run the kitchen—something about not gobbing up the meals." She coiled her hair then secured it with narrow sticks and small clips. "I'll take requests, though. Any cravings?" Head tilted, she swept hair across her forehead. "Or is there another reason you look like someone's rammed a rod straight up your insides?"

"Just steeped herbs," Tash said, hoarser than expected. Closing the door, he dared to move closer. He *could not* be mortified to stand in the same room as her.

"I've got the perfect thing. I'm having a cup myself." Arieve turned to one of the hearths and snatched a towel from the bar beside it. She fussed with the kettle on the rack above the flames. "Mm, more like a vat. I can't seem to wake up today, no matter how much snow I got down my cloak. All I want is to crawl into bed with someone warm and squishy."

Arieve stilled, her hands paused in midair. "That's not a means to pressure you, I swear." She peered over her shoulder. "I meant what I said. I'll wait until you have an answer."

"I understand. I wasn't going to assume it was." Tash settled at the edge of the table where she had previously stood. The tables were large, placed side by side with several foot lengths between them. During the day, they would be covered with food and all manner of dishes. At the moment, the tables were orderly and clean. Thick wooden cutting boards and blocks of knives sat in wait, joined by the wooden bowls and linens stacked along the edges.

The rest of the kitchen was twice the size of the dining room. Counters and cupboards spanned the length and height of the walls. No space was left unused, every shelf and countertop utilized to their greatest capacity. Burlap bags of flour and salt sat in one corner; barrels of ale and mead stood in another. Bundles of herbs hung from twine strung around the room. Pots and pans were everywhere, placed wherever they fit, he supposed. In the back corner of the wall to his right were two doors: one to the room where dinnerware was kept, and one to the pantry where they kept preserves and dried goods, as well as an entrance to the cellar.

In the wall to his left, attached to a cupboard,

was the hidden door that appeared to lead to the dining room. In truth, it was a passageway to the lower levels and a way out of the estate. One of the many, he had discovered.

Tash focused on the crackle of flames while Arieve moved through the kitchen. As she returned to the table, two glazed clay mugs in hand, he struggled to clear his throat. He accepted the cup she offered, the potent scent of painfully sweet winter herbs and fragrant autumn spices rising with the steam.

"You're not coming down with something, are you?" Arieve rested her elbows on the table, both hands wrapped around her mug. "It's something else, isn't it? Someone, perhaps?"

"With such perception, I've no doubt you'd make a good mother." Tash flushed. Those were not the words he had meant to say, and not like that. "That's not to say I didn't think you would. Or will. Or that we don't think you can't—"

Arieve was silent, her fingertips circling the lip of her mug. "We're grown-ups. We can be honest," she said softly. "And honestly, I'm ready. I've been wasting time on someone who's never ready for the serious stuff. I'm always too far ahead, stuck on wanting what she doesn't. I want to be able to hug my own whiny, snot-faced half-pint and mother them till I die. If I have nothing else, that would do me."

Misery splashed across her face, her eyes downcast. He had never seen her so desolate.

"We all go at our own pace." Tash raised her chin and turned her face towards him. "It doesn't mean she'll never want it. Or maybe she does and she can't say it. There's still hope." He tucked a stray white curl behind her ear, letting his fingertips brush her cheek—a test for them both. Difficult as it was to touch her, it was just as easy. "Sometimes that hope needs a nudge from another."

"Like what?"

Tash breathed in. *Someone has to say something. May as well be me.* "Like someone who wants you to have the life you want. Two someones who can help you get there." He drew the back of his fingers along her jaw, delighted that she leaned into his touch.

She clutched his hand, keeping it on her cheek. Her green-brown gaze searched his. "Does that mean what I think it does?"

"If you want it to, yes."

"Both of you?"

"Yes."

Arieve curled her fingers into his palm. "I promise you won't regret it," she said. "We'll do this right. Just keep talking to me. Tell me how I can make it good for you. Anything. Everything."

"You're sweet." Tash caressed her hand, reluctant to pull away. She needed the contact, evident from the relief in her eyes. How starved was her spirit that she took so much from such a simple gesture? If she could trust him enough, perhaps she would tell him what errant paths had left her that desperate. Or Mayr would.

Past aside, she had his attention. He had not lied when he told Mayr he considered Arieve attractive: she was someone he would have lain with before he met Mayr. The more difficult fact was that Arieve reminded him of Inesta in the early days of their relationship, an awkward truth he would keep to himself.

Tash kissed her fingers. "I'll let you get back to work. We'll talk later?"

"Yeah." Arieve blinked, staring at his mouth as he withdrew.

"Thank you for the drink." Mug in hand, Tash forced his feet to carry him from the kitchen. He should have waited for Mayr before saying something. *But her emotions were on display, waiting to be beaten down. I couldn't let her submit to that, especially since I know how it feels.*

He sighed and sipped his drink, falling into step with Gorgan on their return to the stairs. There was more to do, more to say if he could focus long enough.

They ascended the stairs in silence. Lost in thought, Tash turned into the corridor towards the bedrooms, while Gorgan slipped into the corner that was his post. When Tash entered the room he shared with Mayr, the bed was empty, the sheets straight and flat. Candlelight filled the room from his left.

"I was wondering where you'd gotten to,"

Mayr said from the table. "*Please* tell me you brought that for me, whatever it is." Dressed only in pants, he leaned over the washbowl. His face was already wet, his hair still unbound, and both of his hands were cupped in the water.

Tash joined Mayr. "We can share this for now." He set the mug on the end of the table, away from the bowl and the candle next to it. "I'm reasonably certain Arieve's keeping large amounts of it today."

"Arieve?" Mayr splashed more water on his face then grabbed the towel beside the bowl. "What's she doing here?" He grumbled into the towel before drawing it down his jaws and neck. "She's due in at noon like usual."

Tash bit his tongue as rogue droplets rolled down Mayr's naked chest. He could take care of them, no towel required. If only he had the time. "She's in charge of the kitchen today. It seems our beloved Cook is ill."

"That'd do it."

Nodding, Tash turned towards the window. A new writing desk sat beneath the sill—another gift from Mayr—along with the necessary things to write the letter forming in his thoughts. There were hundreds of words, a dozen messages to covey. Not all of them would sound best coming from his lips. Some were meant to be written, captured in corporeal form with ink and parchment, words that were meant to be read and reread, particularly when life was unkind and emotions even more cruel.

"Hey, what's wrong?"

"I spoke to her," Tash answered quietly. "I shouldn't have done it, not without you, but her face… her face said everything. I couldn't let her spend another day like that, so I told her we were in agreement. I'm sorry I didn't wait. I just couldn't…"

In few steps, Mayr was by Tash's side. Lips pressed to Tash's cheek, he pulled Tash into his arms. "If you're worried I'll be angry, don't be. Really wish I could've been there, but I'm not angry," he murmured, nuzzling Tash's ear. "How'd she take it?"

Tash leaned into Mayr's touch. "Pleased. Relieved."

"So we're getting ourselves a girlfriend?"

"Looks like it."

Faster than Tash could blink, Mayr's mouth was on his, softer than Mayr's grip on Tash's hips. "One day at a time," Mayr whispered. "Slow as we need."

"I know." Tash strode across the room to the writing desk. With parchment, ink, and white quill in hand, he returned to Mayr and placed everything on the table before sitting.

"What are you doing?"

Staring at the emptiness of the beige parchment, Tash took a nervous breath. "We need to court her properly. We should at least try to be gentlemen. She needs to hear she's important, that she's someone special. I thought I'd start with a letter, asking her to consider spending time with us and offer her a place in our shared affections." He looked up to Mayr. "It feels right, doesn't it?"

Mayr slid his hands down Tash's chest as he leaned forward and kissed Tash's cheek. "Yeah, it does. It feels more than right." He clasped Tash's hands and drew them across Tash's chest, pinning Tash's folded arms with his own in a tight embrace. "So let's write that letter," he whispered. "Lay our hearts down, dearest love, and let everything else fall into place."

Chapter Eight

Their letter was answered with one from Arieve, filled with so much enthusiasm that Tash could sense her giggles between the words.

Five evenings later, that same glee radiated from her as she sat with Mayr and Tash in the dining room of the estate. Even so, the more they spoke to Arieve, the more nervous she appeared. A deep blush spread beneath the pink powder colouring her cheeks, despite the glow in her eyes that never dimmed.

Tash sipped his mead while Mayr and Arieve discussed the meal. Mayr and he had planned the night to a fault. After playful argument and merciless teasing, Mayr had persuaded Aeley, Lira, and the rest of the household to lend them private use of the estate for the evening. Most of them had found alternate arrangements: Aeley and Lira were at the tavern with Pellon and a band of guards; Ress and Adren were at the temple with their own guards; and staff had gone wherever they pleased. Guards remained at their usual posts, though they operated under special orders.

Mayr had also taken it upon himself to cook.

Tash had erupted in fits of laughter at the sight of Mayr dusted in flour and herbs. Dressed in an adorable white apron, his black hair braided and pinned up in a neat coil, Mayr had been a delightful vision waiting to be undone. When Tash had teased Mayr about his ability to cook, Mayr flicked broth at him, almost staining Tash's robes. That was the last time he dared to enter the kitchen.

The effort had not gone to waste. The food was presented with beautiful care, every garnish and piece deliberately placed. It was a feast of aesthetic to fuel what was to come.

If we ever get there, Tash mused with a frown, studying the room to distract himself. Pristine white linens and candlesticks adorned the long table. Mayr sat at the end, facing the doorway, with Arieve to his right and Tash to his left. Shadows filled the rest of the dark red room, flickering around the glass and gold dinnerware. An elaborate glass vase stood in the centre of the table with a bouquet assembled that morning. Leaves and petals spilled onto the tablecloth, a mix of fresh branches of red-black leaves from the winter garden and delicate pink silk flowers with cream-coloured pearls and white jewels. Their stems were fashioned from dried, golden stalks wrapped in bronze coil, crafted by Orlee who usually sold them at the village market.

Pretty as everything was, the growing hesitation worried Tash. Despite their feelings,

Mayr and Arieve never touched. They spoke like casual friends, desire confined to subtle looks and small movements that never connected. The most contact had been Mayr's fingers interlaced with Tash's for the majority of the meal.

Is he backing out or building up to it?

When Arieve caught his glance again, Tash smiled. With another blush, she lowered her gaze and pushed food around her plate. *It's the early days of courtship all over again: shy and fearful but curious.* Lips pursed, Tash picked at his own dinner. *Then again, I'm not doing any better. We're all frightened to make the first move, too afraid to shatter this before we piece it together.*

Tash squeezed Mayr's hand and raised his goblet. "I'd like to thank you both for this evening. Mayr, for sharing your talents and making me look like a terrible cook, and you, Arieve, for putting up with us."

Mayr raised his goblet to Arieve. "I completely agree. Thanks for trusting I wouldn't ruin it all." He cleared his throat. "And for saying yes. You didn't have to, but you did. That's worth everything," he finished softly.

"I know." Arieve's hand snaked towards Mayr's arm. After a moment, she clutched his sleeve. "I really do."

The next instant, she released him and fingered the loose curls of her hair before toying with the colourful beads in her slim braids. She fidgeted, appearing uncomfortable in her white gown and black leather bodice. The floor-length gown draped gracefully over her shoulders and fell to her wrists in tiers of flared sleeves, alternating between lace and silk. Her bodice hugged her curvy form with a rough touch, laced up both sides with trailing black laces. Somewhere between the delicate fabric that should be peeled away slowly and leather that could be ripped off in frenzy were Arieve's expectations.

Mayr had also dressed for the occasion. In tight black clothes that emphasized all the parts Tash loved, Mayr was as beautiful as the first time they met. His hair was loose, save the strands tied back from his face with red ribbon. He looked willing but uncertain, dedicated but searching for where he mattered.

If Arieve did not want him, Tash would take him, adoring Mayr until exhaustion consumed them.

But tonight's not about him and me. It's supposed to be us, *even with our trepidation. Crafting our future requires words, some which might choke us faster than humility.*

Tash considered his options. Had Arieve been like his former lovers, he would have offered light humour and coaxed her into telling him more about herself to ease her worry.

The days for that had passed. Prior to his relationship with Mayr, Tash had conversed with Arieve in Orae's tavern several times. She was pleasant, thoughtful, and her kind energy swept over his bruised soul like a spring breeze. Since then, Mayr had told him about Arieve, including how Mayr had gotten Arieve the job in the Dahe estate for her seventeenth birthday.

Charmed by her graces, Tash visited the kitchen at the estate or Orae's tavern at least every other day to greet Arieve. While he used the time to thank and bless the staff and their labours, he also took in moments of her. Arieve was easy on his weary mind. Neither imposing nor demanding, she was confident and made him smile, even if no one knew it.

The only thing he had overlooked was the depth of Mayr's emotions for her. In every glance between them, Tash searched for those feelings. In every near-touch, he waited for the spark of their want. The longer they subdued it, the more frustration demanded he do something.

"Arieve." Tash cleared a path among the bowls between them. He reached for Arieve but stopped, resting his hand on the table. She returned his steady gaze, her red-painted lips parted slightly. "You needn't shy away from us. We're here because we want to be. This is a night of safeness: safe words, gestures, and intent. Except it's not safety *from* each other: it's *for* each other." He glimpsed at Mayr. "We must be willing to trust and let ourselves fall within that trust. If we seek to create a life, we must first embrace the hope in that gift."

"Meaning...?" Arieve asked.

"Tell us what you're hoping for tonight." Tash gestured to Mayr. "I know what we're willing to do, but I'd like to hear your thoughts."

Arieve's lips worked soundlessly. "I don't... I just, I mean, I don't..."

"Know?" Mayr finished, his smile crooked.

"No, I know, but..." Arieve eyed Tash's hand, his palm turned up to encourage her touch. "I don't know how to ask or even if I should. This isn't... I'm not used to this. I don't know what's appropriate, or if I'm completely wrong for wanting things." She clutched her head in both hands, staring into her lap as she mumbled. "My thoughts are so lewd I can't even *begin* to describe how rotten I feel. I wanted to be a proper lady about this, but I don't know what that looks like. I thought I did, but it's unraveling."

Tash swore a string in his heart broke for her. Another threatened to snap, teetering on the edge of raw and finely tuned. He recognized her torment, the tip-toeing around the line between what felt right and what others expected.

"Forget propriety." Mayr clasped Arieve's hand. "Whatever you feel, go with it. I promise we'll still be here."

Arieve lifted her head and gazed at their hands. She stroked his knuckles before pulling away. Pain flashed across her features as if someone had strummed a sour note.

"You're allowed to touch him," Tash said

softly. Could that be the issue both she and Mayr struggled with? Was it simply a matter of consent?

When silence answered him, he had all he needed.

Tash pushed up from the table and grasped Mayr's hands. "Come with me." Startled, Mayr followed him to the open area between the table and the doorway. He stopped in the centre of the space and squeezed Mayr's shoulders. "Stay there."

On his return to the table, Tash held his hands out to Arieve. "You, too."

She hesitated before slipping her hands into his, but still she followed as he led her to Mayr's side.

"Wait here," Tash instructed gently, brushing his fingers down her neck with the lightest touch. From the table, he retrieved the salt dish and a pitcher of water. Once he rejoined Mayr and Arieve, he placed the pitcher on the floor. *Emeraliss, please let this work.*

Salt dish in hand, Tash walked around Mayr, Arieve, and the place he would stand. "Goddesses of all that we hold sacred, hear my call," he murmured, casting salt down in a circle. "Bless us with the grace to love and learn. Give us the strength to rise from our past and courage to forge the future. Lend us the wisdom to overcome fear and find reason beyond what we see or touch. Bless this, our sacred space, a place to dream and hope and speak without words."

With a last pinch of salt, he closed the circle and laid the dish on the floor outside the barrier. He took the pitcher and went around again, flicking water above the salt. "Emeraliss, most radiant of hearts," he whispered, "let us see each other in all ways. Help us weave the threads of desire and joy, snagging not on our worries but building from what lifts us high. Give our deepest selves the wings to soar and valour to make the journey."

Closing the second circle, Tash set the pitcher down directly across from the salt. "Here we begin with balance, grounded by the earth, in flux as the water." Tash smoothed his robes before draping his veil around his shoulders. "Let our words flow and give comfort in this space—*our* space. No other may enter. What happens here leaves with us, and may it continue to grow as a flower that has found both root and sun." He took his place in front of Mayr and Arieve then clasped one hand of both. "I'll try to limit how much priest I talk," he said, glimpsing Mayr's confused expression, "but this is how *I* can say what I need you to know. I'm fine with this, what we're doing, and you can be, too."

The instant Arieve looked ready to protest, Tash squeezed her fingers. "You have my blessing to touch and taste, to be together and find what you could've had," he assured her. "I'm thankful to be involved, not cursing what exists. You're both dancing around it with so much care it's excruciating." Tash lifted Mayr's hand to his lips for a quick kiss. "It's sweet but painful."

"Yeah, but you've got a sweet tooth," Mayr argued.

"So stop stalling and I'll put it to good use." Tash lowered their hands. "I've cast this circle so we may state our intentions, shed ourselves of doubt, and take strength from each other. We will give ourselves permission to release our inhibitions. I'll start."

A deep breath settled Tash's nerves while he grasped Mayr's hands and caressed the underside of Mayr's wrists, aware of Arieve as she wrung her fingers. "Mayr, I love you, stubbornly and without apology. You will always have me, come life, death, and every moment between. I cherish the love you give in return. This is our truth, our peace of mind." Tash eased Mayr forward, his fingers creeping up Mayr's arms in circles. "What we do tonight and afterward is a reflection of our feelings. It isn't running away but running towards something we can share. It isn't a suggestion that we don't love each other but a sign that we love so deeply we'll do anything to be happy together."

Tash pulled Mayr close. "It's all right to care for her," Tash whispered. "Showing her love doesn't mean I feel your love any less. It doesn't mean you have less to give me—it means you have more to give *her*. You have so much to offer.

Let me help you do that."

He sealed his declaration with a kiss, drawn-out and tender, until Mayr coaxed him deeper. By the time they parted, both were at the mercy of laboured breaths and a crushing hold.

Despite the fierce desire in Mayr's eyes, Tash guided him back and took Arieve's hands. He stroked her fingers, his touch sweeping across her trembling palms and wrists. "Arieve, I welcome you into the home our hearts have built. We have called you friend, and now we shall call you lover. You shall be a part of us howsoever it pleases you." Tash planted a kiss in each of her palms. "I promise to respect you and honour what you offer. Your place in our life shall be sacred, tended and protected. When you speak, I will listen. Whatever your needs, I will seek to make you happy. I swear you will be cared for."

The kiss he brushed across Arieve's lips was met with surprise, her breath catching as she startled just slightly. As he clutched her hands to his chest, she relaxed into him, her lips trading gentle push for coaxing pull. Their kiss was chaste but warm. She withdrew first, slow to release his lips and hands.

A subtle glint in her eyes suggested something new was finding its way between them. She smiled and dipped her head. Hopeful, Tash looked to Mayr. "Your turn."

Mayr swallowed uneasily and rocked on his heels, hands clasped behind his back. The yearning on his face diminished, hidden behind a mask of alarm. "Yeah, I can't even begin to match that."

"You don't have to," Tash argued. "This is about honesty, not judgment."

"Honesty," Mayr muttered. A long moment passed before he took Tash's hands. "I honestly don't know what to say except this: come the end of the world, I will be here for you." His gaze steadied on Tash's. "I don't want to be anywhere else. I've been there and I hate it, but you've made love worth living again. You make it feel so good it hurts to breathe." He gestured to the three of them. "Whatever comes of this, I'll do right by you. Goddesses strike me dead if I don't. I'll deserve it."

Mayr claimed Tash's lips with unbridled vigour. Tash stumbled, taken by the force of it, until Mayr jerked him forward, answering Tash's moan of approval with his own. Cupping Mayr's smooth cheek, Tash drove the kiss further, wanting Mayr's tongue on more than just his mouth.

"Pace yourself." Mayr laughed lightly against Tash's lips. "This is only the beginning."

"And I've got a plan for where it'll end." Tash nipped Mayr's jaw. "Stop making Arieve wait."

"As if I haven't had help." Mayr turned to Arieve, his smile apologetic. He fumbled as he clenched her hands to his chest. "I'll do right by you, too, Arieve. I've waited so long for this.

Whenever someone digs their way this deep into your heart, it's impossible to completely walk away. A part always lingers. A wish always hangs around." Mayr stroked her cheek. "For years I've wanted to be with you just like this. You've had my love since we were kids, but I couldn't get things right. I couldn't tie you to me when I felt so low. I wanted you to have more—everything you deserve. Now, even when I can give you what you want, I worry I'll mess it up. I promise I'll try not to. I'll do what I should've done before." He glanced at Tash. "No more holding back."

A silent question hung in the air but vanished the moment Mayr leaned down to kiss Arieve. Both hesitated, their arms appearing to be frozen in place.

Once they embraced, their misgivings seemed to melt away. Arieve clutched Mayr's shirt in one fist as she kissed him full on the lips, all of the tension bleeding away, sinking into their deepening touch. Mayr's mouth chased after Arieve's, his eyes opening to peer at Tash as though ensuring he was still there.

Tash smirked and drew his fingertips across his lips. Inside, part of him sighed, satisfied with their progress. Another part of him wanted to touch the places where Mayr and Arieve's bodies met, to take in their heat and meld it into his own, becoming part of them.

It was the most intimate parts of him that

tested his patience, demanding wet warmth and the flood of pleasure. He craved the first touches. He cherished the journey from the new and unknown to the clarity of sureness. Above all else, Tash treasured the precious moments when Mayr reverted to how he was their first night together: vulnerable with fragile trust and the need to be steadied on a new path, everything that had prompted Tash to protect Mayr.

I'll always take care of you. Even if this falls apart, I'll still be here, for both of you.

Arieve parted from Mayr, swaying until he rubbed her shoulders. "I guess that leaves me," she said.

"Take your time," Tash said.

"Huh, time. Funny, that." Arieve's gaze darted back and forth over the floor at her feet. "I've had so much time, and such rough bouts of it." She peered at Mayr. "But this… this is time coming back around. We'll never know what could've been, but now we can figure out new things. Maybe this is how it was supposed to be." Her hands were steady as they wrapped around Mayr's. "You weren't the only one avoiding us. I denied my feelings, keeping you as a friend when I wanted something different. I stole time—I waited for when your heart was broken and took what I could, wishing you'd love me the way I do you. I used to dream of you leaving your lovers so I could finally tell you what I felt, but when the time came, I didn't do anything. I hid behind my own lovers." Arieve kissed his fists. "No more hiding. I'm in this. I've called you family, but I want you to really *be* family."

There was no mistaking the heated way Arieve kissed Mayr, or how she grappled to pull him closer than they could physically be.

Passion and confidence burned in her gaze as she turned to Tash. "Thank you for giving us this," she said, gripping his hands. "I've envied you for having him. I've admired your grace and compassion. Now you're sharing them with me. I will care for you as you do me." Arieve held Tash's hand to her cheek. "I will take your kindness and give it back four-fold. Any child would be incredibly blessed to have you as their father."

Tash swallowed and choked. She had no idea how untrue that was.

He flushed as she kissed him, her desire strong and in control. Instead of refuting her words, he let her explore him with the gentle thrust of her tongue. Arieve's hands traveled down his chest with the warmth he lusted for, and her corset shifted beneath his hands, focusing his attention on the body beneath. Since first meeting Mayr, he had not touched a woman so intimately. Even then, he remembered how good it felt—and how gorgeous Mayr looked with a naked woman in his arms, both of them coming hard and quick.

Pushing Arieve back, Tash cleared his throat.

"I believe we've achieved what we needed." He took her hand, then Mayr's, and kissed their fingers. "We have declared our intentions and sealed them with affection. Blessed be love, the greatest of gifts."

"Blessed be," Mayr and Arieve intoned.

Tash dragged his boot through the salt, breaking the circle. "The sacred space is now once more part of the whole." He led Mayr and Arieve over the barrier. "We should get back to dinner. I noticed someone made an effort at dessert."

"Ha. *Someone*." Mayr snorted and wrapped his arm around Arieve's waist. "I suppose he expects that same someone to suck his cock later. Wonder if he'll remember their name then?"

Arieve laughed, sending ripples of relief through Tash. "To be fair, there are two someones now. Unless he gets us mixed up?"

"I very much doubt that." Tash waited for Arieve to sit before he leaned down to murmur in her ear. "But you'll have to suck my cock first."

Her mouth dropped open. She faced him, catching his lips on hers. "Why, your priestliness, that's the crudest thing I've ever heard you say." Arieve nipped his bottom lip. "I like it."

"He's got plenty more." Mayr reclaimed his seat and tipped back, grinning as he locked his hands behind his head. "He saves it for the bedroom, where it does all the best damage." He winked at Tash. "The real fun will be seeing who screams first."

"And the loudest," Arieve added. "I'll bet it's you, Mayr. I'll even put a wager on it—unless you don't enjoy the pressure of a little friendly competition?"

Mayr laughed. "I love *friendly competition*. I love the pressure even more."

"So we'll put it to the test? You, me, half a day's wages?" Arieve looked at Tash. "Would you like to get in on this?"

"Priests are discouraged from gambling," Tash answered, coiling strands of her hair around his fingers. "Besides, it would be unfair. I've learned Mayr's body but not yours. Perhaps you'll teach it to me tonight?"

The glow in Arieve's silent reply was every answer in one perfect glance.

However stilted the dinner began, its end came with suggestive murmurs and lascivious gazes. Desire played a careful game of chase-and-catch, where even the simple act of clearing the table was spirited with expectation. A comfortable quiet fell as Mayr took the last of the dishes to the kitchen, leaving Tash with Arieve.

In an instant, she was in Tash's lap, arms around his neck. Her mouth distracted his, their unspoken words tangled together as she drew more than one moan from him, grinding hard on his aching cock. For a long moment, he almost believed she wanted him as much as she did Mayr.

That was a fool's wish, lost among the shadows laughing in his mind. Her heart was in Mayr's hands, with Tash to bear witness. They were not equals in her affection.

Still, however he failed in comparison, he would make up for it in touch and whisper. He had once admitted to Mayr that love was the quickest way to kill him and sex was his strength. Arieve was welcome to all that Tash knew of pleasure, even if she never wanted him for anything else.

"Such good thinking, what you did," Arieve muttered between kisses. Her hands crept beneath his veil and around his neck. "I was sure I was getting it all wrong." As his fingers slid beneath her bodice and rested on the small of her back, she groaned. "Thanks for saving me. Us."

"Whatever I can do to make it easier," Tash said softly. "I'll always—"

A knock on the door startled them both, and they jolted apart. Arieve was quick to catch herself before she slipped off his knees.

Metal clinked as the person walked away.

"Merely a guard." Tash offered her a mischievous smile. "Apparently the second part of our evening is ready."

"Dare I ask?"

"You could, but seeing it will be better."

Worrying her lip, Arieve brushed her

fingertips across his mouth. "I don't how to do this, not with the three of us," she whispered. "I have ideas, but that's all. It's difficult enough to share a bed with someone new, but being with two friends is worse. There's too much to lose, too many things I shouldn't do. For all I know, I'll make it horrible. So if I make a fool of myself, forgive me?"

With a restrained sigh, Tash pressed his forehead to hers. Mayr and Arieve were more similar than they realized. "Mayr and I are here for you, however you need. Don't let fear deter you or take away your happiness before you get there." Tash caressed her cheek with the back of his hand. "You are more than enough. The rest will follow if you relax and let yourself experience it. I promise you're not alone: I've held Mayr through his struggles in confidence and my own. If you place your fears in our hands, we'll care for them like they're ours." He cupped her jaws. "There isn't a right or wrong way. We'll find what works for us."

Arieve sank into his touch, rubbing her cheek into his palm. "No wonder he chose you. You know how to suck the pain right out of it."

The twisted, gutting burn in his heart disagreed, reminding him of a hundred bad decisions he had made. Decisions that had caused a dozen types of pain he could never take back.

In words meant to praise him, she dealt him an agonizing blow. He prayed she would never fall victim to his selfish choices and careless mistakes.

Just as he pieced together a reply, the door opened and Mayr slipped into the room. "Here I thought you'd be naked." His roguish grin eased a portion of Tash's miseries. "Not that I'm complaining. I'd like to be the one taking everything off." He held out his hand. "Shall we?"

Thankful for the rescue, Tash helped Arieve up as he stood. She curled her arm around his and accepted Mayr's hand. They led her from the room, their steps echoing in the empty hallway. Every other torch had been lit, casting long shadows into the corridor, though the light brightened as they neared the main staircase. Before dinner, a single torch had lit the foyer, with both the stairs and the floor cleared.

Now, ice-blue petals littered the floor and steps, scattered among vibrant mauve petals on a path up the staircase. Thick white candles sat on either end of every fourth step, their light replacing that of the torch. All else was dark and silent, a flickering picture of serenity.

Arieve faltered at the base of the stairs, her eyes wide. "You're pulling everything out, aren't you?"

"Give or take a few tricks," Mayr murmured, nuzzling her ear.

"You remember *I* approached *you*, right? You don't have to woo the one who started the wooing." Arieve caught Mayr's lips in a brief kiss.

"This is sweet, really, and beautiful. No one's ever done this for me. Thank you."

Taking their hands in hers, she followed Mayr and Tash up the stairs. The corridor at the top was unlit, though a shadow appeared to rush across the opposite end.

Once inside their bedroom, Arieve paused and muttered a curse. Warm light greeted them, emanating from the dozens of white candles placed around the room. The heady fragrances of honey and spice scented the air, their entwined essences a silent call to temptation. The bed looked perfect, smooth with layers of black sheets and pillows under rich mauve blankets. Glass vials containing various oils sat on both bedside tables, their contents golden in the candlelight. Ice-blue petals lay around the bed and chest of linens at the end.

"If we're to offer you commitment," Tash said, closing the door, "we thought we'd start with the clearest of intentions."

"Plus I'm a perfectionist," Mayr added. Stopped between the bed and the door, he drew Arieve into his arms. "But you already know that."

"Since you were fifteen. You're worse than our mothers combined." Arieve nipped Mayr's chin playfully, one hand curled around his neck. "Maybe we'll balance each other out," she said, bringing his lips to hers.

The calm burst into a scream for more.

Through every small movement of Arieve's body, Tash all but felt her surrender: the diminishing tension while she held Mayr and teased him with slow strokes, her relaxed slump into Mayr's embrace as she tilted her head to better taste him. She curved into Mayr as if they melted in the fire of memory and want, molding her to him.

Tash knew the feeling well: the need to clutch what was and lose himself in what could be, giving up everything just to have something. Every intimate moment with Mayr reduced him to that terrifying state, his control torn asunder. Moments when he was so vulnerable, one word could shatter him and a single glance could turn his world inside out.

Like the lustful look Mayr cast him right then, threatening to bring Tash to his knees. A confirmation. An assurance. A promise.

For a moment, he forgot how to breathe.

Mayr parted from Arieve with a sly smile. "Where should we start?" He tugged the laces along her side, undoing her corset.

Arieve clasped his hands. "Show me what you enjoy," she said, "with *him*. Show me how you touch. I want to know how you are together, what I'm going to be part of." She kissed Mayr's fingers. "I'll be here when you're ready, but for right now, go love your man."

Her gentle push sent Mayr towards Tash. Joy shone in Mayr's eyes while satisfaction beamed in Arieve's. With a nod, Tash thanked her for the kindness.

That gratitude fell into shambles, destroyed as Mayr's mouth claimed his. The kiss devoured his will, its neediness demanding a depth Tash sorely wanted to give, even if his lips had to fall off to achieve it. Thoughts of Arieve were lost to the deluge of taste and sound and touch. He sank in the blackness behind his closed eyes, falling mindlessly into blessed familiarity. His body responded to Mayr's every move, greedy for more attention, afraid that one day the attention would run out.

Tash fumbled with Mayr's belt and shirt, the buckle and laces slipping in his fingers. When he finally tore them off and threw them at the door, growling in annoyance, Mayr laughed.

"Guess I should've attended dinner naked, hmm?" Mayr carefully placed Tash's veil on the linens chest in a hastily folded bundle, but made fast work of Tash's first two robes, despite the kisses Tash stole from him, each one harder than the last.

"Naked always works for me," Tash said, breathless as he backed towards the door, taking Mayr with him. A tug on the tie at Mayr's waist loosened his pants, the lowered fabric revealing dark curls and the base of his strained shaft. Tash slid his hand inside to rub drops of pre-release over the head of Mayr's cock, his fingertips slipping beneath the fleshy cover until Mayr groaned. "That's when I know you're mine—

when you scream my name loud enough for the world to hear."

Mayr snarled and yanked Tash's last robe over his head. Before the robe touched the floor, Mayr shoved him against the door. A dull pain shot through Tash as the door rattled with the force.

"They'd better hear it," Mayr said, the words a low rumble in his throat, "because I'm making damn sure everyone knows you're mine." He slapped both hands to the door, trapping Tash between his arms. "*No one's* going to mess with us."

Tash's pants were forced down his hips quicker than he could agree with the sentiment, his naked body rammed against the door. As a knee slipped between his legs, fingers gripped his cock, quick to caress the tip. Mayr's lips came down hard on his neck, his teeth scraping and bruising.

One hand around Mayr's throat, Tash pulled him closer, needing to break beneath him. Desperation guided his other hand as he jerked down Mayr's pants, determined to feel every bit of Mayr trembling in his grasp. Skin slid over skin, hot and hard, their cocks grinding together. Tash moaned, muffled only when Mayr kissed him and clutched the back of Tash's thighs, keeping him in place.

"This needs to go," Mayr muttered, kicking at the fabric pooled around his ankles. In swift movements, he wrenched off his boots and pants then tossed them at the wall behind Tash.

Tash's own boots and pants were next as Mayr removed them slowly, murmuring his approval between kisses as his lips trailed down the insides of Tash's scarred thighs. The boots thumped against the wall and fell onto the pile of Mayr's clothes. Between them, the only clothing left was Tash's bracers—and they would remain until Tash could trust Arieve's reaction, assuming he ever could.

Mayr slid up Tash, his hands gliding over Tash's hips and ribs. "I don't think I've worshipped you enough today."

Tash wrapped his arms around Mayr's neck, then spared a glimpse at the bed. "You're my favourite…"

The words died in his throat, and he swore his blood surged straight to his groin.

"Mayr," Tash whispered. "Arieve."

"What about…?" Mayr peered over his shoulder. He stilled in Tash's hold, his shaky breath caught as he stared.

Arieve stood on her knees on the bed, legs parted slightly. Gone were the corset and gown, discarded on the floor beside the chest. In their stead was delicate lace the colour of spiced cream on her darker skin. Her thin bodice hid nothing, following her every curve as though it were painted on. The lace clung to her shoulders and dipped low in the front, held closed over her breasts by a single pink ribbon. The rest of the bodice hung open, its loose folds framing her stomach and hips, and the short lace skirt to her thighs barely covered the darkness beneath.

"Don't let me interrupt you," Arieve said, drawing her hand between her breasts. "It's been a beautiful show."

Mayr's lips moved, but he said nothing. Flushed, he glanced at Tash and back to Arieve.

"I know," Tash agreed. There was no ignoring her, not when a single look left his insides yearning for release.

How am I going to last the night between them? Tash turned Mayr around and urged him towards the bed. For all he knew, he would lose control or find himself spent before they were done. He could not let either scenario come to pass, not until both Arieve and Mayr were sated and their shared emotions anchored.

"I won't bite unless you want me to." Arieve held out her hand. "Your bed, your choice. Tell me what you want and I'll do it."

Mayr clutched her hand to his chest. Silent, he raked his fingers through her hair and tilted her head back. "Just be you," he said, cradling her neck in his hand. "I fell in love with you just the way you are. I can't stand the thought of losing that." He glided his other hand along her jaw. "Whatever you need, however you want it."

Arieve's lips took to Mayr's, and Tash stifled a groan. His grip on Mayr's hip tightened, their soft kiss setting a fire inside him that only burned hotter the longer they touched, consuming every bit of him with bittersweet torture. He pressed harder into Mayr, the needy ache in his cock finding no relief against Mayr's side.

The moment Arieve led Mayr's hand to the warmth between her legs, Mayr shivered and moaned, his muscles flexing in Tash's grasp. Arieve's pleas for more harmonized with the wet sound of Mayr's fingers slipping into her. She rocked on the bed, thrusting deeper into Mayr's hand while she lavished his neck with kisses.

Where she left off, Tash continued. He trailed kisses along Mayr's taut skin, around his neck and over his shoulder, down the tattoos on his shoulder blades. Sweeping Mayr's hair aside, he licked Mayr's shoulder and sucked hard to leave a mark. With one hand flattened over Mayr's stomach and the other around his hip, Tash rode the rhythm set by Mayr and Arieve.

A groan and whispered "Yes," were his rewards, accompanied by Mayr arching back into him.

Arieve's mouth traveled over Mayr in a path of kisses down his chest, followed by bites up his ribs to his nipples. Over Mayr's shoulder, she cast Tash a mischievous glance.

Before Tash could interpret her meaning, Arieve withdrew Mayr's slicked fingers from her and sucked them clean, eliciting more than Mayr's gasp. A deep, dark need roiled in Tash, spiraling through his wants, hungry to play with her while desire bombarded him with an entire list of things they could try. Images clouded his wanton thoughts as she sat on the edge of the bed and urged Mayr closer. Her lips resumed their quest down Mayr's stomach and over Tash's fingers, their tenderness welcoming his skin to hers.

When her tongue slipped under Tash's fingers, drawing them into her mouth, he moaned and pressed his forehead to Mayr's neck. Her low laugh vibrated through him, teeth raking his fingertips. She sucked him back until he touched the rigidness of her throat then pushed him out only to repeat the motions.

The moment she released him, he mourned the loss, and his fingers chilled in the air as another smile brightened her eyes. "May I?" Arieve asked, coaxing Tash's moist fingers down Mayr's strained cock.

Mayr's breath hitched at the contact. He wrapped one arm around Tash's neck and pulled him in for a hard kiss. In a searing burst of tangled emotions, Mayr's request for permission surged through Tash from lips to heart.

"Yes," Tash replied, gripping Mayr's chin. He wanted to see the spark in Mayr's eyes when Arieve took him in.

The slide of Arieve's mouth down Mayr's cock almost undid Mayr completely, his waning control betrayed by the glimmer of ecstasy in his glance. Eyes wide, body tense, Mayr gasped and moaned. He writhed in Tash's hold, his arm tight around Tash's neck. His lips claimed Tash's, desperate and harsh, searching for relief. His other hand twined in Arieve's hair, gently urging her to take him further. She obliged, sucking and licking and teasing, her fingers stroking him in time.

More than once, she looked up at Tash with the flushed head of Mayr's cock presented on her tongue. Tash groaned curses into Mayr's shoulder and kissed his frustration into Mayr's neck. His whole body trembled. He wanted to kneel beside Arieve and bring Mayr to climax as much as he wanted to feel Arieve's mouth on him, exploring his own sensitive crevices.

He chose the better option.

After a parting kiss to Mayr's lips, Tash shuffled towards the end of the bed and crawled up the sheets to kneel behind Arieve. He slid one hand along the inside of her thigh, his thumb grazing her folds on the way down. She shivered and released Mayr, her breath sharp and loud. As Tash drew his hands up her legs, over her hips, and around her back, Arieve swallowed Mayr once more. Lace stroked Tash like a constant whisper, and curled around her, he felt everything: the rise and fall of her shallow breaths, the heat of her flushed body, the circling of her hips while she rutted against the sheets. In his arms, she alternated between relaxed and tense, eagerly accepting his touch.

Not to leave her wanting, he teased her neck and shoulders with kisses, inhaling her sweet fragrance. His fingertips roved over her with purpose, caressing her hardened nipples, then tugging on the ribbon between them. The bodice fell open as the straps slid down her shoulders. She moaned and shrugged the lace off, lips still around Mayr's cock. Laughing quietly, Tash tossed the bodice to the floor, pleased to find Mayr watching.

Tash glided one hand over Arieve's shoulder and stopped, his gaze locked on Mayr's. It was his turn to ask for permission, to seek Mayr's approval as he often did. Betrothed or not, one hasty choice could ruin what they had.

In silent reply, Mayr covered Tash's hand with his own and interlaced their fingers. A smile graced Mayr's lips before he groaned and clutched Arieve's head. He favoured his bottom lip as his hips rocked faster, giving every sign that time was short, especially if Arieve kept up her pace.

To slow them both and keep Mayr's impending release at bay for even a few moments longer, Tash held Arieve tight and kissed a path down her arm. Hands cupped beneath her breasts, he pinched and rubbed her nipples, alternating rough touch with feather-light caress. She squirmed, responding to him with shivers and gasps. Without hesitation, he slid his hand between her legs to tease her mercilessly, capturing her swollen clit and soaking his fingers in the milky rush of her release.

Arieve cried out and pulled off of Mayr, only for the back of her head to slam into Tash's shoulder. She whimpered and spread her legs while he stroked her, his touch sliding over her moist folds. He slipped one finger into her with ease, joined by a second.

"Yes." Arieve nuzzled his cheek, panting and riding his fingers. "Please, yes. Don't stop. Don't…" As her voice trailed, he squeezed her clit. Her whimper became a whine.

"You're ready, both of you," Tash whispered. He tugged on her skirt. "If you want him, now is the time. Give him everything."

With his help, she wiggled out of the garment and kicked the sheets down the bed. Arieve took his hand as she lay back against the pillows. "I'm ready if you are," she murmured, reaching for Mayr.

Mayr was on the bed by the time she finished. "We all are," he answered. Their mouths crashed together as he lowered his body to hers, aligning himself between her legs and pushing. They both groaned while he slid into her and rolled his hips. The scent of sex filled the air, wet sounds echoing the pace of Mayr thrusts. Arieve cried out and yanked Mayr's head back by his hair. Her other hand clung to Tash's arm, her nails digging into his bracer.

From where he kneeled, Tash caressed Arieve,

his fingers creeping across her waist to where her body met Mayr's. Both of them mewled at his touch, but pressed against his hand as he drew back slowly.

Far from finished, he faced Mayr and bent forward. His lips caught Mayr's hip in an upstroke and followed him down. Nipping and kissing, Tash worked his way up Mayr's hipbone, one hand massaging the inside of Arieve's thigh. Along the expanse of Mayr's ribs, he sucked on the thin skin, biting once. Mayr shuddered and leaned away from Arieve, grunting before he curled his arm around Tash's neck and guided him back until they both were upright. Arieve followed the movement, her hips angled to keep Mayr inside. Lost in the heated kiss Mayr tore from him, Tash heard Arieve's murmured encouragement.

He returned that encouragement the instant Mayr's mouth left his: cupping Arieve with one hand, Tash teased Mayr's cock and toyed with Arieve's damp curls. She struggled with words, breathless while his touch flitted over her stretched opening. Once he spread the folds around her swollen clit with his fingers and thumb, she was his, right where he wanted her. Splayed as wide as her body allowed, with Mayr still inside, she was completely vulnerable, choking on the fight to stay in control.

Sucking her clit between his teeth, Tash stole every bit of control she had left.

Arieve screamed, bucking into his mouth and slamming down on Mayr's cock. In a battle for mercy, Tash wrenched surrender with every lick, focused on her rocking and Mayr's thrusts.

Neither of them lasted long. Arieve's cry sounded first, and moments later, Mayr shouted for Tash to stop. The release of both graced Tash's tongue, their musky, salty come seeping from Arieve in a heady rush. As Mayr pulled out, the warmth gushed and pooled. The familiar taste of Mayr mixed with Arieve's scent overpowered Tash's other senses.

A strong hand jerked him back by the jaws.

"Come here," Mayr commanded hoarsely. He took Tash's mouth with a forceful kiss and licked release from Tash's lips. "We're not done until you come." With his thumb, Mayr rubbed pre-release over the flared crown of Tash's cock, his grip rough as he tugged and twisted. Tortuous pleasure shot through Tash, need threatening to crush him. "Don't think I didn't notice what you did. Don't care *how* considerate you are, you're in this, too."

"Let me in you and we'll call it even." Tash grabbed Mayr's shoulders and rolled with him. Straddling Mayr's hips, Tash pinned him to the other side of the bed.

Mayr snatched a vial from the bedside table. "It had damn well be hard but whatever, I don't care." He poured oil into his hand and Tash's, then stopped the vial and fumbled in his attempts to put it back on the table. "Do it," he demanded, slathering oil over Tash's cock.

Tash snorted as he kneeled between Mayr's raised knees. "As if you command me." He rubbed the oil over Mayr's entrance. "I think this is going—" Tash drove two fingers into Mayr "—to your head."

Hips lifting, Mayr threw his head back and gripped the black pillow beneath his neck. "No, this is definitely going to yours."

Tash pushed in another finger. Mayr cursed, his back bowed with the flick of Tash's wrist. After three sharp thrusts, he withdrew his fingers and teased Mayr's opening with his cock, taking pleasure in the exasperated glare it earned.

He slammed into Mayr without warning, killing that glare with pride.

Mayr hollered and pitched the pillow over Tash's head. Beside them, Arieve laughed quietly.

Propped up on locked arms, his hands on either side of Mayr's head, Tash sank deeper. Mayr rose to meet him, his crossed legs climbing up Tash's back, knees drawn close to his chest. The shimmer of love that glazed Mayr's eyes lured Tash in for a soulful kiss. He was lucky to be privy to the roots of Mayr's being, keeper of his secrets, and a witness to the rawness of his spirit. In that moment, he felt as if he held Mayr's heart in his hands, freshly ripped from his chest for Tash to keep safe.

A caress trailed down Tash's back, jolting him

from his thoughts. A kiss brushed the back of his hand, an unspoken reminder that Arieve was not competition or someone to fear. They wanted the same thing.

Tash thrust into Mayr until need teetered on the brink. His insides burned, ready to burst, and his skin felt too tight, rubbing in all the right ways until it was wrong. In the precarious moments before release slammed through him, he withdrew and sat back on his heels. He grabbed Arieve's hands, pulled her into his lap, and slid into her, catching her as she arched back and took him to the hilt. She whimpered and clutched him tight, riding him gently, his cock buried in her wet heat.

His climax came with a blast of darkness and a rumbling cry. Arms wrapped around him, safeguarding him while he surrendered. On his way down, he realized Mayr held him and Arieve both.

"You all right?" Arieve asked.

Tash swallowed, at a loss for words. "Yes. You?"

She shifted, releasing a trail of come down his thighs. "Absolutely." Arieve kissed him softly, her mouth slow to leave his before she leaned back to kiss Mayr. "Now what?"

"Now I rest my ass and everything else you two attacked." Mayr stuck out his tongue as he lay back and interlaced his fingers behind his head. "Only fair."

Arieve laughed. "Since when?" She withdrew from Tash to lie beside Mayr on his right side, close to the edge of the bed.

"Since I *somehow* ended up in the middle," Mayr answered, glaring at Tash.

"Don't expect an apology," Tash said, stretched out along Mayr's left side. "I'm not sorry."

Mayr protested noisily and gestured to their bodies. "See what I mean? Look at this!"

"Oh, stop your whinging." Arieve slapped Mayr's shoulder then kissed it. "Otherwise we might play without you."

"Not fair." Mayr pouted. "What happened to 'your bed, your choice'? I happen to *come* with the bed, thanks."

Arieve buried her face in his shoulder and laughed, the mattress quivering with her. "That's just too easy. *Please* tell me the after-sex jokes get better." She peered hopefully at Tash.

Tash shook his head. "There's plenty more, and they're worse."

"Hey, still lying here!" Mayr gave Tash a light shove. "And you like my bad jokes. You do me harder every time. Get over yourself, you stubborn, lovemaking… whatever you are." His lips met Tash's in a tender kiss, stealing what little breath Tash had regained.

"So since I'm your lover and all…" Arieve traced circles over Mayr's chest. "Please tell me I can expect a repeat of you two together like that."

She kissed his neck and smiled lazily. "This wasn't a special occasion, was it?"

A throaty laugh burst from Mayr. "Trust me, love, you're the most specialest occasion here. You and your mouth and your beautiful—" His hand slipped between her legs, making her whimper while he fingered her. "Expect plenty of repeats," he said as she moaned and squirmed. "It's the norm for us, me taking all he's got. Maybe not so fast, but tonight it's all you. The things you do to me… us…" He pulled his fingers from Arieve and wiped them on his stomach. His other arm curled around her back as he played with wisps of her hair. "We switch things up occasionally, but this is how I like it. Tash prefers top."

Arieve glanced at Tash, shivering as she clung to Mayr. "Yeah?"

Tash shrugged. "I enjoy giving, especially with him. Since we met, I knew he'd look gorgeous splayed, spent, and raw beneath me."

Mayr grunted. "Yeah, and then I waited forever for you to do it. You kept teasing."

"I didn't want our first time to be cheap." Tash slipped his knee between Mayr's legs before tracing the contours of Mayr's stomach with his fingertips. "I love your whimpers and cries," he said, stroking Mayr's cock, delighted by the arousal it stirred. "When you're rocking and gripping, unable to stay in one place, needing me in you. Then when you finally break, you're all unfettered, clenching and scratching and taking everything like you've done it all your life." He drew his fingertips over Mayr's lips. "That's what I wanted, what I wished for. Nothing else matters."

Catching Arieve's warm gaze, Tash cupped her cheek. "Nothing except what we have right now: an opportunity to explore love in all its meanings."

Arieve leaned into his touch and clasped his wrist. "Blessed be love and hearts so entwined?"

"Blessed be," Tash echoed, leaning over Mayr to kiss Arieve, comforted by the sentiment. They need not tear a hole in love to allow her in: she had already found a way to exist around and between them. Whatever their future, hope had woven her through their hearts—a last thread to pull all others together.

Chapter Nine

Blood, so much of it, streaming down the middle of the cobblestone street, slipping through the cracks. Too much for a severed limb but enough for a body, one that used to be whole instead of the hastily slashed flesh and bone that dangled for all to see. Hanging and swinging back and forth, Tash stared through death, barbed rope looped around his neck. With his dulled blue eyes sewn open, he was forever lost in eternal night.

An inhuman scream ripped through Mayr. A violent sound no living thing could make, it burned his throat like liquid fire and shredded skin all the way up, forcing blood to his lips. No amount of begging "Take me in his stead!" had stopped the torment. No assault against Tash's slayers had mattered: weapons never harmed the shadows. They countered Mayr's every tactic as if he were a toddler trying to kick down a giant. His knuckles were torn apart, shattered bones peeking through, as useless as the rest of his broken body.

Nothing was as broken as his heart. They had left that for him, an ugly sac of misery pounding beneath never-ending bruises and battered breastbone. Death stabbed him, stealing what remained of the splintered life that beat inside. Torture so foul he already felt his place in the Realm of the Dead, flirting with it, staking his claim, writing his name in the blood pooled around his weary feet as his last act.

The torture Tash had endured held a special place in cruelty's domain. There was no last act. No last word. Stolen, everything stolen…

The Shar-denn had collected what was theirs… and the only way out was dead.

Another scream raged through Mayr, pitched loud and high, dropping him to his knees—the sound of his soul going up in flames like Tash's body.

Red. There was too much red. Red blood on a red street. Red-ringed moon bleeding through what was left of his bloodied vision. Red-orange fire devouring his love without remorse. The red long coats of the faction bosses, stretching, cracking, moving with the chains they twirled and flicked. Their one last shot at the man they loathed for escaping their grasp. Shar-denn justice and the death of everything he loved.

The death of love itself.

And in the street, a single white feather sank beneath the deluge…

Mayr forced his eyes open faster than he could draw breath.

The sunlit room spun as the dark red ceiling haunted his blurred sight. The scent of fire seared his nostrils. His head burned, sharp pains laying waste to his focus in flashes, and his heart raced too hard to be anything but alive. His stomach churned, the rest of his insides coiled tight. Acid crept up his throat and scorched as he swallowed it down.

A dream. A horrible, gods-awful dream.

The fourth dream in two weeks to have ended in Tash's death. They were not getting easier to tolerate.

They're just getting worse. Mayr dragged his hands over his face and bit back a groan. The last time he was awake, he watched Tash finish prayers and stoke the fire before returning to bed. Mayr had gone back to sleep with Arieve in his arms, one of his hands in Tash's.

He felt as though he'd not slept at all.

Disgusted, he glanced beside him. Tash lay on his back on the other side of the bed, one arm curled above his head and the other around Arieve's back. Arieve slept on her side between them, her head on Tash's shoulder, one hand on his chest. Her dark hair cascaded over the white sheet twisted around her, the messy curls not far from Mayr's shoulder.

The familiar image struck a nasty chord in Mayr's gut. In the four weeks since first sharing their bed with Arieve, he and Tash constantly kept her between them while they slept. They had laughed at the tendency, insisting Arieve would always be protected.

The nightmares made it less of a laughing matter. It was a necessity.

If I can't protect him, how is she any better off? She's involved now. If something happens to him... to us...

Tash stirred and twitched. His fingers grazed Mayr's arm.

Nausea hit hard and fast, forcing the contents of Mayr's stomach where they did not belong. Wrist against his mouth, Mayr dashed from the bed to the bucket in the furthest corner of the room. Gagging on everything that came up, he cursed his weaknesses. The thought of losing Tash in brutal ways would never settle right. If Tash were caught...

Mayr choked on bile, his throat scorched and raw. He needed to hit something.

Shame that dirty rat Allon's stuck in prison—I'd love to rearrange his face. Mayr spat out the foul taste in his mouth and wiped his lips. *Ae's brother or not, I'd love to finally break his filthy neck. I'm riled up enough to make it hurt real good.* With a grimace, he pushed up from the floor. *Except the coward's not here, so I'm stuck with people who don't deserve to go down.* He studied his shaking hands. *Too much rage today. I can't even begin to put Pell at the other end of it.*

Quiet as he could, Mayr hurried to the table to wash his face. Gripping the bowl in both hands, he stared past the water to the silver bottom. His sight slid out of focus. The silence was all wrong. He was in knots, tied from mind to motion. His skin felt too tight, too small to fit.

The price of paranoia: what it can't reap from your consciousness it takes from everything else.

It was a price he could not keep paying.

As if I have a choice. For weeks, he had tried to ignore his worries about the Shar-denn's silence. He had toyed with the distractions and splinters in his attention, focusing on the good things he needed to nurture, not sacrifice.

Except the longer he avoided his doubts, the more his nightmares assaulted him. Reports from the other four tracts suggested the Shar-denn was quiet only in Gailarin. The Tract Stewards claimed the rates of crime and violence still climbed, consistent with their monthly and yearly accounts, and not all of it was due to the activity of the other two known gangs in the republic: the Cigils and the Glim Takers, both minor players when compared to the growing reach of the Shar-denn. Despite the decrease in arrests in Gailarin, several low-level Shar-denn members had been caught elsewhere, proving the gang remained intact.

Whatever the problem, it was limited to Gailarin. A blessing, the High Council had called it.

Sure, because blessings usually feel like a portent in disguise.

The lack of arrests was nothing to overlook, its significance meaningless without understanding why. From the details provided by Adren and Ress, there were enough Shar-denn members to keep a hundred bounty hunters busy for the whole of their lives. Gailarin was the prime tract in Kattal, hosting both the seats of the High Council and the governing assemblies, as well as being the centre of trade and economy. It was logical for the Shar-denn to operate heavily in the region, especially when they needed to keep control over their territories, punching down the likes of the Cigils and the Glim Takers whenever boundaries were crossed. Two hundred Shar-den members could have easily done the damage they had.

Yet the latest raids had turned up abandoned houses, and the hunters had nothing to track those who should have been there. Even Adren and Ress were at a loss for new leads, saying the Shar-denn had gone into hiding—but where and why now? They frequently taunted High Council and law enforcement, deliberate moves in the Shar-denn's game. The crimes themselves were often invisible but not the disorder. Without the chaos, what did they have left?

They were up to something, but Mayr could not prove it. Most of the High Council scoffed at his concern. Only Severn entertained Mayr's worries, combining her distaste for criminals with her own suspicions. While Aeley and the bounty hunters agreed with him, no one offered a better plan of action than protecting Adren and Ress. If the Shar-denn struck back, they would attack Adren first. As the child of a former faction boss, Adren was the most valuable. Ce knew enough to sink at least three factions and dozens of acquaintances—many that had vanished, taking their work with them.

The best Mayr could do was be vigilant and hold onto Tash as though he would die at any moment. *Arieve, too, because if the Shar ever found out about her…*

Losing them was not an option.

He snatched up the towel from beside the washbowl and dried his face, then glanced at the bed. His gaze followed the curves of Tash and Arieve's bodies, yearning to touch. *They're everything worth fighting for.*

Mayr sighed into the towel, his eyes squeezed shut. More than once, he had feared being with Tash would lock him up in the chains of obligation and habit, paired with expectations and demands he could not meet.

Instead, he felt liberated. They did things together he never would have done on his own. *That's how safe I feel with him.* Mayr tossed the towel onto the table. *That's what I want to share with Arieve—how good it can be. She's already been hurt, treated like she's not enough. I want her to know she's more than that, just like he's teaching me I am.*

He crossed the room to the window and swept back one of the curtains, greeted by the frost that framed the blue-green windowpane. Snow blanketed the yard and trees below, sunlight reflecting off its pristine surface. An image of calm he wished he could be.

What peace he had was wrapped up in Tash

and Arieve. In their safety, in their slumber, in the comfort they offered. Through them he saw the rest of himself: his fears, his secret wishes, and everything that hid deep inside. Together, Tash and Arieve were gently unraveling the most vulnerable parts of him.

Arms folded, Mayr smiled at the flecks of snow that floated through the sky. He had been terrified to pursue Arieve, but Tash had discovered the bit of courage Mayr had stuffed away. Even more, Tash encouraged him. There was no pressure, no shame, and no ultimatum. Mayr was free to share his feelings instead of locking them away.

Marrying you is the best choice I have. Mayr studied his ring, flicking his finger to catch the light.

Feet padded across the floor behind him. Arms encircled Mayr, one sliding over his waist. A hand grasped his and entwined their fingers, matching rings on display side by side.

"I'll kiss it better, whatever it is," Tash whispered, kissing Mayr's neck. He drew Mayr's arms across Mayr's chest and squeezed, his naked body flush to Mayr's. "Come back to bed. Let us ease your burdens." His beard scraped Mayr's shoulder lightly, his cheek a welcome pressure on Mayr's skin.

Shivers rushed through Mayr from Tash's heat—he was colder than he realized. Eyes closed, he rested his head on Tash's shoulder and clasped

Tash's arms. A content sigh slipped from Mayr as he leaned into the embrace. Did Tash realize how perfect his timing often was? How accurately he read Mayr and offered precisely what was needed? Or was it by intuition alone?

"We've slept late as is," Mayr murmured. "You're supposed to be at the temple."

"This afternoon, yes." Tash combed his fingers through Mayr's disheveled hair, tender as he worked around the tangles. "But morning isn't done, not until you tell me what's wrong or come back to bed—preferably both."

Tempting as that is…

"Nothing," Mayr lied. "I'm fine."

"So retching is something to do for fun now?"

"No, it means I'm coming down with something." Mayr bit the inside of his cheek. The last thing he needed was to worry Tash more than he already did. After twenty-three years of the Shar-denn, Tash needed better.

"I suppose you're right… if lying can be considered an illness."

Mayr held back a frustrated breath but whimpered as Tash nibbled his earlobe.

"Keep your secrets for now," Tash whispered. "I'll be waiting to hear them, to make them my secrets."

The grind of Tash's hips against his did nothing to stop Mayr's moan. "Not fair."

"Completely fair." Tash gripped Mayr's hand. "Come, lie down. Maybe you'll feel like talking afterwards."

"Is this a bribe?" Mayr followed Tash to the bed. "You might have to up the payment."

Arieve rolled onto her back, arms stretched above her head. "No one's upping anything until you've washed and eaten something that tastes amazing." She yawned and arched into another stretch. "And priests don't bribe. They entreat with all the sneaky grace of the Goddesses."

Tash laughed and slipped into the bed. "What can I say? It's a skill."

"Mm, I'm sure. It's probably your first lesson." Arieve shuffled up the centre of the mattress, dragging blankets around her. "Morning, by the way."

"Sorry we woke you." With playful tugs on the blankets, Mayr slid beneath what remained of them on his side of the bed. "I'll make it up to you, promise."

"Not necessary," Arieve argued. She sat up and punched pillows into place behind her. "I like seeing you together." Settled against the pillows, she drew up her knees and rested her arms across them. "I've been in your bed nearly every night for a while now, but I'm trying to give you time for yourselves. You need to have your own space, your own time to work things out." She cupped Mayr's cheek and caressed his lips with her thumb. "There's a time for us and a time for you. We need to balance both."

Mayr snorted and propped up on one elbow.

"You sound like him," he said, motioning to Tash.

"That's probably why we get on so well." Arieve clutched Tash's hand against her knee before grasping Mayr's fingers. "I don't want to mess up our relationship, but I definitely don't want to ruin what you have. Not that I don't want to share in it—I do. I wish I could have what you have," she whispered. Sadness crept into her gaze and lingered. "The kind of love everyone can see—the kind that rolls off you. Being here is the closest I've been to having that. It feels so good being wrapped up in all this, like I'm holding love in my hands. It's real, untouchable, yet so strong it defies everything."

Mayr stiffened. He knew that tone. The way her glance dragged over his face then plummeted to the bed. The nervous way she toyed with the blankets, scrunching them and smoothing them out.

"But...?" he prompted.

"But..." Arieve sighed and growled her frustration. She kicked away the blankets and climbed onto Mayr, rolling him onto his back. Gripping his hands, she straddled his hips, then pushed and pulled his arms in an attempt to play. "I have to talk to you, and it's... complicated."

"We're well-versed in complicated." Tash moved across the bed and settled against Mayr's side. He coiled the ends of Arieve's hair around his fingers. "If you say whatever it is, we have a better chance of helping."

Arieve eyed him, weary and doleful. Silence crawled with the weight of the truth she seemed to debate. Her hands went lax in Mayr's. "Coye came to see me a few days ago."

Mayr ground his teeth and held Arieve's fingers to his chest. If he and Coye were ever locked in the same room, things would go poorly. When Arieve had first fallen for Coye six years earlier, he had hoped for the best. For two years, Coye doted on her, making her smile and laugh, giving Arieve everything she deserved... until she left abruptly, abandoning Arieve with vague excuses in a hasty note. Coye said she was confused, messed up, and lost—she needed to escape Arieve to find what was missing. Or, as Coye had written without any measure of kindness: *I need to stop wasting my time. I'm not finding me when I'm stuck down with you.*

The night Coye left, and for two nights afterwards, Mayr had stayed with Arieve in her room at Orae's house, holding Arieve while she cried herself to sleep.

Six months later, Coye returned, equipped with apologies. Despite Mayr's concerns, Arieve all but ran into Coye's arms.

She was out of them almost as quickly. Another breakup befell them after six months. Subjected to a new variation of the same excuses, Arieve wept over Coye again. Once more, Mayr offered his sympathy, cursing Coye's foolishness and his own.

Nevertheless, just as Coye could not commit to Arieve, she could not stay away. She returned and sought Arieve's affections at least twice more before scampering off. From what Mayr could tell, Coye had no more interest in finding herself than she did making Arieve happy.

As much as he wished he could have run Coye off permanently, he kept to himself for Arieve's sake. Given how well she knew him, Arieve had made Mayr promise he would leave Coye alone. Against his instincts, he had agreed. Confronting Coye would achieve nothing but Arieve's fury and disappointment. Unlike Coye, he knew exactly what he had in Arieve.

"What did *she* want?" Mayr managed, unclenching his jaws.

"She heard the gossip about us in the village. She wanted to know if it was true." Arieve traced paths along Mayr's stomach. "So I told her."

Mayr groaned and covered his eyes with both hands. He *knew* the look on her face—the same wounded glance she had whenever she tripped back into love. "Now she wants you back."

"She's been groveling," Arieve whispered. "Real good, too—I swear her knees are bleeding from dragging around on them. I'm trying not to listen, but the begging…" Arieve shook her head. "I liked it at first, but now it's just painful. Every morning, afternoon, and night for the last three days, I've gotten letters saying how foolish she's been. How she's not as important as she thought she was—that what we had is better. She insists she'll prove it, no tricks. Says she loves me and wants to take care of me—with a home and everything. "

"Arieve..." Mayr peeked between his fingers. *Because of course this would happen now, just when I thought we'd figured it all out.*

"I know." Tears pooled in Arieve's eyes. "I'm the foolish one, but I can't... I *can't*." She hung her head. "Here I am, ruining things with you. I'm so happy with what we have—I'd die if I lost you—but I can't help wanting to give her a final chance. I know it'll be useless, but I want to know if... just *if*." Her voice cracked. Curling into herself, Arieve sobbed into her hands. "I'm so stuck. I love you—I love *this*—but I love her, too. If I don't try this time, I'll likely lose Coye forever. It'll be my biggest regret." She wept harder. "I just don't want to give this up."

Tash's arms were around her before Mayr blinked.

"I've got you," Tash said, drawing her off Mayr. On his knees, he cradled her head to his chest and whispered soothing words, his sympathetic glance landing on Mayr.

The fact Arieve cried harder while she clutched Tash did not escape Mayr. Nor did Tash's expectant look.

Mayr grit his teeth. He wanted to refuse the suggestion in Tash's eyes, an echo of the idea that danced around in Mayr's thoughts. He loathed

Coye. If Arieve would not stand up for herself, he needed to do it. If Arieve could not manage the word no, Mayr would say it for her. As her lover, it was only fair.

But then I'd be making decisions for you, and that won't ever do. Better than anyone, he knew how it felt to be at the mercy of someone who made the most important decisions without him, acting behind his back and throwing it in his face. Betta, Sarene, other women he had courted—even Tash had done it. *I won't do the same to you. I can't.*

The thought punched his gut like a thousand fists. He wanted her to be herself with him and Tash, but giving up what made her happiest had never been the intention. Arieve's heart was hers to command, so patient and loving she accepted *both* Mayr and Tash.

He knew what she needed to hear. The words chased each other in his thoughts, pushing at his tongue to say them. Despite the urge to shove Coye into a pit of tar just to get her to stay put, he had to let Arieve make her own decision.

Doesn't mean I have to like it, Mayr countered as Arieve sagged into Tash's caresses down her back and arms. *I'll be damned if I give you up that easily, and Tash is just as stubborn. We committed to this. Coye can kiss my bitter ass if she can't take it. We had each other first.*

"Hey now." Mayr pried Arieve's hands from her face. When she resisted, he pulled harder. "No need to close the door on us when we've gone and torn the hinges off. Especially me, because you *know* I can't be trusted with tools."

Arieve croaked out a laugh. Between sniffles, she sucked in shallow breaths. Her hands trembled as they parted from her face, her cheeks flushed and wet. "Don't look." She whimpered and twisted away. "I'm a mess."

"I've seen this side of you a hundred times." Mayr turned her towards him.

"Yeah, but we weren't sleeping together then. This is just embarrassing." Arieve wiped her eyes with the back of her hands. Tears flowed faster the more she tried to stop them.

"Or it's a symptom of trust," Tash argued. He held her closer, his body wrapped around hers as she settled between his raised knees. "If you don't feel comfortable enough to cry in our arms, we aren't taking very good care of you."

Mayr kissed Arieve's knuckles. "Don't worry about losing us. We won't leave you. I've always been here, and Tash… once he promises to stay in your life, he does. There's always a part of him that holds on so you can find your way back."

Tash pressed his cheek to Arieve's, his arms crossed over her chest. "We understand your pain. We know what it's like to love someone despite their failings. We nearly broke ourselves just to find someone who takes us for everything we are, but we found it, and we've fought hard to keep it, even against death itself," he whispered. "*That's* what we have—the love you want so deeply—and it came at the price of doing what hurt the most. We had to suffer to feel this good."

"Not that we need to revisit it right now," Mayr muttered. Some things were best forgotten, especially on a day he had hurled his stomach into a bucket. He lifted Arieve's chin, stealing her gaze. "What he's trying to say is if you want this chance with Coye, take it. We'll live with it. And if—*if*—she messes it all up, we'll be here to put you back together. We're not going anywhere."

It's only fair. We can't deny you your love when you're letting us have ours. Mayr stifled a sigh. He would rather heal her sadness than rip away her joy.

No matter what Coye did, he knew where his heart was.

The next week did nothing to improve Mayr's mood. By the end of it, he wanted—*needed*—to smash open his skull and release the foulness within.

Mayr buried his face in his folded arms and squeezed his eyes shut against the headache throbbing from one temple to the other. Alone in his office in the Guard House, he hunched over his desk in what was usually the most comfortable chair in the building. Every part of him hated the sitting. His muscles pulled, wrapped in knots so tight they could snap if he twisted wrong. His legs shook as if insects crawled under his skin, their tiny limbs ripping up nerves while they scurried in circles.

Standing was worse. Standing meant looking like rubbish and inviting everyone to question his health. Tash already pestered him enough. Had Arieve stayed overnight instead of returning to Orae's, her inquiries would have pummeled him further.

He had no interest in talking about his persistent nightmares and their lingering effects. Since the nightmare where Tash had been hacked apart and dangling from a noose, three more had hit. Every other morning, they tore holes into his bleary sanity. Talking would not stop them. Only overcoming what prompted his fear could put them to rest.

Except the more I search for solutions, the fewer answers I have. Mayr cursed into his bracer and gently bounced his head on his arm. Each day felt worse. The best sleep he could manage was in the short bouts he stole when no one was looking: in his office, Aeley's study, or the occasional secluded corner—anywhere but his own bed. The nights were unpredictable, a negotiation among tossing, turning, and terrified horror.

After three weeks, he was running out of excuses to hide the truth.

Mayr leaned back and covered his eyes with his interlaced fingers, blocking out the early afternoon light. That morning's nightmare had begun as his wedding but burst into a full Shar-denn attack, ending with the estate in ruins, Tash, Ress, and Adren in the clutches of brutal captors, and a call for payment on Arieve with the intention to sell her to the highest bidder. *Severn just stood there the whole time, letting the bastards hack everything up—cake, flowers, and all. Guess I hate her more than I thought.* Mayr snorted. *Who am I kidding? I hate the whole damn Council, letting the Shar get so much power. They can't even round perpetrators up without hunters holding their useless hands. Meanwhile Severn thinks* I'm *a problem? Ha! Guess they don't give councilmen mirrors.*

At least Ress agreed with him: the Shar-denn would not go down quietly. Any end to their organization would be violent, and no one could predict the amount of suffering.

Mayr growled and kicked his desk, then threw his glance around the room. Small but sufficient, the office was on the main level of the Guard House, just off of the main staircase, down the corridor from the communal kitchen and dining hall. Private quarters dominated the three floors above, each floor sectioned into thirty small rooms that could be shared by two guards comfortably, three during emergencies. Of the one hundred and fifty guards currently in employ, only half lived in the Guard House. The others preferred to live with their families in Dahena or the surrounding villages.

On the floor below were a fully stocked cellar,

storage rooms, and an extensive space divided into four sections for training and exercise. The level below that was rarely used but often tended. Reserved for refuge during attack, those rooms had thick metal doors, strong bolts, and hidden caches of weapons.

Unlike the main house, the Guard House was far from lavish. Built before the Dahe family had garnered enough prestige and wealth to afford elegance, the smaller house had evolved as the need for a larger, stable guard arose. To that end, the Guard House was mere paces away from the main building.

Mayr's office was just as modest. He had inherited the room like his predecessors, along with the worn black desk and its tricky drawers, old red chairs and their matching ragged settee, and faded green curtains. The wall-to-wall bookshelves drooped under the weight of volumes accumulated over generations. The red stain on the light brown walls had faded, leaving dents and scrapes and scuffs on display.

Only the chair behind the desk belonged to him—a necessity he insisted on. Gone were the days he was on his feet for most of his waking hours: as Head of the Guard, he spent more time in his office than he wanted. Orders, reports, and correspondence never wrote or read themselves. No matter how much he wished or stared at them, they never disappeared. He relished the chance to spar and move, to find relief in the training he was accustomed to. Pellon was his greatest adversary in the ring, even more than other guards they had grown up with, guards Mayr trusted implicitly to follow his lead in protecting Aeley and those under her care.

Unless I'm being a complete fool—then they put me into place. Mayr attempted a laugh but surrendered to a groan, one hand pressed to his aching eyes. *Definitely not a day for reminiscing.*

Nor was it a day for visitors. Still, the door rattled under several knocks, reminding him he was supposed to be documenting intelligence for his upcoming meeting with the High Council.

"What?" Mayr hollered. "You'd better make it good or I'm kicking your ass."

The door squeaked open. "How about kissing it instead?" Arieve peered into the room. "I'll present it real nice and everything."

Mayr jumped up, but dizziness nearly sent him back down. "Sorry, I didn't realize. Here, let me—" He hurried to grab the door, watching the wooden tray in her hands.

Arieve's delighted laugh reverberated through him and soothed his pains like a cool salve on fiery wounds. "It's fine. I'm serious, though, because your lips in all the right places..." She winked and sashayed to his desk, the snap of her hips hitting every salacious note inside him. "I'll take whatever I can get."

"You should tell Tash," Mayr said hoarsely, his mouth dry. He cleared his throat and closed the door. "He'll lick you from head to toe and make you beg for more."

In few steps, he was with her. Arms wrapped around her waist, he inhaled the sweet perfume scenting her neck and upswept hair. The thick fabric of her dark blue, floor-length dress under her orange-red shawl and white apron did nothing to stop him from remembering the feel of her sweat-slicked skin on his. He wanted her as badly as he wanted to be unconscious. If the universe was kind, it would knock him out soundly while he lay in the combined warmth of Tash and Arieve. Tash, his future and the one who offered him all the limitless understanding to be himself, and Arieve, a beautiful reflection of the past that anchored him to who he had always wanted to be.

"I'll have to try that. I know how much you love watching." Arieve turned to lock her arms around his neck before she trailed kisses along his jaw. "For now, I've brought you a snack." With the flick of her wrist, she gestured to the tray on the desk. A full tankard sat beside a plate of dried meat, cheese, and bread slathered in minced vegetables and thick cream. "Apparently you ate nothing at breakfast, and that's just insulting. This should tide you over until dinner."

Mayr offered her thanks in the form of a tender kiss. His tongue roved over hers as he slipped his hands down her back, holding tight but hesitant to go further. He yearned to strip her bare and make love to her on the settee, to thrust and tease and make her wail his name for the whole house to hear.

Not without him. Not here, not now.

Without Tash, the motions would feel incomplete, as if he were missing crucial pieces of himself—including the part that loved her without apology, a strand of brilliant colour among the rainbow of details. Arieve was a glimmering thread entwined with the rest of Mayr's soul that Tash had dug out of the mud, rinsed in a waterfall of faith, and sewn back together to make him whole. Now the bit of Mayr that belonged to Arieve was bound between him and Tash, a part of them both.

"Thanks for taking care of me," Mayr murmured, giving into an easy smile. "How was your night at the tavern? How's Orae? We missed you. We came up with a hundred ways to prove how much, including crashing the tavern and bringing you home."

A blush crept across Arieve's cheeks. "That's sweet, and Grandmother's fine, but I wasn't working. I was with Coye." She clenched his arms as though she anticipated a rant. "Just talking, and maybe there was a kiss."

"So you've made your choice?"

Arieve picked at Mayr's black, long-sleeved tunic and thick, black vest. "We'll see how it goes. How much she truly wants me." She flattened her hands on his chest. "You're my focus. I'm not giving you up, not when I finally have you," she assured him, stealing a long kiss. Their lips played slowly, finding a rhythm as they danced over angles.

Parting took away more than Mayr's breath: his aches eased and loosened, allowing him to blink without the urge to fall over.

"I have to get back to the kitchen. See you at dinner." After another kiss, Arieve flounced out of the office and pulled the door closed.

She left him staring at the door, her savoury taste still on his tongue. He needed more than one moment to recall the records he had to assemble by morning. The meeting was scheduled for noon, requiring the usual carriage ride to Vasserey Call, the city that was home to both the High Council and the Sacred Assembly. Between his regular duties and time spent with Aeley, Tash, Arieve, and everyone else, he had finished only half of the documents he intended to take. Lack of focus due to compromised sleep had not helped.

With curses on the tip of his tongue, he settled at his desk and flipped through the stacks of notes from Ress and Adren, grateful their writing was easy to decipher. The last thing he needed was the return of the pain Arieve had soothed.

It was a wish easily made but not granted. Not long after Arieve's departure, more knocks sounded on the door. Heavy, determined.

"I'm dead," Mayr shouted. "Come back later."

"Great, now she's sucking off a corpse," a low voice with feminine air drawled as the door opened. "That makes it *so* much *better*."

Repressed rage numbed Mayr, its bite a gnawing tingle as it skittered through his tightening chest. "Coye," he sneered, pushing up from his desk.

The door closed loudly behind her. "It's been a while," Coye said. She stopped in the middle of the room, dressed in two thick brown cloaks and layers of fawn and grey clothes. Her golden-blonde hair was longer than he remembered, curled tightly around her ears and neck rather than cropped close to her scalp as it had been, but the darkness of her green eyes and the thin line of black paint around them remained the same. Although most of her deep tan skin was hidden, she appeared to have lost none of her muscular frame developed from tree felling as a logger.

Because if there's anything she knows, it's killing things and running away.

Mayr crossed his arms and pressed his thighs to the desk, determined not to move. "To what do I owe *this* honour?"

Coye snorted. "Like you don't know." She cleared her throat, her expression softening. "I love Arieve. Might not seem like it, but I do. She says she'll give me one last chance...but that she's staying with *you*, even if we get back together." Her face lowered with her gaze. Taking a shaky breath, she raised her chin and pulled back her shoulders. "I'm here to beg you to let her go. Not asking you to stop being friends, only lovers. I want to take care of her, but I need you to step back and let it happen. Let us be happy. It won't work if I have to compete with you."

"*Competition?*" Mayr laughed. "Out of everything, *that's* what you're worried about?"

Lips in a grim line, Coye narrowed her eyes. "There can't be *us* if she's stuck on *you*. I'm here now. I can give her everything she wants. She doesn't have to settle for whatever you are. But instead of her dropping your ass, *I'm* the one who has to play second favourite. Or third, considering the situation, you greedy bastard." Her lip curled. "I can either accept that she's sleeping with you or leave her be. *Or* I can throw away my last shred of dignity and ask *you* to leave *her* so we have a better chance. Funny, I kind of hate all the options."

"Funny, I don't care." Mayr gritted his teeth. "I'm *not* making the hard decisions for you, and I'm not leaving her. She's made it clear she wants to be with us—there's no way I'm fighting that. I'll give her whatever she wants. Arieve told you her choice. Go take this up with her."

Emotions collided on Coye's face, clouded by a flash of rage. A dark flush shot across her cheeks. "That's how much you care, isn't it? *So* much you'll dump your selfishness on her because you're not man enough to back off!"

Snow flicked from Coye's boots as she

stomped closer. "Do you even know what makes her heart beat faster? Everything that makes her laugh so hard she's crying and dance so funny she falls over? Has she told you her secrets, like she's afraid of watching her family grow old and die because she can't do anything about it? That she's worked hard to make sure they *always* have the best they can?" Coye waved her hands erratically. "Do you even know how to take care of her other than spreading her legs? Because that's what she is to you, isn't she? Just a place to stick it because your man isn't good enough!"

"*Where* in the *blessed Four* do you get off on using a mouth like *that*?" Mayr roared, slamming his hands to the desk. "And *you're* lecturing *me* on using Arieve? *You*, who's broken her heart more times than I've broken my face?" He thrust one hand towards the door. "*Her. Whole. Life. That's* how long I've been here for her. I even stood over her cradle, calling her the prettiest damn baby! Yeah, I know why she works hard. I helped her *get* the job here because I knew how much she needed it. I know a realm's worth about her — except how she can waste time on *your* sorry ass."

There they were: all the words he had waited to shout in Coye's face, an onslaught he had struggled to control for far too long. After every breakup, he had focused on soothing Arieve's pain instead of avenging her. On Arieve's behalf, he had practiced a gentler fight, standing at her side while she battled her emotions. He had expected Arieve to find better than Coye—someone who would protect her in love.

Now that someone's us. I'm sorry, Arieve, but I can't keep my mouth shut anymore. I'll say everything you won't. Everything you can't.

Mayr jabbed his finger at Coye. "Don't you *ever* talk about Arieve or Tash like that again, and don't ever question my loyalty to her. You're the problem. *I* didn't take my *selfish ass* into the woods and hide. *I'm* not the one who threw her away with half-assed excuses. I don't play that game."

Coye huffed. "*Fine,* I ran away. I couldn't take the pressure. Go ahead, call me worthless, unfit, useless. I'm messed up, all right?" she shouted, throwing open her arms. "I don't get all that 'my stuff is your stuff is our stuff' rubbish. I have commitment issues, I *know that*. I don't know how to be part of two when it's difficult enough being one."

"So why are you back? What's different this time?"

"I'm sick of being a loser." Coye raked back her hair. "No one's even half as good for me as Arieve. No one's like her at all, and being without her is killing me. I get one more chance. It *has* to be the one I don't mess up."

Sarcasm forced its way from Mayr in a rumbling laugh. "I *love* how it's *now*, when she's moving on." Mayr snorted. "That's it, isn't it? She's moving on without you and you can't take it."

"Maybe, or maybe it's because I finally need to settle down with someone I can't live without. Maybe it's the punch I can't keep ducking."

"Yeah? Great, you finally clued in."

"Piss off. You're only special because the Tract Steward thinks you are." Coye glowered at him. "Look, I didn't run because I don't love Arieve; I ran because I *do*. I just haven't loved myself any. I'd hoped she'd wait for me, that she'd be here once I figured myself out." She folded her arms and dug her boot heel into the floor. "I was wrong, unfair. I should've risen up to her level, not dragged her down to mine. She *knows* who she is and what she wants. I should've trusted her to help me. It's not like she hasn't offered—I've just been too cowardly to accept. So yeah, Arieve moving on scares me," she said softly, "because I know who I could be with her."

A dozen mangled curses exploded across Mayr's thoughts. If Arieve were there, she would beg him to listen. Ask him to be kind.

As if I could deny her.

"If she's not leaving us, we're not leaving her." Mayr ground his teeth and sucked in a breath. "But we don't control her. That's not what we're about, her and us. If you want her, you're free to court her." The words left a bitter taste as he continued. "Just remember that you, her—this whole running away thing—it's *our* business now, especially if she gets pregnant. Or did she leave that part out?"

Coye shook her head. "She said. I just don't like hearing it."

"Yeah, well, that's your problem. I'm more concerned with making sure she's happy. Making sure my husband's happy." Mayr tucked his fists into the crooks of his arms, his voice leveled. "Arieve's ready for a family, with or without you, and we'll be there every step, every smile, every scraped knee. If you want in, you'd better be sure you're sticking around."

"I get it."

"Really? You don't seem to care about that part. You're talking competition and having for yourself instead of what Arieve's after." Mayr leaned over the desk. "Hint: kids won't make that better. If you can't take it, leave now. We'll be focused on our family, not playing your 'do I, don't I' bit."

"Stop patronizing me," Coye hissed. "I'm not *that* much of an idiot."

"Hard to tell where the line ends." Mayr splayed his hands over the parchment on his desk. "*I'm* not the one hurting her. That's all you, so get it together." His finger was steady as he jabbed it at her. "*Don't* keep breaking Arieve. She's family. You can be part of our family, but you'll have to *be* part. Be present. We'll be open with you, and honest, but if you mess around with any of us, I'll step in and fix it. I'll legally keep you from Arieve." A smirk tugged his lips. "I know *all* the right people."

"You're a complete ass," Coye snapped. "How does she even put up with you?"

"Go ask her. She's the one with all the power in this. If you've got a problem with that, maybe you shouldn't be in a relationship."

"By the Four, you defend her like a *husband*!"

"Yeah, well, I've always been the marrying kind."

Unspoken expletives hung in the air, sinking through the silence.

"Forget this." Coye stormed out of the office and slammed the door closed.

"You're welcome!" Mayr yelled. For a long, seething moment that dragged its way into a series of even longer, brooding moments, he could do nothing but stare at the door, years of anger poking at his every frustration, wanting the fight to continue. *So many things to say, never the right time—*

He clutched his head and clamped his jaws against the sharp pains stabbing holes in his thoughts. What aches Arieve had eased returned three-fold. He needed rest, solid and deep.

What I need *is to get these papers done and pass out until morning. Then Aeley can haul me to Council by my feet.* With a sigh, he sank into his chair, his forehead cradled in one palm as he willed irritation to bleed itself out in the silence. Whatever awful feelings Coye's presence had stirred up had to wait, at least until he finished his work and could deal with it all later—

preferably away from everyone else, but most likely ending in him hauling Pellon into the training room and going a few rounds until one of them surrendered and bought the other one a round of drinks—or five, knowing them. *Until then...*

There were too many other things to focus on, too much that had to be done now, not later. It was his responsibility to present new intelligence on the Shar-denn factions to Severn and the rest of High Council—Aeley and Lira were too busy to compile it. Their presence at the meeting was the most they could spare, leaving the details to him while they dealt with even larger matters.

"Running themselves ragged," he muttered, settling with his quill and parchments. To succeed as Tract Steward, Aeley had to fight for every step she took. If politics was not the problem at hand, the games of society were. Keeping Gailarin in order was no easy feat. The best he could do was be where she needed him, however she needed him, and keep their guards in line.

Guards that were pounding the floor above him, stomping like giants.

"Really?" Mayr seethed and scribbled, desperate to concentrate. He was going to kill someone before the day was out, he was sure of it.

The first three shouts he took with the grinding of his teeth.

The angry cries to be let go were another

matter.

He fled from the office for the staircase to his right. To the deafening ruckus of yells and whistles, Mayr climbed the stairs two steps at a time. The wooden floorboards vibrated with the commotion of more than a dozen guards. Gathered halfway up the hall, the guards hollered and jeered in a blur of bodies in various states of dress. More guards rounded the corner at the other end of the corridor to join the crowd, their faces flushed with excitement. Others remained in the doorways of the rooms, appearing to debate if they should get involved.

At the centre of the fray, two bodies rolled and wrestled on the floor, fists pounding whatever they could.

"I told you to back off!" one man shouted, followed by a slap.

"And I told you to stop going around with my girl!" his opponent roared. A body slammed the ground, shaking the floor. "You should've kept your vile ass cock in your damn ugly pants, boy. I'll rip it off and make you eat it!"

"I didn't do anything!" the first voice countered, pitched higher. "I don't even *like* women that way."

Another hit, a harder slam. Grunts and groans. Three guards rushed to pry the fighters apart.

Mayr gritted his teeth. How many times had he instructed the guards to settle their differences without their fists unless they were in the training ring? How many times had he told them he would kick them out of the Guard House if they insisted on using it for brawls? The onlookers were no better. They all needed a refresher in rules and camaraderie.

"Would you quit it?" Mayr bellowed before he elbowed and shoved his way through the crowd.

The fighters continued, even in the clutches of the guards that attempted to stop them. Fists cut through the air, cracking where they landed. Only the onlookers backed away, blushing as they avoided Mayr's glance.

In the centre of the widening circle were Gorgan and Lisreft, kicking and growling.

Mayr snorted. Normally he would have bet Lisreft would kill Gorgan, given Lisreft's size and experience. His fists were brutal like hammers to the balls. For Gorgan to hold his own in the fight was impressive.

Yeah, except forget impressed. Let's go for damned foolish beyond reason. Fingers to his lips, Mayr whistled, shrill and loud.

Bodies stopped. Shouts silenced. The crowd shuffled back.

Lisreft stopped mid-strike, the collar of Gorgan's dark green shirt in one fist, his other fist aimed for Gorgan's bloody face. Beneath Lisreft's twisted, kneeling body, Gorgan stiffened and stared at Mayr, one eye swollen and his bottom lip split.

"*What* is *going on*?" Mayr yelled. "You—" he jabbed his finger at Lisreft "—here. Gorgan, stay put."

Hunching, Lisreft obeyed. Taller than Mayr by a foot and larger in stature, Lisreft was Gorgan's senior by five years, one of the first guards Mayr had trained after becoming Head of the Guard. Lisreft's brown hair fell to his shoulders in the back, while the sides of his head were completely shaved. Dressed in a loose grey shirt and pants now mussed and bloodstained, Lisreft should have been asleep in preparation for his night shift, not fighting. His brown eyes focused on Mayr, a hint of apology at their edges.

"Little brat was running his hands up my Revie's skirt," Lisreft snarled, wiping his swollen mouth and ruddy cheek. "They were in his *room*, door *closed*, murmuring and *giggling* like dirty little lovers. *All* the guards saw her leave. She was all pleased and glowing and all that filthy rubbish!"

"So you figured punching his eyeballs into his skull was the way to go?" A rumbling growl slipped from Mayr. He sucked it back with cold air between his teeth.

Lisreft flinched. "I wanted to make it clear. If he doesn't keep his hands off, I'll hack him to pieces."

Gorgan snorted and choked, launching into a fit of coughs. With a groan, he pushed up from the floor. The curls of his blond hair were unkempt, his pants and shirt disheveled. "Yeah, Revie *was* in my room." He glared at Lisreft and wiped the blood trickling from his broken nose. "We were *talking*. She knows my mother's experienced in midwifery. She had questions."

"Questions?" Lisreft's fists tightened. "*What* questions?"

"You should ask her." Gorgan bit down hard, one arm wrapped around his ribs. "You'll need the answers in seven months anyway. A whinier little you to contend with, Goddesses save us."

Confusion swept across Lisreft's face with a scowl.

The moment he understood, emotions ripped across his face. Lisreft paled, his eyes widening. "Oh, by the blessed... We've been trying, but I didn't think she was..."

"Happy now?" Mayr shoved Lisreft towards the stairs. "Go and see if she's all right. Start acting like a father before you become a complete disgrace. Next time, keep your fists to yourself or you're on lock-down."

Still dazed, Lisreft nodded. "Sorry, Gorgan," Lisreft mumbled before he stumbled down the hall, raking one hand over his shaved head.

Mayr snapped his fingers and thrust out his arm. "The rest of you, clear off!"

The guards faltered.

"*Now*," Mayr barked, "or I'm handing out punishments you won't be thanking me for."

Murmurs filtered through the hall as the

group disbanded. One of the guards accompanied Lisreft down the stairs, her hand on his arm to steady him.

"Overgrown scrappy mutt," Mayr grumbled, turning to Gorgan. "You all right?"

"I'm upright." Gorgan licked his lips and winced. "Nothing some horrible poultice and a face full of snow can't cure."

"Sure. I've been there a few times."

"Suppose so. Can't be Head Guard if all you do is knit pillows and hide in the stuffing." Gorgan limped up the hallway. "Thanks for intervening. I'll just go and die now." He threw a lopsided smile over his shoulder. "After I get Stuck to bandage me. She's the best of the bunch. Rarely ever bites."

Yeah, but she kicks like there's no tomorrow. "You need anything, I'm downstairs," Mayr said, holding back a snort. "And I'm scolding Lisreft about this later, so don't run off or you'll miss it."

One hand up in acknowledgment, Gorgan rounded the corner and disappeared into the back corridor.

Alone in the hallway, Mayr stared after him. In less than two years, Gorgan had changed from the quiet, uncertain youth he used to be. The training with his fellow guards and extra lessons with Mayr and Pellon were paying off in confidence. In his first weeks, Gorgan had uttered few words and gaped at his comrades rather than risk punching them. He had been new to the village at the time, still finding his place. Since then, he had learned to relax, joke, and strike back.

Hello, adolescent me. So nice to see you again. Mayr snickered and started for the stairs. Only Pellon knew that Mayr saw parts of himself in Gorgan. *Then again, Pell was there to torture me into comfort. Aeley to my right, Pell to my left—it's a wonder I survived. Still trying to figure out how Allon dragged through life without getting pummeled to death. Korre, Korre, Korre. You probably would've loved to have me and Pell as sons instead of fathering that coward.*

Partway down the stairs, Mayr leaned against the railing and bit his cheek. His memories raged, gnawing on his fiery aches and tearing open old wounds that would never fully heal. How did filth like Allon remain alive while good people like Korre were snatched away? How could the monsters of the Shar-denn still exist when kinder souls were torn from life itself? How could all that death balance *any* scale in any world? They had more funeral pyres burning every year for innocent people than there were criminals in the prisons.

The world was cracked in all the wrong places and goodness was oozing into the voids.

His bad mood slid from worse to the rancid, scorching need to sharpen his favourite weapons on the bones of his least favourite people. He was tired of playing games. Was it too much to ask to be happy without anything tripping him up?

Releasing his frustration in a dull roar, Mayr slipped into his office and kicked the door shut.

The instant he sat in his chair, the door rattled. More knocks.

Mayr slammed his head onto his folded arms. "G*o away*! I hate everybody equally today. No. Special. Favours!" He bashed his forehead against his leather bracers. "Next knock, I'm ripping *all* your hands off."

The door opened and closed. Quiet footfalls approached the desk before a cool hand caressed the back of his head. Fingers glided through the loose tail of his hair and settled on his nape, kneading with familiar weight.

Mayr lifted into the touch with a sigh. "Except you," he said, closing his eyes. "I love your hands."

"I should be so lucky," Tash whispered. His fingers trailed down Mayr's jaw to his throat, tender as they lifted Mayr's chin. "And may my lips be as adored. Goddesses know I cherish yours."

His soft kiss brushed across Mayr's lips, asking for affirmation.

Mayr's strangled whimper answered, drawing forth more than Tash's mouth: the vibrations of Tash's throaty laugh played through their lips, urging their kiss to bypass chaste and settle for deep and longing. Stealing Tash's breath rooted Mayr in comfort, but sharing the same breath filled him with all the reasons why he needed to keep working.

"What can I do for you?" Mayr sat up straight. Tempted as he was, he would *not* make love to Tash on the desk, even if the High Council annoyed him enough to offer them parchment stained with sweat and come.

Bundled up in his red long coat and cloak, Tash's nose and cheeks were just as red from the cold weather. His eyes held all the warmth winter was missing. "I heard from Keeper Felensa. He's requested I bring Adren to the Sanctum. He was quite insistent, in fact." The easiness of his laugh rolled through Mayr's headache like a cooling wave. "I should forewarn Adren that ce has a new, rather excitable, friend."

Mayr leaned back and scowled. The Sanctum of the Mortal Divine was a full day's carriage ride from Dahena, too far for his liking. The trip required at least two night's stay in the Sanctum with its secrets and sacred library, secluded from the nearest town, Eleonne. In all, the journey required at least three days, though more were often required. The priests of the Sanctum frequently entreated Tash to stay longer.

The excursion was too long for Mayr to support given his nightmares. Images of corpses lingered in the back of his mind: bodies littering the road, limbs smashed, faces broken beyond repair. He could almost taste the ambush to come, every strike itching beneath his skin, pricking his intuition like a bed of needles.

Yet he hated to deny Tash his chance to learn the truth about Adren and cir Goddess-touched lineage. The Sanctum held all of the knowledge Tash craved. By the oaths of a priest, Tash was sworn to serve Adren to the fullest of his capability. His duty was no less worthy than Mayr's, particularly since Adren was considered an ally and priceless informant.

An informant Mayr was not sure he trusted, not like Tash did. Not like the priests chose to. *If Adren ever cheats us—if ce ever puts you in danger—I'll make cir pay for it so fast, I don't care which goddess rages on my hide.*

Mayr ground his teeth. If Tash wanted to go, Mayr would accompany him as he always did. He refused to sit at home and wonder if Tash would return unscathed. *Especially with Adren there, and where Adren goes, Ress goes. All three of them out in the open for days at a time, available for the taking... No doubt it's what the Shar's waiting for.*

"We can leave in three days." Mayr forced his gentlest tone and a weak smile. "Let me wrap things up with Council and we'll—"

Tash shook his head. "Sweet love, we're leaving tomorrow."

Mayr blinked. The words crashed in his thoughts, toppling more than his patience. "Tomorrow?"

"Keeper Felensa requested we come for the day after tomorrow, yes."

"To-mor-row."

"Yes."

Heat raced up Mayr's neck and flooded his cheeks. "Tell him no. Pick another day."

"I can't," Tash said, clasping his hands before him. "Keeper Felensa has business elsewhere in Kattal for the next month, and he's leaving in three days. He requested we visit him now so he can search for answers while he's away. I've already sent word that we would."

Mayr's fingers curled, his nails digging into his palms. This was *not* happening. "You agreed without talking to me? Didn't bother *asking* if I was even available to escort you—you just assumed, didn't you? Sure, it's fine to go traipsing wherever you want, whenever, consequences be damned. Your priestly needs are all that matter. Who cares if I can't be there—you'll just run headlong into foolish decisions!"

Tash stepped back, the corners of his eyes tightened. "No, I considered it. I also considered the other options."

"Other *options*? Because there's *so bleeding many*." Mayr pushed up from his desk. Blood-soaked images assaulted what was left of his clarity, set to the tortuous sounds of Tash's screams. Tash's last breath, ragged and painful, his last whisper, snagged on Mayr's name…

Some days he wondered if Tash truly valued what they had. For each time he led Mayr to believe they loved to equal depths, there were just as many days Tash did something so foolish Mayr wanted to choke his damned pride. Did Tash *care* he made himself a target? Did it *ever* occur to him that he nearly broke Mayr's heart every time he left? Did he *want* to get caught? He said he wanted to spend his life with Mayr, but all he seemed to offer was his eventual death.

His promises to always take care of Mayr—were they *that* empty? All of the whispers in the dark about having a child—did they mean *nothing*? Words were easy illusions that said anything they had to, but actions were intent itself made real. If this was Tash fighting to stay, he was waving every flag that said otherwise.

Control snapped in Mayr like frayed rope, the jagged ends tearing holes through his overwrought nerves. Agony gorged on his composure with barbs and talons, clawing a tortuous path from headache to heartache. His back ached from having to keep his fist from going through the desk.

"Real good timing, Halataldris," Mayr yelled, words bursting forth in an avalanche of hurt, "because *forget* the meeting I've got with Council—a meeting I told you about a *hundred times*—and *forget* the fact I can't miss it. Let's all just drop whatever we're doing to make some egotistical little priest happy."

Anger clouded Tash's gaze. His fingers flexed, but his voice remained calm. "Dare I assume that Felensa's the so-called egotistical little priest?"

"Who else would it be?"

"Considering I'm the one who runs headlong into foolish decisions, perhaps you need to spell it out."

"I don't need your condescension," Mayr snapped. "Not when you're running around like no one cares. You'll do me, play me, placate me when it suits you, but forget *respect*. Forget I have people to protect, including *your* targeted ass. Forget I'm trying to make things safer *for you*. You jump whenever the other priests tell you to. You're such a good boy, doing whatever they want, but forget that *I'm* the one trying to *keep you alive*."

Softness returned to Tash's features as he let out a slow breath. "Mayr, what is this really about?"

"I can't go with you, that's what!"

"That's all right," Tash said quietly, "because I'll take other escorts. *That's* the other option."

"Foolish, inferior escorts." Mayr growled. "Gods-awful children with weapons, that's what they are." He smacked both palms on the desk, his knee ramming the drawer. "You going without me is unacceptable. You going *anywhere* is unacceptable. You're begging for death. The fight in Araveena *won't* be the last. Mark my words," he hissed, jabbing his finger at Tash. "Ress and Adren will drag your ass into *everything* you left behind. One of these days, the debt's coming due and you'll be skinned right alongside them."

Tash moved forward, one hand raised. "Mayr—"

"Don't!" Mayr flung out his arm, gesturing towards the main house. "It's bad enough that since your reunion with Ress, you're depressed and weepy on the most random days—all because Ress makes you feel like a useless little bitch of a rat. He *isn't good for you*, no matter *what* you think. He'll get you killed," he sneered, "and I'll beat him so far into the lowest realms of the blessed ugly dead he'll *never* get out."

Mayr snorted. "Don't even get me *started* on Adren. You want death? Spend more time with cir and it'll come. Ce's a beacon for the Shar." He leaned forward, spitting out words between clenched teeth. "I can't keep dropping everything to play caretaker to some magical little felon, especially one I can't even *begin* to trust with your life. I don't care *whose* blood ce's got, ce's *not my problem*. Stop expecting me to help your nuisance of a pet."

Flinching, Tash stepped back. Lips drawn in a tight line, his hands in fists, he glowered at Mayr. Emotions danced across his face in a shifting mask of shadows. Fury, disappointment, disgust—they flowed into each other, forging something deeper, darker. "Good to know where your superiority lies. I'll be sure to remember."

Tash's lip curled as he continued. "Adren's not a nuisance, and ce's *no one's pet*. Don't you *dare* say that again," he snarled. "I used to *be* like Adren—I won't abandon cir. Ce needs all the friends ce can get." He took another step back, his chin lifted. "I'm still going. The other priests in my generation have never met a Goddess-touched, and it's been decades since our temple encountered any. I'm honoured to be entrusted with Adren's life, and I'll continue to protect cir— even from you. Ce wants a new life, so I'll help any way I can. If I *ever* consider wanting your opinion, I'll be sure not to ask for it."

When Mayr opened his mouth to argue, Tash raised his hand. "It's just as well you can't come. If you're going to be moody and mean, I don't want you there. I *won't* have you ruining this for Adren *or* for me." He backed towards the door. "I'll take Pellon, assuming you can spare his *inferior* ass. At least he won't throw a fit."

Tash flung open the door in an instant and slammed it shut the next. The doorframe shook from the force.

Mayr kicked the desk hard enough to jam the bottom drawer.

"Forget you and your morals," he seethed, slapping parchments off his desk. The tray from Arieve crashed to the floor. *Forget the Goddess-touched, forget his stubbornness, and a* huge *forget this to his asinine loyalties!*

He fell into his chair and shoved his feet against the desk. The chair squealed backwards, slamming into the bookcase behind him. Knees bent with his feet on the desk, Mayr glared at the papers strewn across the floor, his hands tucked into the crooks of his arms. *This* was more like it, the pain he was used to. Not the longing pain of leaving a lover's bed. Not the sweet pain of hearing how much someone loved him. Not the exquisite pain of having everything and not knowing what to do with it. This was the deep ache, the hurt that froze the blood and spurned self-loathing. The kind of pain that injured and bruised and sucked joy from him until all that remained was a gaping hole dripping with disdain.

And he goes on about us being soulbound. Ha! Soulbound this, you ass, and you can soulbound your arrogant servitude while you're at it. Because what is soulbound really?

"A short chain calling us to heel," Mayr mumbled. Where Tash's duty went, Mayr's acceptance was expected to follow. His opinions mattered little when the treasures of divinity were waved in Tash's face. Anytime the priesthood demanded his obedience, Tash gave it without hesitation, sacrificing Mayr's hope.

Tash swore he would take care of Mayr, but not once did Tash consider that protecting himself was part of it. Now there was Arieve to consider: her happiness, her safety, and the family they hoped for. An entire life waited to be held in their hands.

It only works if you're alive to enjoy it.

Mayr dug his annoyance into his desk with the heel of his boot. What was he thinking? His relationships never lasted. Tash and Arieve would be no different. Everything went away, love was always a casualty, and he was the one who stoked the pyre.

Muttering half-formed curses, he pulled his chair back to the desk and gathered the documents from the floor. *Forget them. Tash and Arieve can do each other all night for all I care. Won't be able to get it up anyway, so what's the point?* Mayr slammed the papers onto the desk. *Forget everyone else, too. I'm too messed up to be around anything that breathes. So suck on that, Goddesses, and I'll get back to you when I'm ready to take your rubbish again.*

Chapter Ten

Nothing eased the ache lodged in Tash's chest, regret seeping from his misery. Though considering he already had a lifetime of regrets, the additional guilt should not have weighed as heavily as it did.

Especially when I know how his temper works. Tash folded one last robe before he packed it in the brown leather travel case on the bed. *Mayr yells first and thinks later. Then the apologies follow, profuse and genuine.*

He also knew Mayr never attacked without reason. Mayr was not careless, dealing emotional damage because he derived pleasure from conflict. If anything, Mayr was too giving, too kindhearted, twisting himself in every direction to protect his loved ones from harm. Outbursts like the one that day indicated injury and fear more than pride and self-importance. For his anger to be directed at Tash with such ferocity suggested something haunted him, latched onto hidden wounds.

Still, it hurt.

Tash pressed the pile of robes further into the case and sighed. Bearing witness to Mayr's rants could be informative and darkly comical, but being on the receiving end stripped courage from his soul. Ten years in the Shar-denn had taught Tash to withstand confrontation and outrage with rigidity. He had adapted to being screamed at and derided by gang members, including those who had trained him to guard their faction boss, Colare. The cruelest castigations had been by Colare himself, who never spared compassion unless it was to test his guard's resolve or exact a harsher penalty. That same Colare had coerced Tash, Ress, Nimae, and Varen into swearing fealty to the Shar-denn. Shortly after threatening their adolescent lives, Colare had stabbed Ress and left him to bleed all over the tavern floor.

Even after all that, Mayr's wrath hurt more. Instead of bleeding out, Tash's insides shattered into tiny fragments. Mayr's words had stung worse than his tone.

A tone Tash returned at the end, punishing him.

He never wanted angry words to be the final thing he said to Mayr. If the Shar-denn had taught him anything, it was the value of life. The preciousness of a single breath was worth a hundred lashes. The lasting impression of love was worth humility. Any moment could be the end. He never wanted Mayr's last memory of him to be one of contempt.

With another weary sigh, Tash slipped the books he needed into the travel case: two leather-bound journals that contained what he knew of the Goddess-touched and a raggedy volume of whimsical stories gifted to him by his parents, an artifact from his childhood. The book was a touch of them wherever he was, whenever he needed them.

Now would be good. They could tell me their secret to staying together, even when fight gets in the way. Tash buckled the case shut and sank onto the bed, then gazed around the bedroom he shared with Mayr. Bathed in light from the hearth, the room looked the same as it always did, though its ambiance was empty and colder than the winter wind. The closed curtains hid the night sky but not the truth: Mayr was avoiding him.

After the confrontation in the office, Tash had returned to the temple to finish preparations for the trip to the Sanctum. While his duties normally included training novice priests and tending to the altar rooms dedicated to Emeraliss, Kee had decided Tash was required elsewhere. More specifically, Kee had instructed him to help Adren and Ress acclimate to a new life. Most of Tash's days were to be spent with them, assisting them while they worked for the High Council and continued doing their community service in the village. Together, the three of them helped villagers with mending their homes, tending their gardens, moving or fetching items, and being useful in whatever way they could.

The most solemn of his responsibilities was to

safeguard Ress and Adren with all the shrewdness he possessed. Kee did not trust the High Council's methods, nor did she trust Severn to abide by the conditions of amnesty. To deter the councilmen from reneging on that amnesty, Kee placed the care of Ress and Adren in Tash's hands when she was not present. He had earned his role, Kee had told him, after the Temple of the Four gave him refuge at his time of greatest need. She expected him to be a paragon to those who sought redemption.

That role ended at the boundary of priesthood and left a delicate man on the other side, one who had needed assurance once he returned to the estate, determined to make up with Mayr. Expecting to see him at dinner, Tash had practiced all manners of apology and soft words. He had intended to whisk Mayr into a walk through the moonlit conservatory, arm in arm as they discussed what truly worried Mayr, followed by the drawn-out kisses they savoured and another night with Arieve.

Mayr never showed. He sent a message on a torn piece of parchment instead, saying he would miss dinner due to *reasons*.

And that he was not to be bothered.

By anyone.

Crushed, Tash ate alone with Aeley, Lira, Ress, and Adren, picking at his food until they finished and went separate ways. Aeley and Lira retired to Aeley's study, alone and mischievous.

Ress and Adren had settled down with cards and discs, gambling with Ress's earnings from whatever he crafted for the High Council, a confidential project kept in a room on one of the estate's lower levels.

Reminding himself that he was always Mayr's exception to the rules just as Mayr was his, Tash had gone to Mayr's office. A hastily scribbled sign hung from cord on a nail in the door, practically shouting for visitors to leave. Inside, Mayr hummed and grumbled, and the floorboards creaked as feet shuffled. Tash had tapped on the door and tried the handle, only to find it locked. Worse still, his efforts were completely disregarded.

Mayr never ignored him. Even when they were too angry to look at each other, Mayr never ignored him.

Nevertheless, Tash had pressed his palm and forehead to the door, pleading to be let in.

He never made it over the threshold.

Eyes blurred with tears of resignation, Tash had run to Mayr's room. For all the talk of protecting him, for all the anger directed at people he insisted would hurt Tash, Mayr cared more about carrying on the fight than spending time together.

Disgust at Mayr's hypocrisy burned in Tash. It left a foul taste on his tongue and abhorrence in his core. What a betrayal of the simplest emotions between them.

Tash growled out his frustration and held his face in his hands, elbows propped on his knees. Evening prayer had not soothed him. Packing only distracted him as long as there were things to pack—and he had exhausted the list, an easy feat given his few possessions. As for tears... those stopped and started, wetting his cheeks before he knew he was crying.

"More of the weeping he hates so much," Tash sneered.

No, it's not the weeping he hates, he corrected bitterly. *Just Ress and Adren and everything to do with my priesthood.*

None of which he could separate from himself, not without losing pieces of who he was. They proved he still had value, that he was worth *something*, even if it was just a speck of dust in a bucket. Those pieces meant nothing to Mayr, but they were the price of life to Tash—his second chance.

He was humbled by the faith others invested in him. His Uldana Trials had been a means to find absolution, but expectation had turned the universe on him. Like looking in a mirror, he saw truth reflected back in his actions, choices, and the care he showed others. By the time he started the Trials, the Goddesses had already determined his worth. Not only had Emeraliss claimed him as a servant, She watched over him through every step of his Trials, testing how much he treasured love and how deeply he desired Mayr.

Prior to the third trial, Navara had weighed his soul on the ethereal plates of the Onamarre, a judgment Tash witnessed during the fourth trial. The scales of fate had tipped in his favour, despite his mortification and doubt.

Even then he could not shake the need to prove himself. Since childhood, the itch to find his place plagued him. Worried he would never fully belong, he had ached to feel equal to everyone else — to *be* like everyone else.

For a time, he had found self-acceptance in the warmth of brotherhood. Ress had lifted him up when he stumbled and scraped his pride. Varen had taught him how to laugh at himself without slicing his confidence on the edges of self-deprecation. Nimae had made him feel safe, as though Tash was unique and special, no matter what he did with his life.

Perhaps he would have been a tailor, clothing the wealthiest Grand Families in the latest fashions. Or he could have worked in the metal shop with Ress, courted Inesta like a gentleman, and married her. He would have spent his life showering her with gifts and teaching their children to make beautiful things.

Maybe he would have been a collector of tales and song, performing at festivals and feasts as a bard, given his fair voice and passable skills with a harp and sifter's skin drum. Or he would have traveled Kattal in search of its mysteries, picking apart the universe one secret wonder at a time.

Once the Shar-denn claimed him, however, self-acceptance had faded into a dream. The gang harvested his pride in chunks and left him with a battered soul. It was prove himself or die, and he was too stubborn to give up. He had fought the Shar-denn for the right to be himself, foisting hate upon them with a vengeance.

All he got back was approval. They wanted his rage. They valued his fury. They spelled out his worth in the language of violence and rewarded his hunger to survive.

The price of that survival was one he would never live down, no matter who believed in him. The weight of the cost had never been on his back alone. Like a coward, he had allowed innocent lives to pass him by. He had allowed the possibilities to save them to slip through his hands, his heart closed to freedom no matter what he witnessed or how he felt beneath his hate.

Like Ress, he could never forget their crimes. They were accomplices to horrors no one deserved, and they had ruined too many families by giving into the Shar-denn. Not just their own, but those of the people who were taken from their homes, markets, alleys, and roadsides only to be broken and sold as slaves. To his shame, he had lost count of how many times he helped drag people to the sordid houses where the Breakers did everything possible to make them obedient. He bore witness to more violations than he could stomach: brutal beatings that left the floors soaked with blood, mind games that twisted and scorched even his mind, threats of rape and the vile act itself, and the death of the weakest member of a group to make the stronger ones comply.

I walked away every time. I left them there to scream, to rot and die one poisoned moment at a time. Tash glared at the floor, his sight blurred with tears of disgust. *I forfeited all their souls and for what? Loyalty?*

No, not loyalty. Never loyalty. It was fear that stopped him from fighting back. Had he intervened, he would have been the next one broken, along with his family and everyone else he loved. Only seventeen at the time, he had forced himself to comply. The Breakers had pushed him to the edge of his tipping point, testing how much he needed to be damaged from the inside out before he shattered completely.

How he had any sense of self left was beyond him. His training as a guard never helped. At nineteen, he killed his first man in the training ring, and not by accident. Pride had gotten the better of him, the need to prove himself too strong to ignore, and taunts from the other guards only prodded his need for revenge. From that day forward, he swore he would work his way up to a better position instead of remaining a grunt. If he was going to lay down his life for the Shar-denn, he wanted the gang to pay him handsomely for it, if not in respect or the blood of other members then in funds and leniency. Along the way, he broke whatever he needed to, whether it was a face or neck or back. Respect accompanied his efforts and earned him a place on Boss Colare's team of private guards, which kept not only Colare safe but his wife, their six children, and his two brothers.

In Colare's service, he learned what it was to spill a thief's entrails onto the floor and let scavengers have at it. He knew how to rip back the scalp of a traitor and hand them over to body workers for skinning. Colare was happiest when his enemy was in the greatest pain, and Tash had been another one of his well-trained beasts.

Those were his worst days, terrifying years he wished his memory would block. He had never needed a talon to tear into people—his passion to survive had done all the damage, and Colare drunk in every victory like the smoothest ale. The horrid dichotomy between what Tash was with the Shar-denn and who he was with Inesta and his family had always been deranged. He never wanted to see another drop of blood, to handle another weapon. The fight in Araveena Ford to save Ress and Adren had tortured him enough with nightmares for three weeks afterwards. Sometimes even sparring with Mayr pushed him too close to the edge of misery, raising the ghosts of dead emotions. Tash felt the shadows reach for him, poking at his calm, threatening to escape from the places he had trapped them.

He had always known what he was doing was wrong, and perhaps that was the worst truth. Whenever he had been with family or out among the villagers, he loathed himself, shamed by his choices and horrified by his actions.

But when he was with the Shar-denn, the darkness had come easily. Violence was a familiar friend, his rage an insatiable fire. No matter how wrong he knew his actions were, he had slipped into the skin of a monster, falling further and further from the man he could have been. In the search for himself, the gang opened every locked door and broke everything he had. How he could have loved Inesta at the same time was beyond him. There was little space for love. By the time he worked his way through the ranks to stand by Colare's side, he barely recognized himself. He forgot what it meant to be human.

It was that twisted, grotesque self he had heard reflected back in the sickening screams of the children he refused to kill on Colare's behalf—ten children who had died anyway, regardless of Tash's attempt to save them from his gang brothers.

The same men who had taught him how to fight also taught him to value rebellion, and he had invested it into sparing lives. Young, innocent lives that had been snuffed out with knives to their throats, their bodies discarded with the rest of their family.

After that night, his worth was reduced to

how much flesh he lost to punishment. For every child he had tried to save, he screamed mercy, but not for himself. Instead, he had begged the Four to grant the children peace and a kinder new life. Their unfortunate relation to a faction boss at war with Colare was not their fault.

He would never regain what he had lost, and he could never restore what he had taken. Those ten years stole who he would have been, replacing life with shadow. The boy he used to be had dreamed of what existed beyond the stars but died the day he met Colare. That boy was still kneeling in Ress's blood, desperate to tie a tourniquet made from his shirt.

All the reason why he knew Mayr's anger was justified.

I can't even disagree, not really. Tash groaned and leaned forward, hanging his head. As much as Mayr despised his priesthood, he had nothing else to show for himself.

If Mayr thought Tash was fearless, he was wrong. Tash was fear walking. The gang's memory was long and clear, but he could not spend the rest of his life hiding. There were promises to keep. He had to move on.

"I want you to move on with me," he whispered, wishing Mayr was there. "I need you to, because Ress isn't the one that's not good for me—it's me. It's always been me." A sob wrenched free from Tash and snagged in his throat. He rubbed tears from his eyes, defeated as more spilled over his fingers. He was falling apart without someone to catch him. That someone was elsewhere, hating his choices. Hating the trouble he brought.

It was not far from hating him.

He had seen what Mayr would do to protect him, but there was a limit to Mayr's understanding. His patience would run out.

We're supposed to be getting married in two months, but now it feels like forever. What if it becomes never?

Raps on the door jarred him.

"Yeah?" Tash croaked, wiping his eyes.

The door opened slowly. Arieve entered, dressed in an intricate, pale green bodice woven from various fabrics and a heavy, dark blue dress, its hem grazing the top of her black boots. Her tousled, unbound curls tumbled over her shoulders, strands of tiny silver beads shining among them. "Just wanted to check on you. Can I...?"

Tash nodded and moved the travel case to the floor. The door latched shut behind Arieve before she crossed the room to sit beside him.

"You looked upset earlier," she said, removing her boots. Arieve drew her legs up onto the bed and dug her heels into the edge of the mattress. "I went to check on Mayr, take him dinner, but Aeley and Pellon beat me to it. They're in his office, talking."

Stabbed by her words, Tash's heart threatened

to bleed itself dry.

Arieve cupped his jaw. "I know something's wrong. I don't know what, but I'm here, and I'm pretty sure you shouldn't be left alone." With her thumbs, she caressed away the lingering wetness on his cheeks. "I'm not him, but I'm good at listening. I've heard so many of his woes. It's time you share yours."

When he said nothing, Arieve's lips brushed across his cheek. Whisper-light, the string of kisses left a blazing trail. "I'll be here if you want me to be," she said, sweeping his veil over his shoulder. "We don't have to talk. If you want me just to hold you, I will. Tell me what you need."

All of his silent answers collided together, smashed against the walls of *don't*, *can't*, and *shouldn't*. He hated being alone. Half his life had been spent feeling lonely, convinced no one understood what he had been through or wanted him enough to be there when he crumbled. Mayr had been the first to stay, the first to care.

Mayr, who hid behind his anger, far from where Tash needed him.

"Stay," Tash whispered. "Please. I can't…"

Arieve's arms slipped around him. "Can't be alone?" she finished, cradling his head against her shoulder. "You don't have to be. I'll stay with you, just like this, just keeping you in my arms."

Tash squeezed his eyes shut and breathed her in. Perfume clung faintly to her smooth skin, mixed with fragrant soap and savoury aromas from the kitchen. While he could not tell Arieve what horrors haunted him, he wanted to accept her comfort. The warmth that spread through his chest demanded it, teasing him with possibility.

He knew that feeling, a lightness that struggled to overpower an unyielding heat. Familiarity and need pushed and pulled, commanding he open himself to let someone in. Since his youth, he had needed that feeling, craved it. It was what had led him to Mayr and why he had almost lost Mayr. Now it was the part of him that wanted Arieve.

He was falling for her, and there was no stopping it.

Even knowing Mayr's feelings for her, despite knowing she loved Coye, he desired her. He knew her body from memory alone, adoring how she sought his touch, and her taste lingered in his thoughts. The laughter she could never seem to contain and the lilt of her voice offered more than notes—they were a remedy for what ailed him.

Tash may not have spent years dedicating pieces of himself to Arieve like Mayr, but he wanted to. In the quiet moments, he saw everything Mayr saw: she was colour and light, brilliant and blinding with the rarity of a falling star. She was a gentle call to love rather than a piercing cry of lust. Earnest and welcoming, she was a part of them, staking her claim inside their hearts. Although she loved Mayr, she also saw Tash. What all she found in him gave him pause, knowing she could leave if she knew the full truth, but she saw him, included him. Instead of breaking them down, she built them up.

Clutching her close, Tash buried his face in the heat of her throat, lulled by the rise and fall of her chest. Being with her was the last thing he should do, given Mayr's temper, but he needed peace, just for a while.

"This might be more comfortable lying down." Arieve pulled his veil away and tossed it over the chest at the foot of the bed. Her hands glided over his shoulders, consoling him. "Let everything else go and the rest might come."

"Are you sure you've never considered becoming a priestess?" Tash smiled weakly, following her off the bed, his hand in hers. "Sometimes you sound like one of us."

Arieve laughed with a light snort. "What a catastrophe that would've been." She made quick work of removing his outer robe and unlaced the second robe, pushing his hands away when he tried to help. "I might scream the Goddesses' names when I'm losing my mind, but that's all the worship I can manage. The rest…" With a shrug, she slid the second robe down his shoulders. "It's never been something I've spent much time on." A blush raced across her cheeks. "Not that it's not important or I don't care or anything. Because I do, and you make a wonderful priest, you have no idea. But I—it's just—"

Tash lifted her chin, leaning down to kiss her. "I won't judge you, gentle one. It was a compliment."

Her blush deepened. "Thanks," Arieve muttered, divesting him of his remaining clothes before skimming her spread fingers down his chest.

Want blazed in a quiet fire, his body ready to be wrapped in her heat. Every night she had come to their bed, he offered himself. Whenever she whimpered for his touch, he indulged her with wickedness. Each time she kissed him, he returned the gift with fervour. Anything she wanted he gave, and in return she let him make love to her as though she truly wanted him.

Tonight was not one of those nights. Arieve's hands did not tease. Her lips did not press to the tender spot beneath his collarbone that made him shiver and moan. There was no heated glance. She untied her bodice and stripped off her dress, then discarded both in a heap with her boots and thick emerald-green stockings. Her sleeveless black under dress slipped off her shoulders and pooled on the floor. In the firelight, her skin seemed to emanate a soft glow all its own. Her eyes shone brighter than other nights as she ushered him into bed and urged him to lie against her side.

"That's it, just like this," Arieve murmured. She flipped the blankets over them. "I'm here for however long you need. Let me make it easier, whatever it is, no matter the worry." One of her hands passed over his back in slow circles; the other sank into his hair, massaging the sensitive places behind his ear and down his neck.

On his stomach, one arm around her waist, Tash nestled closer and rested his head on her breast. Beneath him, her heart beat out a steady rhythm, serene like a lullaby. Her touch lingered after every stroke, warding off the ghosts taunting his selfishness, and her scent wafted around him with a hint of something he could not identify, no different than the other subtle changes he had noticed in her since their first nights.

If his feelings were even a fraction of what Mayr felt for Arieve... There was no doubt why Mayr loved her. Beautiful as she was to look upon, she was even more gorgeous inside. Her greatest gift was the tender companionship that wrapped around Tash warmer than any blanket.

No matter how much fear argued what he was doing was wrong, everything about it felt right. The three of them could share a connection beyond pleasure. In the effort to forge a family, they were bound to find the rest of each other.

Dreaming was safer than facing the day. If he opened his eyes, he would have to face the truth: Mayr was not in bed and things between them were still not right.

Tash swallowed a sigh and shifted his arms around Arieve. At some point, they had turned onto their sides, her back against his chest. She slept soundly in his embrace, one hand in his. There was no other weight, no other sounds.

The lack of relief suffocated him. Memories of the previous day slotted themselves between harsher recollections. He could still hear Mayr's anger.

We shouldn't be here like this, not without him. Tash silenced a groan. *If he's still in a mood, this'll start the second round of yesterday and we'll lose twice the ground we could've gained. Me turning to her without checking with him, not respecting that he loved her first... Blessed be Emeraliss, because I've got none of Her grace.*

However poor his choices, he could not stay in bed. He was to depart with Ress, Adren, and their escorts by mid-morning—assuming Mayr had bothered to assign guards. When Tash had spoken to Pellon before dinner, Pellon promised to discuss the details with Mayr. For all he knew, Mayr could have done nothing, determined to make his point.

With a sigh, Tash rolled onto his back and forced his eyes open. The faint light of dawn slipped through the slight part in the curtains, the blue and green windowpane glowing softly. Tempted to kiss Arieve's shoulder and steal a moment of comfort, Tash watched her sleep, telling himself he needed to leave her alone. Even without making love, he had taken advantage of her.

He turned onto his right side and stared at the wall, fingers fisted in his pillow. He had done enough damage. Doing anything more without Mayr's approval would drive a wider wedge between them. Mayr and Arieve deserved better. Tash needed to *do* better.

The tune of my life and I still haven't figured out all the right notes.

Tash raked his fingers through his hair. He needed to get up and be useful. *Morning prayers, clothes, and something that resembles breakfast, even if my stomach disagrees…*

His thoughts trailed, the list forgotten as he glimpsed his armoire.

Mayr.

Agony exploded in Tash's chest like a metal fist smashing his breastbone. Curled up against the doors of the armoire, Mayr huddled under the heaviest of Tash's discarded robes, his head resting on his raised knees. The robe hid most of Mayr's black clothing, his dark hair fanned out over his shoulders. In the pale light, he resembled a child desperate to avoid the cold.

A child that became a man the instant Mayr lifted his head and opened his eyes. His hesitant gaze met Tash's, shadowed with exhaustion.

Mayr's shoulders sagged. His glance plummeted.

Tash's heart went with it.

"Mayr," Tash whispered, reaching for him. Hand outstretched as far as it would go, Tash's joints pulled until they ached. His fingers trembled in the cold silence.

The robe fell away as Mayr pushed up and crept to the bed. At the edge, he sank to his knees and interlaced his warm fingers through Tash's, steadying them. Mayr kissed the back of Tash's hand. "Pellon will be here soon," he said quietly.

Relief forced out the breath Tash was holding. "Why aren't you in bed? How long…?"

Mayr smiled sadly. "Neither of you woke when I came in. I didn't want to disturb you. Figured if I stayed there, I couldn't possibly miss saying goodbye." He drew his hand down Tash's arm and bracer. "That and I didn't deserve to be here."

His forlorn tone unraveled the sickening knots in Tash's worry. "Come to bed," Tash said, tugging Mayr's hands. "That's the best send off I could ask for."

No other words were needed. Mayr stripped while Tash shuffled into the middle of the bed, nudging Arieve. Turned onto his side, Tash shivered as Mayr slipped into the bed behind him and curled his arm around Tash's waist.

Tender kisses trailed up his neck. "I'm sorry," Mayr murmured. "I shouldn't have said what I did, and never like that. What I said about Adren… I went too far." Rough morning stubble raked Tash's shoulder before Mayr settled his cheek on Tash's arm. "It wasn't fair and it wasn't your fault."

Peering over his shoulder, Tash caught Mayr's troubled glance. "You could have told me what was bothering you. I would've listened."

"That wouldn't have been fair, either," Mayr said. "*I* was the one who needed to listen. Instead, I hurled my anger at you and took your needs down with it. Then you were there after dinner and I could've made it up to you, but I let you walk away. I didn't even tell you why."

"I wanted to know if we were all right." Tash slid his hand over Mayr's and interlaced their fingers. "If you needed something I could give."

Mayr buried his face in Tash's hair, his sigh hot on Tash's nape. "I needed time, Halataldris." Tash stiffened, not sure he wanted to know the rest, but Mayr pulled him closer. "Not because I was angry. It was this damn meeting. I needed to finish preparing for it, and I couldn't do that with you there." He lavished Tash's spine with light kisses. "You're every distraction I'd die for and every excuse I couldn't afford. Council needs this information—*we* need it if we're going to make a difference."

Gently turning Tash's face towards his, Mayr rolled Tash against him. "I'll do anything to keep you safe. *Anything*. If I could take the Shar down myself, I would. I'll give Council whatever I can to protect you."

Whatever reply Tash wanted to give drowned in an ardent kiss. They parted only when shallow breaths became a struggle.

"I'm sorry," Mayr whispered. "Go to the Sanctum, and of course you'll take Pellon—him and eight other guards. I can't expect you to give up your life when you've fought to have one." His lips roved over Tash's temple. "We wouldn't have us if you weren't you. You survived, endured. Now you have to live. I don't have the right to steal that away, no matter how frustrated I am."

"It doesn't mean you don't hate what I do." Tash cringed, berating himself for arguing. "It doesn't mean you don't hate Ress and Adren or the priests."

"No, Halataldris. I don't hate them." Mayr cupped Tash's cheek. "I don't *trust* them to keep your safety in mind. I worry they'll sacrifice you if it's between their lives or yours." He let out a shaky breath. "Truth is, I'm uncomfortable with the things you do, putting yourself out there. We can't predict what'll happen, and I can't always be by your side. I'm afraid I won't be good enough, that you'll come to harm anyway. *These* are what I feel but not hate." His eyes shone with unshed tears. "Don't think for one moment that I hate *you*, because that's so far from the truth, it's not even possible."

Grief flitted over Mayr's face as he closed his eyes. Tash brushed a kiss over his eyelids, catching the rogue tear that clung to his lashes.

"I believe you," Tash whispered. "You needn't apologize anymore."

Arieve coughed, jolting Tash and Mayr. "Guess that means I can turn over now," she said hoarsely. "Right?"

"Dammit," Mayr muttered. "Sorry."

"It's fine." Arieve rolled over and propped up on one elbow, her eyes heavy with sleep. "You had things to discuss. Breaks my heart to see you so sad," she mumbled, sweeping Tash's hair over his shoulder.

"How much did you hear?" Mayr winced. "How much explanation do you want?"

"Most of it, but you don't need to explain. Not right now." Arieve reached over Tash and stroked Mayr's cheek. "You look like death kicked in your face and took your horse. Explanations can wait until breakfast, though I may have to apologize…" Her thumb hesitated on his lips.

Mayr kissed her fingertips. "For what?"

"Being here without you," she answered quietly. "Maybe I overstepped the boundaries, but I knew *something* was off. Neither of you should be left alone when you're upset. After I found Aeley and Pellon keeping you busy, I figured he needed me."

Tash held his breath and watched Mayr's expression down to the tiniest nuance, waiting for signs of a jealousy he prayed they could avoid.

Confusion crept across Mayr's face, followed by sadness. "If you're looking for permission, you don't need it. Neither of you," he said, prodding Tash's ribs. "Quit looking at me like I'm supposed to be angry. I don't need your apologies. You did nothing wrong."

With a languid kiss, Mayr claimed Tash's lips before offering Arieve the same. "I'm happy you're here, taking care of him." Mayr cupped the back of Arieve's head while she steadied herself on Tash's chest. "I messed up. I'm mad at myself for putting you in this position, for making you think you have to feel guilty. You don't have to be. We said we were in this together—I still mean it."

Mayr's attention swung towards Tash. "She's got such a good heart, one I want you to feel the way I do. This is the family I want—open, honest, loving. No hate or shame. Just this."

A slew of emotions threatened to do Tash in, tears and all. He choked on words that fell apart on his tongue. The best he could do was nod.

When Arieve hugged him and tucked her head beneath his chin, Tash almost lost what little composure he had left.

"I can do that," Tash whispered, his arms curled around Mayr and Arieve. How easily they worked, filling the voids in the silence with what their hearts knew. Like perfect pieces in a puzzle, they fit snugly together. No jagged edges, no frayed corners, no pieces missing in between. The frame of their relationship was solid and the picture clearer each day.

"Now I have to confess something," Mayr said. He groaned and dropped his face into his palm. "I did something on this side of messed up. Coye…"

Arieve lifted from Tash's chest, her leg slipping between both of his. "What about her?"

Mayr grimaced. "I ripped into her." His face reddened. "She came to break us up. I wasn't having it, so I made it clear… with an extra helping of you'll-get-my-foot-up-your-ass."

"Mayr!" Arieve sat up, elbows and knees jabbing Tash.

"I know!" Mayr grabbed her hand. "When I go ass-bastard, I go the whole way. I needed her to understand what we have is more than fooling around. That if she wanted in, she has to be just as serious."

Arieve eyed him warily. "Possessive much?"

"Not possessive," Mayr whispered. "Protective. They're not the same thing." Sorrow clouded his gaze as she withdrew her hand. "I don't want to own you, or Tash, or anyone. I don't even own myself, but I'll lose my mind just to keep you safe. Anything less hurts."

Lips pursed and arms folded, Arieve regarded Mayr for a long moment. The tension passed over Tash with an icy chill.

"Fine." Arieve sighed. "You win—for now." She scrambled off the bed and dressed quickly.

"Wait—" Mayr fumbled over Tash towards the end of the bed. "I'm sorry. I'll grovel if it helps."

"I'm sure it would. I've always loved the idea

of you on your knees, usually with something else involved..." Arieve snorted and yanked on her boots. "Relax. I'll be back." She combed her fingers through her tangled hair. "I'm going downstairs to make us some of the strongest steeped herbs I can find and see about helping Cook with breakfast. I won't have either of you starving." Fists on her hips, she scowled. "Then I need to check on Coye before she leaves for the lumberyard. I have to make sure she's all right. Kiss the bruises."

The moment she turned, Tash sat up. "Wait," he said, crawling down the bed to kneel at the edge. Once she accepted the hand he offered, he pulled her against him. Leaning into her, he pressed his lips to her ear. "Will you take care of him while I'm gone? Be here for him like you were for me? Please?"

Warmth spread across his chest where Arieve rested her flattened palms. A smile greeted him, followed by a kiss, her lips teasing his with reassurance. "Without a second thought."

She was gone the next moment, slipping into the hallway. The door closed quietly behind her.

"Lovely." Mayr huffed and fell back onto the bed. "Just call me the Steward of Really Awful Ways to Wake Up, outranked only by my other title, Councilman of *All* the Bad Ideas."

Tash straddled Mayr's thighs. "No matter the title, you're mine and hers. Ours."

"Yeah, I am."

"So you're not bothered by finding us together? You're truly not upset?"

"Bothered? A little, yeah," Mayr admitted, sitting up, "but not for the reasons you think." His hands glided down Tash's spine and settled in the small of his back. "I'm bothered because I wasted time sulking. I'm bothered because Arieve and I could've *both* been here, taking care of you. Instead, I was alone and selfish, freezing in my office with a headache gnawing holes in my head." Mayr toyed with the ends of Tash's hair, curling strands and releasing them. "But I'm not bothered by you being together. We wanted this. We *hoped* for this. The closeness, the trust—all of it. We didn't lay down a hundred rules for a reason, and I don't *need* a hundred rules to tell us what we can and can't have. She looked perfect lying in your arms," he murmured, his lips on Tash's, "and *you* looked perfect holding her."

Their kiss came and went like a summer breeze, its warmth lingering as Mayr drew back.

"It feels good, doesn't it, this thing with Arieve?" Mayr whispered, grasping Tash's hips. "I know Coye makes it complicated, but we're still in it together, still with each other? You'll still marry me even though I'm a complete jerk?"

The vulnerability in Mayr's eyes stole Tash's breath. From the waver in his voice to the faint tremble in his fingers, he was a stunning image of fearful uncertainty and wishful dream.

Tash cupped Mayr's face with both hands.

"You're so beautiful, but you don't have any idea how much, do you?" He pressed his forehead to Mayr's. "I'm not giving you up that easily."

They gazed at each other, their lips close but not meeting. A wealth of words descended on Tash, none of them finding their way to his voice. They were in the language of feeling rather than syllables, whispers gleaned from memory and passion. He knew what blossomed between Mayr and Arieve. More than that, he felt their connection. Being with them softened the sharp edges of life, as inviting as the thought of dancing beneath a clear blue sky, caught in a silken cascade of feathers and pink petals. The power in their generosity was almost addictive.

Yet sharing Mayr meant more than reveling in the enticement of love. To let Arieve in meant risking the loss of Mayr altogether.

Or finding the part of him he fears to reveal, bringing us even closer. Kissing Mayr as softly as he could, Tash willed his silence to say what words could not. He pressed closer, needing to follow the rise and fall of Mayr's chest with his. The kiss deepened, tongues entwined in a slow dance, hypnotic and seductive. Every moan sent waves through him, ripples of want that crested at the crown of his hardened cock.

Just as he loved Mayr, Tash treasured what their relationship with Arieve did to him. Imperfect and frightening as vulnerability and uncertainty were, they were perfect and captivating when Mayr surrendered to them, especially when he gave Tash his complete trust—

Mayr bit his neck, teeth scraping with intent.

A groan tore out of Tash as he rocked against Mayr's hips, rolling with his tempo. He tilted his head back and bared his throat. The next assault was wet and hot: Mayr's mouth took to the flesh above the hollow, sucking without mercy.

Desperate for more, Tash clasped both hands around Mayr's neck and quickened his rhythm. His throbbing cock slid along Mayr's, a reminder of everything he had missed the previous night. With Mayr and Arieve, he fell blissfully into the arms of need, craving the bond between touch and safety at their hands. Unlike the other times he had offered himself to the play among three people, he sensed a dark, delicious depth he wanted to experience. None of the other times had given him reason to want romantic attachment from more than one person at once, only sexual desire. Even then, he had wondered where love could factor into it—how it would feel to share that much without compromising himself or them.

The answers were making themselves known, even as Mayr's low moans against Tash's throat set his lust on fire. In giving Mayr and Arieve a chance, Tash had unleashed possibility.

His reward was a new side of Mayr, a new depth of love. From the perspective of three came a new meaning of what it meant to be selfless. There was more to it than feeling secure in a committed relationship: there was freedom, found only from giving in and giving over.

Until his doubts screamed, reminding him that nothing good lasted.

Grinding his teeth, his body aching for release, Tash gripped Mayr's flushed cock and dragged his fist up its length. Mayr moaned and writhed, clawing Tash's back as his warm pre-release flowed over Tash's fingers. They rocked hard, their bodies colliding with every tortuous twist of Tash's wrist.

This was how he needed Mayr, always: in his arms, rasping his need, and screaming no other name but Tash's. No matter what Mayr felt for Arieve, no matter how much Tash cared for her, he could not lose Mayr. He *would* not.

Still, insecurity taunted him. What about being soulbound? What if he lost Mayr like his other loves? What if he was not enough?

I've been fooled before. Tash yanked Mayr's head back by his hair and flicked his thumb over the tip of Mayr's cock. Mayr roared his approval, bucking into Tash.

Without warning, Mayr's mouth attacked his, tongue and lips finding whatever angle they could. Focused on their moans, Tash squeezed his eyes against the noise of excuses in his head. He rose into Mayr's fist, wishing he could escape the past as Mayr worked his cock in alternating bursts of hard and soft clutches.

He loved watching Mayr thrash and come when they were with Arieve. In truth, he loved seeing them together—their touches, tenderness, and the fluid movement of their bodies were enough to lead him to climax.

But soulbound. Soul… bound.

Tash came with a cry, come spattering across Mayr's chest and spilling over their hands. Body clenched tight, he ground against Mayr to wrench out the rest of his release, panting Mayr's name. He loosened his grip on Mayr only to clasp Mayr's sac and roll its heaviness in his palm.

Mayr's nails dug into Tash's shoulders as he embraced Tash, his cry muffled in Tash's neck. Liquid heat painted Tash's chest, streaming down his stomach to pool between his legs. Coated in Mayr's musky scent and his own, he wanted to believe they could stay together forever, bound by soul, sex, and surety.

On his life, he swore he had spent a dozen lives waiting for Mayr.

"You're the piece of me that's always been missing," Tash whispered. Slicking back Mayr's hair, he plundered Mayr's mouth for a kiss deep enough to lose himself. Would he never stop being terrified to make mistakes? Could they survive the relationship with Arieve?

"Like you're mine, always mine," Mayr muttered.

The metallic bite of a ring thrust Tash into his

right mind. As Mayr's marriage ring raked over the feathers tattooed into his back, reason chastised Tash for entertaining paranoia. Emotions could not bury the truth: their wedding would bind them, and Arieve would float through their oaths, drawing them to her while ensuring they never parted. Arieve was comfort. She was promise. They were in it together, wherever the end waited.

Mayr leaned his forehead against Tash's chin. "We need to get up. Washed. Dressed. Food."

"And Pellon."

"Nnnn." Mayr nipped Tash's throat. "That oaf will probably knock down the door any moment because he's cruel."

"And doing what you requested him to."

"I guess there's that," Mayr grumbled, shuffling out from under Tash to crawl off the bed.

Tash let him cross the room towards the washbowl, unable to look away while Mayr stretched his arms and back. Mayr's black and red tattoos flexed with every motion of his toned body, enhancing his nakedness and funneling Tash's gaze to his taut buttocks. Things seemed to be right between them again—except for the bit that was still wrong.

He's holding back.

Perhaps it was Tash's paranoia. Perhaps he was reading too far into nothing.

Or maybe he really is keeping secrets.

He still evaded Tash's questions about his health. There was also how quickly he had thrown Ress and Adren in Tash's face. Everything he had yelled came from somewhere. Trust was one thing; spiteful insults and fury were another. If this was the state of things before Tash visited the Sanctum, what would he find when he returned?

Chapter Eleven

The day-long journey to the Sanctum of the Mortal Divine had been tiring and cold, but the walk from the dining hall to the library the next morning was worse. The ardent glances of the Sanctum's priests almost burned holes through Tash.

Too much attention, none of which Adren wants or needs. Tash gritted his teeth behind his forced smile, his steps steady as he led Adren, Ress, Armamae, and their entourage of guards down the wide corridor. Sunlight streamed in from the high glass ceiling, catching on the silver and gold specks in the pristine white marble floors and walls. From the spiraled columns to the finely detailed glass statues of the Goddesses in each corner, everything glimmered as if built from the ethereal dust of stars. The vestments of the priests took on their own glow, a stilled sea of vibrant red and pure white.

Although the priests were calm and quiet, their unwavering gazes betrayed their awe as they backed towards the walls on Adren's approach. Each priest bowed their head and clasped their hands, frozen in place until Adren passed.

Awareness crept down Tash's spine, anticipation slithering between his bones. Familiarity awoke the guard he once was, his reflexes at the ready. He sensed the weight of the blades he used to carry, his fingers flexing as though ready to wield a knife. *Too many eyes, too many unspoken words. Ce should be in the shadows, not the light. We're the ones who watch from the darkness, not the other way around.*

On instinct, he slid his hand over Adren's back, the black leather of cir long coat cool on his palm. Adren jolted but continued walking down the middle of the corridor.

With Tash to cir right, Ress to cir left, and Armamae shuffling along behind, Adren appeared collected and in control, cir back rigid and chin raised. Dressed in black and channeling cir quieter, masculine air, Adren offered a starkness the Sanctum rarely encountered. Adren looked the part of a faction boss's child, arrogance and scrutiny presented in the polish of a high-collared shirt with stylish cuffs, shin-high boots and woven leather belt over tailored pants, and the generous hood pooled around cir neck beneath cir coiled red hair. On each finger, Adren wore a ring of sentimental value, and black paint ringed cir eyes. What softness Adren frequently displayed had been usurped, yielding to the part of cir that resembled cir father and brothers.

Adren's confidence was another matter: ce

was uncertain and nervous, no different than Tash or Ress.

At least we know who our blood families are, and our allies. Tash glanced over his shoulder to Pellon, who remained close behind him. *Adren doesn't have much to go on except for a growing list of enemies. I'm not even sure ce trusts me completely.*

Anxious like the first time they met, he feared he would make a mess of Adren's situation, ending in cir death or his. *We're walking a fine line between imprisonment and guarded freedom. I'll do everything to keep the one from becoming the other, but it doesn't change what we are. I can't afford to fail in any way, not when Mayr, Arieve, and I are trying so hard to...*

Panic coursed through him, sharp and biting. *If Adren ever went back to the Shar or turned me in... if our family got hurt, even just by accident...*

He would lose everything.

Tash swallowed hard and coughed to disguise his discomfort. Mayr would never forgive him if Adren or Ress betrayed them. He would leave Tash, fast and full of rage, and Arieve would stay by Mayr's side as Tash's replacement. Disgust would be thrown in his face, sending him back to where he began: alone, loathed, and lost.

Trying not to alert anyone as he breathed deep to calm his nerves, Tash fussed with his veil, pretending to struggle until it fell in an acceptable way. He would not be an emotional mess, not when the long-overdue meeting with Keeper

Felensa could change Adren's life for the better.

Think better. Bigger. Happier. Tash guided Adren around the corner of the long corridor and into another. At the end were the ornate bronze and gold doors to the library.

On command, his chaotic thoughts shifted into a cascade of relief. Contrary to Mayr's concerns, the ride to the Sanctum had been uneventful. The only assault came from the barrage of priests eager to meet Adren, an excitement Tash handled with all the patience he could muster. Snow and ice had slowed the carriage and six guards on horseback, but they arrived safely, albeit late. By that time, the evening meal and prayers had ended and Keeper Felensa was detained by business.

Regardless, the priests had received them graciously with a warm meal, friendly conversation, and soft beds. Adren had one of the largest quarters, a grand suite of white marble and ice-blue crystal with a sunken bath, a stately hearth beneath a jewel-encrusted mantel, and an elegant silver bed on a raised platform, surrounded by voluminous red silk curtains. It had taken three priestesses, two priests, and both Ress and Tash to convince Adren ce could accept the room. The argument ended once Ress pulled Adren into the room and locked the door.

Tash, Armamae, and Pellon had rooms of their own in the same hallway as Adren and Ress's suite. Their rooms were smaller and less majestic, lacking the crystal and metal decoration. Meant for the attendants and guards of the Goddess-touched, the rooms were centuries old, built when the Sanctum had entertained others like Adren. Since the war that sent the magical families into hiding, the Sanctum had few visitors. The rooms in which they stayed had not been occupied in several generations. Still, they were well-kept and welcoming, lit by white candles in stunning bronze lanterns and stocked with more blankets and pillows than Tash had ever desired to use.

The eight guards that accompanied them were split between four rooms. During the night, the guards had rotated watch in pairs, and Tash had listened to their quiet footfalls until dawn. Unable to sleep, he spent most of the night on the floor inside a circle of candles wearing nothing but a white silk sheet. With materials from the Sanctum priests, he had crafted two bracelets. The first took the longest, its earthy-coloured yarns plaited and entwined with gold embroidery. The second was of thick gold thread, polished red and brown wooden beads, and bronze toggles. Once they were finished, he had moved to the windows overlooking the snowy courtyard and written to Mayr.

Tash completed the letter by sunrise, filling it with the reassurance that he had arrived safely and in full health. More than that, the message had blossomed into a love letter that encompassed both his deepening affections for Mayr and his burgeoning adoration for Arieve. Words spilled over pages he had never intended to write. He had scribbled furiously, pouring images into prose, stretching emotions as far they would go. Every letter and space between gave life to sentiments he could not speak.

At dawn, he had wrapped the letter and bracelets in white canvas, then asked one of the Rese-level priests to deliver the package to Dahena. Although the package would arrive the day before Tash returned, the tokens were necessary, meant in love and apology for leaving so rashly. He was accustomed to doing things the instant they needed to be done, without negotiating with a partner. At one time, however, he had known how to be more than a lover. For half of his time with Inesta, he had considered what it was to be a husband. How it could feel. Her ultimatum had come shortly after he decided to ask her to marry him—a proposal that never made it from his lips. Instead, he had choked back the words and drunk them away.

Now he was considering every meaning of marriage and partnership. His duty was to Mayr as much as it was to the Temple, but the invisible boundary between them wavered. It was never clear, never set. He needed to be both husband and priest, to be everything to everyone. Yet the line constantly divided one from the other as though they were not connected. One day he would be forced to choose between them once again—a choice he would have to keep making.

"Hey," a deep voice said. Fingers gripped Tash's shoulder. "You sure we need to keep walking? I'm pretty sure the library's right here."

Jolted by the interruption, Tash blinked, surprised to find the open doorway to the library to his right instead of in front of him. The fanciful carvings of twisted birds at play and winding vines with bursts of tear-shaped petals stood out from the bronze and gold doors, exquisite in their craftsmanship. Clusters of red and white jewels formed the birds' eyes and the centres of the flowers.

How he could have passed it was a wonder. If his thoughts continued to be elsewhere, what else would he miss?

"Thanks, Pellon," Tash muttered. Clearing his throat, he turned and gave Pellon a strained smile. "And thank you for being here. I appreciate your help."

Pellon's grin complemented the laughter in his blue-green eyes, as intense as his red hair. Taller than the others in their group, Pellon was impossible to miss, his broad, muscular frame obvious under layers of dark, long-sleeved tunics, quilted brown leather vest, and dark brown long coat. The boyish honesty and mischief in his gaze only made him seem less menacing. "Aw, come on. I've always got your backs." He elbowed Tash gently, his voice lowered. "You don't have to keep thanking me. What's important to Mayr is important to me."

"Still, thank you."

"Quit it." Pellon waved both hands, his tongue sticking out playfully. "Go on, get leading. I'm just here to look pretty."

Adren snorted. "Like *that's* possible."

"What?" Pellon pouted. "You don't think I'm pretty?"

"I can't even…" Adren grunted and stared at Tash. "Can we just go? I'm about to say something I'm going to regret. Badly."

To the sound of Pellon's laughter, Tash led Adren through the doorway. They stopped in the middle of the antechamber, the rest of the group falling into place around them.

Adren turned slowly, cir jaw dropped. "This place really doesn't pull punches, does it?"

Tash smiled his agreement. Grandiose and bright like the rest of the library, the antechamber served as a reading room. Long boxed seats with plush, deep purple cushions and silver tassels were spread out along the white walls, beneath the silver-framed windows. Above, circular windows in the ceiling formed red and white spirals. Strands of crystals hung from the centre of the ceiling to the corners, connected by a glass orb speckled with crystalline dust, casting a multitude of colours through the room.

"Only the best for the descendants of the gods," Tash answered.

"Particularly when they come a-calling," Keeper Felensa's voice added from the second doorway. "Sparing nothing is only a portion of what we owe our benevolent Four."

Felensa entered the antechamber, his robes sweeping across the floor behind him. Slender and slightly taller than Tash, Felensa moved with grace and little sound. His long white hair fell to his hips and ended in tight curls, stark against his rich brown skin and red veil. Dressed in full vestments like Tash and Armamae, Felensa wore the regalia of a Keeper of the Sacred Assembly: a white gold circlet crafted from intricately twisted metal and bright red jewels, a thick choker of white and red diamonds, and a set of gold rings on both hands with matching bracers. Each finger bore an engraved ring and delicate gold chain that draped over his knuckles and attached to a ring on the back of his hand, forming a web. From that ring, a single chain connected to a gold bracer formed from three narrow cuffs, the bands joined by tiers of fine scales up Felensa's bony forearms.

"Greetings, and welcome to our humble Sanctum," Felensa said, stopping in front of Adren with a bow. "Brother Halataldris, Brother Armamae, welcome to the home of my heart." His grey-green gaze shone before he dipped his head towards Tash.

A cue, not merely a formality, Tash realized as Armamae tapped his elbow. *Those who escort the*

Goddess-touched announce them… and I'm already late on that.

Tash cleared his throat and offered Adren his hand, relieved ce accepted. He lifted Adren's hand towards Felensa. "Keeper, it is my greatest honour to introduce the Goddesses' divine child, Adren of Elsove Hillock, blood of a lineage yet to be named. Descendant of a magnanimous heart, ce is touched by the sacred."

Felensa bowed again, low and steady despite being twice Tash's age. "It is my honour to receive you, Descendant Adren. May our work please your Goddess Mother." He stood and clasped his hands. "In my humility, I must ask for your forgiveness twice-over. I intended to receive you last night but was called to a meeting I could not leave. I also failed to receive you properly this morning for the same reason." Tight lines pulled around his smile. "It appears my trip has snuck up on many, including the other Keepers." With a third, shorter bow, Felensa pressed his hand to his chest. "Please accept my sincerest gratitude for coming."

The antechamber fell silent, Felensa's expectant gaze never leaving Adren's.

When Tash squeezed cir hand, Adren's face reddened. "Yes, of course," ce said. "I don't see why you're…" Adren withdrew cir hand from Tash's. "It's fine, honest. I'm just here to talk. Or listen. Something."

"Whatever you wish, Descendant." Felensa

nodded to Tash, his glance flicking to Ress.

If Felensa was testing Tash's ability as Adren's guardian, Tash suspected he was already failing. "Keeper, I would also like to introduce Ress of Araveena Ford, blood of an Untouched lineage, through Sebina and Telumic. Ress is Adren's companion."

"Well met, Ress." Felensa bowed his head, though his gaze lingered on Ress.

Curious to know why he was transfixed, Tash followed his line of sight: the skull and fist of the Shar-denn tattoo on Ress's left forearm, visible in its entirety since Ress had rolled up his sleeves at breakfast.

Ress turned down his sleeves, saying nothing.

Felensa's attention broke. He peered over Tash's shoulder. "It's also a pleasure to see you again, Pellon Emeranth. I don't often speak with anyone of the Langalose-Emeranth lineage, save your fathers a month ago. Sorys and Wynn are well and send their regards."

Tash jerked back, his skin prickling. *Names? Formal lineage? Since when does he have those?* Even Ress's eyes widened before they narrowed in Pellon's direction.

Pellon cursed loudly.

"You can't possibly be Goddess-touched, too," Tash said.

A dark flush coloured Pellon's cheeks. He rubbed the back of his neck and rocked on his heels. "Worse: a regular boring aristocrat," he mumbled.

Murmurs sounded from the guards behind Pellon, and the hue of his embarrassment deepened, his gaze darting across the floor. "I'm the not-so-grand son of a Grand Family and so completely estranged in the most special of ways," Pellon said quietly. "*No one's* supposed to know." He glowered at Felensa then turned away in a rant of unfinished expletives.

"It seems Sorys wants it to be known. He asked me to address you as such the next time we met." Felensa frowned. "Although it sounds like I should apologize. I was under the impression it was on better terms."

Pellon's snort led to a strangled laugh. "I'm sure it was, for your part. Makes me wonder how he knew you'd met me."

Felensa grimaced. "My fault, I'm afraid. We were at a gathering. Sorys looks so much like you, I asked if you were related. When he realized I knew you, he was quick to offer conversation."

"I'm sure he was. He's real good at that, especially when he wants something." Pellon crossed his arms. "He can get *anyone* to talk, including those who should know better." The fury in his eyes raged, his glare sharp with intent. For all their sakes, his soured thoughts needed to be diverted.

"Pellon, look at me, no one else." Tash grasped Pellon's wrist and squeezed gently. "Does Mayr know? Aeley?"

Pellon blinked as the corners of his eyes softened. "Yeah," he said. "I was sent to train with Korre's guard. I was supposed to go back home and run their guard and secure assets." He stared at Tash's fingers around his arm. "I stayed with Korre instead. I've never wanted the plan my fathers have for me, not when I'm with people I care for. The best thing they *ever* did was ship me to Korre's doorstep. Other than that, I'm all but disowned." His weak smile looked lost on his sad face. "It's why I love spending time with Lira. She gets it."

A scowl blew his expression away. Pellon whirled around and jabbed his finger at the whispering guards, silencing them. "If *any* of you share this, I'll skewer and pickle your balls and tits, and Aeley will make sure you *never* work again. Understood?" He growled, deep and long. "*Under. Bloody. Stood*?"

The guards nodded and mumbled their agreement.

"*Now*," Pellon said, turning back to Tash, "can we stop picking on my sorry ass and get back to business? Sooner this happens, sooner I'll forget wanting to skin someone."

Or drink it off and forget completely, Tash wanted to add, noting the truth scrawled across Pellon's face. Never had he seen Pellon so defeated. He was usually cheerful, always in control, and rarely spoke with such hate.

Perhaps it was a carefully crafted illusion like

the image Tash put on for others.

"Allow me to introduce myself, Descendant Adren." Felensa cleared his throat, drawing all gazes back to him. "I am Felensa of Garsy Isle, one of four Keepers of the Sacred Assembly. Like the other Keepers, I manage the affairs of the Sacred Assembly and assist in the needs of the Temples of the Four. However, my main responsibility is this Sanctum and all matters pertaining to the Goddess-touched." He gestured to the antechamber with both hands. "Welcome to my home, where I spend half my time. When I'm not with my fellow priests, pestering government officials, or on the hunt for information, I am here. This is my life."

"But it's a library," Adren muttered, "and from what I hear, you don't have many Goddess-touched to deal with. I'm sorry it must be boring."

"Ah, but that's in the eye of the beholder, and you haven't seen everything." Felensa's bright smile made him appear years younger. "The Sanctum is more than a library: it's a sanctuary from the mundane, protected by old magic. It's filled with secrets and story and wonder. In the forty years I've been Keeper, I've lost myself countless times in these pages. I've dreamed among the artifacts, whisked away by legend and awe. I've stood ready to serve, waiting for someone who might need help." His hand trembled as he reached for Adren, hesitating before he tapped cir hand. "And here you are,

Descendant. In you, the Sanctum once again fulfills its purpose, offering knowledge and shelter. You may even find the rest of yourself."

"Maybe." Adren breathed out. "It can't be any less helpful than anything else. I don't have much to lose."

Ress pulled cir close, one arm around cir waist. "Hey, now," he murmured, kissing Adren's neck. "Keep working on positive thoughts, dear heart. Maybe this place will make an optimist out of you."

"For my benefit or yours?" Adren snickered and ruffled Ress's dark hair.

"How about both," Ress grumbled, smoothing his hair back. "You owe me for that. I can embarrass myself just fine, thanks."

Felensa chuckled. "Please, follow me."

Tash guided Adren forward, flanked by Pellon and the other guards. They entered the next room, the usual heaviness of their boots muted.

As sunny as the antechamber and even larger, the second room was filled with black wood tables and benches for research and writing. On each long table stood two crystal candelabrums, one near each end, holding eight white candles of various lengths. White leather cases sat at the centre of each table, containing multiple white quills and inkwells with various shades of red, black, green, and blue ink. Beside them, blank sheets of beige parchment lay in stacks under white stone paperweights. Spiraled book stands fashioned from white marble stood close to the windows, where frosted glass panes spanned from floor to ceiling on both sides of the room.

They strolled through the doorway at the end and stopped in a corridor. In front of them, the wall resembled a sheet of ice engraved with the image of the Goddesses. When viewed from the leftmost angle, the images glimmered with silver veins as though they bled metal. From the rightmost angle, the veins shimmered like liquid gold. Every angle in between yielded a different metallic shine, and a soft white glow emanated from below.

Tash swallowed back the memories that taunted him. The glass offered nothing as surreal as the truth, despite its magic. The artistry was sound, but it missed the mark on reality.

Still, all four deities were represented in painstaking detail. Emeraliss, Goddess of Love, stood barefoot in the middle, draped in layers of wispy gown and precious jewels. Her hair tumbled to her thighs in a cascade of untamed waves and tiny braids decorated with ribbons and beads. A majestic scepter rested in her right hand, while Halataldris, the Father of All Birds, perched on her left forearm. In a flourish of feathers, tail, and opened wings, Halataldris looked ready to take flight and sing. His longest and most complex song was reserved for when the entire world needed to be lulled into peace.

With the silkiness of every fallen feather, he dispersed hope. With the quietest warble, he could pull any heart from despair.

Beside Emeraliss was Laytia, the Goddess of Wisdom, in a sleeveless pleated gown. Her tiered skirt was embellished with cords of nuts and fruit, and its ghostly hem faded into the background in airy tatters. Strands of dew drops and tears hung from the lace sash around her waist, between chains of rings and tree-shaped charms. Laytia's knee-length hair was twisted and bound in four sections, secured with plaited twine like the bundles of stalks at harvest. She clutched a scepter in her left hand, while the six Eseldeer seeing stones were presented in her outstretched right hand. Believed to be the oldest stones in existence—shards snatched from the birth of the universe as its predecessor burst at the seams—the Eseldeer granted the power to see past, present, and future within the invisible webs that bound them. When set together to form the thread that connected all things, the Eseldeer became the spindle around which time wound. If one of the Eseldeer were lost, life, death, and the worlds in between would bleed into one another, blending into a new consciousness, chaotic and uncertain. Should all of the Eseldeer be lost or destroyed, the universe would unwind, unravel, and collapse into a new darkness without end.

To the left of Emeraliss stood Hastal, the Goddess of Protection, in armoured plates over a thick bodice and hide dress. Like her open cloak, the layered strips of her knee-length skirt were trimmed with jagged rows of teeth and sharpened claws. Over her short hair, Hastal wore an elaborate headpiece made from four curved antlers and dangling shards of bone with feathered edges. In her left hand stood a staff; in her right, She carried a shield, the ancient script on its face a match to that engraved on Hastal's breastplate. Named Talean the Unbreakable, the shield had been forged from time itself in the fires of a dozen suns and polished with the angry breaths of a thousand storms. Even when Talean had tumbled into the molten abyss at the centre of their world, striking every rock and scathing jewel on the way to the roiling core, Talean remained intact. It was only after Talean had drifted on the liquid earth to the Caves of the Found inside the southern mountains did Hastal find the shield gleamed like the stars, blinding all who dared attack.

Navara, Goddess of Justice, stood to the right of Laytia, dressed in a patchwork gown of chain mail and silk, finely threaded with veins and sinew. The petal-shaped scales and circular links in her girdle fell in tiers, tied around the middle with a belt woven from locks of hair taken from every living creature. A circlet of frozen embers adorned her forehead, the rest of the band lost in the tight curls of her short hair. While Navara gripped a staff in her right hand, her left hand held up the Onamarre, the balanced scales of fate. The plate on the left represented the weight of falsehood, paired with the plate of truth on the right. Crafted from a world's worth of lost souls, their essences captured in the voids of ethereal dust, the Onamarre balanced on a frame of bone fragments taken from the spines of the most just and the least kind. Every judgment was weighed on the backs of the cruelest spirits and the most selfless hearts, allowing fate to tip in whichever direction it desired.

With all the luck in the world, my fate tipped the right way. Tash looked away. He would always kneel to Emeraliss without hesitation, but Navara would never cease to frighten him.

"Welcome to the library proper," Felensa announced, his arms spread. He pointed to the closed gold doors on either side of the corridor. "To your right is the Library of Descent, where we keep ancestral records and everything to do with lineage, including documents of births, deaths, and marriages. Family banners, crests, shields, weapons, and tools. Each room in that library is dedicated to the descendants of one particular goddess." Felensa lowered his arms and turned left. "We'll start here, in the Library of Memory," he said, pushing open the doors and sweeping into the room.

Close to stepping on Felensa's heels, Adren followed and whistled low. "Then there was a *library*. My tutors would cry if they saw this."

Ress snorted a laugh as he hobbled inside. "All I see is *a lot* of tinder."

"*Ress*," Tash warned, following them over the threshold and across the room. The vastness of the library hit him like it always did, as if it were an endless world. The air smelled of leather and paper, thousands of years at the ready. Black marble shelves with blood-red veins spanned the room from end to end, all the way to the ceiling. On every shelf were stories about the Goddess-touched and the Goddesses that birthed them. There were volumes of every sort, from history and legend to myths and treatises, the world of an entire race contained between the pages. Tash had read less than a dozen volumes of the hundreds available.

"What?" Ress peered over his shoulder. "Relax. I'm not going to *do* anything. I'm not *that* mean."

"Which will help you immensely," Felensa said, claiming his spot beside a white marble table beneath one of the wide, circular windows. The table had nothing on it save the candelabrum in the centre, and there was ample space for their group to gather around it. The closest bookshelves were ten paces away on both sides. "Try to set fire to these and you'll roast in eternal flames."

Ress stopped short and leaned on his cane. "As in…?"

"Magic will not be your friend," Tash replied, sidling up to the side of the table. Armamae shuffled beside him, as silent as he had been at breakfast. Crossing his arms, Tash cast Ress a wry glance. "As in 'Ow, ow, ow, my soul is burning. Help me, save me. Oh, bollocks, I'm dead.'"

Adren and Pellon laughed in unison. Ress rolled his eyes and draped his arm around Adren's shoulders.

"Yes, something like that, though I've never tested it." Felensa smirked. "In any event, I suggest being kind to the books." He snickered and turned to Adren. "If it's all right by you, Descendant, I'll keep this first foray into your lineage on the lighter side. There are plenty of books we *could* go through, but I would prefer to narrow things down."

"Yeah, sure." Adren glimpsed at the shelves to cir left. "I wouldn't even know where to start."

"Why don't we start with the basics?" Felensa suggested. "I know you've told Brother Halataldris, but I'd like to hear the details myself in case something comes to mind."

"There's not much, except for the magic." Adren shrugged as ce pulled into cirself, hands jammed into cir coat pockets. "All my life I thought my parents were my parents. I've never known any different. I don't look like them, but I was told it didn't matter. It wasn't until I talked to Tash that suddenly it *did* matter. When he said everyone in my bloodline would have magic like me, it kind of busted things *wide* open."

"Sorry," Tash mumbled. He remembered their

first meeting well—its intensity and how the energy sparked in their first touches had nearly burned him. Adren had been afraid of everything and everyone. Calming Adren down and telling cir what ce was had sapped his strength, his body wearied by the touch of cir magic. That night, he had staggered around as if drunk and collapsed onto his bed before midnight, only to lie unconscious until noon the next day.

Adren protested with a strangled noise. "Stop apologizing. You told me what nobody else would."

"So you have no clues?" Felensa asked. "None?"

"Except for what I look like and what I can do." Adren folded cir arms. "My parents aren't exactly up for sharing."

"Something about prison," Ress muttered.

Felensa's head snapped to the side. "Prison? Your Goddess-touched family—?"

"No," Tash answered softly, "Adren's Shar-denn family. They raised cir."

"Shar-denn," Felensa repeated.

"Yeah, Father's a faction boss and all." Lips pursed, Adren glanced at Tash. "So he looks surprised. Mind sharing?"

Tash breathed out. To shield them all from unnecessary complications, he had kept particular details about Adren's life in the Shar-denn from Felensa. The fewer people who knew cir exact connection, the better. "I *may* have held back a little."

"I see. Playing guardian, indeed." Felensa's lips twisted. "Is there anything else?" He faced Ress, his gaze on Ress's arm. "Perhaps *your* affiliation, companion?"

Ress stepped back. "Me? I've got nothing to do with this."

"Except sharing my bed," Adren noted dryly.

"Fine, if that's how we're playing it." Ress leaned his cane against the table and folded his arms. "So you saw my tattoo, and yes, I *was* in the Shar. Not anymore. I'm under amnesty with Priestess Kee, so let's keep this friendly or you'll be hearing from her." He motioned to Adren. "That goes for both of us. Him, too," Ress added, flicking his finger towards Tash. "Kee's pretty fond of him."

"Yes, I'm aware. You needn't worry—I'm not accusing you." Felensa's brow furrowed. "It's just…"

"What?" Adren moved closer. "What's wrong?"

"Nothing's *wrong*, merely… odd," Felensa answered, rubbing his throat. "Then again, perhaps it's a matter of fate, because wouldn't *that* be the way of things." Lost in thought, he stared across the room and tapped the largest red diamond in his choker.

No one spoke. Tash's attention remained on Felensa's pinched, twisted expression.

"Keeper," Armamae said, "perhaps this would

be a good time to share your wisdom?"

Felensa blinked. "Yes, I suppose so. Wait here."

Quick on his feet, Felensa disappeared among the sea of shelves. On his return, he cradled a black leather-bound volume to his chest.

"I'm sorry if I fade in and out. It's not every day a resurrection happens," Felensa said, laying the thick book on the table. Green and black ribbons stuck out from between the pages, some of them faded while others were frayed. "It's funny you should have fallen into the roles you've assumed. Brother Halataldris and Ress; one is a guardian and the other a companion. Both protectors. Allies." Head tilted, Felensa laughed quietly. "Here you are, fulfilling the role of the Shar-denn and you don't even realize it."

The hairs on Tash's neck stood on end as an icy shudder coursed through him, rippling under his skin. It took everything he had not to run.

Felensa motioned to Ress's forearm. "Why did you get that mark?"

The puckered scar on Ress's right cheek flexed with his jaws. "Because it's the Shar's symbol."

"No, why did *you* get *that* particular mark?" Felensa flipped through the book, muttering under his breath. "Show me your wrist."

Annoyed, Ress jerked back his sleeve and thrust out his forearm. The closed-mouthed skull perched on a fist had once been whole. A scar now clove it in two, only one of his lasting injuries from the attack in Araveena Ford.

"Cover the fist," Felensa commanded. As Ress complied, Felensa turned the book around and pushed it forward. "Does it look familiar?"

The left page was covered in words scribbled with brown ink. At the centre of the right page...

Tash's memories plummeted into darkness. Hope crashed. A sickening chill blasted down his spine, numbing his limbs.

The Shar-denn skull stared up from the spotted brown parchment. The same skull they had been trained to fear, to serve, to bleed for. The same curves around the same sockets with the same menacing depth. The same cracks in the same jaw bones. The same ugly mouth with the same crooked teeth.

If not for the table edge digging into his thighs, Tash would have needed to sit. Ress and Adren appeared no less confused.

"The Shar-denn you know added the fist," Felensa said, "but the skull wasn't theirs. It belonged to the original Shar-denn—those chosen by the Four to protect the children of the divine. They were shields for the Goddess-touched, sacred in their own right. In the language of the gods, 'Shar-denn' means '*Blood guard*.'"

At the other end of the table, Pellon cursed softly.

"I don't... This doesn't make any..." Adren jammed the heels of cir palms against cir eyelids and shook cir head. "If that's true, how do you even *get* from one to the other? *How?*"

"Greed, anger, bitterness. People who wanted control over the High Council and saw a way to get it." Felensa smiled sadly. "The Volarsaa War was not kind to anyone. Although it was meant to liberate our nation from the larger whole of Arminloa, it shifted the lines of social imprisonment and split more than countries. Our republic gained autonomy from Arminloa's abuse and neglect, but at a high price. Kattal earned its name during the War, and in doing so, fragmented its people." He tapped the book. "The Goddess-touched families absorbed much of the harm it took to become a free nation. Once they realized the War Council and High Council had taken advantage of them, playing their magic and divine lineage against innocent people and hurting families in Arminloa, they made their mutual agreement to hide from the rest of the world."

"But where does the Shar-denn come in?" Ress asked. "If they were guards, they would've gone with their charges."

"Yes—if the world was perfect and terror not so effective." Felensa frowned. "The Goddess-touched left everyone behind, Shar-denn and priests included. They trusted no one. The guards were left with no one to protect. Those same guards rallied and demanded restoration from the High Council, but received nothing." His fingers traveled over the pages in thoughtful caress. "To make matters worse, the Goddess-touched had already started wiping memories, erasing their existence from the minds of the War Council and other parties important to Kattal. While the guards fought to get their charges back, the Goddess-touched put increasing distance between them and everyone else. The guards couldn't recover what people didn't remember."

Adren stared at cir palms, cir expression dark. "They never had a chance," ce mumbled, clenching cir hands and tucking them into the crooks of cir arms.

"No, they didn't," Felensa agreed. "To make amends, the Shar-denn tried to take justice with the sharp claws of revolution. Along the way, they made new friends: people with influence who claimed they believed in the cause." He sighed. "Those same people abused the plight of the guards, twisting it into a gross perversion that spread like wildfire. They never cared for the Goddess-touched, only power and monetary gain. They warped the name of the Shar-denn, focusing on violence and control instead of duty," Felensa said angrily, his age showing with his scowl. "By the time the true Shar-denn realized their mistake, the damage could not be reversed. Those who tried to fix it were killed for not playing along. Without help to right the wrongs, the Shar-denn's purpose withered into what we face now."

Tash licked his lips, willing his voice to work.

"Who else knows about this?"

"I'm one of the precious few," Felensa admitted. "The Shar-denn was meant to be a secret guard. They were trained to rush through shadows and move light on their feet. When they stood in the light, no one really knew who they were except their charges. The priests gave the Goddess-touched guidance, but the Shar-denn kept them alive."

Armamae nodded and rocked on his heels. "I see why you are fascinated with this, Keeper."

"Indeed. Halataldris and Ress in this Descendant's life, in this capacity… it's astounding." Felensa shook his head. "Maybe there's more than a pinch of fate involved—a different issue for another day, unfortunately. Since time is limited, perhaps we should resume the discussion of Descendant Adren's bloodline? While I haven't met a Goddess-touched in decades, I'm not at liberty to waste your time." He bowed low. "I apologize, Descendant. I will defer everything to your familial needs."

"All… right…?" Adren took a shaky breath. "Though I wouldn't mind talking about the other thing, honest."

"Perhaps I can answer some of your questions at dinner?" Felensa suggested. "If you're open to indulging my curiosity, I'd like to start on your lineage before I go away, since I'll be visiting certain repositories of knowledge that might lead us in the right direction. But once I come back, we can sit down and talk about everything for as long as you'd like, if you'd do us the honour?"

"I guess, if you say so," Adren said, though Tash recognized the disappointment in cir tone before ce cleared cir throat. "What else do you need?"

"We could spend time teasing apart the details of your magic," Felensa replied. "I'm told you experience a change in time. Manipulations, reversals, cessation. You also feel variations in temperature and discomfort?"

Adren's laugh was halfhearted. "To put it nicely."

"It's a good start," Felensa argued. "Temporal distortion usually runs in families, just as the sense of temperature does. They already narrow the list of possible bloodlines."

"What about my theory?" Tash asked, grimacing at the crack in his voice. Shock clung to his insides and pulled his skin taut. "About Adren's relation to Navara or Emeraliss, I mean. The reason why Adren can't kill, the fact we were Araveena at precisely the same time—I don't think that was coincidence."

Felensa appeared thoughtful. "A possibility, yes, but all options are possible, especially since the families marry into each other." With another quick smile, Felensa patted Tash's arm. "Patience, brother. These things take time, and sometimes they're not what they seem. If we work together, we'll find Descendant Adren's family. Perhaps you'll even learn enough to replace me one day. Who knows what the future will hold?"

If only Tash could have known. Maybe then the knots in his stomach would have stopped tying over each other.

After half a day of rummaging through dusty volumes and inhaling the scent of old, tattered bindings, Tash was more than ready for the break Felensa suggested. A headache destroyed his clarity, brought on by lack of sleep and too much reading, particularly after scripts that were difficult to decipher. Had someone thrown him a pillow, he would have curled up in the closest corner.

Even then a pillow is unnecessary. Tash shook his head at the thought. He could not shirk his duty, even if he *still* could not stomach the concept of being Shar-denn once more, despite leaving them behind—or how he would tell Mayr without setting off another verbal explosion.

There was also the matter of how he would get any sleep without considering every implication of every detail in every part of his life.

He was drowning in murky thoughts, a slew of half-formed ideas sinking in fully formed emotions. *I need to make sense of all this before I let anyone down. I have to sort... clear... deal... Wish we could go back to how everything used to be, but the wedding's so close, and we were safer before, and it used to be less complicated. Now there's too many people, too many things, and Mayr's keeping secrets, I'm still Shar, Arieve's too perfect for us, and I'm a selfish bastard for traipsing around like this, and... And. So much and.*

Fingers clasped Tash's shoulder. Jumping back, Tash all but tripped over Armamae.

"You look weary, Halataldris." Armamae gestured to the open door of the library. The rest of the group was already leaving to join the Sanctum's priests for a light meal. "Come, let us walk and ease some of your burdens."

Tash nodded and followed Armamae. Of all the priests in their temple, Armamae was the one he had naturally drifted towards as a mentor and confidant. More than three decades separated their ages, and Armamae was nothing like him in past, personality, or even in their servitude. Since his youth, Armamae had known the Temple was where he belonged, following in the steps of his aunts. He served all four goddesses equally and resembled a walking library with what he knew. Above all, Tash trusted Armamae's unflappable patience and understanding.

"Let me just..." Tash tapped Pellon's arm before they slipped out of the doorway together.

Pellon turned and flashed a smile. "Yes?"

"Brother Armamae and I would like to take a walk." Head tilted, Tash watched Pellon's face for hints of his mood. From what he could tell,

Pellon's anger was gone, replaced by his normal calm. "We'd also like to talk alone."

Pellon's gaze clouded with a darkness Tash recognized. "If by 'alone' you mean a two-guard team, then fine, walk to your heart's content. Inside, no outside," Pellon said, leaning against the doorframe. "I need to stay with Adren and Ress, but I promised Mayr I'd keep both eyes on you even if I have to yank them out of someone's skull." Both his chin and voice lowered. "And like I told him: my rainy-day intuition is tingling things these days it shouldn't be, so I'm hoping you'll humour me. Any hint of trouble, you holler and I'll come running."

Tash exhaled slowly, counting to five to keep from saying something he regretted. "Thank you," he said, avoiding the argument part of him yearned to start. He was not defenceless or unskilled, as illustrated in his weekly sparring matches with Mayr. Nor was he naïve: his own intuition had been on alert for twenty-three years without reprieve.

With a whistle, Pellon caught the attention of the guards in the corridor. "Stick and Stuck, you're staying with these two."

The two guards retreated and stopped in front of Pellon. Stick was the quietest and least intimidating of the two. Tall and pretty, he was slenderer than most of the other guards. Tash knew him better as Ralaern, unable to forget his ice-blue eyes and kind face softened by a youth that refused to let go, even in his late twenties. Ralaern's white-blond hair was short and styled neatly around his face and black collar. Three sets of the several small gold hoops in his ears peeked out from beneath his hair.

Beside him, Surie was a stark contrast: her shoulder-length brown hair framed her bright green-gold eyes, and she bore more muscle than Ralaern, packed into a short but sturdy frame. Her nickname, Stuck, had come from her tendency to get stuck to the people and causes she believed in, including Ralaern. The guards also called her Other Mother, respecting that she could put her boot up their ass to steer them away from trouble as swiftly as she tended their wounds after a fight.

"Keep our priests safe and don't get up in their face," Pellon instructed. "Let them breathe. If you don't, I *guarantee* this one bites." He pointed at Tash and laughed wickedly. "I've seen the teeth marks."

Surie laughed but quickly coughed it back. "Sorry. I mean, yes, will do."

Pellon rolled his eyes. "Stuck, don't make me haul out my digging skills. It's too cold to go hiding your dead body." Without looking back, he strolled through the hall to Ress and Adren.

"Pfft, like he would." Surie grinned, a sparkle in her eyes. "I've only heard a hundred variations of that in the past ten years. Funny, he *still* hides his goods from my reach."

"Punch a guy once," Ralaern muttered, "that's all it takes." He stepped away just as Surie attempted to smack his arm. "After you, Priest Tash, Priest Armamae."

Tash chuckled and brushed past both guards with Armamae. They followed the group ahead of them through the library suite, but where that group continued forward into the main corridor, Tash turned right.

True to Pellon's commands, Surie and Ralaern stayed back by more than a dozen paces. They spoke too low for Tash to make out words but loud enough to remind him they were there. From what Mayr had told him, they had endured eleven years of service with steadfast commitment. They were highly regarded by Aeley and had helped put Aeley's brother, Allon, in prison. If anyone should attack, he suspected Surie and Ralaern would counterattack even harder.

Likely the same reason Mayr had assigned them as escorts.

Sighing, Tash eyed the marble floor, his hands clasped before him. Long ago he had been the one assigned to guard others, but being the one guarded was infinitely more frustrating.

"There it is: that long trouble with the short patience," Armamae said, his shuffled steps matched to Tash's slowed pace.

"Is it that noticeable?"

"Certainly to me, though Sister Kee mentioned

the same, which is why I came along. I hoped you might share what weighs you down, away from things that could deter you."

"This place isn't any better," Tash mumbled, "not with all that back there. This visit was supposed to *help*. Now I'm going back confused by too much information I can't do anything *with*. This Shar-denn thing..." He snorted. "I thought I had it all figured out, but now... *now* it's not so simple. It's sneaky and convoluted and feels like fate jerking me around. I *stopped* being Shar, but suddenly I'm *still* Shar, just not the way I know it. I'm all twisted up and backwards again. It's like staring at my own back, wondering how I'm supposed to stab it."

Tash stopped and faced Armamae. "It's got me wondering if everything else is tangled up and false. What if Mayr and I aren't soulbound like our temple brethren think? Or what if we *are*, and it isn't what I think it is? What if our triad isn't what I believe? What if *none* of the good things in my life are *actually* what I've made them out to be?" Arms folded, Tash circled his boot heel into the floor. "What if I'm missing the important things because no one's telling me the truth? And what if *none* of this makes *any* sense because I'm rambling right now, spinning in circles and wondering why I'm so dizzy."

Armamae squeezed Tash's shoulders. "You are exhausted, Halataldris," he admonished gently. "You are also trying to make sense of too much at once. You need to rest, sleep, and stop over-thinking. Let yourself *feel* the answers. You are more in harmony with that." He frowned and drew away. "We need to address the underlying factors, however. Your relationship, the soulbound supposition—*these* are what have been bothering you?"

"Yes." The heat of embarrassment surged across Tash's face. "This is why Uldana priests aren't allowed romantic relationships. This is *exactly* why the rules are there, to stop this ridiculous, painful…" Tash dropped his forehead into his palm. "I'm becoming the example the Temple needs to keep enforcing the rules, because the boundaries… the *boundaries*."

"Which boundaries?"

"The ones that say I can't be a husband while I'm serving the Temple."

"The ones you have permission to ignore."

"Yes, and I *have* been ignoring them, but what if I'm abusing that permission?" Tash asked, hating how his voice cracked. "Am I even representing the priesthood and living our values anymore? Am I making a mockery of you and everyone else? How can Sister Kee even begin to look at me, let alone congratulate me on our family? She shouldn't, not as Overseer, not with all the rules." Miserable, he sucked in a painful breath. "The Sacred Assembly said I could *stay* with Mayr, but they said nothing about a family. What if I'm forced to choose again, between him and my priesthood? I need both," he whispered, "and they're intimately connected."

"A painful quandary, yes, but there is more bothering you," Armamae said.

Tash grimaced and resumed walking. "We're still working out how to share a life—how to be ourselves within a single entity. Now there's Arieve, and *her* relationship with Coye, and the child we want... It's frightening. We're giving things up just to have others." Rubbing his temples, Tash wished his headache would subside and offer his worries a break. "Sometimes it feels like another way to hurt each other. I'm scared we'll find ourselves at odds, too far to bridge the gap. We have to find balance, but we can't give up everything that makes us who we are—even if it means tearing each other apart."

Armamae nodded while he followed. "Permit me to offer some advice?"

"*Please.* I need someone else's voice in my head."

"You are young," Armamae stated, blunt but kind. "You are learning, and others are learning with you. Patience, time, and love: these will guide you, one day after another." He tapped Tash's elbow. "Dare I remind you that Emeraliss instructed you to follow your heart? In your heart, do you truly *want* to marry Mayr? Do you *want* to be a father?"

"Yes," Tash admitted, "and it goes beyond want. They feel like the air I breathe."

"Then that is what matters," Armamae said. "It all comes from the same place and ends with the same thing. Do not impose mortal restrictions on a divine match. Nor should you build a cage for happiness." He clasped Tash's shoulder. "The Sacred Assembly granted your priesthood knowing where your match with Mayr could lead. It is rare for a goddess to intervene in our Trials the way Emeraliss did for you, especially when it is obvious you are one of us. To honour Her wisdom, we agreed not to limit your freedom. She sees something in you, and we chose to protect that, not push you out."

Tash's shoulders sagged as he lowered his gaze to the floor. *There they are: all the things I should already know.* Once more, he felt like a child in Armamae's presence.

They turned down a short corridor before encountering another long, empty hall of gleaming marble and glass, the noise from their boots echoing quietly. Surie and Ralaern were silent, their presence a rough reminder of everything Tash was afraid to say—all the words he needed to put out into the world and see what they brought back.

"I don't think we're doing so well with it," Tash whispered finally.

Armamae peered around his veil, one grey brow arched. "With what?"

"The soulbound thing. We're violating it. That's why all this turmoil is busting up my gut."

"What makes you think that?"

"Because I gave Mayr my heart on the solemn premise that I wanted to be his everything... and I still want to be. I never want to stop, even if it kills me."

"However?"

The breath Tash sucked in rattled him. "I like having Arieve with us. So does Mayr." A shiver surged through him. "But it's against the soulbound ideals. Two souls entwined, beyond life, beyond death. If he and I *are* bound, we shouldn't be doing this. If we're bound, we're *bound*, just him and me. Not him, me, and someone forced into the middle."

Armamae pulled Tash to a stop, his hand tight around Tash's wrist. "You may believe you are bound, but you do not understand it," he said, mixed emotions tumbling across his face. "You know the word but not what it means."

Sympathy and sorrow flickered in Armamae's eyes. "You have the spirit of a priest, devout and sincere, but sometimes your inexperience works against you. You confuse expectation for truth, leading to unnecessary limitations," he reproved gently. "While I have never desired anyone as you do, nor craved romantic attachment or carnal relations, I *have* spent a lifetime studying all loves, including those people might scoff at or dismiss." Armamae's brow furrowed as he urged Tash to continue walking. "The belief in soulbound entanglement is one of these. Not everyone agrees it is a true thing, not even priests."

"With the way our sisters and brothers mention—"

"They tend to believe it on the good days, but the majority of people do not, even in our temple. Many people do not believe it exists. Most do not realize it *could*, particularly since not everyone feels it. Rarity does not breed clarity."

Disappointment stabbed at Tash, slicing his hope into tiny pieces. "Then why say it at all?"

"Because it is a beautiful thought, never having to be alone," Armamae answered softly. "The words of Emeraliss have suggested such a connection, albeit briefly in one particular tome, but there are no explanations. The concept of soulbound is more of a myth, a relic in the mysticism underlying our beliefs."

"So how does anyone...?"

"Know?" Armamae tapped Tash's forehead. "Feelings, words of the heart and soul... and some help from those aware of that particular tome of interest." He clasped his hands, steadying the constant quiver of his fingers. "No one knows how souls are bound or why, but a select few would theorize that in a past life, you or Mayr were once Goddess-touched and formed a bond. Or perhaps you were cursed by an enemy to spend the rest of your existence bound but never finding each other. There are plenty of theories, none of them proven or disproved."

"Helpful," Tash muttered.

Armamae's light laughter filled the hall. "It could be. There is debate there, also." Another smile brightened Armamae's pale green eyes. "As a concept, it is comforting, gentle, a notion that clutches the inspiration of romantics." His smile dimmed. "In practice, it can be a nightmare, unkind and damaging. It does not appear to hold true for all. Even if it did, we hear of so few such relationships, suggesting people may not be finding their partners. It hurts, being connected that deeply to someone but never finding them."

How well Tash recognized that hollow feeling, having been lost in such an emptiness for much of his life. Even with Inesta, Naliss, and Erithe, an invisible weight had pushed him to emotional depths he could not avoid. His love had never been enough, not even for him. There had always been sunken holes of loneliness in what he offered, but his heart had no means to fill the gaps. Until Mayr, he had accepted it as the way he was.

Once his soul found its voice and the words it had desperately needed to say, everything changed. The weight lifted and voids were filled. Love became enough. It had a name, a home.

"*There* is why it is often brushed aside," Armamae said, motioning to Tash's face. "Dreamy hope. It is less harmful to never believe in such a connection and focus on what *is* than believing and never finding it. It is better to take love where it presents itself, not wither over what may be missing."

The thought made Tash's heart ache. Without Mayr, he would be alone and convinced it was the best he could have.

"Because we want to be optimists for the greater good," Armamae continued, "many priests and scholars do not believe in soulbindings. A vast number of philosophers have spoken against it, saying it is something else: the mind playing tricks or justifying the need to fight—or not fight, as it may be. Others say it is an illusion to rationalize the depth of one's feelings or why they feel so easily. Many deny it because it is too painful to consider, especially for priests bound to their faith."

Tash felt the pointed look Armamae cast him. This was more than a spiritual lesson meant to make him a better priest: this was Armamae telling him to stop soiling what he had. He needed to punch out his doubts before they ruined everything.

"Soulbound relationships are also not limited to two people, just as having multiple partners is not limited to the Goddesses," Armamae said, stepping closer. "Whatever your perception of the ties, there are cases where three or more have found their counterparts tied together, each of their spirits uplifted by the others. There is a group of four living happily in the Eruelme tract. Groups of three are even more common." Head tilted, he regarded Tash with a pensive expression. "Even *within* those relationships, certain individuals feel a special pull while the others do not. It is not restricted to couples, nor does it dictate exclusivity. It simply *is*. What those lucky few do with it is completely up to them."

Armamae guided him into the hallway to their left. "Then again," he started, "soulbound does not mean romantic or sexual ties. I know of some who prefer the intimacy of friendship without such desires. I have even heard rumour of enemies being soulbound. It is more complicated than you think."

Tash twisted his marriage ring around his middle finger. He swore he heard Mayr's voice demand he relax and let his thoughts wander. "This is where you tell me the rules aren't set, just like the rules of love aren't clear."

A smile teased a glint from Armamae's eyes. "You are learning."

They drifted to the rectangular seats aligned against the wall beneath the windows. Vivid purple cushions provided thick padding on the dark red wood frames, the seats high enough to lean against rather than bend low. Ralaern and Surie leaned against the opposite wall, their glances everywhere but on Tash and Armamae.

"Soulbound is not a restriction." Armamae patted Tash's hand. "It will take more than a shared lover to destroy what you have."

"Meaning we should let it run its course."

"If your lover feeds off and *into* your coupling,

is it necessary to pull it apart? Perhaps if you were splitting yourselves in twine to appease one relationship or the other, maybe, but if you are creating a new entity then perhaps you should revel in it."

Revel. Tash sighed and dropped his head into his hands, his elbows balanced on his thighs. He wanted to enjoy the delight in Mayr's eyes when the three of them were together, to lose himself in Arieve's warm, lazy smiles while she lay sated in their arms. The best he could tell, they were not losing themselves or each other—they were finding a deeper connection.

"We are complex creatures," Armamae said, "complicated by emotions, physicality, and needs. Sometimes those needs can be met by a single person, but sometimes not, no matter how much you try. Perhaps your spirits have discovered a new and enlightened self, shared among hearts rather than split."

Or we're simply in it for sex.

Tash shook his head. He wanted to believe they were more than that. *Especially with how we were when I left. Arieve's so open, so kind, never forcing her way in. She's there, where she's needed, where she's wanted. The thought of letting her go…*

Groaning, he bounced the back of his head against the wall. If he was not falling in love with Arieve then he was in trouble, because he had no other word for what he felt. He needed to kiss Mayr *now* and admit everything. He needed to embrace Arieve and tell her what she meant, how wonderful she was.

"Is it truly that bad?" Armamae chuckled.

"You have no idea."

"So is the rebel that is love. It does not obey by imposed lines, no matter how clear we draw them." Ankles crossed, Armamae leaned back against the window frame. "Rules are what we create to make sense of love, to tame it, born from our need to sort complex matters and remove complication. Love is vast, ever-consuming, and so deep we *must* restrain it. Otherwise, it is a terrifying beast that threatens our struggle to keep control. Yet love does not surrender power. It keeps track when we do not."

Maybe this is our path, sharing our life with Arieve, Tash realized. *Maybe we're supposed to leave fear and everything else behind. What if we're all soulbound and don't know it?*

Of all the possibilities, he wanted their relationship to be more than lust. If he had dreamed up their love and believed in a hallucination…

Just the thought cracked his heart.

"Halataldris, look at me."

Tash obeyed, peering at Armamae from beneath the folds of his veil.

"You cannot read Emeraliss's mind, nor can you read the energy of love. You can only feel it and see the result. Everything else is instinct and raw emotion." Perched on the edge of his cushion,

Armamae tapped Tash's knuckles. "The why of your relationship is not important; taking care of one another *is*. For all the control we strive to harness, fear taunts us. It is love's darker twin. The key is to not let fear overcome love. Hiding in the shadows is no safer than dancing in the light."

Armamae stretched with a groan before he stood. "If you take anything from our discussion, it is this: your relationship is experiencing growing pains. Like Mayr, you are obstinate, loyal, and dutiful. Yet you are loving and protective, particularly towards each other." He offered his open hand to Tash. "The day will come when you will never doubt your connection again."

Nodding, Tash accepted Armamae's hand and stood. If only he could accept everything else with that much ease.

Chapter Twelve

Nothing gave Tash relief like the estate's foyer. Its familiarity was a welcome mercy after spending the day in a carriage on snow-covered roads, tucked beneath a blanket and fighting to stay awake.

Tash sighed and rubbed at the ache in his neck, pushing the front door closed behind him. They had left the Sanctum after breakfast but traveled slow with several stops to stretch and give the horses rest. For most of the trip, he had been cramped in a corner with Adren and Ress beside him, across from Pellon and Armamae. Midnight had come and gone by the time they reached Dahena. He wanted rest and warmth, both of them better with companions.

If he only knew where Mayr and Arieve were.

Tash frowned at the staircase. While Ress and Adren went off with Pellon, Tash had hurried into the house, hoping someone would greet him.

There was no one, not even the household steward, Haydin. The spacious foyer was well-lit by torches, but he stood alone at the double doors, dripping snow all over the floor.

Disappointment pooled in his chest, spreading

an uncomfortable heat through his gnawing aches. With another sigh, Tash unwound his red scarf, unbuckled his long coat, and unbuttoned his short coat. After hanging them on the wooden garment stand to the right of the entrance, he started for the stairs.

Doors slammed. Metal clinked. The click of heels accompanied voices as a blur of dark fabric burst into the hall left of the staircase. Arieve barreled up the corridor from the kitchen, running as if a vicious beast pursued her. Mayr followed, yanked along by Arieve, his hand in hers.

Tash barely saw her face as she threw herself at him. They crashed together, knocking him back several steps. Unable to balance on the slippery floor, Tash swerved and slammed his hand against the wall, then curled into Arieve to keep from falling and taking her with him. Pain seared his cold fingers as they burned with tingling numbness.

"You're home!" Arieve held tight around his waist, drawing him forward. "Goddesses, I missed you."

He returned her embrace, burying his face in her warmth. She smelled of soap and a touch of perfume, combined with her own scent that he wanted to lick and taste…

Fingers crept between Tash's cheek and Arieve, calloused and doused in the scent of metal and leather. Mayr's touch slipped down his jaw, lifting his chin.

In a breath, Mayr's lips were on his. Soft and seeking, Mayr took the kiss deeper, staking his claim with undeniable seriousness. Even as Tash's tongue sought his, he refused to play. Mayr pressed harder, overcoming Tash's advances for anything else.

Tash's emotions melted around his insides. Had he pulled away, he was certain he would find the rest of himself in a viscous puddle on the floor.

In his arms, Arieve shifted to nuzzle his neck, her hands offering a caress he sorely needed as they traveled over his back, keeping him close. When Mayr's mouth left his, Tash's desperation screamed to continue tasting and teasing. His gaze followed Mayr's swollen lips, joined by his fingertips. He needed to touch, worship…

Arieve nipped his throat and giggled, shattering what remained of his thoughts. As she stood on her toes, Tash tilted her chin up, meeting her partway with a kiss. A quiet fire greeted him, her sweet sensuality a perfect complement to the intensity of Mayr's passion. The vibrant memories of both tangled together in an exquisite dance.

She parted from him slowly. "Welcome home," Arieve said, her voice husky. "We've been waiting."

"I apologize. We took extra time to make it back safely." Tash drew the back of his hand down her cheek. He could get used to having someone wait for him at home, wanting him there. The only thing more breathtaking was having *two* someones.

Arieve squeezed him in another hug. "You made it, that's all that matters."

"Absolutely." Mayr wrapped his arm around Tash's back and pressed his forehead to Tash's temple. "Alive. Safe," he whispered.

Turning into Mayr's touch, chasing Mayr's mouth with his, Tash moaned at the effect his homecoming had on everything below his waist. Sleep could wait. He needed to make up for lost time.

Before he could say as much, Arieve moved away. "Thank you for the gift. It's *gorgeous*." She raised her left arm, the bracelet of beads tied around her wrist. "I've been wearing it ever since that nice priest delivered it last night." Arieve laughed and bounced on her toes, leaning into Tash. "I can't stop playing with it. It's been *such* a long day."

Her laughter stopped short, cut off by her sobered expression. Arieve's eyes glistened with unshed tears. "It's beautiful. Perfect. So is Mayr's, even if he's not wearing it."

"Hey!" Mayr glowered at Arieve. "Stop getting me into trouble." He jerked up his left sleeve. "Especially," he grumbled while he loosened the laces of his bracer, "when it isn't true." After digging under his bracer, he shoved the black leather upwards, revealing the swirled red-brown roots of the tree tattooed into his forearm. The plaited yarn bracelet slid down his wrist, its various green and brown hues rich on his tan skin.

Just seeing the bracelets was enough to drown Tash's worries. A piece of him was on them, close to their hands, small enough to carry in their palm.

Arieve slipped her arms around Mayr's waist. "I'm sorry. You said you put it somewhere safe, and I thought you meant something else. Forgive me?"

"I suppose." Mayr sighed dramatically and wrapped his other arm around her shoulders. "I'll let you know when I finally grow a spine where you're concerned."

"Last I checked," Arieve murmured, drawing her hand down Mayr's back, "it was right here and—" Mayr yelped and jolted from whatever her fingers did. "—perfectly functioning."

"Dearest, you are *cruel*." Mayr pressed closer to Tash.

"No, cruel would be finding all the ways to keep you from coming till your balls bust." The mischief in Arieve's deep laugh was difficult to miss. "But we're getting off plan, and we're making our poor boy stand here." Arieve clasped Tash's hand. "We need to feed you. I put aside a plate, all the fixings, just the way you like it. Although wait..." She cupped his cheek and frowned. "You're freezing. You need a hot drink

and rest and to warm up. Let's get you—"
Tugging his hand, she stepped towards the
kitchen.

Tash resisted and pulled her into him,
laughing softly. "Honestly? I just want to lie
down and stretch out, sweet one." He toyed with
the thickest of the dark curls around her face.
"The Sanctum sent us home with enough things
to feed us for two days. Right now, I'd like to
enjoy being home."

"We can do something about that," Mayr said.

There was no hesitation, only Mayr's grip on
Tash's hand as he led Tash and Arieve upstairs,
and the fervent glances between Arieve and Mayr
spurred Tash to match their pace all the way to
the bedroom. He saw the door open and close,
but his head spun as determined hands dragged
him into the fire-lit room. Needy kisses attacked
him just as quickly.

"I missed you," Mayr muttered before nipping
his way down Tash's throat, one hand around the
back of Tash's neck. He sucked at the hollow of
Tash's throat, his other hand heavy on Tash's hip.

Tash trembled and glided one hand over
Mayr's thick braid, frustrated he could not rake
his fingers through Mayr's hair. With a yank,
Tash freed the tie keeping the braid together and
hummed his satisfaction as the plaits loosened
into ebony waves beneath his touch. Sinking his
fingers into the cascade was like stroking silk
doused in the scent of spiced honey fruit.

They groaned together as Tash traced the curves of Mayr's body with both hands, down Mayr's spine, over the small of his back, and around his hips. When Tash's thumbs brushed Mayr's hardened cock, Mayr cursed and claimed Tash's mouth with his, demanding more than a kiss.

"We both missed you," Arieve said, turning Tash towards her, one hand on his elbow. The next moment, her lips were on his, both of her hands around his neck.

Tash surrendered completely. Hesitations aside, he unlaced her bodice, the ribbons easily undone. Behind him, Mayr's body pressed to his, a hint of a caress while he removed Tash's veil before a nudge at his ankle warned of Mayr's intentions. Tash complied, lifting one foot then the other to allow Mayr to tear off his boots and stockings. Where they landed, he could not tell, though he heard them as he shoved Arieve's bodice down her arms and to the floor. More dull thuds followed, accompanied by the clink of belt buckles.

Mayr's touch was gone one moment and back the next, a quick caress before he slid both hands around Arieve's waist and kissed a path up her jaw. Without waiting for Tash and Arieve to part, Mayr's lips met the corners of theirs and eased into their kiss, the tip of his tongue teasing theirs.

How easy it had become, finding the angles that allowed them to share a moment as equals, entwined as three, not simply two.

There would be more time for that later, Tash decided, withdrawing to allow Mayr to finish the kiss with Arieve as he started on Mayr's pants, untying them with Arieve's assistance. Together, they stripped Mayr of vest, long-sleeved shirt, and lightweight shirt, stealing kisses between efforts.

Before they could remove Mayr's pants, Mayr grinned and sank to his knees. Expecting Mayr's attention to be on Arieve, Tash sucked on her bottom lip, resuming the kiss he had abandoned. Firm hands slid up Tash's legs, urging his robes upwards. Lips followed the path, up the inside of his calves and over his thighs, coaxing Tash to moan and shudder. Mayr worked the tie of Tash's pants, slow as he tugged the fabric down.

In an instant, the pants pooled around Tash's ankles and Mayr's mouth was around his cock, taking his length to the hilt. Tash choked on a cry, hand fisted in Mayr's hair. He clawed Arieve's back with his other hand, in need of an anchor to keep from coming. She laughed and kissed him harder, swallowing every gasp.

Caught in an aching wave of want, Tash rushed to rid Arieve of her dress and under dress, only to toss them aside and growl at the effort. Completely bare, she pressed against his side, her fingers interlaced with his where they cupped Mayr's neck. Mayr played Tash's cock with every trick, his teeth, tongue, lips, and fingers working in perfect strategy. Release was near, rattling Tash's insides, ready to burst.

Relief was denied. Mayr pulled away with a cruel smile and stood, condemning Tash to shiver and hiss. While Mayr stripped Tash of his robes, Arieve kneeled to rid them both of their pants. More than once she teased their readied cocks, swirling her tongue around their leaking tips.

By the time all of them were naked, Tash wanted to defy nature and pound into them both at the same time, splitting himself in two if that was what it took. As Mayr's lips crushed his once more, his salty essence on Mayr's tongue, Tash urged him as deep as they could go without wrenching their jaws apart.

A tug on his left bracer stopped him. Tash squeezed his eyes shut against the sensation of Arieve's fingers on the laces. He clenched her wrist, halting her. Never had she forced the issue of why he wore his bracers, nor had she demanded their removal. Her sudden focus on them baffled him.

It also made him wonder *if.*

If he took them off, would she curl her lip and walk away? Would she laugh or shame him or consider him a lesser person? If he trusted her with that truth, would she still want him? Or would she stop caring because they proved he was a mess?

If he were honest, would she be kind?

I don't want to keep hiding. I want to trust her. I

want… Tash opened his eyes to find Mayr's gaze on him, their lips still pressed together. He wanted what he had with Mayr: full disclosure, even if it took time. Mayr already had that with Arieve. *If he trusts her that much…*

Maybe it was time to try.

She's seen the rest of the damage, and she's still here. All she's said is…

He could tell her when he was ready.

"I don't need to know, not until you want me to," she had said.

Maybe he wanted her to, in little bits at a time. *For now…*

Tash released Arieve's wrist. Diving into another kiss with Mayr, Tash turned his forearm upwards and stroked Arieve's hand. Distracted, he barely felt the laces loosen.

He did feel her ease the bracer off. With a muted whimper, he broke from Mayr to watch Arieve's face. She held his hand while she noted the marks: a series of dark horizontal and diagonal lines around his forearm, a mix of shallow and deep scars that started from his wrist and ended past his elbow. His left arm bore four thick scars more pronounced than all the others because of their depth. There was one puckered line for each love he had lost. The longest, deepest scar was from the day he told Mayr they could never be together.

His right arm fared no better except for the faint fourth scar. After the damage to his left arm, severing things that never should have been touched, he had been unable to finish the last line. The knife had slipped from his fingers faster than he could regain his grip. That night, misery made it clear what he had with Mayr differed from his love for Inesta, Naliss, and Erithe. If he had continued harming himself, he would have caused worse damage than the persistent numbness in his left arm.

"Hey." Mayr turned Tash's face to his and pawed his cheek. "Where did you go?" He leaned his forehead against Tash's. "We're here, Halataldris. We're good." Subtle panic flashed across his face as he glanced at Arieve. "Maybe don't do that," he said, clutching her hand. "A different time, when he's—"

"It's fine." Tash grasped their hands. "I just needed a moment. Please, don't…"

He gnawed on patience while Arieve's caress flitted over the damaged skin as though it were delicate parchment.

"When you're ready, you tell me," Arieve said, kissing his wrist. "For now, we just touch. Good touch. Words can wait. Sometimes they need a little help, and that's all right, too."

Had Tash swallowed back his relief, he would have missed the words *I love you* dancing over the tip of his tongue.

None of them were ready for that. Not yet.

Instead, he helped Arieve remove his second bracer and surrendered. The passion in her kiss seared his fears before she pulled him flush against her. As Mayr wrapped around him from behind, he was at perfect balance between them. What battles raged inside him reached ceasefire. He was exactly where he needed to be and wanted nothing more…

Until Arieve guided him back to the bed and pushed him onto the end of the mattress. Once she fell to her knees and sucked down his cock, the twisted claws of need returned with a vengeance, ready to shred balance into delirious joy.

Watching her only made matters worse. Settled between his knees, she slid one hand between her legs and moaned. Vibrations rippled through him while she rocked on her fingers.

The sound of her pleasing herself nearly undid him. He had always loved the wet, primal sounds of sex. Wet meant an essence he could taste. Touch. He craved both.

Tash fell back, groaning as Mayr caught him.

"Yeah, I know you like that," Mayr whispered. On his knees behind Tash, Mayr shifted on the bed and pressed his chest to Tash's back. "I know what else you like." Slipping his arms beneath Tash's, Mayr bent his arms up and back to rake his fingers through Tash's hair. He gripped Tash close to the scalp and forced his head back, pinning Tash against him. "You two together, I want to see that." Mayr pushed Tash's head back further, craning Tash's neck and straining the muscles in his shoulders. "Show me she's yours."

Between the pain from Mayr's fists and the pleasure of Arieve opening his legs wide, Tash was split down the middle, one cry from begging for someone to take him. Either. Both. Any way they wanted.

Arieve laughed as she glided her fingers over the juncture between his hips and legs, down the inside of his thighs. Her lips crept up his stomach and chest, his scent accompanying her mouth to his exposed neck. Her own musky scent wafted around him as she tweaked his nipple.

Torture. This is torture.

A torment he would endure gladly.

"You want me?" Arieve raked her nail down his throat.

Tash shuddered and nodded as much as Mayr's grip allowed.

"You've been riding in a carriage all day," she murmured. Her tongue passed over his collarbone, slow, hot, and full of promise. "Perhaps I should ride you?"

"Any...way..." Tash whispered, struggling with each syllable. Words were pointless. They had him pushed to an edge he wanted help jumping over, not talking his way through.

Actions were a different story. He managed those, fast and effortless. In moments, he was lying on his back, Arieve's moist heat sinking down on his cock. She was a perfect image of raw beauty, settled upright with her palms flat on his stomach, the bounty of her breasts cradled in both his hands and Mayr's. With Mayr on his knees behind her, they touched her together, through the valley between her breasts to her stomach and further to the damp curls between her legs. Their reward was a series of moans in time with the rise and fall of her hips, pressing Tash deeper into the bed.

When Mayr drew away, Tash cursed the lack until he noticed a vial in Mayr's hands. The vial hit the blankets before Mayr's oil-coated fingers disappeared behind Arieve. Her insides clenched tight around Tash. She rose into Mayr's touch then let out a long breath and rolled her hips. Tash felt the flicker of Mayr's fingers between them, a rough caress that teased his cock without any measure of mercy. He bit back his cries, battling his release despite how much he had to come.

Between them, Arieve panted and whined. By the time Tash realized Mayr's intent, Mayr had eased Arieve forward and down by the shoulder. Arieve smiled and leaned onto Tash, lifting slightly.

As Mayr breached her second entrance, Arieve's breath hitched. She choked on a sob and broke into a string of curses between staggered mewls. While Mayr pushed deeper, she squirmed and arched into Tash, scraping his chest with her nails.

Tash gritted his teeth, partially against the

shredding of his skin, but mostly to counteract the extra pressure. He felt Mayr as though they shared the same space inside her. Arieve's body contracted and pushed hard, fighting to stretch and accommodate and *do* something. The tension was an even sweeter torture than earlier.

"I didn't think you were ready to do this *yet*—" Tash cursed loudly as Mayr slid in further, almost to his full length. He snapped his head back, every part of him taut as his back bowed from the intensity.

Mayr's rumble of a laugh was cut off by a moan. He guided Arieve back into him, both hands on her hips. "Nearly there," Mayr said softly, caressing her shoulder. "Bear with us, love. Just a little..." At the same time he gave a final push, Tash joined him.

Arieve cried and whined, rocking and writhing as Mayr and Tash found a gentle rhythm. She ground against them then froze. One arm wrapped around Mayr's neck, she clawed Tash's thigh and exhaled deeply. "Good now," she whispered.

Mayr's response was a tender kiss, his flattened hand over her stomach. She laced their fingers together and held tight.

"We practiced a bit while you were away," Mayr said, his attention back on Tash. A mischievous grin spread across his lips, and he pulled out slightly. "After we got your gifts and really touching letter—" Mayr gave a gentle thrust, making Arieve cry out and buck forward until she hit Tash's chest. "—we thought we'd give you a gift of our own."

"Because…" Arieve panted as she pushed up and back. "We missed you."

Moans overcame words as they moved together, steady even when they quickened their pace, Arieve accepting them with growing ease. When Mayr withdrew almost the whole way and slid back into her even harder than before, Arieve fell forward again. Tash caught her face in his hands.

"This feels… so good…" Arieve rasped, straining upwards to kiss Tash. She ground against him, her clit a whisper of needy touch.

Touching her was irresistible. Not touching her was ludicrous.

Sorry… and so very not sorry. Tash slid his fingers between Arieve's swollen folds and spread her wide.

Arieve screamed, clawing his chest hard enough to draw blood. At the same time, Mayr thrust into her.

Heat exploded around Tash, seeping with wetness. Arieve came once, then again, fierce and tearful. From the desperation on Mayr's face and his trembling, he was close to release.

I can't… hold… Not anymore—

His world crashed into a dizzy, shrieking existence of blacks and whites and spinning stars. Tash jerked Arieve against him and wrapped his arms around her head, covering her ears as he hollered his release.

Soon after, Mayr came, panting and cursing. Arieve complained Tash was suffocating her. Everything else was a blur, woven together and spiraled out, a mess of noise and colour punched out by gaps of silence. They were done for.

All three collapsed, Arieve sprawled on Tash with Mayr draped over Arieve's back.

Yeah, it's definitely time for bed. Tash closed his eyes. His thoughts crafted pretty pictures, shifting colours back into place. Hands and arms and flouncing dresses waved in the breeze, decorated with silk ribbons and beaded strands of jewels in every imaginable hue. The noise yielded to silence, drifting into the darkness. Tranquil and beautiful, he floated on a sea of stars, birds singing on the horizon…

"Tash?" an airy voice called. "Wake up, love."

Tash groaned in protest and opened one eye. Arieve stood beside the bed, leaning over him.

"There you are." Arieve brushed hair from his cheek. "We're going to finish washing and we'll join you. You seem to be having such a lovely dream."

Tash frowned as she walked away. Dream? Had he fallen asleep? He had closed his eyes for only a moment…

A moment long enough to clean him of come and blood, he realized. He lay under the blankets, more relaxed than he had been for days.

Tash closed his eyes again and listened to Mayr and Arieve talk quietly. Once they crawled into bed, they fell around him. Mayr and his calming warmth curved into Tash from behind, one arm around Tash's waist. Arieve lay in Tash's arms, facing him, her playful energy bundled up inside. Their legs and feet shifted over one another, finding a strange but comfortable position.

With a sigh, Tash sank into their embrace. Ignoring everything he wanted to say, he surrendered to bliss.

Waking to the painful sounds of someone retching was far from what Tash had hoped for the next morning.

He forced his eyes open, groggily meeting the soft light of day. Across the room, Arieve was on her knees, bent over the same bucket Mayr used for his own bouts of illness. Mayr hovered beside her with words of comfort, holding her hair away from her face.

Not much for me to do. He's already got it handled. Tash rolled onto his back, his thoughts scrambled. He remembered falling asleep, but nothing in the way of dreams. Hopeful that Arieve and Mayr would return, he remained still and watched them.

"Sorry," Arieve said hoarsely. "I think it's over

now." She stood and swayed into Mayr's arms. "Ugh, I swear I'm not usually this much work."

"It's *fine*, promise," Mayr assured her. He retrieved a towel from the table and wet it in the washbowl. After wiping her hands and face, he dabbed her lips. "You're not work, not even a little. You're perfect."

Mayr threw the towel onto the table and grabbed Arieve's hand. They crossed the room to the black chairs near the window, blue-green light playing over their nakedness. Before she could speak, Mayr snatched up the grey wool blanket from one chair and wrapped it around her. Under the folds of heavy fabric, Arieve stood covered from shoulder to floor, snorting back a laugh.

When Mayr swept her up into his arms and fell into the furthest chair, she squeaked and struggled to get free. "Mayr!"

"You're fine. See?" Mayr leaned back and settled her in his lap, draping her legs over the arm of the chair. Tash waited for Mayr to laugh and joke.

There were no jokes. Mayr was solemn and quiet, his gaze on the floor. He cradled Arieve in both arms and rocked gently. Without further complaint, she curled into him, her head on his shoulder, one of her freed hands around his neck. They were a heartwarming image of trust and familiarity.

We're good together, all three of us. With him, I

feel complete, but with both of them… It transcends words. It's like tasting divinity.

As though Tash had spoken the words, Arieve's glance caught his. She cast him a weak smile and a small wave. Tash returned her smile and waved back.

"Sorry." Arieve cleared her throat. "Not the best thing to wake up to. I tried to fight it, but it all just… ugh."

"Stop apologizing." Mayr kissed her forehead. "We'll take care of you. We're good at it, I think. Sort of. Maybe?"

Tash slipped out of the bed and hurried across the cold floor to join them. "He's right. You are no burden," he insisted, pressing the back of his hand to her lukewarm forehead. Whatever ailed her was not due to fever. "You grace our lives, gentle one." His lips replaced his hand on her forehead, trailing light kisses along her hairline. "You're nothing less than wonderful."

"And you're much too agreeable in the morning," Arieve mumbled as he kneeled. She clasped his hand and turned his arm upwards. Her calloused fingertips traveled up his forearm, tracing and skipping over scars.

Tash held his breath. No matter what she had said, what she truly thought…

His heart raced while she kissed a path over his wrist, never once stumbling across the damage.

"There are things going around," Arieve said.

"I'm pretty sure I've caught one of them." She tucked Tash's hand into her chest, then led Mayr's hand to his and laced her fingers with theirs. "I feel achy and disgusting—and not from last night. *That* was amazing. This is probably whatever Cook had. Or what you've had," she added, glancing at Mayr.

Mayr's expression darkened. "No, I'm pretty sure it's not what I have. If it's contagious, we have bigger problems."

Awkward silence fell between them. Once more, Mayr kept secrets, too stubborn to let Tash in.

Not that I'm one to talk, Tash realized soberly. *I'm doing the same thing. I want to tell them both what I learned about the Shar and how I feel, but I can't. I don't want to ruin this.*

"It's not a surprise," Arieve said, breaking the tension. "I get sick every winter. This is the same old thing." She sighed and pushed out of Mayr's arms. His grasp followed her, fumbling to pull her back. "I'm going to go home and get a long bath, then start up a cauldron of broth and drown in steeped *everything*." Paused next to Tash, she held the blanket around her. "It always gets worse, so I'll probably stay home for a few days. That means I won't be here with you," she said with a pout. "I don't want to make either of you sick."

"I don't mind," Mayr argued. When she tossed the blanket over the second chair and retrieved her clothes, he slumped forward, his doleful gaze clouded with disappointment.

Guided by heart alone, Tash held Mayr's face in his hands and offered a tender kiss. Mayr relaxed beneath his touch, enough that on their parting, Mayr's eyes were clear with relief. He stole a second kiss, even as Arieve stood beside them, fully dressed.

"I'll come back. Just give me some time," Arieve said, drawing her hand through Mayr's hair. "And I should probably tell you, since you're both here: Coye's decided to stick around. What you said… it shook her up. She's willing to stay, to work at it. She'll also be escorting me to your wedding. This is your two-month warning to play nice."

"Great," Mayr grumbled. "I'll try my best."

"You'd better. I know what your best looks like—absolutely breathtaking." Arieve kissed their foreheads before walking away. "I'll heal up quick," she said, opening the door. "Once I'm better, we'll get right back to it. I won't ever run away, not after waiting all this time."

With a quiet "I love you," she was gone.

Mayr sighed. "I wish she could stay forever, even when she needs the space. If only she had a room here, some place she can go that isn't Orae's."

Tash shifted on his knees and rose up between Mayr's legs. "We can always ask her," he said, resting his arms on Mayr's thighs. "I wouldn't object."

"You're too good for me," Mayr murmured, his lips gliding over Tash's. Their kiss deepened in an instant, urged by muffled moans as Tash caressed Mayr's hips. Mayr shivered and raked his nails across Tash's shoulders, his legs wrapped around Tash's back.

"The bed," Tash whispered, coaxing Mayr forward by the elbows. "Need to be in you…"

The words faded on his tongue. Out of the corner of his eye, something stole his attention: bright white where none had been earlier.

Pinning Mayr to the chair, Tash glanced at the table. A small box sat on the edge, white as snow with silver gilding, glimmering as though sprinkled with crushed jewels.

Tash froze, paralyzed by the icy chill surging down his spine.

"What's wrong?" Mayr turned and blanched. "Where did that come from?"

"I don't know."

"You think—?"

"I don't know."

"We should probably—" Mayr was out of the chair and dragging Tash along before Tash could reply. They stopped beside the table, gazes locked on the box. No longer than their forearms and almost as wide, the metal box was beautifully crafted, every corner rounded. Engraved on each side were the swirls and vine-like markings of Emeraliss, accompanied by silver-streaked feathers in the corners and colourless crystal flowers on the lid. "Do we...?"

"I would think so. I don't think it's meant to be stared at."

"Ha, funny." Hesitant, Mayr reached for the box. "If I lose my arm, it's your fault." Holding the box in both hands, he pressed on the seam of the lid.

A puff of crystalline cloud burst out of the box and dissipated around them. The gust passed over Tash and Mayr like a feather sweeping across the skin.

Inside the box, two bracelets lay within gleaming folds of white silk and glass petals. At Tash's best guess, they were half the length of his bracers and just as thick, forged from the same white metal as the box with a heavier layer of the sparkling dust.

Tucked between the bracelets and the white down that lined the back of the box was a folded piece of parchment. Woven from threads of glossy silver and radiant gold, the parchment was similar to one they had seen before.

Mayr plucked the note from the box. "There's only one person... entity... thing I know that uses this." After a ragged breath, he opened the message. The glow of amber ink rose from the parchment. "Wedding wishes," he whispered, tilting the parchment towards Tash, "from Emeraliss." He laid the note in Tash's hand. "Your goddess is giving us gifts."

Too numb to move, Tash held his breath. The bracelets were an early wedding gift, the message said, meant to bring them luck.

You need them now, not later, Emeraliss explained in the same script Tash recognized from countless notes protected by the Temple. *To enjoy their full effect, put them on, clasp hands, and kiss.* Her name was scrawled across the bottom in gold light and red diamond flourishes.

Tash nearly choked. Once more they had the attention of a deity—and he had no idea why. Few people received such regard. More than that, gifts were usually reserved for the consorts of the Goddesses, not insignificant servants like him.

It can't get any more terrifying.

"We should probably do what it says, shouldn't we?" Mayr asked.

"That's probably a good idea." Tash laid the parchment on the table. As he accepted a bracelet from Mayr, his hands felt as if they belonged to someone else. They slipped the bands around their right wrists and secured the three silver clasps on the undersides.

"Something like this?" Mayr suggested. Pressed flush to Tash, Mayr clasped their hands between their chests and interlaced their fingers. The bracelets were warm, soft on the inside as if crafted from fur and not metal. A white glow emanated from where the bands met, its intensity growing the longer they held hands.

In the blink of an eye, strands of white light

burst forth, hot and cold and everything in between. Minute bolts of lightning raced around their hands like narrow ribbons in a summer's gale. Spasms skittered through Tash, shocking his nerves.

Tash claimed their kiss with full force, scared to question what was happening.

Magic slammed into him, around him, through him. It ripped his insides apart and rammed them back together. His thoughts shattered, whisked away by a thousand voiceless questions. He was nothing and everything, the emotions of entire lifetimes shoved into him until he exploded. Nowhere and everywhere at once, he was liquid soul, squeezing through the voids between worlds, screaming Mayr's name in a never-ending chase.

He moaned, sobbed, wept into the kiss. Touch faded, taking Mayr's lips with it, his hands gone.

Hurled into a blackness so starved of life he choked for air, Tash clawed and scratched, desperation thrown back as if it had hit a mirror. His heart throbbed, convulsed, deflated. It sank into itself, robbing him of life and identity until all that remained was death...

Sucking in the darkness, his heart pulsed back to life, hammering fast, beyond the simple beats of drums and breaths and time. The stuff souls were made of.

Before he could make sense of any of it, threads of white light spun webs sticky with purpose. In a flash, he was blind.

From the depths, a second heartbeat drummed in harmony with his, filling his ears and vibrating his skin, stitching together the shreds of his being. Every beat was a word and every word a feeling. Joy. Sorrow. Uncertainty. Determination.

And love. Above all others, the lightest feeling was love. Not *his* love, which pounded in his chest, bashing his breastbone. No, it was not his love shocking his spirit. It was Mayr's.

The name screeched through Tash's mind, echoed in a hundred pitches like a chorus of screams. Truth bombarded him with memory: their first touch, their first kiss. The first time they made love and destroyed the barriers between them. Beneath it all, his feelings floated on a calm of recognition. He felt Mayr's emotions seep into his, becoming one. Somewhere between horrified and stunned, he was safe.

His calm wavered. Panic butted against the song playing between him and Mayr, souring the sweetness with sharp cries and flat effort. The heaviness pushed down, clawing apart their safe space. In the shadows, despair danced on fear's feet, taunting the rhythm, always two beats off.

This is what it is to be bound, a familiar voice told Tash. *To dance and sing and live in tune, fighting against all odds.* Pitched high and light, Emeraliss's voice was femininity balanced by a soulful, masculine undertone, graced with a peculiar lilt. Her voice was more than sound: it was a presence, a connection felt more than heard. It was the resonance of the heavens crashing down.

Tash could not speak, only feel.

You are soulbound in the truest of ways, your link crafted by my own hands. Of this you can be certain, for now and always, Emeraliss continued. *This is my gift to you in this lifetime: a chance to feel how closely tied you truly are. Your chance to touch what is most sacred in its rawest, most intense form.*

Emeraliss appeared beside him, a whisper of cool air and amber light devoid of discernable form. *These bracelets are connected only to the two of you. Through them, you shall know the strength of your connection, translating spirit into sensation and imprinting two lives within the same self. Such are the bonds that hold your souls together, too fragile to be seen, too strong to ignore.* Reaching into the nothingness around them, Emeraliss moved as though She plucked the strings of a harp.

A harp that played love at the price of every breath he took.

Tash gasped. Dizzy with weightlessness, he struggled to remain upright.

Emeraliss laughed, the singsong girlishness offset by the hoarse cackle of a crone. *The worries in your minds are echoed in your hearts, but it is the soul that knows best. Your love needs your faith, not the shadows of what was and what isn't. Release the burdens of your doubts and fall into absolute trust.*

The bindings will catch you. She reached out once more. Her fingers wound around an invisible thread that slowly became visible, flowing like water. *You need not worry about Arieve, either. She offers love you may take into your binding—love that neither diminishes nor taints your connection, but forges the links tighter. Allow your feelings to live, and they will fill you with a light so warm you shall never be lost. You will always have a way home. Your bond is your guiding star, your life. Never fear to follow it.*

In a whisper, Emeraliss was gone. Nothingness spun into radiant colours and loud noise. The heaviness of skin wrapped around bone, weighting Tash in consciousness.

On his lips, Mayr's lips, hard and bruising.

In his hands, Mayr's throat, soft and real.

Around him, Mayr's arms, tight as they trembled.

The veil lifted between debilitating, otherworldly awareness and stark mental clarity. Tash slid his hands around Mayr's neck to clutch him tighter. Tears dampened their cheeks as they shared the same breath, needing to hold on. Pressed together, slicked with sweat, they were more than flesh: they were pure emotion, entangled inside and out.

Mayr pushed away. Just as quickly, he groaned and hauled Tash into him again. "Feel you," he mumbled, his face buried in Tash's neck. His shaking fists settled in Tash's hair. "In me. You…" Voice hitching on a sob, Mayr dug his nails into Tash's shoulders. "All of you, in here. She said... She told me... It's you and me, together."

Once more, Mayr drew back, his eyes red and swollen. He held Tash's face in his hands. "Never leaving you, *ever*." Mayr flattened Tash's palm over his chest. A swell of emotion coursed through Tash, overpowering his own feelings. "You feel that? I'm always with you. *Always*."

"I know," Tash murmured. He peered at their bracelets. Gone was the white metal. In its stead were coloured bands: Mayr's was black with thin silver and blue markings, while Tash's was red with black and gold markings.

"Guess these really do belong to us," Mayr muttered. In a fit of sniffles, he wiped his face and turned towards the box. "That wasn't there..." He turned back to Tash, a second piece of parchment in his hand. "Apparently our messenger isn't finished."

"Emeraliss tends to have many things to say," Tash joked, followed by a grimace. "What does it say?" He stepped around Mayr to read over his shoulder.

Written in ink resembling liquid amber, the words were easy to decipher:

Tell him, Mayr.

An addition appeared, inscribed in a trail of golden light:

Tell him what terror feels like.

Fear washed over Tash, flowing beneath his confusion. Shame and guilt rode the wave, bumping into his curiosity.

The emotional deluge was Mayr's, not his.

"I don't understand," Tash said. "What...?"

"It feels like you dying," Mayr said softly. "That's what terror feels like." His eyes were glassy as he glanced at Tash. "I've been lying to you, and Emeraliss is calling me out." He tossed the note aside. "Nightmares—that's what I haven't been telling you. Worst ones I've ever had. You die *every. Single. Time. That's* why I've been sick, why I've been in a mood. It's also the reason I yelled at you, and I'm sorry. I should've told you, but I couldn't take you there with me. I wanted to give you better." His shoulders sagged as he looked away. "I'm just sorry I failed at it. Failed you."

"Nightmares?" Tash stared at him, pushing past the regret that crept between their fears. "That's it? *That's* what you've been holding back? Mayr..." He pulled Mayr into a hug. "You didn't fail me, or us," he whispered, surrendering to an onslaught of tears. Whatever doubts he'd had crawled back into the painful holes in his judgment. Armamae was right: he had no cause to worry.

He only hoped the strength of his forgiveness made it through the bracelets. Words would never be enough to say it all.

Chapter Thirteen

Two months rolled by in a blur as Mayr counted down the days and battled his worsening jitters. The next thing he knew, the wedding was upon them, along with his sister's fussing.

"Would you quit fidgeting?" Estara slapped Mayr's shoulder then gently tugged on his hair. "You're worse than my children."

Mayr stuck out his tongue at her reflection in the mirror standing before him. The mirror was as tall as him, with a thick black frame and spotless glass. Simple and pristine, it matched the rest of the room provided by the temple for his pre-ceremony preparation. "If you wouldn't take forever to *do* something, maybe we'd behave."

Estara pulled his hair, yanking his head back as he yelped. "Yeah, that's right," she chided, her white lace cuffs sweeping across his shoulder. "You're at *my* mercy. Or perhaps you'd like me to rearrange your face and not just your pretty locks?"

"Ha!" Pellon snickered and leaned against the wall to Mayr's left, peering out the window into the sunny spring afternoon. Dressed completely in white from his embroidered tunic and thigh-length vest to his fitted pants and shin-high boots, Pellon's red hair seemed to blaze like fire. "You might want to save the fight for later, Mayr. Tara looks fit to make the worst happen."

"Fine," Mayr grumbled. He sat straight in his high-backed chair and tugged at his shirt, the dark red fabric pulling taut over his chest and stomach. How he missed his black attire. "I'll *try* not to move while you make a mess back there."

Lira crossed the room to stand behind him, laughing lightly. Her white gown fell around her in a cascade of silk and lace layers beneath a soft bodice with white and silver ribbons. "Actually, it looks beautiful." She drew her hand over the plaits that hung down Mayr's back. "I admire your talent, Estara."

I'll give you that. Mayr eyed Estara's hands as she continued to braid and twist his hair. Despite his teasing, he appreciated her help in making him presentable. She had practically jumped out of her skin when she accepted his request. He could still feel the tightness of her hug.

Then again, he had denied her the chance when he married Betta. The secret ceremony in the woods had robbed their family of the joys from the event.

Not this time. This time everyone's here and we're really doing this… Letting out a slow breath, Mayr glanced around the room. Like most of the private chambers in the temple, the room was small, no different than the room Tash still kept.

Every wall was of the same bright, pure white marble that formed the rest of the temple, the smooth surfaces gleaming in the light. The room was furnished with modest pieces, limited to a dark wood bed against the furthest wall, a bedside table, an armoire in the corner opposite him, and a writing desk near the window. Thin white curtains billowed around the window that opened out onto a garden, while mild floral incense filled the room, offering a calm he needed.

I'm actually getting married again. Mayr flicked his gaze upwards, wondering if Emeraliss read his every thought. *Please let this one stick. I can't take any more heartbreak. But that's the whole point, isn't it? To move forward instead of always looking back, because that's all Tash and I do. Get stuck. Fall back. Dance around what we need.*

Not anymore.

He had promised Tash no more avoidance, no more clinging to the past. The bracelets from Emeraliss had revealed the truth of their partnership: there was no escape, no easy way to split their connection. If one gave up, the other would follow. What they had lost with past loves was nothing compared to what could destroy them.

Mayr rubbed his right wrist, envisioning the magical black band where it would have been had he put it on. The silver and blue markings burned in his mind, thin and mysterious ribbons of what he supposed were the emotional roads of Tash's soul mapped onto his. Since the first time he had worn the bracelet and heard Emeraliss speak, Mayr had surrendered completely. He was blissfully and hopelessly lost in Tash. No more secrets. Tash knew everything, including Mayr's fears of the Shar-denn, especially after Tash had told him of the Shar-denn's origins, along with the rest of what Felensa had revealed at the Sanctum. With all that mattered to them now out in the open, their marriage would be the cleanest of slates.

Assuming I stop being nervous. Mayr stared into the mirror, the why of his anxiety still difficult to pinpoint. Tash wanted the marriage as much as he did. *The bracelets made sure we know* exactly *how much we want it, and when we're touching, coming…*

A blush spread across his cheeks. There was a reason they were eschewing the bracelets for the wedding. In the quietest moments, wearing the bracelets meant existing as a single entity formed from twice as many emotions. Their effect was overwhelming, even when Mayr and Tash were asleep. Those nights, their dreams were overcome with ethereal beauty.

But when they wore the bracelets in their most intimate moments, magic overrode reason and reality. Sex became an otherworldly experience. Coming was cataclysmic, addictive like a drug, and the result was an ecstatic nightmare, a rush of life and death spun together in a sticky ball. Mayr likened it to his body imploding while the force of a collapsing mountain slammed through his cock. The consequence was devastation and bewilderment while they lay paralyzed, their bodies too shocked to function beyond strangled breaths. Given how elated Mayr and Tash both were over the wedding, the bracelets would remain in their box and sit on the altar during the ceremony.

Later, when it's just us... Mayr grinned at his reflection. He had plans, most of which included enticing Tash to have him every way he wanted from that night to the next. Although he appreciated his wedding attire—all red as custom dictated—the clothes would look better scattered across their bedroom. His long-sleeved shirt, blood-red with embroidered vine patterns of darker red around the hems and cuffs, would pool well in the centre of the room. His well-fitted pants, so dark they were almost black, would drape perfectly over the chest of blankets at the end of the bed. His blood-red, knee-high boots would fly well in all directions, keeping him from being anywhere else but in Tash's arms. The yarn bracelet from Tash would be the only thing he kept on.

"Hey," Aeley called from across the room, "stop thinking about getting off."

Startled, Mayr blinked as Aeley's reflection approached his. "Why? It's what I intend to do with my *husband*. Don't know *what* you do with your wife."

Aeley punched his shoulder. "Don't even think about it. I'd hate to chop your brain into teensy little bits." She gazed lovingly at Lira before smacking Mayr's arm. "You've got enough to play with. Keep your mind out of my love life."

Mayr rubbed where she had hit. "You're certainly excited today. At this rate, I'll lose limbs."

"Hey, I'm allowed to be happy." Aeley scrunched her face at the mirror and straightened her clothes. As was custom for wedding attendants, she wore only white. A leather bodice cinched her bell-sleeved tunic at the waist, and her loose pants were tucked into her boots just under the knee. Only years earlier, Aeley had been a bride and Mayr her attendant. Prior to that, Mayr had been attendant at both Estara and Loftin's weddings.

How time toyed with them.

Without turning his head too far, Mayr watched the others make last preparations. Tradition required the marrying parties to have at least two attendants each to help them and assist in the ceremony. Often those attendants were siblings, other family, or close friends.

Mayr and Tash had five attendants each. Neither could play favourites. For most of his life, Mayr's siblings had consisted of Estara, Loftin, and Aeley. Since his adolescence, he had taken to Pellon as another brother. Now, Lira was like another sister. He could not choose one over another.

Tash faced a similar impossible choice. Allaysia was his sister and Ress the closest thing to a brother. He had grown up with Covran and Bremary, his family latched to theirs. They were cousins in addition to friends.

Then there was Arieve, the one who most needed to be present. Her place was by Tash's side, next to the altar. Nothing less was acceptable.

"Here," Lira said, stealing Mayr's attention. She made her way through the room to Aeley, Estara, and Pellon, offering each a traditional floral crown. Bright, iridescent blue flowers the size of Mayr's palm formed the crown with small, deep blue flowers bunched in chains between them. White and silver ribbons trailed from the back of the crowns, several curled while others hung straight amidst strands of white crystals on white gold chains.

"Thanks," Estara muttered around the hairpins between her lips. She paused to put on her crown and sneered at the ribbons caught in her curled hair. "One last bit..." Her fingers sifted through Mayr's hair once more, plaiting quickly as her crown slipped to one side.

Lira's voice drowned Estara's quiet curses. "I'm going to take this to Loftin," Lira announced, holding up the last crown. "I'll be back. Don't kill each other." The next moment, she was out the door and closing it behind her.

"I'll just kill this," Estara hissed, pushing her crown back into place. "Don't mind me if I toss it at someone mid-ceremony."

"Throw it at my guy and I'll toss *you*." Mayr met Estara's gaze in the mirror. "You can take out your husband, though. He likes you rough."

"Ha! Bet you think you're funny." Estara snorted as she tied and pinned the braid in her hand. "You're not, by the way. We just let you think you are." With both hands, she smoothed his hair and brushed loose strands forward over his shoulders. "Almost there." She motioned to Aeley.

Several steps from where Mayr sat, something clicked. When Estara's hands neared him again, a strong fragrance followed—a floral scent not part of the crowns.

"Oh, *no you don't*." Mayr pushed Estara's hand away. "I *don't* do flowers or fluffy things. That's always been your thing, not mine."

"Stop being a jerk," Estara snapped. She thrust her hand in his face. "Take a look at it. *Really* look."

In her palm sat a single flower the size of her hand. White starburst petals formed three tiers around the golden centre. Each petal bore bright purple and gold streaks.

Tash's favourite. Mayr sagged in the chair.

Estara drew back the flower. "It's *supposed* to be *romantic*."

Yeah, it is. Mayr peered at the yarn bracelet on his left wrist. There was nothing he would not do for Tash.

"Go ahead," he told her quietly. "But if you put in ribbons or strands of those awful tiny jewels that get all tangled up and yank things out, I'll find someone to curse you with three more children, *none* of whom will grow up. They'll stay toddlers and the *only* word they'll say is *no*."

Tsking at him, Estara worked the flower into his hair. "Fine, I'll just cut *all* your hair off. Won't have to worry about a thing after that."

Mayr snorted back a laugh. "Do that and Tash will unleash *all* the wrath of his inner priest. He'll curse you until the end of days. At least *my* threat was temporary."

Pellon's deep laugh rumbled through the room. "You two are hilarious." He stepped up to Mayr's side, arms folded. The ribbons of his crown dangled down his chest to his waist. "Neither of you has the guts to do a damn thing, but I'll give you points for entertainment."

"We'll give you pillows and you can bash this thing out," Aeley said from her place next to Estara, her glossy lips turned up in a grin. "Round one: the wedding takedown."

One brow arched, Mayr glimpsed Estara's exasperated expression. "And you accuse *me* of not being funny?"

"Poor Tash," Estara said as she took something from Pellon. "Someone ought to tell the poor boy to run. We're all cracked." She shoved a silver mirror with a handle into Mayr's hand. "Here, look at your vain self."

Mayr obeyed quietly, standing and turning around so he could use the smaller mirror to see the reflection in the larger. Half of his hair hung straight past the middle of his back. The rest was up, more elegant than he had ever attempted to appear. Strands had been twisted and pulled away from his face, then exquisitely draped over a wide, flat braid and pinned to an intricate cascade of narrow plaits in a mirrored pattern. The flower sat in the centre where plaits and twists met.

It was more than he deserved. Never had he wanted to appear delicate or hide behind fashion and glamour. His hands were dirty, his roughness a shifting layer beneath his skin.

Tash saw past it all, regardless of any veneer. He insisted Mayr was beautiful, even in the worst moments. Mayr's polished appearance would no doubt capture Tash's attention, especially where Tash's hands were concerned.

"Thanks, Tara." Mayr passed the mirror to Aeley and hugged Estara. "I know I'm a pain, but you're a really good sister. You can throw your crown at anyone you want."

Estara laughed and gave him a tight squeeze. "I'll hold you to that."

Taps sounded on the door before it crept open. "Knock, knock," a quiet voice said. "Can I come in?"

Mayr's heart skipped beats as Arieve slipped into the room, a radiant vision of white and brilliant blue. Her dark hair was curled tighter than usual, tumbling around her shoulders and down her back, the white-blonde streaks brightened by her floral crown. When she moved closer, the vivid green in her hazel eyes shone in the light. Lush, deep pink paint on her lips complemented the faint pink powder colouring her cheeks. Beneath it all, she appeared to glow.

He flushed, recognizing her gown from the first night she had slept with him and Tash. The gown flowed as it did that night, though she wore a white sash instead of a corset. Formed from long, loosely plaited lengths of white lace, the sash clung to her waist, and its unbraided ends trailed behind her along the floor.

Mayr was certain he looked foolish, red-faced and stuck on staring.

"This is where we step out." Pellon offered his arms to Aeley and Estara. "Shall we? Don't really need to see this next bit."

"Don't I know it," Estara agreed, looping her arm around Pellon's. "I saw enough of things last night at dinner. I'm surprised the three of them came up for air."

Aeley cast Mayr a pointed glance. "We'll be back. Try and keep your clothes on?"

"Thanks for the advice." Mayr shooed them from the room and threw the door shut.

Arieve was in his arms an instant later, melting into his embrace as he tilted her head back, cradling her neck in his palms. Her lips met his with a kiss, its solemn essence wrapped around restrained passion. For what felt like forever, he had wondered how it would be to marry her and be happy together. He had never expected to find the answer, and never like this. His heart was whole, the fragments welded together by Tash and Arieve's relationship. Despite the fewer nights she had spent with them in the last two months, she was a part of them he would die to keep.

Mayr drew back to caress her cheek. "I'm surprised you're here. How's Tash going to get on without you?"

"Considering he's ready and waiting on *you*, he'll be fine." Arieve smirked. "Besides, the last kiss I gave him should keep his thoughts scrambled long enough to start missing me."

"Are you suggesting I'm holding things up?"

"Not suggesting. Telling."

"You're so mean," Mayr breathed. "I'm getting married today, you know."

Arieve shrugged. "I'll be nice tomorrow." She coiled the ends of his hair. "Actually, make that whenever you finally surface from bed. One day won't be enough."

"Can't argue there." Mayr teased her nose with his and pouted. "Is Tash truly ready to start? He's not pacing the hall, fending off annoyed guests, is he?"

"*Mayr*," she reproved. "You really *are* nervous, aren't you?" She cupped his face with both hands. "He's having a moment with his parents. If he weren't so proper, he'd be jumping around like a little kid. I've had to calm him down twice." She gave him a gentle hug. "I'm so happy for you," Arieve whispered. "I wish I could describe how much I want you to have this."

He clutched her as if she were the last person he would ever see. "Even though I'm not marrying you?"

Honesty crushed him, his question punching him in the gut. Mayr grimaced and buried his face in her hair. *Dammit. Dammit, dammit, dammit...* They were far from ready to go there. Not only was he not ready to ask, he wanted to dote on Tash with their marriage, not make him share absolutely everything. He doubted Arieve was ready to consider marrying him and Tash as it was. For all he knew, Arieve still wanted to marry Coye. She could not be in two marriages at once, not by Kattal's laws, and a single marriage with all four of them would never work. Mayr preferred to keep Coye at arm's length, and she felt the same about men in general.

It was too soon. They were too new. There were so many unanswered questions...

Arieve slid her hands around his neck. "I don't have to marry you to be yours," she said softly. "I belong with both of you, I know it. If I didn't, I wouldn't be desperate to hold onto you. I wouldn't seek you and Tash out or wish I could see you every moment of every day. I lie awake when I'm not with you, remembering how you say my name like it's worthy of something more than just me."

Her fingertips glided over his smooth jaws. "I cherish you both, and I'll stay as long as you'll have me. No one else offers what you do, not even Coye. Her love is a different gift, one I can't breathe without." Arieve's lips claimed Mayr's, light and uplifting. "Her love sustains my days and brings me peace of self," she murmured, "but your love is time unfolding, winding back to recover everything I thought I'd never have. A love that's *there*, so easy to share and curl up in. With you and Tash, I feel…"

"Different?" Mayr suggested.

"Secure. I feel secure with you." Arieve's pensive gaze searched his. "Even if we don't last for some reason, I know you won't abandon me or each other." She grasped his hands and kissed his fingers. "I also know you'll give everything to our baby. You'll never leave, never stop loving. You'll lay the whole world at our child's feet."

Assuming we get that far, especially with your time split between us and Coye. Though every couple days I wonder if you might be… just a bit…

Mayr kissed her before he asked the one question he dared not voice, not without getting their hopes up or sabotaging what could be. He settled for the sweetened taste of her lips on his, words echoing in his thoughts. Something was off in her tone, but he was too nervous to ask why.

Arieve pushed away with an assuring grin. "I should get back to Tash. We'll talk later, promise. I love you."

Moving aside, Mayr ushered Arieve out of the room. Lira waited in the hallway, hands clasped. Beside her, Aeley and Pellon leaned against the wall.

"Love you, too," Mayr whispered, watching Arieve return to Tash's chamber several doors down. He nodded at Aeley. "Shall we finish?"

"We shall." Aeley flounced past him, headed for the bed.

Lira swept into the room with Pellon. "All of your guests are here. The priests are ready to start whenever you are," she said, stopping in the middle of the room. While Aeley sorted through the items on the bed, Lira flashed Mayr a smile. "Your mother is being well cared for. She's having a wonderful time. Your father's been pacing a storm, however. Loftin assures me it's expected."

Aeley snickered and joined Lira, a red leather coat draped over her arms. "Weddings and Malary aren't exactly friends," Aeley said. "He appreciates what they mean but dislikes the wait, especially when his only role is father. But enough of that." She held up the coat. "Time to finish dressing."

With Aeley's help, Mayr slipped into the

blood-red long coat as Lira maneuvered his hair out of the way. The coat's hem brushed the toes of his boots, and its cuffs hung loosely around his wrists. Similar to the long coats worn by the High Council, his bore elaborate black vines that spiraled around a shield on his back and coiled down his arms. Where the High Council's coats boasted the emblem of the Council, his displayed the Dahe crest. Of all his wedding attire, the coat was one of his favourites, having been a surprise gift from Aeley and Lira.

"There." Mayr lifted his arms and spun slowly. "Looks good? Gentlemanly?"

Lira smoothed Mayr's hair over his shoulders. "Very. It's definitely you—as perfect as the two of you getting married." Her smile faltered. Tears wet her eyes before she wiped them away. "Thank you for asking me to be an attendant. I've never been a witness for anyone. Seeing as I'll never be one for my brothers or the friends I don't have, this means something."

"Hey, now, no crying until the ceremony starts," Mayr chided gently, drawing Lira into a hug. "You've got more friends than you know, but you're also family. We do this sappy stuff. It's in the rules. Well, the good ones."

Her reply was a sniffle interrupted by a laugh. "They're the ones that count." Lira kissed his cheek. "Thanks."

"And thanks for getting married by an actual priest this time." Aeley arched one of her blonde brows. "As much as I *loved* witnessing that first time, I'm enjoying this wedding infinitely better."

"Thanks for rubbing it in," Mayr muttered. It was awkward enough that Betta and Iliane were at the wedding.

Aeley kissed Mayr's cheek and embraced him. "Only good wishes for you, brother. We'll always cheer you on." After a wink, she gestured to Pellon. "Grab the sword. It's time to do damage."

"Aye, aye, Steward," Pellon said with a toothy grin. Humming a happy tune, he rushed to the bed to retrieve the sword Mayr would give Tash at the ceremony and its black leather scabbard. The hilt was forged from yellow and white gold adorned with black and red jewels in a spiraled pattern. The blade was crafted from brilliant silver, save the colourless crystal in the centre. Engraved along one edge was the word *Always*, with *Soulbound* engraved on the other.

Mayr forced himself to breathe. When he married Betta, a simple knife had been the best gift he could afford. As Head of the Guard, his wages granted him a taste of the extravagance enjoyed by the Grand Families. He only hoped Tash liked the sword, fancy as it was.

"We're off," Aeley announced, gliding out of the room with Lira.

Mayr and Pellon followed. Together they strode through the corridors between the private chambers. Every hallway looked the same: long stretches of white marble interrupted by white wood doors, all of them shut. The varied aromas from incense and candles on the small shelves in the corners blended and shifted from section to section, a woodsy fragrance underlying them.

Once Mayr turned into the corridor that led to the altar, he nearly froze.

Tash stood at the other end. Arieve, Ress, Kee, and Armamae waited with him, all of them gathered beside the tall, spiraled pillars that denoted the sacred space of worship. Tash had traded his religious vestments for traditional wedding attire tailored by his parents. His long-sleeved shirt was of the same shimmering red fabric as his robes, embellished with gold embroidery at its hems and cuffs, while red ribbons and pearl toggles laced the shirt closed at his throat. The shirt fell to his thighs, guiding Mayr's gaze to deep red pants that hugged Tash's legs beneath knee-high boots of a slightly brighter red, tied up the side with red cord. Over it all was a sleeveless leather coat, its high collar turned up. The coat hung open and trailed along the floor, a series of gold and pearl closures down the front.

Mayr slowed on his approach. The waves of Tash's blond-streaked brown hair were more pronounced than usual, playing over his shoulders at different lengths. An antique hairpiece made from intricately entwined lengths of silver was nestled on the bed of twists and plaits at the back of his head. Thin strands of silver dangled from the hairpiece into his hair, offering flashes of white and red jewels. An heirloom, Tash had said, passed down through his father's family. Tash's father had worn it when he married Tash's mother, and Tash would pass it down to *his* child.

Reality slammed into Mayr, clarity tumbling as he stopped before Tash. The child who inherited the heirloom would be *theirs*. The significance nearly knocked him over.

"Mayr," Tash whispered.

Mayr all but melted at the hope in Tash's eyes before he spared a glance to the others in the hall. Arieve let go of Tash's hand to urge him forward, while Ress stood behind Tash in white tunic and pants, his cane nowhere in sight. A long, black box with gold latches sat in his grasp instead.

To Mayr's left, Armamae and Kee appeared as they did every day. A small glass dish rested in Kee's hand.

Everyone else waited on the other side of the pillars behind them, watching the exchange. The other attendants formed a semi-circle around the black altar in the centre of the room. Clothed in white, family and friends stood in a wide, near-closed circle around the attendants, taking up half the space of worship. Around them was another circle formed entirely of priests, full and dense with Tash's peers from the temple and the Sacred Assembly, including Keeper Felensa. The priests stood back as far as they could, several pressed against the pillars. Guards from the Dahe estate stood along the walls, dressed in white and holding wooden staves. At the request of Kee, the guards had left all other weapons at the estate.

Consumed by a sea of bodies clad in red and white, the entire area seemed to have shrunk from its normally spacious expanse.

No pressure whatsoever.

He would do this right, nothing left to interpretation.

Mayr removed his marriage ring and caressed the blue diamond in the band. Tradition called for Tash and him to bow to one another and present their rings for blessings during the rite.

It was too little for so great a gift.

Before anyone spoke, Mayr sank to one knee and offered the ring to Tash in his cupped palm. Head lowered, he ignored the gasps and light sighs that broke the silence. He prayed no one noticed his trembling.

Tash's fingers slipped beneath Mayr's chin and lifted his head. A thin layer of tears glistened in Tash's eyes as he accepted the ring. Bowing low to level their gazes, he brought Mayr's palm to his lips and replaced the weight of the ring with the heat of a kiss. A hint of perfume wafted around him, subtle with a pleasant musk.

Mayr held his breath. A metallic clink accompanied his ring as Tash slid it into the glass dish, followed by the sound of Tash's ring.

Kee's smile stunned Mayr, its youthful glee far from her serious demeanor. "Thank you. You may proceed onto the Walk of Union." She spun away in a flurry of robes and headed for the altar with Armamae.

Tash pulled Mayr up. Palms pressed together, Mayr leaned his forehead against Tash's. He needed the calm, the reassurance.

"Ready?" Tash asked, nuzzling Mayr's cheek.

"Are you?"

Tash squeezed Mayr's hands. "I have no doubts, only determination." He took his place to Mayr's right and laced their fingers together. "Let's take our stroll."

They moved between the pillars and through the opening in the circle of priests. Aeley and Arieve followed, flanked by Pellon and Ress. With matched steps, Mayr and Tash turned left and walked through the space between the priests and the inner circle of guests. Slow as their steps were, Mayr could barely sort one face from another, unable to focus on anyone except for his father and mother, who sat in a chair close to the front of the altar.

The first part of their walk ended where it began. They passed through the inner circle and walked around the altar, only to stop in front of it. Aeley and Arieve took their places in the empty space between the altar and the line of attendants, with Aeley to Mayr's left and Arieve to Tash's right. Pellon and Ress stepped into the middle of their lines, each holding their respective gifts in flattened palms.

Kee and Armamae stood in front of the black stone altar. At the back corners of the altar stood two priestesses, one with black hair to her waist and the other with red curls that framed her face. The black-haired priestess held a gleaming scepter of silver and glass in both hands to represent Emeraliss and Laytia. Her counterpart held a silver staff with elaborate engravings, a symbol of Hastal and Navara.

Behind Kee and Armamae, the altar overflowed with wedding cheer. Spiritual tools blended with nuptial items, bathed in a soft red tint from the circular pane in the ceiling. Four wide, white candles sat in a line across the centre of the altar, each with four lit wicks and a colourful crown of lush spring flowers around their base. Instead of goblets and bowls filled with offerings from worshippers, four colourless glass goblets of rich mauve mead formed a square around a fifth goblet. Three red glass bowls accompanied the goblets, the first filled with white and silver feathers, the second with water, and the third with red earth. By them, a stick of woodsy incense burned on a black clay plate.

Behind the bowls and goblets sat items from Mayr and Tash's relationship, including the locked box of feathers from their bedroom altar. Next to the feathers sat the box containing the bracelets from Emeraliss, left open to display the colours. In front of both boxes was the love letter from Tash during his visit to the Sanctum after their last confrontation. A pile of tightly plaited white and silver ribbons lay in front of the goblets, coiled beside a second glass keepsake box that shone with gold and silver flecks. Beside the ribbons was the glass dish with their rings.

Four copies of their marriage record lay on the right side of the altar, along with an ink well and white quill. High Council would retain the first document in their Records Hall. The other copies would remain in the possession of Aeley, Mayr and Tash, and Kee, partially to ensure that Tash was never cheated out of what was rightfully his, and partially to keep what was theirs in the possession of any children they had if the worst should come to pass. Both were possibilities Mayr hated to think about but had no heart to ignore.

"Very good," Kee said, lifting Mayr and Tash's clasped hands. "Yours is a strong, confident walk. Now we must bind that strength."

With Armamae's tap on Tash's elbow, Mayr and Tash faced one another, Kee's hands wrapped around theirs.

"Friends, family, community of the sacred, I welcome you to this most blessed celebration," Kee said loudly. "We have gathered to share in this solemn act, tying together two hearts so the rest of the world may know them as we do. In all the power I possess on behalf of the Goddesses, and with deepest blessings, I am overjoyed to fasten the lives of Mayr and Halataldris, whom I am proud to call my holy brother. Blessed be love."

"Blessed be love," the assembly responded, along with shrill whistles and cheers. Mayr swore he saw handkerchiefs already wiping away tears.

Kee waited until silence returned. "Under the gaze of the most radiant Emeraliss, you are here to become legally recognized as one. It is with mutual consent that you take such a step. You may make your intention known to all, however you wish."

Mayr did not need to be told twice. He took to Tash's lips quickly, but as Tash deepened their kiss, Mayr struggled to avoid doing what he truly wanted. *Keep it chaste. No tongue, no tongue, no—*

Tash's tongue swept through his mouth, slow and sensual. A groan escaped Mayr before he could stop it, and he fought against the weakening of his knees until Tash answered with a quiet moan.

When Tash pulled away, Mayr was nearly undone.

Amusement brightened Kee's eyes as she laughed. "Indeed." She withdrew her hands from theirs. "You may now declare your affections with such vigour. Brother Halataldris?"

Without hesitation, Tash fluttered kisses over Mayr's knuckles. "Thank you for asking me to marry you," he whispered. "I cherish your courage, taking these steps forward after being pushed back so far." He clutched Mayr's hands to his chest. "I will never make you regret it. There is sacredness in what we have. Being with you feels like worshipping at Emeraliss's altar every moment, tasting everything She offers. Through you, through *us* and our families, I better understand Emeraliss and everything priests are meant to give. What *I* can give." Tash pressed his forehead to Mayr's, his fingers gliding over Mayr's hair. "You've given me the rest of my life. I owe you every lifetime to come."

"And you've put me on the spot," Mayr murmured. Focused on the warmth of Tash's short, light breaths as they danced over his lips, he barely noticed the silence around them. He blinked back tears that refused to go away. "I can't offer the kind of words you give—I'm not good at it—but I can offer you everything I have and show you my love. You're part of me, deep inside every thought and action, every glimpse of the future." Cupping Tash's jaw, he drew him closer. "I may have given you the rest of your life, but you pulled me from darkness and gave me light. The night we met, you asked me to trust you. I was yours from that moment, and that won't change."

Before Kee could give her next instruction, Mayr slid his lips over Tash's, imparting all the passion he could muster without losing control. Tears slipped down Tash's cheek and pooled on Mayr's fingers.

Giggles from the crowd prompted Mayr to pull back. He cleared the moist trails from Tash's cheeks with his thumbs, earning Tash's smile in return.

"Blessed be your luck in finding each other," Kee said, waving the stick of incense over and around them.

Bowl in hand, Armamae flicked water in a circle around their feet. "Blessed be the hope that guides your path."

A string of prayers followed, one to each goddess. Afterwards, Kee and Armamae took turns singing tales of Emeraliss's most celebrated consort, Valaster the Unburdened.

Mayr's heart burned from the sentiments behind the stories, all of them chosen by Tash for their ceremony. Valaster had sworn to commit himself to Emeraliss only when the vastness of love filled his heart, unimpeded by impurity. He traveled the world on foot four times over and sailed the waters in a tiny boat with a single sail. On land, Valaster had collected a handful of dirt for his every woe and whispered the grains into gold. In the span of a thousand dawns, he scattered his regrets on the wind and dropped a golden trail of generosity to ease the burdens of others. On the seas, Valaster had drunk a cup of water for every guilty thought and cried tears of pearls, releasing his despair to the tides and offering a gleaming grave to those who drowned. At the end of his journey, Valaster sank into Emeraliss's silken lap with the lightest soul a man ever had, devoid of darkness. Together they birthed a dozen children, each with a spirit lighter than the last. Their final child had been born as pure soul, wispy energy that drifted far into the universe on its first breath.

The last song ended on a sweet phrase of harmony, though the warmth of its significance lingered. He needed no explanation for why Tash had chosen those particular tales. Deep within their pretty words was everything Tash wanted to say.

Mayr glanced at Tash, mesmerized by his noticeable adoration of Kee and Armamae. Later, when they were alone, he would entreat Tash to serenade him with the same songs. Where Kee's voice was harsh and Armamae's voice wavered, Tash's singing voice was gentle and smooth, comforting like a lullaby.

Kee raised her arms towards Pellon and Ress. "We shall present the offerings. Mayr, you may begin."

Pellon stepped forward, the hilt of the sword tilted towards Mayr's right hand. In Mayr's firm grip, the sword slid easily from the scabbard. He presented the sword to Tash, the blade flat on his palms. "With Emeraliss's blessing, I offer you this sword, a symbol of protection, security, and balance. May it serve as the line we never cross, the united front we present to the world, and the strength in our duty to one another."

Tash's fingertips wandered over the sharp edges and paused on the engraved words. "It's beautiful," he whispered. "Thank you."

Mayr sheathed the sword and waited as Pellon placed the sword across the front of the altar. Once Pellon resumed his place, Ress moved to Tash's side and opened the black box he held. A gold talon ring lay inside, a twin to Tash's silver talon. Every ridge was finely detailed, the smooth curves flawless.

"With Emeraliss's blessing, I offer you this ring," Tash said, holding the talon towards Mayr, "a symbol of faith, determination, and loyalty. You are to me what Emeraliss is to Halataldris: trustworthy companion and steadfast spirit. May it represent the clutches in which our union is held safe, the power of our happiest joys, and the softness beneath our hardest layers."

"I'll go with that." Mayr stroked the ring lovingly. "I will always treasure it. Thank you." He nodded additional thanks to Ress, knowing well he had forged it.

Tash beamed as Ress set the box on the altar. When everyone was back in line, Kee and Armamae blessed the rings with incense and water. They recited another prayer, alternating verses until Armamae turned around, the dish in hand.

Kee picked up both rings. "These carry your words, a symbol of beginnings with no end and ends with new beginnings." She opened her hands to present the rings in her palms. "Falter on your path and they will lead you back to the beginning. If you think you see the end, look ahead to what you left behind. Alone, they are voids; slip them on and they become whole. Just as you complete them, fill your marriage with what they represent."

Mayr retrieved Tash's ring and slid it onto Tash's middle finger, then waited as Tash returned his. Beside them, Kee and Armamae disentangled long lengths of white and silver ribbons.

"Hand in hand, present your arms," Kee instructed.

The ceremony was nearly finished. Mayr shivered and took Tash's hand, grinning at his slight tremble. While Kee tied and knotted the end of one set of ribbons around Mayr's right elbow, Armamae did the same around Tash's left. In a graceful flow of motion, Kee and Armamae looped the plaited ribbons together and wove them around Mayr and Tash's arms. Their hands moved over and under in an elegant dance. An elaborate web of crisscrossed ribbons radiated from a tight, spiraled pattern down Mayr and Tash's forearms, holding them together. The design ended at Mayr and Tash's wrists, the loose ends knotted.

"Love is a promise of self," Kee said. "Strong and delicate, it is a gift beyond worth. It is like wings, uplifting as it moves us from one place to another. It is as the divine, rooted in our soul, entwining us together. So are you bound."

The rest of the ceremony was a blur to Mayr. Kee removed the ribbons and placed them in their glass box, then Mayr and Tash toasted their union with a goblet of mead. He recalled signing his name on multiple documents, followed by Tash kissing him to a roar of approval. Their guests whistled and sang, clapping and stamping their feet while they tossed petals everywhere.

Somewhere in it all, he told Tash he loved him, dropping the words with such fire and honesty they branded Tash's name on every piece of his heart.

Propriety be damned if anyone says anything about this. If relaxing with my husband is inappropriate, they never should've let me get married.

Mayr sank deeper into his heated kiss with Tash, a breathless gap in time that tasted of berry preserves and clotted cream drowned in smoke-laced syrup. Settled sideways on his chair at their table, Mayr's legs stretched across the abandoned chairs next to him, previously occupied by Aeley and Lira. He had intended to rest before they resumed thanking their guests, but lifting his legs had led to leaning into Tash, followed by Tash's playful assault on Mayr's neck, jaw, and lips. At the mercy of touch and moan, Mayr had twisted himself into Tash's embrace, crossed his ankles, and wrapped one arm around Tash's neck to keep steady.

What snickers and chuckles he thought he heard were forgotten. The din of the wedding feast continued, the multitude of voices meshed with melodies from the musicians. For what precious moments they had, he was finally alone with Tash.

Mayr nipped Tash's bottom lip and chuckled at the groan it earned. All things considered, he could not complain even if they were interrupted. The feast was perfect. After the ceremony, all of their family, friends, and guards returned to the estate for the festivities, accompanied by most of the priests. Given their families had planned the feast and kept most of the details secret, Mayr had worried over what to expect.

His concern vanished the moment he and Tash entered the ballroom.

Their families had spared nothing. Soft, ethereal whites and blues filled the room, with touches of gleaming crystal that stole focus from the room's earthy greys and dull silver. The table for the wedding party and their escorts sat on a dais, facing the long tables arranged through the room, save for the empty space reserved for dancing. White tablecloths with bright blue runners covered every table to the floor, while chairs were dressed in white silk and delicate, iridescent blue sashes. On the back of each chair was a spray of white feathers and different tones of blue ribbons, fastened by a white jewel pin.

Extravagance spilled over every surface. The dishes were of pristine glass, the goblets colourless crystal—all of them heirlooms of Aeley's family, used for every Dahe wedding, birth, and funeral. The walls were decorated with thin, billowing white and light blue fabric, long lengths of draped and cascading ribbons in the brightest blues Mayr had seen, and strands of white crystals with silver beads. Among them, tapestries depicted Emeraliss in various scenes, including one of Emeraliss and Halataldris in flight. Gifted to Tash and Mayr by Tash's family, the tapestry's shiny blue threads picked up the light from the fire, torches, and candles.

Not one corner had been left unadorned. Had Mayr not known better, he would have taken it for a feast for a councilman or one of the Grand Families.

It's even worse than Ae and Lira's, and I planned half of that.

Mayr parted from Tash and laughed softly, caressing Tash's whiskered cheek. The night could not have been better. The dinner had consisted of their favourite dishes in copious amounts, followed by a casual celebration that allowed everyone to mingle and converse in comfort. The music was lively with various drums, flutes, fiddles, pipes, and a harp Tash had carefully fondled and plucked beautifully, the bright notes as endearing as his nervous smile while he played quietly. Where Aeley and Lira's wedding had relied on the usual stringed ensembles found at aristocratic festivities, Mayr and Tash's feast had all the playfulness of a barn party. If anything, the celebration proved how well their families knew them.

Out of habit, Mayr eyed the guards stationed along the walls and near the doorways. Second shift was almost finished, with the third to switch on at any moment. To allow every guard the chance to enjoy the evening, he had scheduled four shifts with the instruction to avoid inebriation. Far as he could tell, everything was under control.

His back protested his contortions, echoed by the ache in his legs. Grumbling his annoyance, Mayr swung his legs down and sat up straight. He gazed over the crowd, relieved to recognize most of the guests. The priests were the only exception, though Tash knew them all. Everyone else was considered safe. If they were not family, they were friends from the village and surrounding towns, including Orae's staff from the tavern, various merchants, the families of the guards, and friends of Mayr and Tash's parents. To Aeley's credit, she had not invited any of the High Council, sparing them all a headache, though Mayr was still split on the choice to not include the few bounty hunters he appreciated. Their distrust of Tash was the only reason they had not been invited.

He *did* think it regrettable that the one

mercenary he liked, Gren, had been unable to attend due to what his letter called 'family complications,' notably with his adopted son, Playe. From that alone, Mayr gathered Playe was acting out again, his adolescence in full effect. No doubt he was running his adoptive mother, Tracel, to absolute aggravation. Tough as Tracel was, Playe tested everyone's patience, a trait honed by years of living on the streets with youths not much older than he. *We'll come around when things calm down,* Gren had written. A wrapped box had accompanied Gren's letter, filled with fragrant creams, oils, and salves from Tracel.

It was just as well: Mayr was unsettled with the idea of Playe being around Iliane, especially with her being so young, impressionable, her life wrapped up in however twelve-year-olds saw the world. Playe, on the other hand, was nearly fifteen and used to fighting rules more than following them, and while Mayr appreciated his circumstances, sympathized with them, Mayr still hoped to keep them apart for a while yet. Preferably until Iliane was closer to sixteen, with several sparring sessions to her experience, though those were another matter entirely, one Mayr intended to approach Betta about in a year, maybe two. One day Iliane would lose the innocence of her childhood, and when that day came, he would make certain she could defend herself against trouble and lies.

Able to sense where she was, Mayr found Iliane quickly. She danced in front of the musicians with his niece and nephews—her cousins, he insisted. As Efae and Alith stomped and flailed their arms, Iliane's arms were looped around Dayla's waist. Together they pranced and hopped and flicked their feet in a shoeless blur of white skirts and stockings. Betta and Barin also danced, hand in hand as they moved across the floor.

Despite the crowd, it was Iliane that kept his attention, her round face lit up with a grin. Her dark, thick ringlets were tied back with curled white ribbons and a jeweled hair clasp. The white gold necklace he had given her hung around her neck, its red and white jewels shining as bright as her brown eyes. Whenever she spun, the top layers of her white dress floated upwards and fell gracefully, the image so soft and sweet he wished he had the means to keep the damaging, painful things in the world well away from her for the rest of her life. Every time she looked at him, there was a smile, a wave—something to tell him their relationship was all right. That he was far from a stranger.

Once more, he said a silent thanks to Betta for keeping her word. Their past had been a mess, and though he still loved her, he liked this Betta more.

Sipping his lukewarm gaffa nectar, Mayr searched for the others he was most concerned about. His parents sat at one of the closest tables with Tash's parents, all of them laughing and sharing what he supposed were family stories.

A disaster we'll pay for later, he almost muttered, continuing onwards. Most of the children danced spastically or raced through the room, pushing through the crowd and playing games. Aeley and Lira were engrossed in conversation with Loftin, Orae and her three sons, and Estara's husband, Teneth. Gathered around the end of a table in the middle of the room, he suspected they traded the latest gossip.

Further away, safe in a quiet area near Iliane, Arieve and Coye danced slowly. Arieve looked as radiant as she had at the ceremony. Her smile seemed to be permanent, just like the glow in her eyes.

Likely due to Coye, Mayr realized, disappointed. In the last month, Arieve had spent more and more time with Coye. Some days he wished Coye would leave for good, but most days he was entirely too relieved Coye was back. There was no denying the joy Coye brought Arieve or the dreamy way Arieve spoke of her. Although he and Coye had yet to exchange words since their confrontation, he would show Arieve he could be civil. His chance would come soon: he and Tash still had to officially thank them for attending the wedding.

We'll do that once I'm ready for more talk. Mayr rested his head on Tash's shoulder and nuzzled his throat. Neither of them wanted to dance, but Mayr was not much fonder of large gatherings. His interests lay in intimate conversation. With Tash, he could say a wealth of things without uttering a single word.

"Soon," Tash murmured. He slipped his arms around Mayr's shoulders and huddled close. "A few more guests and we'll be done."

"Good thing we aren't expected to stay all night or *that* could get problemsome."

Tash's deep chuckle played through Mayr, chased by a shiver. "Let's try 'problematic'?"

Mayr rolled his eyes. "No, problemsome. You can have 'some' problems, but who in the Four's blessed world has 'atic' problems?"

"I think someone's had too much to drink, or maybe not enough."

"Who made *you* Keeper of all wordage?" Mayr pressed his hand to Tash's stomach and glided his palm downwards to Tash's hardened cock. When Tash's head fell back and he rose into the touch, Mayr hummed. "Yes, I can see my language bothers you. Perhaps I should make up some other words to relieve the frustration? How many words do you think we can make from 'suck,' 'my cock,' 'and come—'"

The words tumbled into a moan as Tash attacked Mayr's mouth again. Hungry and commanding, his tongue and teeth besieged whatever Mayr intended to say.

By the time they parted, Mayr had no words,

his conversational skills too scrambled to function. To quench the blaze under his skin, he finished the rest of his drink and poured another from the decanter next to him. He downed that round as if it were air. Contrary to what Tash thought, Mayr was far from drunk. His choice to drink gaffa nectar instead of mead, ale, or wine was strategic. The nectar's only effects on Mayr were a sweet aftertaste and delightful tingle.

The downside to not being drunk was being sober enough to recognize an oncoming catastrophe when he saw it: off to the side of the room, Estara, Orlee, Allaysia, *and* Bremary stood together, talking and laughing like the best of friends.

All four of them. In the same space. Without supervision.

Mayr whimpered. "By all that's sacred, *get them away from each other.*"

"Who?" Tash asked.

"Our sisters." Mayr motioned to the group. "They might've helped plan the wedding, but the end of days is imminent whenever they're together." He scanned the crowd for Pellon. "If I send Pell charging into their little party, maybe they'll scatter…"

Tash's throaty laugh twisted Mayr's insides. "I definitely need to get you out of here. You're starting to see things." He tugged Mayr's hand. "Let's go finish with the guests then I'll make you forget about the end of the world. I hear I can be a *very* good distraction."

"You have *no* idea," Mayr said, standing with Tash. "One look is all it takes."

"You'll have to show me which look," Tash whispered against Mayr's ear.

The answer on Mayr's tongue never made it past his lips, interrupted by the vibration of footsteps. The dull thud of boots sounded from Mayr's right, accompanied by softer steps.

Arieve strolled across the dais, her face flushed. Passing behind the chairs, she pulled Coye by one hand, the ribbons of her floral crown tangled around her shoulders. "Since you look ready to escape, it's a good time to chat." She stopped at Mayr's side and stole a hesitant glance at Coye. After Coye's subtle nod, Arieve stood on her tiptoes and brushed a kiss over Mayr's mouth, then Tash's.

"And by chat, she means give you your wedding gift," Coye said, crossing her arms and uncrossing them. The deep golden hue of her short, curly hair was dark against the embroidered white collar of her long tunic. A wide belt of thick white cord hung loosely from her hips, twisted and woven to resemble a lattice. Her loose white pants, tied up the sides in a crisscrossed pattern of thin cord, disappeared into boots up to her knee. Her green gaze flickered away and down before returning to Arieve and Mayr.

Amused by Coye's nervousness, Mayr focused

on Arieve's empty hands. "I don't know," he said, clutching her fingers to his chest, "but I think we've already been gifted these and all the lovely things they do. Unless there's something special we're meant to do with them?"

"You've done quite enough already," Arieve said. "What trouble we were aiming for we've got now."

Mayr stilled, his lips hovering over Arieve's knuckles. Her tone… Its playfulness was gone. The way she straightened her back, the tension in her grasp, the odd note in her voice—she meant something more solemn than a wish for a happy marriage. The awkward pause stretched into an agonizing silence. None of them moved.

Not until the corners of Arieve's mouth twitched with the smile she fought to hold back.

"Arieve…" Confusion twisted Mayr's emotions. "What's going on?"

Arieve crooked her finger at him and Tash. They both leaned in and pressed their foreheads to hers. "We wanted a family," she whispered, cupping their cheeks, "and come the end of summer, we'll have a little one to spoil shamelessly. This is the only gift here that'll keep giving, and it's the only one you can't give back."

Mayr stopped breathing. There was no gasp, no choke, just a painful lack. Arieve's words echoed in his mind, bouncing his sluggish thoughts around happiness and shock. He shuddered, caught between her meaning and the disbelief that raced after it.

A sideways glimpse confirmed he had not misheard: Tash's stunned expression was frozen, a mirror of what Mayr felt, right down to the hint of terror.

"You're pregnant?" The question barely made it from Mayr's mouth.

"Roughly three months," Arieve replied. "It's why I've needed to spend so much time with Coye. When I got sick… it wasn't what I thought. It didn't go away, then I realized…" She raked her fingers through his hair. "I wanted to wait, to make sure. I wanted *now*, this moment. The healer gave me something to control the sickness so I wouldn't ruin the surprise when I was with you." Arieve turned and clasped Coye's hand. "We've been getting our relationship ready. It's going to be very real very soon."

"Such an understatement," Mayr muttered. "Come here." He pulled Arieve into his arms and buried his face in her neck. "This is good. *So* good."

Tash's arms slipped around both of them from the side. "I don't know what to say," he mumbled against Arieve's temple. "Thank you isn't enough. Though I love you…" His hold went rigid before he cleared his throat. "We owe you every gratitude, every blessing, and I'm sorry I have no better words."

Arieve rubbed noses with Tash. "It's fine. Words aren't everything. As long as you're happy—"

"Ecstatic," Mayr interjected. "We're ecstatic." Still clinging to Arieve's waist, he studied the shine in her eyes. "I was right."

Arieve gazed at him quizzically.

"The morning after Tash came home from the Sanctum—you, me, the bucket. When you said it was something you'd picked up, I knew. Well, thought I knew." Mayr shrugged. "I didn't want to ruin our chances, so I didn't say anything. Then I thought you actually were sick. Then you weren't. *Now*…" Hesitant, he drew a hand down her waist. His nerves steadied once Arieve pressed his fingers to her stomach.

Coye leaned against the table, laughing quietly. "Yes, the healer's assured us it's true."

As Tash rested his hand over Mayr's on Arieve's stomach, a strangled noise of approval escaped Mayr. "I guess that means you're staying," Mayr said, glancing at Coye, "right?"

The smugness Mayr expected was nonexistent in Coye's sincere smile. "Yes. Staying as in staking my feet to wherever Arieve is and being a parent instead of a child." Head tilted, Coye regarded Mayr with a hint of surrender. "Nothing like a pregnancy to bring out the jealousy—it's putting me in my place *real* good."

"That jealousy better be on lock-down." Mayr's eyes narrowed. "Remember what I said."

"Mayr…" Arieve whispered.

"He's right." Coye raised both hands. "I'm in

this, full-out, for Arieve and the baby."

"For Arieve and the baby," Mayr agreed, his chest tightening. Just saying the word, imagining all the crying, the sleepless nights, every first...

Everything he had missed with Iliane he would do this time, not one day wasted.

A baby. Theirs. All the time he had forfeited with Arieve made up in a single life. The future he desperately wanted was almost close enough to touch.

Blinking back tears, Mayr hugged Arieve. "I do have a question," he murmured. "Move into the estate with us? *Please,* for our family. Coye can be here, too, just..." He held Arieve tighter as a trickle of tears warmed his cheek. "Everything you need, all the people you want. Let us take care of you—"

"Yes." Arieve pushed Mayr back to hold his face in her hands. "I've just been waiting for you to ask."

Lips overtook Mayr's, first with an excited kiss from Arieve, followed by Tash's tender calm. Pressed between them, he was rooted to the spot. If there was anywhere else he was meant to be, he never wanted to know about it.

Chapter Fourteen

Even after four months, Tash still barely believed it was real.

In the middle of Orae's tavern, he sidestepped the table to his left and grasped Arieve's hand, then pulled her into him. They collided gently before he slipped his arms between her heavy breasts and ever-growing stomach. Savouring the time alone, they swayed together in the open space between the tables and the bar.

Bathed in the early summer light, the empty tavern looked different during the day. It appeared larger than usual, the contrasts of dark red wood and light brown panels more noticeable. The scent of sweet nut bread and glazed berry tarts lingered with a hint of warm spice cake, nothing like the usual aromas of roasted meat, herb bread, and ale. Instead of lanterns, bouquets of flowers the size of his palm brightened the tables, as festive as the pink and yellow petals that littered the floor.

The stillness stirred Tash's attention the most. Without anyone else present, the tavern was oddly silent save for the sounds of chatty villagers passing by.

Yet it was the multitude of ribbons in every imaginable colour that made him smile. They draped about the room from corner to corner, complemented by a long banner above the tavern entrance that screamed congratulations in bright blue, purple, and green paint. The softness seemed out of place, leftover from the party hosted by Orae and Arieve's mother, Vilady. Not only had every woman from Arieve's family attended, Mayr's and Tash's families had joined them, along with Arieve's friends and anyone else who wanted to shower her with gifts.

Arieve chuckled and set a wicker basket of cloths and stuffed toys on the table beside her. "This isn't moving things to the wagon," she scolded, fingering the sleeves of his robes. "I imagine Mayr will have something to say about taking everything himself."

"Likely, but a moment won't hurt." Tash glided his hand down her belly, smoothing the folds of her emerald-green dress. Already in her seventh month, Arieve was heavily pregnant and pleased to be kicked furiously from the inside. Hoping to feel one such kick, he slid his fingers over her. When a small bump met his touch and jerked away, he could not help but laugh. Mayr promised the day their child was born would far surpass every day before then, though the moments where Tash felt their child's existence were already well beyond anything he hoped for. "Besides," he said, brushing his lips over Arieve's throat, "we're not in any rush. With everyone else gone up ahead, we're allowed to linger. Not that you can't linger whenever you please."

Boots scuffed the floor inside the entrance, followed by Mayr's laugh. "Here I wondered why you weren't shoving baskets at me, telling me where to put them. You're *busy*. Though it's funny, because you're practically glowing—and *she's* the pregnant one." Mayr sauntered through the dining area, thumbs hooked around his belts. "Of course, taking care of our girl… that's better than hauling baby stuff. Gah, there's *so much stuff*, in case you didn't notice. This baby's already worse than Ae, and she's been around *forever*." He reached for Arieve, looking pleased as she accepted his grasp.

"Oh, hush," Arieve admonished. "We'll need all these things." She moved to punch Mayr's shoulder but retracted. A sharp breath followed. "Ili wasn't any less needy. I remember your house, all her things everywhere."

Mayr gave a dramatic sigh and rolled his eyes. "I surrender—but only because I know arguing with a pregnant woman gets me nothing but hurt."

Arieve snorted a laugh and fanned herself. Her back tensed, and Tash held her a little tighter. "A little wisdom goes a long way."

"Absolutely, especially after I learned it the hard way." Mayr grinned and slipped his hands around her belly. "The things I can teach our baby. They'll be so smart."

"And they'll know fifty ways to use a knife by the time they're five." Arieve took a long breath accompanied by a second.

Tash loosened his hold and scowled. "Are you all right?"

"Feeling a bit off, but I'm fine," Arieve said, patting Tash's arm. "Just need to stay still a bit, that's all." She nodded towards the entrance. "How about you get the rest of these things into the wagon and we'll head up to the estate? I'd hate to miss the dinner Lira's putting on." Her smile hid the bags under her eyes. "I'm being spoiled today. First the party, now dinner… I'll be worn out by the time the sun sets."

Mayr kissed Arieve quickly. "Let's go, husband. Sooner we're done, sooner we get fed. I'm *famished*."

Tash released Arieve with a kiss to her cheek, feeling her take another long breath. "Famished for food, flesh, or something else altogether?" He swept back his veil and followed Mayr to the dark-stained wood chest on the floor. Together, they carried the chest of quilts, wool blankets, and infant clothes through the tavern with Mayr walking backwards.

"Wouldn't *you* like to know?" Mayr chortled and groaned. He shifted his grip as they stepped out the front door. "I'm dying for something edible. Those cradles aren't anywhere near as light as they appear—and there are *four*. One isn't fun enough."

"They *are* useful, though. We can put them everywhere we need them." Tash waited for Mayr to turn towards the small black wagon they had left on the red dirt road in front of the tavern. "One for Arieve and Coye's room, one for ours, one at the temple, and one in the Guard House. I'd expected we'd purchase a couple on our own, but to receive them all as gifts from our mothers… we're terribly blessed."

Mayr grunted and set his end of the chest on the back of the wagon. "Yeah, I know." He helped Tash push the chest against the side, next to a deeper black wood chest of clothes and blankets. Once the chest was secure, Mayr swiped his arm across his damp forehead and wiped his hands on his shirt. "I'm just being a pain. Ignore me."

"You're impossible to ignore," Tash said softly, "and with Arieve unable to share our bed, you're all mine. What aches the furniture gives you, my hands can soothe." He slid one palm around Mayr's neck and worked his fingers down Mayr's spine, finding the point that never failed to make Mayr arch into him.

"Blessed be the horrible weight," Mayr said, closing his eyes.

Tash surveyed the mostly filled wagon. At the front were four white cradles, separated by mounds of colourful pillows in pale tones. Four wooden chests of various hues sat along the sides of the wagon, a dozen baskets of every size between them. In the centre of the wagon, secured by a pile of cloth sacks, stood a white wood heaven's horse on curved legs, its slightly open wings curved around a small black seat. Beside the horse was a wooden ice-slider beast on six curved legs, three horns extending from its forehead. Its bisected tongue spiraled out of its mouth as wood and encircled its body in waves of white leather. The ice-slider also had a small seat, though of bright red. Tash suspected several stories of both animals would be in the books gifted to them by Aeley and Lira.

Fingertips settled on his jaw. "Hey," Mayr said, "where'd you go?"

"Here." Tash returned his attention to Mayr. "This really is happening, the four of us raising a child together... I never thought I'd call myself a father."

When Mayr opened his arms for an embrace, Tash stepped into them happily. "I know," Mayr murmured, his hold tightening. "It'll take a few good cries before you believe it's permanent. You'll curse the days when you can't get a moment's peace, but by then it's so real there's no going back to how you used to do things." He drew back to kiss Tash. "We can go into that more tonight. Right now, I'm going to check everything's packed in tight. You grab a couple more baskets. I'll come get the rest and Arieve. She'll need Coye to do something about her ankles."

"Hands, too," Tash added on his way back to the tavern. "They've been swollen lately." Had he been more versed in healing, he would have found a way to take the swelling away. All he could manage was treating what aches were relieved by a soak, oils, and massage.

With a sigh, he crossed the threshold and strolled into the dining area, expecting to find Arieve fussing over toys or refolding clothes.

Nothing prepared him for her lifeless body on the floor.

"*Arieve!*" Tash rushed across the room. She lay on her side, one arm out and the other across her hip. Whether it was lucky or damaging, he could not decide. Kneeling, he pressed against her throat. Both her pulse and breath were weak. "Arieve," he called, brushing her cheek with the back of his hand. "*Arieve.*"

He peered over his shoulder. "Mayr! Get in here, *now!*" In his grasp, Arieve trembled.

No, it's not her. It's me.

Behind him, Mayr's footsteps pounded the floorboards and stopped. A moment later, he was out the door.

"Come on, Arieve. Wake up, kind love." Tash gathered her into his arms, panic a spark that set fire to every feeling he had. Cradled against him, she remained unresponsive. He rocked gently, touching her face and hands and neck. Every few moments he stilled just to feel her slow breaths. There had been no warning, no time to prepare…

Except she felt off, she said. Tash cursed his ignorance. He should have asked her to follow them to the wagon. *But then she could've smacked her head on the doorframe or tripped.*

At least he could have known sooner. Wasted time could kill.

"Arieve, *please*," Tash whispered. His hand shook as he slid his fingers over her belly, wishing for a kick, desperate for a sign of life. He searched for the bump of the elbow or foot he felt earlier. There was no blood that he could see, no wound or sign of an early birth, not that it made him feel better. There was nothing. Nothing to work with, and nothing he could do.

He hated being helpless.

At least in the Shar-denn his adversaries had names. They'd had reasons, too, and weaknesses he could exploit.

This was worse than the Shar-denn. This was true helplessness.

Emeraliss, Lady of Love's Light, I seek your benevolence and grace...

In the eerie silence, he almost missed it: a shift in Arieve's breaths, a small hop from one to another.

"Arieve?" Tash tipped her face towards his.

Ragged breaths answered, then a strangled moan. Arieve's lashes fluttered. She blinked until her eyes stayed open, her brow furrowed. "Why am I on the floor?"

"I don't know," Tash replied quietly, "but I

need you to stay here. Mayr loves you—*I* love you—and we need to get you checked first. We can't put you or the baby at risk."

A ghost of a smile swept over Arieve's lips. She played with the trim hairs on his chin, her touch weak. "You love me? Really?"

Guilt punched Tash in the gut. What used to be whispers of feelings for her were now shouts loud enough to shatter hearts. Still, he had not openly admitted he loved her. The last time the words slipped out had been at the wedding feast—and no one mentioned them afterwards. Why had he wasted time? Why had he left the words for when she could have been dead and not staring like she wanted to hear them again?

"Yes," he said, caution thrown against the wall of regret. "I'm sorry I didn't tell you, not like I should have, but I'll tell you often from now on. Mayr and I both—"

Feet stomped into the tavern and through the room. "Got her," Mayr announced, breathless as he sank to his knees beside Arieve.

A tall woman with dark tan skin and golden eyes hurried around them, her deep orange-red hair pulled back in a thick braid that hit her lower back: Karane, one of Dahena's best healers and midwives, as well as Arieve's chosen healer.

"Mayr says you were on the floor when you weren't before." Karane kneeled and set down her healer's case, its thick shell an iridescent blue against her charcoal-grey dress and apron. "Can you tell me about that?" she asked, clasping Arieve's wrist.

Arieve blinked. "I don't know. I... Everything went blurry. Had some problems getting a good breath. Dizzy, definitely dizzy. I spun around to get something and reached and... that's it. I woke up here." She winced and rubbed her belly. "I feel horrible. Aching *everywhere*."

"I see." Karane brushed her fingers around Arieve's neck. "Have you been eating properly? Working too hard again? Doing something I've strongly suggested you shouldn't?"

Arieve scowled. "I can't seem to *stop* eating, though sometimes it's coming right back up. As for work..." She huffed while Karane's hands traveled over her breasts and down her stomach. "I haven't done much. Spent some time in the estate's kitchen, but not as much as I'd like, and they've got me doing the easy jobs. Cook won't let me do anything else. I've stayed out of the tavern except for today. Mother and the girls threw me a party. Grandmother turned away business for three days to do this, even the rooms..." Tears spilled down Arieve's cheeks. "Now I'm ruining dinner."

Tash squeezed her gently. "Shh, don't think about it. It'll wait. *They'll* wait."

"Promise," Mayr added as he rubbed Arieve's arms. "You haven't ruined anything. Karane?"

Karane offered a reassuring smile. "I hear today's all about you and the baby. Of course they'll wait for you, but we need to do this." She flattened both hands on Arieve's stomach. "Do you have any pain here?" When Arieve shook her head, Karane's hands moved to her hips. "How about here?"

"Just the one." Arieve gestured to her left side. "It wasn't hurting earlier."

"She landed on it," Tash explained.

Karane returned her hands to Arieve's belly. "So you were light-headed, having vision problems. Is this the first of it?" Arieve's head shook again. Karane sighed. "How long and how bad? Tell me everything you've felt since we last talked a couple weeks ago."

A blush coloured Arieve's cheeks. "Um, well, I've been tired and getting so warm I wish I could strip everything off and bathe in ice. I've been getting swollen feet a lot, and it's happening in my hands and face. Today's not so bad. Actually, it's been an all right day. This came on so fast, not being able to stop the room from spinning… Normally it goes away."

"'Normally'?" Karane repeated, drawing the word out.

"I've felt funny for a few days," Arieve admitted, "but usually it's fine after I sit or lie back. The dizziness goes up and down, though I guess it's getting worse. It feels longer. I'm still having those terrible headaches—whatever you gave me isn't working."

Karane cursed under her breath. "You should

have come to me."

"I was going to tomorrow. It's just little things brought on by all the excitement." Arieve glanced at Mayr and Tash. "I figure all this is regular pregnancy stuff, especially since the baby's getting *really* comfortable," she murmured.

Without warning, she jolted. Arieve grabbed Tash's hand and pressed his fingers to her stomach. A solid thump hit his palm.

Relief washed over Tash, dripping into the crevices worry had carved.

"I've been feeling funny all day, to be honest," Arieve continued. "It got worse after the party, then I ended up here." She frowned at Karane. "There's nothing to worry about, right? I just need better sleep?"

Karane let out a long sigh. "No, and I've seen it enough to be concerned."

Arieve paled and clenched Tash's fingers. "That doesn't sound good…"

"Here's the plan," Karane started, resting her hands on her knees. "For the next week, slow down and be cautious. Have someone with you at *all times*. If this happens again, you'll need help. If the symptoms continue—and *especially* if they get worse—you fetch me *immediately*."

"If they do continue?" Mayr asked, his quiet voice wavering.

"Bed rest, medicine, and constant supervision," Karane answered.

Mayr grunted. "'*Don't assign me a guard*,' you

said. '*I don't need to be followed*,' you said." He lifted Arieve's chin. "I'm assigning you guards as of right now, love. No way out of this."

"Fine," Arieve grumbled.

Karane shook her head. "Let me check some other things and we'll get you on your way." She held up one steady finger. "I'll give you some time to enjoy the dinner, but under my supervision and guidelines. Nap first, followed by a thorough examination, then a *short* stint at dinner. I won't have extra stress doing you in. It'll give me a chance to see how bad things are."

Tash swallowed uneasily, his stomach flipping. Nothing about Karane's counsel sounded reassuring. Her stern expression may as well have been grief for all its warmth. He only hoped it stopped there.

The weeks had not been kind nor were they getting easier. Hopes for Arieve's quick recovery had been abruptly quashed.

With nimble fingers, Tash worked his finest needle through the soft white fabric in his grasp, continuing a line of near-perfect backstitches as he rocked his chair. Piled in his lap, the embroidered material was tinged with purple and blue hues from the stained-glass window beside him, the afternoon light as warm as the summer day. Thanks to the time spent sewing his own robes over the years, his skills were sharp and consistent. At the rate he was going, the blanket would be finished within the month, and he could move onto the baby blessing gown.

Providing there's a baby to wear it. Tash stifled a sigh and peered at the bed. Curled up in a thin, cream-coloured sheet, Arieve slept soundly in her daily noontime nap. Once she awoke, he would place the blanket aside and escort her on a walk around the estate before ensuring she ate something. To occupy the rest of their afternoon, he supposed he would either read to her or find something else, though he was running out of new ideas.

He knew how frustrated Arieve was. Being confined and restricted to light movement was far from easy and even less enjoyable. For one week after the gifting party, they had followed Karane's instructions, but Arieve's condition did not improve. Her aches and light-headedness only worsened, prompting Karane to prescribe constant rest balanced by short walks twice a day and a series of stretches.

After two weeks of the regime, Arieve's patience was wearing thin. She wanted to do things, not waste her days. To her annoyance, Tash, Mayr, and Coye not only reinforced Karane's instructions, they had adapted their routines to her needs. Tash and Mayr stayed with Arieve during the mornings and afternoons, alternating days to allow Mayr time with the guards and Tash with Adren, Ress, and the Temple. The nights were overseen by Coye after she returned from felling trees and moving logs. Together with a crew of guards and household staff, they kept Arieve company and fetched whatever she needed.

The changes drew more than one fit from Arieve, resulting in tears and gushes of apology. They were being too thoughtful, too kind, too honourable—too *everything*, according to her. She wanted them to go on as if nothing had changed.

Except something *had* changed, and while she argued they did too much, Tash believed they did too little. Not that there was much else to do. He could not carry the child for her or bear her symptoms.

Arieve was not the only one frustrated—she was simply the only one who dared show it. Regardless of how ragged and exhausted they were, Tash, Mayr, and Coye had made a pact to offer Arieve only lightness.

At least she's here at the estate. We're never far from everything she needs. Tash tugged on the needle and tightened the white thread, then wedged the needle through thicker stitches and laid the blanket down. He stopped rocking to flex his fingers and stretch his shoulders, stiff as they protested being in the same position for too long.

Relieving the tension in his neck, he gazed over the large bedroom. The walls were of the same grey stone and red wood panels as his and

Mayr's room, with the same red ceiling and a hearth in the wall behind him.

The similarities ended there. From the colours of the windowpane and layers of emerald-green curtains to the black cushions and trinkets on the mantel above the hearth, everything was different. The room and its smaller adjoining room had once been Aeley's bedroom and her childhood playroom. Up until her wedding day, Aeley had kept the rooms rather than take over her father's. Once she married Lira, however, Aeley assumed her father's abandoned suite and completely accepted her position as head of the Dahe family.

Both rooms belonged to Arieve and Coye now. They had moved in two weeks after Mayr's request, and Tash appreciated his wisdom: as Arieve's pregnancy progressed, there had not been enough space in Mayr and Tash's bed for the three of them to sleep comfortably. Arieve had also wanted Coye to remain close.

To Tash's relief, Aeley not only supported their decision as a family, she shared her home. Even more, she surprised them all, offering rooms with personal meaning instead of one of the smaller rooms reserved for guests. According to Aeley, she had intended to give Mayr her old suite once he settled down. Things had come to pass more or less as anticipated.

The rooms granted Arieve and Coye plenty of space. A set of red doors in the wall behind the bed offered access to the smaller room, a nursery decorated with pale colours. Located across the hall and in between the Head of the Guard's room and the suite meant for the head of the Dahe family, the chambers were often occupied by the most vulnerable family members. More often than not, the rooms were passed down to children. The conjoined room had served multiple purposes in the past, from nursery and playroom to sitting room, study, store room, and collections display.

The suite was not the only thing passed down, Tash recalled, glancing at the thick, wooden bed frame. The rooms were furnished with matching pieces that had been polished and re-stained. Crafted from hard, deep red wood with a black tinge, each piece of furniture boasted elegant carvings of wolves, bearcats, and hawks among ferns and flowers. The high bed frame had smooth, gold-plated corners, similar to the gold rings around the legs and arched backs of the round table and six chairs behind him. Four armoires stood along one wall across from the dresser covered with jewel cases and boxes of ribbons, beads, and other baubles. Close to the bed sat two bedside tables occupied by candles, books, and dishes of candied vegetables and fruits Arieve craved. Across the room, by the hearth, were three high-backed chairs, each covered with black cushions and emerald-green blankets, their vivid tone the same as the curtains chosen by Arieve. Black footstools accompanied each of the chairs.

To balance the dark tones, Arieve had chosen cream-coloured linens and decorated the corners with draped gossamer, the long lengths of pale blue complemented by a shimmer of bright blue. One of the white cradles stood between Arieve's side of the bed and the outer wall, away from the doors and window.

The rocking chair in which Tash sat matched the cradle. The chair was a gift from Mayr's family, all of it cut, carved, and polished by Loftin and Teneth. They had chiseled cubs and pups down the back with fine artistry, along with narrow leaves and small buds. Padded with white cushions sewn and stuffed by Estara and Orlee, the chair was more comfortable than Tash could have guessed. It also had a twin, kept in Mayr and Tash's room.

Gathering his focus, Tash withdrew the needle from its resting place. As he tugged the fabric taut inside the embroidery hoop, small stitches stretched over the faint lines drawn in pale yellow ink. He was halfway through embroidering the top layer of the blanket, the shapes of flowers and feathers sweeping around the long, graceful lines and curls of a vine. When the embellishment was complete, he would add a thick middle layer and thin bottom, all quilted together by a simple pattern of petals. The blessing gown would match the blanket, layers of white fabric with hints of silver thread to make it glimmer.

If only he could have an easier time of making it. His calloused fingers ached. The thimbles on his middle finger and thumb slipped at the worst times. The thread would not cooperate: he continued to struggle with almost-knots and fussed with the spool. He had better luck making clothes for himself.

Still, it helped carry the weight on his mind. Beneath his forced composure he worried about *everything*. Not only was Arieve's health at risk, the baby's was as well. One or both could die.

I shouldn't even be here, not after what I did to Ines, refusing her needs because I was too caught up in the Shar. Now Arieve's getting the raw end of the deal. I always want what I shouldn't have.

With stark clarity, he remembered the rejection in Inesta's teary eyes when he had denied her a child. She had come to him with sweet honesty and asked if he loved her enough to start a family. He had held her and admitted he loved her more than life itself, but a family was out of the question. It was a messy headache he could never afford. The Shar-denn was rubbish enough; a child would have only made their lives a disaster.

Now… now I can't wait. The thought of Mayr holding our child in his arms, seeing Arieve be the mother she wants to be… It feels right, but I'm horrible for what I put Ines through, all that hurt. I stole her life. Tash frowned and rocked the chair harder. *It's just as well. A child would've tied her down worse than she was. I still might have run away, leaving her to fend for them, and Ress would've had to take them both in. Even if I'd stayed, I'd be dead or so unfeeling we'd have separated anyway. Saying no was the best choice. My leaving saved us all.*

Leaving was the last thing he wanted in the present. Tired and fearful as he was, he intended to fulfill his promises to those who relied on him. Their needs pulled him in every direction, stretching his focus and straining his calm. Somewhere among the chaos he was still himself, his identity woven through the pieces. Whatever complaints he had he kept secret, aware of the weight on Mayr and Coye's shoulders. Mayr's control of the household guard required time, and his work with Aeley and Lira took effort, particularly when they traveled to High Council Hall for meetings. On the days Mayr sat with Arieve, stacks of reports and schedules accompanied him.

Coye was under another sort of stress. Work required her to be away from the estate every day, distanced from Arieve for six days of their eight-day week. While Tash and Mayr stayed close to the estate, Coye's location could change on a daily basis. Usually she was in any one of the forests in Gailarin, though there were days when she was in one of the nearest lumberyards, replenishing their stock. Other times, she traveled for most of the day, transporting logs to woodcutters, millers, and anyone who needed them. By the time she returned home each evening, she was fatigued and often sore.

Hope, that's what I need to focus on. Tash retrieved a pair of scissors from the sewing basket beside the chair and snipped the thread from the needle. As he rethreaded the needle, he commanded himself to think solely about Arieve and the baby. Not only did he need to grasp hope, he needed to channel it into beauty. It was not enough to cleanse and bless the blanket once it was finished; he had to infuse positive thoughts into every stitch rather than darkness.

There were things he wanted to do with their child, a thousand things he wanted to share. *Like how the Four truly are. The fact that statues and tapestries and paintings won't ever get it perfect, not when the skin of the Goddesses changes in the blink of an eye, hues layered on hues that run so deep it's like staring into an abyss. Not when their eyes slide from white to black in a breath, hitting every colour in between. Not when their clothes and armour are made from everything that makes the world and holds it together.*

A memory slaughtered his concentration. He knew what it was to be on the divide between life and death, where the world seemed to begin and end at the exact same moment, spinning yet standing still.

More than that, there's what I saw during my Uldana Trials. How wondrous it was to pass over the precipice between life and death and wake to love at my fingertips. It gave me clarity like never before. That's *what I want to give our child: the chance to see the world for themselves and let them know there's always more. To make sure they can reach to* become *more.*

He wanted to share everything he knew. Without a doubt, he wanted to make another journey to the Shatterlands and show Mayr, Arieve, Coye, and their child the stupendous, terrifying beauty. They could travel to the sandy red shores of the shimmering blue-green sea and wade in its salty warmth under a sky filled with playful flocks of golden birds. He could show them how to slide over the glassy black and amber terrain without falling. They could explore the winding puzzle of amber glass caverns and meet their inhabitants: tiny, silver-scaled creatures the size of a wildemouse with silver-green wings and bright orange tongues that flicked and curled and latched onto things with all the softness of silk rope.

Just as much, he wanted to share the view into the grandest of the Shatterland's canyons and its echoing depths. Around the canyons, massive walls of crumbling black stone rose from where the earth had burst apart centuries earlier. Split into three, the destroyed earth had spilled its insides across the landscape, the deluge of amber blood devouring everything in its path. Where there once had been expansive woods and thriving villages, there was only weathered stone and slippery glass, the twisted forms of ancient beasts, people, and trees entombed beneath. Horrifying as it was, the Shatterlands preserved the past and offered the present a new perspective on the future. Perhaps that was its true beauty; the real lesson meant to be learned during the first Uldana trial.

That same trial had also brought him pain. Viciously mobbed and pummeled after his visit to the Shatterlands, Tash had tried to fight off the men who attacked him on his return to the temple. His escape had been a precarious mix of luck and skill, resulting in brutal injuries. Recovery had been difficult, soured by flashes of violent memories he was unable to stop or ignore.

During those days, the brightest light in the darkness had been Mayr. In his selflessness, he had come to Tash's aid and waited by his side while he slept. It was then that Tash's love for Mayr had burned with a vengeance, desperate to hold onto the care and security Mayr offered. No one protected him the way Mayr wanted to. No one had ever tried.

Two years later, the fear and agony from the Trials still haunted him, no less hurtful than the Shar-denn. There were lessons to be learned from both. He would never be proud of his past, but he would not dismiss it. Perhaps when their child was old enough to fully understand right from wrong, he would share the experiences that had burned their morals into his life. He would teach their child to not only help others, but to protect themselves without taking advantage of anyone. Greed, malice, and the bloody quest for power were not worth the pain inflicted. *You take the weight with you. There's no easy way to shake them once they poison your blood. This is what I'll pass along. This is my legacy.*

Although he should probably tell Arieve of his past before he mentioned it to any child.

The needle pricked his uncovered forefinger on his left hand, a sharp stab worth the curse he flung at it, scolding himself in the process. He was scared to tell Arieve everything about him. Mayr had taken the truth better than Tash anticipated, but that meant nothing when it came to anyone else. On the day they received the bracelets from Emeraliss, he had told Mayr what happened at the Sanctum, including the revelation about the Shar-denn's origins. Given their discussion then and an even longer conversation since the wedding, they had agreed not to tell Arieve of Tash's past while she was pregnant, and certainly not during bed rest. They would save the disapproval and anger for later, once they all could think clearly.

Sighing, Tash rubbed his eyes and glanced out the window, glimpsing the buildings of the village in the distance and their various coloured roofs. On the other side of the great expanse of village was the temple, though he could not see it from where he sat. The temple was a fair distance from the estate, but he appreciated it all the same. Often he walked between them to clear his mind. At the moment, he sorely needed one of those walks.

Three soft knocks on the door to the hallway jarred his attention. Arieve stirred, moaning as she turned over.

Before more knocks woke her completely, Tash left the blanket in the chair with his thimbles and hurried across the room. He opened the door and leaned against the doorframe, surprised to find Lira and Adren. Their escorts, Ralaern and Surie, waited on the other side of the corridor with their arms folded.

"Fancy meeting you here," Lira greeted, sweeping back the loose curls of her dark hair. Her pale pink gown was a dainty sight of tiered cuffs and bright pink sash compared to the white dress Adren wore beneath a loosely slung black belt, thigh-length black leather vest, and bronze chains draped from cir hip to back. "We're off to get a light snack and thought you might like to join us. Call it a well-earned break from our meeting while Aeley has a private conversation with Mayr, Pellon, and Ress."

Adren snorted. "Try not-so-private argument. My money's on Aeley. The boys don't have a chance."

Lira beamed. "I always bet on Aeley. The men tend to cave. Right, Tash?" She tilted her head, the corners of her grey eyes strained. "Especially when they know what's good for them."

Her words could not have been more pointed.

"I suppose so," Tash answered, peering over his shoulder to the bed.

A gentle hand settled on his forearm. "She'll be fine," Lira assured him. "We won't keep you. We only want to chat." She moved closer, her grip tight on his wrist. "Mayr worries," she murmured. "When one doesn't eat or sleep as they should, their husbands send reinforcements. At least I'm mostly harmless and Adren likes you—Mayr could have sent Pellon and Aeley to tie you up and knock you out."

Tash let out a defeated breath. Convincing Mayr he was fine was a lie he had yet to perfect.

"Go on," a voice added from Tash's right. Gorgan stood from the chair set against the wall mere steps from the door. Dressed in dark clothes like Ralaern and Surie, a short sword and knife strapped to his belt, Gorgan brushed blond curls out of his eyes and offered a shy smile. "It's why I'm out here, anyway. Least you could do is make me work. Mayr'll have my balls in a jar if I'm not pulling my weight."

"Aw, come on, half-pint, you're pulling." Surie nodded at Tash, the high tail of her brown hair swinging with the sharp turn of her head. "Our HG knows this one's stubborn as anything. That's why he sent Lady Lira and Pretty Feisty to drag him to his culinary death—I mean *satisfaction*."

"Stuck," Ralaern chided, nudging Surie's

elbow. "Manners?"

"Left them downstairs, and quit doing that." Surie elbowed Ralaern's ribs. "Priest Tash appreciates a plain speaker. Goddesses know everyone here prefers plain speak, right?" Her hopeful glance met Tash's then flitted to Lira's and Adren's.

Adren shrugged, cir hands shoved into cir vest pockets. "Blunt and honest works for me. The game's always in the fancy words, though some people know how to play them without being complete asses." Ce smirked at Tash. "So? Shall we?"

Tash looked back once more. His stomach was ready to devour everything in the pantry and exact revenge on his lack of appetite. Surely he could leave and return without anything happening…

Gorgan patted Tash's shoulder, his blue-green gaze sympathetic. "I've got this. If anything happens, I know what to do."

The confidence in Gorgan's quiet voice eased Tash's doubt. Mayr had assigned a team of guards to stay with Arieve when no one else could. Gorgan had the daytime shifts due to his mother's experience with midwifery. According to Gorgan, he had acquired the same skills as an assistant to his mother. When Karane had primed the guards for their position, Gorgan was the only one who conversed with her in the words of a healer.

"Give me a moment," Tash muttered, turning into the room. On his way to the bed, he met Arieve's gaze as she turned towards him.

"What's wrong?" Arieve asked groggily, wiping her eyes. The bed sheet tangled about her legs, while the low neckline of her light blue dress skewed towards one shoulder.

"Nothing." Tash kissed Arieve's forehead. "I'm stepping out for a bit." He swept back the mussed plaits of her hair. "Go back to sleep, gentle love. I'll be back shortly."

"You'd better." Arieve's sigh was sleepy, her fingers weak as she caressed his jaw and lips. "Love you."

"Love you back." After a tender kiss, he waited for Arieve to curl onto her side. Although he loathed taking his gaze off her for even a moment, it hurt seeing her look so small despite the life she carried within.

Perhaps he needed a break after all. Maybe Mayr had sent him exactly what he needed.

In silence, Tash waited for Gorgan to settle in a chair by the hearth before he left the room and closed the door. Without complaint, he followed Lira and Adren through the hall and down the stairs. Ralaern and Surie strolled alongside them, their voices hushed.

The dining room was fully prepared by the time they entered, the red walls brightened with candlelight. Platters awaited them with an abundance of food, including three types of pastries that overflowed with thick cream and colourful preserves, a mixed-grain trencher filled with melted cheese and diced vegetables, and several plates of sliced summer fruit drizzled with honey and herbs. Goblets and pitchers sat at the ready, spread out across the long table.

Already planning the plate he would take to Arieve, Tash settled in the seat across from Lira, closest to the end of the table where Aeley usually sat. Adren sat to his right, and once Lira glowered at Ralaern and Surie, they sank into the seats to Lira's left.

Following Lira's lead, Tash filled two plates with every option on the table. He set one plate aside for Arieve with a pitcher of berry juice and picked at the food on his own plate.

"Well, at least you're *touching* the food." Adren bumped cir shoulder against his. "How much will it take to get you talking? Apparently you're not so good with words lately. That's all sorts of terrible considering we usually can't shut you up."

Tash arched one brow and peered at Adren from around his veil. "It's a full intervention, then?"

Adren shrugged, nibbling on a jelly-filled pastry as red as cir plaited hair. "If you'd talk to your damn husband I wouldn't have to call you out." Adren licked cir fingers and swung cir legs over the side of cir chair, facing him. "Spill, priest, and get eating. Don't make me go Goddess-touched on you. I'm getting better at it, all the magic that can break things into pieces and assemble them all weird. Important things, things Mayr might like to play with."

Across the table, Surie choked on a laugh. "Best threat I've heard *ever*. I like you. You can stay."

"Don't encourage cir." Tash scowled at Surie. "I thought you were supposed to protect people, not ambush me."

"Right now it's the same thing." Lira leaned back, her goblet in hand. "If you truly don't want to talk, I'll respect that. However, if you're amenable to friends who want to help you the way you help us, we're happy to listen. I hear it's what family does."

Tash recognized the strain in Lira's voice. She did not offer the words lightly: not only had her parents all but disowned her for not being what they wanted, her brothers had intended to kill her and take advantage of Aeley's position as Tract Steward. Her happiness came with a painful price.

Compared to her, he was luckier than he had a right to be. Three times in his life, he had been blessed with a kind, loving family who valued his happiness and safety: his parents, sister, Ress, Varen, Nimae, and their families; the priests; and now Mayr, Arieve, and their loved ones. They included him even when he pushed the world away. He owed them more than words—he owed them trust.

"I'm frustrated, that's all," Tash admitted, prodding food around his plate. "There's not much I can do for Arieve. I can't fix what's wrong. Mayr and I got her into this position, but we can't make it better. I'm afraid it'll take its toll on her." He sighed and sat back, fingers laced together in his lap. "As a priest, I'm sworn to help however I can and solve problems. As a father, I can only do so much."

"She's stronger than you realize. Mothers usually are." Lira reached to him from across the table. "Arieve comes from a long line of tough women, and you're helping the best you can. Have faith. Surely you have more of it to spare."

"Should be bottomless, the way you are," Adren argued. "Then again, you like complicated, so maybe there's more to being a priest I don't get. Like how you can even *begin* to balance a relationship with Mayr and Arieve in the first place. Add Coye and the baby… How do you keep it under control?"

A slow smile crossed Tash's lips. "It isn't as complicated as it sounds, and we've found ways to include Coye—mostly by backing off so she and Arieve have the time they need. A short list of rules helps. So does conversation and compassion for what we all feel. We've agreed to keep things simple and stop unnecessary tension before it starts."

Adren lifted one red brow. "I think your

simple and everyone else's may be on different planes of existence."

For the first time in what felt like days, Tash laughed, the knots in his emotions uncoiling. "Perhaps that's true. Mayr and I care for Arieve deeply. Our hearts recognize her as something between an old friend and a wife. She's only one document away from being the latter. She's also very much *ours*, someone we love together. At the same time, we're strengthening the foundation of our relationship." Tash gazed at the smears of honey and jam on his plate, his laughter giving way to solemn truth. "We love Arieve in our own ways, and we want her to have everything she desires. We'll sacrifice what we must. We'd trade our entire lives to keep her and this child alive," he murmured, slipping his hand into Lira's outstretched palm. "I'd stake my life on carrying this child for her if I could."

As Lira squeezed his fingers, Ralaern and Surie cast him sympathetic glances.

"It'll be all right," Lira said. "Good things come to kind souls, and yours is kinder than most."

"If not being smacked by the romance stick a little too hard," Adren said before sipping cir mead.

Another laugh escaped Tash, low and long, deep in his throat. "Maybe it has been. Emeraliss knows it's one thing I love most about Mayr." He dipped his head in Adren's direction. "Like his essence in my life, Arieve has seeped into our relationship, lingering like an embrace. Always there, always a comfort, bridging divides we never knew existed."

Adren smirked. "You're talking priest again. You must be feeling better."

"I suppose it's my version of romantic, where Mayr's is about deeds," Tash said. "Truthfully, I've never considered myself a good speaker. When I was in the Shar, I was consumed by emotions I couldn't express, except with my fists. I communicated through violence, bruising anyone who got too close." He cleared his throat, avoiding Ralaern and Surie's keen expressions. Just how much did the guards know of his affiliations? "I was angry, miserable. Lost. They conscripted me at a prime age, when my view of myself was fragile and malleable. They used it against me, and I let them."

Tash gripped his goblet of water and stared at the reflections on its surface. "Becoming a priest allowed me to find a better, more eloquent way to express myself. I've learned new words, new perspectives. I think in a different way than I used to. I've learned to say what I feel, even if I use too many words and they sound like riddles."

"Until you get talking about the Shar," Adren argued, "then you sound like one of my father's men."

Tash snorted softly. "Doesn't matter how long or far I run, no one can gut the Shar in me. There's no killing it," he said, letting his tone slip. Darker and deeper with traces of the man he used to be, the words flowed from his lips. "To be honest, some days I want to do damage. There've been people I wouldn't mind punching straight into dead and ripping things apart. Now I have Mayr for those things. He's set on protecting whatever humanity I've rediscovered."

"So he beats them and you pray for him?" Ralaern asked, playing with wisps of his white-blond hair and the thick gold hoops around the shell of his ear. He seemed oddly fascinated.

"Essentially, yes. We're well-paired."

"Which is why everything will be *fine*, you'll see." Lira tapped the back of Tash's hand, his fingers trapped under hers. "It's terrible how alike you and Mayr are, going to the ends of misery and hitting every cliff along the way." She clutched his hand in both of hers. "As I've told Mayr: this household is blessed with stubbornness and hope. We're survivors, compelled to live and love and keep going. But you can't live today if you allow the fears of tomorrow to control everything. Tomorrow will come and we'll sort it, then we'll sort the day after, and the day after that. If all you see is the potential disaster instead of enjoying what you have, you're not living—you're waiting to die. You're waiting to lose. You're waiting for all the wrong things when the good is here and now."

Lira released his hands. "Faith, Tash, isn't that what you tell us? 'With faith, all things have a foundation; all happiness has an anchor…'?"

"'And all spirits find their way,'" Tash finished, gazing at the white table linens. He recalled the first time Mayr, Arieve, and he had dinner. *"If we seek to create a life, we must first embrace the hope in that gift,"* echoed in his mind. It was no less true now, even while he lost himself to grief not yet earned. Arieve was alive, as was the baby. Despite his what-ifs, they had every chance of survival. To lose faith meant he was giving up, and he never intended to do that. He had given up once before.

Never again.

"I know I'm an ass, but tell me again: *what* do you say if the priests threaten to keep you?"

"No, thank you," Tash answered. He laughed at Mayr's question as he slipped a handful of books into a wooden travel case and wrapped them in linen. Buckling the case shut, he glanced around his chamber in the temple, certain that he had everything for the Sacred Assembly's meeting. His clothes were already packed at the estate.

"Right and *why* is that?" Mayr folded his arms and leaned against the closed door. The worn brown sword scabbard strapped to his waist scraped the wall. In the sunlight, his black clothes were stark and defiant against the gleaming white stone.

"Because I have to get home before my husband comes looking." Tash's lips twitched with a smile. He spun to face Mayr, his fingers itching to release Mayr's long tail of hair and fan its silkiness across his shoulders. "He'll storm through the House of the Sacred Assembly with all the fury of wings and fangs and claws."

Mayr's features twisted. The tip of his tongue stuck out as he pushed off the wall. "No wings—just fangs and claws." He crossed the room to join Tash. "As long as you *come home*," he said, sliding his hand beneath Tash's hair to cup the back of his neck. His fingertips danced up and down Tash's nape, making Tash shiver and arch into his caress. "Today and tomorrow, that's it, right?"

The worry in Mayr's voice was nothing compared to the concern in his grey eyes.

Tash drew him close, focused on the warmth of their shallow breaths. "I'll be home tomorrow evening," he promised, his lips lingering over Mayr's.

Neither of them moved, their mouths flirting with the anticipation of a kiss. Mayr's need for assurance mirrored Tash's own anxiety. After one month of bed rest, Arieve was ready to wreak havoc on the world simply to feel alive. In recent days, her mood had been more erratic, prone to smiles and laughter one moment, tears and emotional breakdowns the next. Just that morning she complained of new aches in her back.

Thankfully Coye's home today—she can do something about that and we can do this. Tash claimed Mayr's lips in a hard kiss, urging it deeper with every angle and thrust he could manage. Mayr's fingertips raked down the back of his robes, leaving a blazing trail of want along his skin. In their efforts to care for Arieve, pleasure had been cast aside. What free moments they had together were invested in rest and discussion. Most nights, they were too preoccupied to pursue anything beyond kisses.

Now I'm going away... though we still have the rest of this morning. Our little group isn't leaving until mid-afternoon, so really.... Tash chuckled as his thoughts sank to filthy depths. He could not miss the meeting of his fellow Uldana priests and the Keepers, nor could he allow them to hold him hostage for further meetings, but he *could* have his way with Mayr before then. The ride between the Dahe estate and the House of the Sacred Assembly was short, but he craved the distraction memories would serve. The thick, salty taste of Mayr on his tongue, the slick heat of Mayr's cock between his lips—they would ensure he kept his trip short, hungering for more.

Mayr eased him back. "What's so funny?"

"Nothing." Tash stole a wet, messy kiss. When he pulled away, Mayr's lips glistened. "Merely considering how to use our time wisely," he said huskily, coiling Mayr's hair around his hand and tugging. Mayr tilted his head back, his tattooed throat exposed. "I'm done with my meetings here." Tash kissed Mayr's neck. "Ress is at home teaching Adren a new recipe. Sister Kee and Brother Armamae are preparing for the meeting." He licked a path down Mayr's throat to the hollow. "No one's looking for me until later. I'm all yours if you want me," he murmured against Mayr's collarbone.

"Tempting," Mayr breathed. "Even more tempting if we were at home. In bed. Locked door."

"If that's what it takes to get you naked."

"Always is." Mayr stepped back and motioned to the room. "Have everything you wanted?"

Tash cast another glance over the stripped bed, dresser, writing desk, and the white and red tapestry on the furthest wall that depicted the Goddesses frolicking around a silver fountain. "Yes, just these books from our library. I can brush up on details on the way to the meeting."

The last thing he needed was to look unprepared in front of his peers. The Sacred Assembly was the quintessential gathering of spiritual leaders in Kattal. Their discussions could go for days, bringing every Uldana priest into a single space to work out issues, pursue changes to society, and shape the future of religious practice. To be part of the Assembly was an honour, and he needed to be at the ready with worthy thoughts.

With a sly smile, Tash pressed a chaste kiss to Mayr's lips. "Let's go do something unseemly."

"You're trouble," Mayr mumbled. "I wish I was going with you."

"I know, but Arieve." Tash nuzzled the soft skin behind Mayr's ear. "One more month until the baby comes. We can't *both* be gone if something happens. Pellon and I will be back from the Assembly tomorrow, I swear."

"You're *absolutely sure* you have to go?"

"Mayr." Tash sighed. "I promised. I missed the last two."

"I know, I know. You have to represent the temple, plus Felensa's got things for Adren. I'm only whining because—"

Frantic knocks rattled the door. "Tash! Mayr?" a man's voice yelled. More pounds sounded.

"What in the—" Mayr rushed to open the door.

Gorgan hunched over in the hallway, gripping the doorframe and gulping breaths. His blond curls were a mess around his red face, his clothes askew. "Arieve—" he rasped. "Baby's coming." He motioned into the corridor. "I found Karane, sent her up."

A chill surged through Tash faster than his heart could stop. He choked and sputtered. His mind… frozen, gone like the rest of him.

Tash hurried to Mayr's side, tripping over his own feet along the way. His knees were there somewhere, keeping him upright. Thoughts…

There was nothing. He was functioning on nothing.

Mayr's jaws dropped. He stumbled back. "I—She's—" Mayr gaped at Tash, a stunned silence between them. It was as agonizing as the gnawing, burning need to be by Arieve's side. "But it's too early. A month…"

"A month you don't have." Gorgan backed out of the doorway. "Come on!"

Forget the meeting. Grabbing Mayr's hand, Tash ran from the room and yanked him along. They kept pace with Gorgan, charging through the hallways to the main entrance of the temple. Without looking at the worshippers in the altar space—without seeing much of anything—Tash forced his legs to keep moving. They could not miss the baby's birth. Nothing and no one would stop them.

"Started before my shift," Gorgan said.

The hoarse words were almost lost to the noise drumming in Tash's head. His heart was working again, but the rest of him…

They burst through the open entrance and fled down the long staircase of wide, white steps. Tash and Mayr were little more than a hand's length from catching Gorgan's heels and tumbling them all.

Another chill blasted down Tash's spine, colder and darker than the last. In an odd moment of clarity, he heard a faint hiss. Over his shoulder, he glimpsed a blur of villagers who milled about the temple steps. Others dashed towards the woods that surrounded the temple.

Can't lose focus. Just keep going. Tash obeyed Mayr's pull, his arm threatening to rip from its socket before they reached the last step and hit the red earth with heavy feet. The baby was early and anything could happen. They needed to help Arieve—

A deafening roar split the air. Thunder slammed down around them, raining screams and shouts and piercing cries.

The earth shook violently, cracking open beneath their feet. Veins of shadowy voids burst from a hungry core. The stairs blew apart, hurling stone in every direction. Pressure assaulted Tash from behind and below, tossing him as if he were a doll, lifeless and insignificant.

He slammed to the ground, unable to yell, robbed of breath. Ribs dug deep. Every gasp seared. Warmth seeped from his nose as blood filled his mouth, and his eyes burned, gritty and dry. Sharp, ringing pain stabbed the insides of his ears.

White dust clung to the air as rocks and bodies were everywhere at once, flying and falling, landing with sickening thuds around him. Blood splattered his hand, heat dropping from the sky...

And then silence, lethal and furious.

Death had come to play.

Fighting to grasp life, Tash reached into the terror and drowned in darkness.

Chapter Fifteen

Mayr groaned, his body all but fused into one big ache. Pains jabbed and flared behind his eyes in ribbons and chunks, flashes of colour fuzzy in his heavy daze. The ringing in his ears muffled what sounded like wails. Had a carriage landed on him, crushing half his ribcage? More than one of his ribs was jammed against the hilt of his sword. His right arm was pinned beneath his waist; his left arm was sore from an angle that offered nothing but tension. Though his legs were attached, they protested his efforts to move. None of his limbs seemed broken, but that provided only partial relief. When had he hit the ground?

We were running... Mayr coughed and spat out dirt. *Arieve, the baby...*

He pushed up, gasping and snarling as his muscles battled back. Whatever the damage, he would drag himself home, broken clarity and all. Cursing with every foul word he knew, he maneuvered into an upright position. Red earth soiled the front of his clothes. White and red grit covered the rest of him.

In an instant, a headache rushed him, burning and punching at his skull. A cry of agony tore through him before he thrust his palms against his eyes. The priests could give him something to soothe the aches. He peeked at the temple.

It took everything he had not to scream.

There was no temple, only fresh ruins littered with bodies. Gaping holes filled with destruction. Each majestic column was destroyed, every wall blasted apart. Several still toppled, throwing white dust into the air, and the roof lay on the ground, glass panes gone. The staircase to the temple was cracked and upturned. Dozens of the red trees that surrounded the temple were obliterated, the gardens buried. White stone was splattered red as sickening grey smoke swirled, dulling the sunlight. The glass statues of the Goddesses that had once guarded the entrance were nowhere to be seen.

Among the rubble, battered figures crawled and hobbled, unsteady as they tossed marble aside. Screams for help pierced the fogginess between Mayr's ears, and it took him a moment to realize the top levels of the temple had caved into the lower levels. Tattered red fabric waved in the slight breeze—priests lay among the sea of worshippers, injured and unmoving.

Panic raced through him. *Tash.*

Mayr scrambled to stand, almost falling over twice. He gazed at the debris around him, rubbing away the dirt and hot tears stinging his eyes. There was nothing but chaos. Pummeled earth and broken stone. Ragged limbs discarded, lacking bodies. Torn parchment and clothes that fluttered away. A dozen footsteps to his left, a priest lay face down, the skin-coloured bracer of one arm unhidden by his soiled robes.

"Tash!" Mayr hurried through the rubble and tripped, crashing to his knees beside Tash's lifeless form. Hissing at the fiery pain slashing through him, he rolled Tash over.

He wanted to retch and cry and yell. Tash was little more than dead weight, his face smeared with blood from his nose, mouth, and a gash along his hairline. Faint breaths slipped between his split lips.

"Come on, Halataldris. Don't go out like this," Mayr ground out through clenched teeth. He tore off Tash's ruined veil and wiped blood from Tash's face. There was no telling how long Mayr had been unconscious, let alone Tash. *Please, please, please. Not now. Not ever...* "You'd better damn well wake up or I'm sending you to the Realm of the Dead *myself*."

Tash twitched. One of his hands lifted to Mayr's chest. With a moan, he peered at Mayr. "Doubt it," Tash rasped. "I'm already there."

"You and me both," Mayr muttered. He raked his fingers through Tash's hair and down his neck, feeling for wounds and bumps. "Stay still, just a quick check." His hands glided over the rest of Tash, pressing tenderly.

"Most of the damage is inside, love." Tash winced as Mayr grazed his ribs. "You can't fix that."

"I can try." Mayr continued down Tash's legs, satisfied nothing was broken. Sprained was another matter, and they both were bruised and scraped for certain, but his head gash…

Before Tash could argue, Mayr snatched a knife from his belt and pushed back the hem of Tash's first layer of robes. He sliced through the second layer and ripped fabric all the way around. The ragged strip was wide enough to fold twice and wrap around Tash's head. Knotted, the makeshift bandage was just taut enough without causing further damage.

"You sit here for a bit," Mayr instructed, easing Tash upright. "No falling asleep, no lying down, no standing. I'll be right back."

After tearing another piece from Tash's robe, Mayr went in search of Gorgan. He found him sitting more than twenty paces away, closest to the dirt road that led to the village. People already crowded the road and shouted their will to help, their stunned expressions marred by horror.

Mayr kneeled in front of Gorgan. He stared past Mayr, his gaze empty. His ashen features were lax, swollen lips parted. Gorgan shivered, his hands tucked in his lap, drops of blood on his knuckles. The tremble wracked his entire body.

"Gorgan." Mayr gripped his shoulders and shook him gently.

Gorgan's focus slid to Mayr, weighted with

confusion. "All these people... I don't understand...?"

"I know," Mayr said softly, "but we don't have time to talk. I know you're in shock, I know you're hurt, but I need your help. Can you get up?"

"I—" Gorgan lifted his left arm to his chest, grimacing as he cradled it with his right. "My arm... doesn't feel right. The elbow... my shoulder..."

Not waiting for Gorgan to finish, Mayr fashioned a sling out of the fabric in his hands. He slipped it carefully around Gorgan's neck and injured arm. "Your legs?"

"I think..." Gorgan dragged his knees up. "They work."

"Good." Mayr loathed every syllable of his next words. "Enough to run?"

"I—" Panic splashed across Gorgan's face. "I guess."

"Come on." Mayr helped him to his feet. Once Gorgan was steady, Mayr grasped his shoulders and stared him in the eye. "You're the only one I have. I need you to do *exactly* what I say. You have to do *three things*. You hear me? Three things."

Gorgan nodded.

Mayr sucked in a ragged breath. His heart thumped painfully. "One: run to the village and send help, anyone and everyone. You scream it until they start moving." He pinched Gorgan's chin, holding Gorgan's gaze to his. "Two: go to the estate, tell Pellon. Do you understand?"

He received another nod, though it gave little relief. If Gorgan managed those instructions, they would have all the help they needed. Pellon would protect Aeley and Lira, no hesitation. He would also split the guards up: half would remain at the estate; half would bring supplies and wagons to the temple. Meanwhile, the Kattal soldiers in the village would defend the villagers from any possible attack.

It was the third item that killed him. Just thinking the words brought tears to his eyes, blurring his sight.

"Third thing, Gorgan," Mayr forced out, his voice shaky. "Go to Arieve and *stay* there. We'll come home as soon as we can." He swallowed hard and choked on the agony clawing at him. He would never witness the baby's first breath, their first wail, their first glimpse of the world.

The only thing worse is being dead.

It was duty against duty, personal desire pitted against what was right. If he had been someone else, maybe he could have run from the destruction, abandoning the wounded for their child.

Instead, I'm the one who stays.

"Do you understand?" Mayr shook Gorgan again. "Village, Pellon, Arieve—in that order. If *anyone* tries to hurt Arieve, you rip them apart. Shove their bones into their face until they're nothing." He cupped Gorgan's cheeks. "You protect everything Dahe, got it?" When Gorgan nodded, Mayr released him. "Repeat the instructions."

Gorgan winced as he straightened. "Send villagers, tell Pellon, protect Arieve."

"Good. *Go.*"

Gorgan hurried away awkwardly. *As long as everyone else is safe, that's what's important*, Mayr told himself, wiping tears from his cheeks. This was his role, his purpose. He protected others, taking little for himself. Lives came first, not want.

Though I'd really love to know what in the tarnished name of the Four this is.

Mayr scurried back to Tash. The temple had exploded, he gathered that much. His last encounter with such violent destruction had been during Aeley's ambush on her brother at the smaller Dahe estate in Oly Valley. The attack was meant to rescue villagers caught in Allon's attempt to coerce power from Aeley, but Allon's people had tossed explosives down like insignificant pebbles. They had blown holes throughout the house in attempts to kill Aeley, Mayr, and their comrades. Since then, Aeley had fixed little of the property.

This...

Who hated the priests *that* much?

He helped Tash stand, grateful that Tash had stayed put. Around them, villagers fumbled through the rubble, calling out to the wounded.

"You all right enough to help? Or do you want to wait for a healer?" Mayr held Tash up, one arm around his back. If only he could take Tash home, fuss over his injuries... *But we can't, and I'm not sending him alone. He'd probably fall down dead halfway there.*

Tash lowered his chin. "I can help." He curled his arm around his ribs, grimacing as he drew a sharp breath. "Stop me if I try to be a hero. My body can't take being that clever."

Mayr pressed a gentle kiss to Tash's bandaged temple. He needed to keep Tash by his side, especially if his injuries took their toll. "So we won't be clever—we'll be smart. Come, walk with me. You know all the priests that should be here."

As Mayr turned them towards the centre of the wreckage, Tash splayed his shaky hand over Mayr's chest.

"It's all gone," Tash said, voice cracking. "There's nothing..." Overcome by a sob, he hid his face in Mayr's shoulder.

"I know."

"Arieve, she's... and they're..."

"I know that, too." Smoothing Tash's hair to soothe them both, Mayr struggled to stay composed. There was no time to break down or heal his wounds. No time for tears, shock, or anything beyond compassion. The last thing he needed was to focus on the reality: they could have died had they stayed in the temple, leaving everyone they loved behind.

Thank the Four for Coye. If we were dead, she'd be the only one Arieve has. She'd be the difference between Arieve raising our child on her own and having a family.

Mayr blinked, realization blazing a path of stark clarity through his instincts. Perhaps he had underestimated Coye's worth in their lives, too angry to see her role in Arieve's future. They might never completely get along, and he refused to apologize for defending Arieve, but he could not deny Coye gave Arieve someone else to turn to. No longer was it a question of happiness—it was a matter of survival.

"We should get helping," Mayr mumbled. Reflection was a luxury in the wake of what was.

To Mayr's relief, Tash nodded and followed. Tash was quiet except for his cries at what they found. Mayr could not blame him: at their feet lay twelve years of Tash's life, the place he had called home.

That home was becoming a grave. Broken possessions and shredded, bloody fabric lay among the upheaval, scattered around lifeless bodies. Glass shards crunched beneath Mayr's boots everywhere he stepped. Plants lay in bits, colourful petals strewn everywhere, sticking to everything. Books and parchment had been reduced to tatters. The altar had fallen over, cracked through and splattered with food, wax, and blood. What remained of the furniture had been tossed in every direction, depositing splintered wood, soiled linens, and dented metal where they did more damage.

Mayr picked a path through the rubble, pulling Tash by the hand. The first people he found—two young men and a woman—were wounded but intact, pinned beneath stone pillars. After dragging them out and bandaging them with pieces of robe, Mayr instructed them to await a healer at the edge of the fray. The three hobbled off without peering back.

The next six bodies were not so lucky: all dead, and more than one suffered from a cracked skull. The three people after them were unconscious and unlikely to survive. The two priests after that were barely put together, limbs and torsos torn asunder, veils and robes drenched in so much blood the fabric looked black.

Steering Tash away from the grisly sight, Mayr cursed under his breath. *No one attacks the temples. There's nothing to gain except a messy death, a cursed afterlife, and agonizing punishment during every life after that. What could this possibly achieve?*

Mayr continued on, relieved when they discovered a group of stunned priestesses buried under the remains of one of the libraries. With their assistance, the women crawled out of the mess of fallen shelves, overturned tables, and damaged volumes then helped each other limp to safety.

His relief died the instant he spotted Kee

thirty paces away. Among the crumbled walls and bookshelves of her private study, Kee sat beside Armamae's still form.

"Damn, damn, damn." Mayr hurried to Kee with Tash in tow.

Blood coated Kee's left cheek from the jagged wound around her eye, and her eyelid was swollen shut. The rest of her face was a mess of small wounds. The backs of her hands were torn, and her ripped veil hung low in her disheveled black hair. Next to her, Armamae appeared to be asleep, bruised with his robes askew.

Surprise brightened Kee's face. "Thank the Four's kindest graces," she murmured, reaching for Mayr. He clutched her gritty fingers lightly. "I was worried everyone might be done for." Kee smiled sadly at Tash. "Brother Halataldris, may you always find such favour with the Goddesses. You are certainly held in esteem."

"I don't feel like it." Tash fell to his knees beside Armamae. "You're hurt, Sister, and Brother Armamae, he's…" Hesitant, he laid his hand on Armamae's chest.

"He's alive, Halataldris." Kee rubbed Tash's shoulder. "He breathes, though it's weak. I found him under my desk. I fear he's hit his head." She caressed Armamae's scraped cheek. "It's too early to tell if he'll come out of this," she said softly. "His age does not lend itself to sufficient healing. We may yet count his name among the dead."

The words alone broke Mayr's heart, but

Tash's sob nearly destroyed him altogether. They owed Armamae more than they could offer in return. For him to die for no reason...

Mayr ground his teeth. If he ever found who was responsible, he would make them pay in every imaginable way.

"We need to bandage you." Mayr muttered a prayer as he bent down and tore long strips from Armamae's robes. Kee remained still while he dressed her wounds. Once he finished, she resembled a pale imitation of herself, half of her face and both hands bandaged.

Kee rummaged through the rocks and wood beside her. "I found this. It might be helpful." She dropped something warm into Mayr's palm. "There are several pieces scattered about, none of which matches anything in my study, though it's stuck in everything. Perhaps you'll know what it is."

The heavy metal fragment needed no thought: shrapnel, sharp and black. He had noticed shards of it in the rubble and sticking out of bodies.

Seeing it up close, his entire body throbbed with anger. It was not shrapnel from the usual types of explosives, composed entirely of metal. The fragment in Mayr's hand was reinforced with veins of white and pink diamond—the kind found in the most expensive pieces of jewelry ever worn, owned by few people in Kattal because the price was too high for anyone else to afford. The same kind of diamond used for rare weapons. Such precious stone claimed the lives of miners due to the extreme methods required to obtain it. It would not be in explosives unless the person responsible could sell their entire life for a small rock.

Or hire someone with magic to do it.

Mayr's face burned. Rage itched beneath his skin. *Adren helped the Shar create new explosives — ones that do the worst damage. Ce said they're worth more than the most precious jewels.*

More than one of them would have destroyed the temple.

Those gut-sucking, ass-cracking bastards from the rank depths of Kiss My Filthy Hole! With a deep growl that morphed into a shout, Mayr kicked a chunk of white stone at one of the toppled pillars. As the stone hit the pillar and fell, he yelled obscenities at the piercing pain that surged through his toes. *I knew those bastards weren't done. Now we're sitting on this disaster.*

Mayr glowered at the shrapnel in his grasp. The longer he held it, the hotter it got.

Someone would pay harder than they ever thought possible.

"What is it?" Tash asked.

"You don't want to know." Mayr clenched his jaws. He wanted to see Adren immediately. Ce needed to confirm what his intuition screamed.

It was as infuriating as the feeling that he was being watched.

Mayr's skin prickled. In slow movements, he

cast his glare over the wreckage and beyond.

His gaze stopped at the edge of the woods. A man stood among the trees in plain brown travel clothes, staring at Mayr from behind untouched branches.

No, not just staring—

Smirking. Laughing. Enjoying the chaos.

His clothes and weathered face were average and forgettable, dusty and worn as though he was simply passing through the village. A hood covered his hair; a cowl hid his neck. Only his hands were notable, tattooed in black and red ink from wrist to fingertip, as filthy as his malicious smirk that made Mayr's insides crawl.

Mayr could almost taste the rancid rot that was the Shar-denn.

The man's smirk melted into a snarl before he turned and shot through the woods.

Tossing the shrapnel, Mayr raced after him. Pain stabbed at Mayr, protesting the pursuit. His headache pounded, echoing the noise of his feet over the uneven rubble.

None of it mattered. He crossed the border where wreckage met woods, determined to close the gap between him and the stranger even if it killed them both.

Among the long, dense branches of blood-red leaves and white blooms, the stranger's clothes were visible enough to track his movement. The path of the chase meandered, curving around stands of trees, sliding into gullies, and fumbling through thick brush.

Had Mayr been able to stop and laugh, he would have. For all of the cleverness the stranger thought he had, the awkward route allowed Mayr to catch up. Neither could run forever, though the stranger lost stamina with every turn and decision.

The creek changed everything like a shiny gift from the divine.

Caught on the slippery decline towards the water, the stranger hesitated and stumbled over the rocky edge. By the time he turned left to cut through the clearing towards flatter land, Mayr had closed in from the side, less than thirty paces between them.

Yeah... I'm done with this. Mayr grabbed a knife from his belt, took a quick breath, and let the weapon fly.

The blade sliced through the stranger's lower back, knocking him forward. His hood fell, revealing dark, shoulder-length hair. The man shouted and jerked out the knife. He scrambled to resume running, one blood-smeared hand pressed to his side.

Mayr charged through the distance and tackled him at the knees, slamming both of them to the ground. In a flurry of fists, teeth, and feet, Mayr punched any part of the stranger he could reach. Winded and heavy-headed, Mayr struck hard and fast. They tumbled over the dry grass and leaves, rolling and pitching each other in every direction. Distorted grunts and yells met Mayr's in noisy challenge. Whenever the stranger escaped Mayr's hold, Mayr yanked him back. Beneath Mayr's assault, the stranger weakened. Blood from the man's gritty wound coated Mayr's fingers, warm and sticky.

Between punches, the stranger toyed with a thong of leather around his neck, snapping it. Through the blur of hits, Mayr caught the movement of fingers across the man's mouth.

A knee caught Mayr in the hip. In an instant, Mayr was on his back, his shoulders and arms pinned by the man on his chest. The man's dirty, swollen jaws worked laboriously, chewing behind split lips slicked with blood.

"The Shar says hello," the man rasped, disheveled hair plastered to his sweaty face. "We'd really like Taldris and those other traitors to die. Adren belongs to us. Ress, too." He punched Mayr's throat, making Mayr choke and gag. "Taldris survived this time, but we'll keep at it, no matter how many priests we have to kill. They'll look so pretty dead." The man wrapped his hands around Mayr's neck. "We know where he is now. Should've chosen a different husband." The man snorted and dug his knee into Mayr's chest, shifting his weight to crush Mayr's ribs.

Gritting his teeth, Mayr pulled on the man's wrists and pressed hard as he wrenched their bodies to the side. They rolled through the ragged clearing, stopping only when Mayr rammed his knee into the man's groin and grappled to get top position.

Beneath him, the stranger coughed and choked. "See you in the bloody pits of the dead," he rasped. Frothy white foam spilled over his lips. The coughs became wheezes. In moments, he was convulsing, sputtering in Mayr's grasp. A groan, a gasp, and a final shudder ushered the man into death.

Mayr jumped back, caught in a stumble until he found his feet. Words pounded terror through him, his thoughts spinning faster than the haze of colour before his eyes.

The temple had been destroyed to kill Tash.

Had they succeeded… if Gorgan hadn't shown up…

His nightmares were coming true and punishing innocent people in the process.

"I hope you all die, *you sick twisted pieces of cock rot*!" Snarling and spitting, Mayr stomped on the corpse. He thrust his boot heels into the ugly face and kicked in the ribs until he no longer felt his toes. When boots felt too kind, he snatched the corpse by the collar and punched the face over and over again until the cheeks caved, the lips were all but pummeled flat, and the nose was too disjointed to be pieced back together.

Only when he finally pulled back did he realize tears soaked his face and lips. Through his blurred vision, he stared at his trembling hands. Raw and likely broken, the knuckles of his right hand ached fiercely beneath thick blood.

They were nothing compared to the rest of him. His body vibrated, fueled by pure rage. He had never been so terrified, so numb.

I'm messed up, and if Tash finds out…

Mayr collapsed, barely catching himself on his hands and knees. If Tash knew why the temple was destroyed, they were done. He would lose Tash for good.

It'll devastate him. He'll run away or fall apart or tear into himself to make up for it. For all I know, he'll slice open both arms and bleed out. He sacrificed his life to be free of them and now…

If Tash did not disappear or die, he would push Mayr away.

He did it before, and he'll do it again. Even if he stays, he'll stop being Tash. He won't be mine. He won't be himself. He'll be a shadow, some sick reminder of what could've been. He'll give up everything to make amends, everything we have…

Choking on his sobs, Mayr battled the war inside his head. He needed to tell Tash the truth, but it would ruin their lives. Their marriage gave Tash every reason to leave, but their child was every reason to surrender. If Tash's past actions held true, he would choose both, condemning their family to live without him.

In the end, love would be their death.

Chapter Sixteen

The temple had been a safe place, compassionate and generous.

Now it's been violated like it didn't matter. Tash surveyed the damage wearily, Armamae's limp hand clasped in his. Helpers arrived from all directions and climbed over the rubble. The panicked screams had subsided, replaced by moans and sobs.

And Mayr's run off. No warning, no reason, just gone.

Tash winced and eyed Armamae's pallid face. Compared to his battered emotions in seeing Armamae unconscious, Tash's physical aches were less excruciating. If only Mayr were there to lull him with optimism. *I'd take a boldfaced lie—anything to make this bearable.*

"Sitting here will not improve matters, Halataldris," Kee said softly. "I can't move very well, and I won't leave Armamae, but you can still help. People need you." She squeezed his arm with one bandaged hand. "There were priests and worshippers in the lower levels. They need rescue, especially if..." Kee eyed the ruins, her worry splayed openly.

"Everything collapses further," Tash finished. He gazed over the wreckage. Groups were gathered where there had been temple entrances. Dozens of people dug through the rock, but if more hands were involved, rescuers could save those trapped beneath.

Assuming anyone can *be saved.* He looked away, unable to stomach his doubt.

"I know it looks desolate, but we are Uldana. We hold onto faith when no one else can." Kee pushed him gently. "Go be their strength. We need the servants of Emeraliss to remind us to keep going."

Desperation crept through Kee's insistent tone. With a shiver, Tash stood and peered over his shoulder in the direction Mayr had gone. No doubt Mayr wanted him to stay with Kee, out of the way where Mayr could find him, but he could not wait when people suffered beneath his feet.

Tash headed for the group at the entrance to the long corridor between altar rooms. Located two floors beneath the decimated main levels and protected by thick stones, he supposed the altar rooms could be intact. The level above had housed mostly libraries, all of them reduced to split wood and paper.

The staircase to the altar rooms was only partially buried by debris. Determined to make his injuries worth something, Tash hauled rocks with the diggers. Two priestesses worked beside him: Esaline and Goyanne, both clothed in the white attire and red sashes that signified their Metah level, novices he still hoped might achieve the Rese level of priesthood, and perhaps even Uldana. Their clothes were soiled, but both were unharmed, saved by their errands in the village at the time of the explosion.

A small mercy. Tash said a silent prayer of gratitude and carried a chunk of marble away with one of the men from the village. Not all of the priests had been present. They were homeless but not hopeless.

As they cleared the stairs, sounds carried through the barrier. At least three voices yelled for help from the other side. They calmed once the diggers leading the effort—a man and woman Tash recognized as a glassmith and carpenter—shouted back. Chatter was kept to a minimum while their group of a dozen helpers moved in steady rhythm.

Cries of relief split the air as a hole formed and a dirty, scraped hand reached out. The diggers continued until the opening was large enough to crawl through.

Tash held his breath. Bodies climbed and wriggled through the makeshift entrance. Covered in dust, the survivors were worn and bruised, but few showed signs of dislocated joints and other injuries. First to surface was a group of seven, two of them first-level priests new to the temple, each of them sobbing their thanks while they embraced everyone on their way up the stairs.

Quick to follow were two groups of five, each led by an Uldana priestess: Wrenna and Jaylone, two of the priestesses who had conducted Tash's Uldana ceremony and helped him adjust to his responsibilities. Wrenna ushered her group up the stairs, her tone soft. Her long, tight blonde curls were disheveled beneath her skewed veil, the fabric torn like her red robes. Jaylone looked as stalwart as Kee usually was but even more annoyed. She flanked her own group, strands of her wavy black hair stuck to her sweat-slicked face.

"May Navara and Hastal burn every metaphorical hide of whatever's responsible," Jaylone muttered, stopping beside Tash partway up the staircase. She hugged Esaline and Goyanne before clasping his hands. "Thank the Four you were here. We worried it'd be our tomb. Let it be known I'm now afraid of closed spaces. No more locked rooms for me."

"I don't blame you," Tash answered, gripping her elbows to steady her trembling. "Is that all of you or are there more?"

Jaylone shrugged. "I think there's one more, maybe two. They didn't join our groups, not that I saw." She motioned to the entrance. "Half of the rooms are still intact. The last two on the left and the last on the right are done for. I don't think anyone was in them, though. Even if they were, they wouldn't have survived. I'd go back in and check but..." Shuddering, she glanced back.

"No, I'll do it." The words tumbled from Tash's lips, too fast for him to stop. "None of you should go back in. Get to safety."

While I go do something I shouldn't. I'll never learn.

Tash held back a sigh as Jaylone joined Wrenna at the top of the staircase and headed across the ruins. Mayr would yell at him for being careless, and Ress would call him damned foolish hero. *But I'm no hero. I'm just a stubborn ass who tends to mess up in a relatively useful way.* It was not a trait he wished upon their child.

A child he would be lucky to see, assuming they all survived.

Stepping up to the ragged entrance, Tash peered into the darkness. Everything was wrong. He was in the wrong place, led by duty to do what was right. Meanwhile, he was abandoning Arieve. As she brought life into the world, he and Mayr were surrounded by death. At the first test of loyalty, they were failing her.

If the baby's come too soon...

The possibilities hurt more than his injuries.

I can't think about this. I can't do anything with it. Tash climbed over the barrier. He needed to push forward, not panic. The priests were family, too.

Followed by Esaline, the carpenter, and the glassmith, Tash assisted each of them into the temple. The corridor was partially lit, revealing cracks in the walls, chunks of ceiling scattered across the floor, and swirling dust clouds. Shadows extended beyond, towards the mountain of collapsed stone that had devoured the furthest end of the hallway. If he listened hard enough, he could hear the sharp sound of rocks tumbling through the crevices.

"Spread out, check every room. Pull out anyone you find." Tash pointed to the left side. "Altar rooms for Hastal and Navara are up here. There are eight, but the last two aren't safe." He started for the rooms on the right as their group divided. "Esaline and I will take Laytia and Emeraliss's rooms."

While Esaline hurried to check the first four altar rooms, all dedicated to Laytia, Tash ran to Emeraliss's rooms. The first chamber was empty, lit by a single white candle by the door. Of the white statues kept in each of the four corners, one had fallen over. Its smashed torso lay in fist-sized pieces around the dented silver bird that once perched on its hand.

The second room was also empty. The silver candelabrum on the table against the back wall lay on its side, wax from its still-lit candles pooled around a wooden bowl of offerings. The vase of flowers had shattered, bright-coloured petals strewn among the glass shards. The black and white marble altar in the centre of the room was cracked, straight through the bust attached to the side. The fissure split open the face of Emeraliss that was carved into the stone, its serene likeness marred by gaping blackness.

Tash fled the chamber. He had tended the altar rooms with diligence, cleansing them, preparing them, and using them for prayer. To see them destroyed…

The scent of incense had never been so sickening.

Crushed by dread, Tash charged into the third room, intending to leave the next moment.

He was not alone.

Tash stopped short. All but one of the statues had toppled over in their corners. Flowers lay in a soaked pile on the table at the back of the room, one glass vase on its side near the edge of the table. A second vase was in pieces on the floor. White candles lay on the table in a haphazard mass of wax and flame.

The man at the altar was just as still.

Kneeling with his back to the door, the man resembled a shroud-draped sculpture, his broad body covered by dark, baggy attire. Tears in his long-sleeved shirt revealed light brown skin. The soles of his dirty boots were too worn to be useful much longer, and a mass of fabric lay on the floor beside him—a cloak, possibly. There were also three leather belts, one for the waist and two for the thighs, all bearing sheathed knives of different sizes. A short sword waited to his left.

Tash stepped closer. Dark hair tumbled down the man's back to his waist, tangled and greasy.

Long strips of frayed near-grey fabric dangled from his few narrow braids. He gripped the edge of the altar with both hands, a silver chain wrapped around his right hand as he shook and curled into himself, leaning against the altar. A sob broke the silence, followed by another.

Something was familiar about him. The weapons nagged Tash's memory. Danger and caution found balance with the shock of relief. The sobs... he needed them to stop. Listening wrenched his gut into knots.

"I'm sorry," Tash said, moving through the room, "but we need to leave. It's not safe."

The sobs paused as the man peered over his shoulder. "That's the whole point," was his hoarse reply. In an awkward turn from the waist, he stared Tash down. Contempt and anger clouded his features, the depth of his disgust on full display.

Nimae. Alive and here. Alone.

Stark realization washed through Tash in an icy wave. His thoughts reeled and screamed, desperate to wage war against the cruelty. They had once been like brothers, facing life and the Shar-denn together with Ress and Varen. Circumstance had bound them, and time had strengthened their camaraderie.

Choices had split them apart, ones Tash could never take back. Whatever their childhood oaths, there was no returning to brotherhood. In one bad decision, Tash had taken Varen's life.

In one swift move, Nimae could exact revenge.

Ress had yet to forgive Tash for turning them in. Nimae would never entertain forgiveness if he knew the truth.

Please, don't let him know. Tash shuffled back, holding his breath. *Please let this be a brutal coincidence. Let this be anything but what I think it is.*

"Nimae? How are you here?" he whispered. Never had Nimae looked so sickly and bedraggled. He was thinner than Tash had ever seen him, and his dark beard only distorted the image further. While Nimae had always worn his hair long, he had insisted on being well-groomed with a trace of scruff to keep Varen happy.

All of that polish was gone. Even Nimae's tear-swollen eyes—one green, one brown—resembled that of a different man. A miserable, defeated soul with too many lines etched into his face as if they kept score of failures.

"Nice," Nimae spat out, rising to his feet. He clasped the silver chain around his neck and slipped it beneath his shirt. "All I get is a half-assed question when you know I deserve apologies. You're not worth *any* words and you *know it*." In a blink, Nimae withdrew a knife from his boot. The blade gleamed as he neared, holding the knife flat and unsteady, directed at Tash's heart. "So maybe I'll stop talking and just end you. *That's what you deserve!*"

Tash held up both hands, only two paces

between him and the blade. Instincts told him to run; the nagging voice of intuition commanded him to stay. "Nimae—"

"Don't start." Nimae jabbed the knife at Tash. "I know about Varen, and I know *you're* responsible. *You sent him to his death!*" Nimae stomped forward, forcing Tash backwards. "You surrendered him to save your own ass, but he wasn't yours to do *anything with*. He was *mine!* My life, all the good I had left. *Damn you* for selling Varen out. Selling me and Ress, too, after we loved you, missed you, had every faith in you!" He growled low. "I've waited for this moment, Council whore. I'll rip out your guts and shove them into your skull. Rearrange your limbs."

Nimae closed the space between them and grabbed Tash by the collar of his robes. He shook Tash violently before the tip of the knife jammed against Tash's thigh, just short of piercing his skin. "Here you are, not even fighting back. Lost your bite? You'll suffocate us with prison, but you won't *bother* doing the damage yourself? Is that all we are to you? Just names to barter?" Nimae's voice cracked. His hold weakened. Tears rushed down his weather-beaten cheeks. "Are we *that* much of nothing?"

Fear ripped through Tash like lightning. "Never," he whispered, wrapping his hand around the fist at his neck. He dared not pull away, not with how badly Nimae trembled. "The three of you were worth everything, even giving in to the Council to save you."

Slow and calm, Tash turned into Nimae and shifted his feet. He guided the knife towards his knee at an angle more difficult for Nimae to exploit. "I never meant to hurt you and Varen..." Tash cupped Nimae's cheek, his wiry beard moist to the touch. "You were supposed to live, *all* of you, away from the Shar, away with each other, with me. We were supposed to end up on this side together, free as much as we could be, but it all went wrong. I put my hope in the wrong people, and I'm sorry. I only wanted to save you."

Tears slipped from Tash's eyes. "Ress knows why I gave you up. You'll probably never believe me, but I swear I did it to save you, to get you out. There wasn't any other way, but the Council ruined *everything*. They made Varen think you three were headed to prison, but you *weren't*. They promised... and I trusted them," Tash admitted hoarsely. "Now it's killing you, and I'm sorry. You deserve so much better, but now... I miss Varen. I miss you. I miss how it used to be. If I could bring him back, I would've done it already. I'd do anything to have you back, too, even stand here when I should run."

Nimae blinked, his sorrowful gaze locked with Tash's. His lips twisted and quivered. "It hurts," he whispered.

With a whimper, Nimae dropped the knife. He threw himself at Tash, sobbing as he locked his arms around Tash's shoulders. Tash returned the embrace without hesitation, unable to stop his own tears.

"I miss him so much," Nimae croaked, grappling to hold him tighter. "I can't stop hurting. It won't go away. I never got to say goodbye—he was just gone. I can't be alone, not anymore. All this pain… Make it go away. Just take it, *please*."

Tash sucked in a sharp breath. Varen had been emotional but not Nimae. Nimae had always been composed like Ress, ready to plan his way out of problems. For Nimae to fall apart in his arms…

"I'm sorry," Tash murmured.

Nimae clung to Tash's robes with both fists. "He went and died, leaving me behind." His words came out in pieces, separated by cries and sniffles. "The first time I told him I loved him… me asleep on the floor in his room and him waking up so scared, so terrified of his own dream… I couldn't take it. Crawled into his bed and held him, wishing it away. The next morning, I asked him to be mine, and he said yes. He didn't even think about it—just kissed me and said yes. So surprised, so happy, like when I bought our tiny piece of land…"

Thumping his fist against Tash's back, Nimae cursed. "And the Council—those wretched bastards with their gods-awful hunters—they raided the estate he was at and took him. Just barged in, took everyone. I wasn't there to protect him. I couldn't save him from that nightmare. He was alone because I wasn't *there*."

"He loved you." Tash squeezed his eyes shut. If only he had known about Varen. If only he could undo those last moments. "Varen wouldn't leave you without a good reason. He would've given everything to keep you safe. You were his world; the hope that kept him alive whenever the Shar ripped into him. You *know* that, and he'd want you to remember it. Every day, he'd want you to keep going, even when it hurts to try."

"No point when all I want is dead." Nimae pushed back. Strands of dark hair stuck to his wet cheeks. "Since I'm here—" He held out his wrists. His sleeves shifted upwards, revealing jagged, puckered scars similar to those on Tash's forearms. "Take me to the Council. I'm ready for the execution. Finish what you started."

"Nimae…" Tash bit back the rest of his words. No matter how much he understood the request, he could not see it through. Nimae's life could not be snuffed out with such little regard. Varen would have told them to fight it. He would have demanded Ress talk Nimae into saving himself. "Let's go see Ress, you and me. No Council. We'll sit down and talk. We'll get the rest of our family back together."

Nimae snorted. "Family. Goddesses, I hate that word. It's such a lie."

Brow furrowed, Tash looked over Nimae as if

seeing him for the first time. Too many questions gnawed holes through him, but he feared the answers. The knots in his stomach twisted on themselves, pulling his insides taut. "Nimae, why are you here? Did you come to kill me?"

"Not you," Nimae answered. "Me." His gaze flickered away. "I wanted to go out praying for Varen, to be with him on the other side. Figured I'd get buried and be too dead to care about much else. I set the explosive above this room *myself*, but the damn thing *still* didn't go off." He picked up his knife. "All the other explosives went off. This one…" Shouting a mangled curse, he tossed the knife across the room and knocked one of the candelabrums off the table.

A chill skittered down Tash's spine. *If he's here…*

"Nimae," Tash started slowly, "who set the other explosives?"

"Old friends." Nimae's stony glance sent a shudder through Tash. "You made a good game of hiding, but it's over. The Shar's got you now."

Warmth fled from Tash, and he felt the blood drain from his face. His joints locked as his body refused to function beyond shock, panic holding him captive.

No. No, no, no.

"You blew it with Ress," Nimae continued, "pulling him out of Araveena with Rivane's heir." He flung out his hand. "The lookout *saw you*! He recognized your damn robes, saw your face—you didn't even *try* disguising yourself, *you idiot*! He ran off and reported *everything*. Didn't know who you were, but they sent scouts to *every* temple in Kattal. They found you here and rumours went flying." Nimae snorted and swayed on his heels. "Every faction went at it, trying to figure out who you were. Then the old bastards in our faction got involved and that settled it. *I* was yanked around by bosses trying to get information *I didn't have*."

"I'm... I..." Tash blinked, unable to focus. The room seemed to spin, the ground unstable.

"This was to get rid of *you*!" Nimae growled and jerked Tash close with both fists, his ale-scented breath hot on Tash's face. "*This* is what happens when *every single faction* wants you skinned. Whatever life you've had, it's *over*." He shoved Tash back. "The temples are *nothing* to the Shar but a means to kill you. You might survive today, but don't count on tomorrow."

Choking on a cry, Tash pressed his wrist to his lips. He swallowed once, twice, fighting the nauseating taste that surged up his throat. They knew where he was. Retribution had begun, taking innocent people with it.

Because of me. Tash spun away. His gut felt as if it was being punched by a thousand fists fashioned from razors. The hiss he heard before the explosion, the people he saw leaving the temple... All of it meant to kill him.

"Brother Halataldris!" a voice called from the doorway. "We need to leave!"

Tash snapped his head up. Esaline rushed into the room, her long red hair a mess like her face and white gown. She beckoned with a frantic wave.

"Come on. You're being hollered for." Esaline clutched Tash's hand and tugged. "You're the only ones left. Let's go."

"After you," Nimae mumbled.

Tash snatched Nimae by the arm. "*With* you." Before Nimae could protest, Tash pulled him along with a grip that only grew tighter. Nimae fought his grasp, but Tash dragged him, his fingers aching from the effort. Once they reached the hole to the surface, Tash shoved Nimae through the entrance and up the stairs, barking at him to stop insulting Varen's memory.

At the top of the staircase, Tash gazed across the ruins. More groups had formed, twice as many as earlier. Among them were republic soldiers and Dahe guards, all of them occupied with either rescue or helping healers with the wounded.

His glance stopped on Mayr, who stood with three guards where Kee and Armamae had been. Mayr looked pained while a guard bandaged his right hand. Blood stained his left hand and cheeks; dirt smeared his clothes. Leaves and grass clung to his hair.

Whatever Mayr had done, Tash preferred not to know. Not yet. He needed something more than answers. One hand around Nimae's wrist,

Tash hurried over the rubble. If anyone spoke, he did not hear it. When Nimae protested with a tug, he ignored it. Only when he reached Mayr did he acknowledge anyone else.

"Hold him," Tash instructed, pushing Nimae towards one of the surprised guards. Without a second thought, he grabbed Mayr in a tight embrace, terrified to let go.

Mayr gasped and returned the hug. "Are you all right?"

Cries Tash had stifled burst forth, muffled in Mayr's shoulder. Tash shook his head, tears falling in a hot cascade. The weight of the truth was crushing as it clawed through his insides. How was he going to tell Mayr they were in danger? How could he have ruined everything? Even though he survived, knowing he was responsible was murder enough.

"It's my fault," Tash sobbed. "They did it to get back at me."

Mayr tensed and took a sharp breath. "I know," he murmured. "I really do know." He eased Tash back, his face marked with fresh cuts and bruises. "We'll talk tonight. So much has to change. Right now, I have to take you home." With the thumb of his left hand, he wiped tears from Tash's eyes. "I need you to stay at the estate from now on. No trips. No gallivanting. No nothing. Become Aeley's advisor and stick to her. Stay where I can protect you." Mayr drew Tash against him. "*Stay. Home.*"

Nodding, Tash buried his face in Mayr's neck, taking comfort in his heat and bittersweet scent. He would enjoy them as long as he could, however long he had left.

Goddesses, grant us peace. All these innocents... It's like I never left the Shar—I'm still hurting people.

Tash's stomach turned. If he could hold onto Mayr long enough, maybe salvation would come. Amid any darkness, Mayr was his absolution, his clarity.

Everything the Shar would take... unless he gave it up first.

He had never felt so dead.

Nothing about the estate brought Tash consolation. Not the heavily protected entrances with guards as solemn as the four that escorted Mayr and him. Not the chaos within as household staff rushed about, gathering supplies and making room for survivors. Not the eerie silence from beyond the main staircase.

Despite all the confusion, there were none of the screams or wails Tash anticipated from Arieve or the baby. Each hurried step he took up the stairs with Mayr was frightening. No one they passed said a word about Arieve's state. Instead, they eyed Tash with pity and offered condolences.

None of it eased his conscience. He was

covered in dust, blood, and grit, sick reminders of death and suffering. Innocent people had been dragged into a fight he started, yet he was alive, left to witness the destruction. The last thing he wanted was pity. He needed something to lift his heart, not smash it into tinier bits.

With all the words not said, Tash feared what waited in Arieve's room. Silence meant death. They had lost either Arieve or the baby—or both.

His world was falling apart.

Tash faltered at the top of the stairs, too terrified to take another step.

"Hey," Mayr said. He squeezed Tash's hand and sidestepped a group of guards carrying baskets down the stairs. "We're almost there. Come on."

Closing the distance to Arieve's room only made matters worse. By the time they reached the closed door and the two guards who stood at attention, Tash felt trapped, his skin like ice. His fingers trembled in Mayr's grasp. His body refused to move.

The guards' faces mirrored his feelings. Ralaern stood on the left, his white-blond hair slicked back, his youthful expression sombre. To the right, Lisreft towered over Ralaern with a rigid form, his brown hair tied back from his tightened features. Both wore black leather armour and metal bracers, fully armed with swords and knives. There was nothing joyful to their presence, no measure of reassurance.

"Mayr, Priest Tash," Lisreft greeted, bowing his head. "Thank the Four you're alive."

"Thank the Four you're where I need you," Mayr said. "It's going to be a long night. An even longer few weeks."

"We'll do whatever we have to." Ralaern nodded at the door. "You ready?"

No. Tash swallowed back the answer. *No more death. Please.*

Ralaern's expression softened. "No need to be frightened. The screaming part is over." A smile crept across Ralaern's lips as he opened the door.

Lisreft clapped Mayr on the shoulder. "Go on. They've been waiting. Bless their patience because I wouldn't have any."

Tash's heartbeat lunged into a hard, quick rhythm. He held his breath and followed Mayr into the room.

The tension faded as they entered, as if they stepped through an invisible wall. Arieve came into his sight, propped up on the bed by a mound of pillows.

Tash's breath tumbled out in a quiet whoosh. She was alive. So was the bundle in her arms, a wiggling source of tiny, muffled noises that were something between cries and whimpers.

"You're home!" Relief flooded Arieve's face before she glanced at the ceiling. "Blessed be everything good. I couldn't take the thought…" The worry in her voice dissipated with a weak smile, her eyes wide as she gazed at Mayr and

Tash. "You're here now. You're with us."

As the door closed behind them, Tash stopped beside Mayr, partway between the doorway and the bed. Flushed and covered by a pale blue nightdress and layers of blankets, Arieve looked exhausted. Darkness coloured the skin beneath her eyes as though she had not slept for days. Her hair was tied back with ribbons, rogue curls sticking to her moist forehead. Coye sat next to her with a balled up white cloth in her hand.

They were not alone. Karane scurried around the room as she moved sheets and clothes, discarded bloodied linens, and placed items into her blue healer's case. Every few moments, she checked on Gorgan and tugged on the faded yellow blanket draped around him. He sat pale-faced in a chair beside the bed but appeared alert, his right sleeve rolled up. His hair was wet, face and hands washed of dust and dirt, and his left arm rested in a clean sling.

Surie stood by the window, dressed for battle in black leather armour, gloves, and weapons. A grin cracked her solemnity, relief evident in her green-gold gaze. "Good to have you back." She motioned to the bed. "Take your time. Pell doesn't want to see you till it's good and late."

Mayr laughed quietly. Tash simply stared at Arieve. Inside, he was a disarray of opposites. Happy as he should be, dread suffocated his joy. Pride nudged his emotions, but shame dragged them down.

Arieve reached for them. "Come meet our daughter."

"We have a girl?" Mayr's face brightened with a childlike glimmer.

"Unless she says otherwise," Arieve replied. She caressed the baby's cheek. "You'll always be beautiful, little one, no matter what you decide."

"Absolutely," Mayr agreed as he crossed the room, pulling Tash along. Once they stopped beside the bed, he kissed Arieve's forehead. "I'm sorry. We tried so hard. We didn't want to miss it," he said, his voice cracking.

"You're alive." Arieve cupped Mayr's jaw and forced him to look her in the eye. "You're still here, *that's* what matters." She offered the baby to Mayr. "Now you need to hold her."

Beaming, Mayr cradled the baby with his left arm, her bottom propped on his right wrist. When she whimpered and fussed, he cooed and swayed. "I know, sweet baby. It's not easy being little," he murmured, turning towards Tash. "Let's go see your other daddy. You can tell him all about it."

Time seemed to stop as he placed the baby in Tash's arms. "You hold her first. You've never held a child that's yours. You need this."

Tash choked on surprise. Overwhelmed, he struggled between holding the baby tight and not wanting to crush her. Swaddled in a white blanket, the baby fit in the crook of his arm, her body the length of his forearm. Tawny hair peeked out from beneath her white knit cap. Though her eyes were barely open, he caught a glimpse of her blue irises. Her pudgy cheeks were ruddy, her pale golden-brown skin smooth and warm, and her nose resembled Arieve's. Everything about her was small and pinched, a burst of life squished into a tiny body.

She was worth every breath he could not take.

Mayr chuckled and brushed back Tash's hair. Pressed against Tash's side, he swept his fingers along Tash's neck and down his arm. "There it is, written all over your face," he whispered. "The feeling I wanted you to have."

Tash leaned into Mayr's touch. "Was Iliane this small?"

"No." Mayr wrapped his arms around Tash's waist. "But she was full term, so it's probably not a fair comparison."

"This one's more impatient," Coye said with a smirk. "She's going to be a handful."

"Yeah, but she's *our* handful." Mayr grinned. "We'll teach her all the good tricks. She'll be *brilliant*."

"Great," Arieve said dryly. "When she's sixteen and tearing up the world, we'll let you deal with it."

Karane laughed from where she stood behind Gorgan. Surie snorted and leaned against the wall. Only Gorgan appeared to have trouble enjoying the moment, his eyes glassy as he watched silently, reminding Tash of what he had let himself forget.

Tash slipped his finger into the baby's hand. Her fist closed in a weak grasp, the simple act too precious to ignore. Holding her, reveling in what she represented... he was trading harsh reality for the whimsy of a future he might never have. Twice he had lived on stolen time. Now he had to pay the price. In his carelessness, he had made her part of the cost.

How could I be so selfish, pursuing a family when I knew the Shar still wanted me? Tash blinked back tears and caressed the baby's fingers, sharp aches rippling through his chest. *How are we going to protect you, little one? They know where I am. They know I'm with your father. They likely know about your mothers and you. How do I survive to see you grow up? How do we keep you alive when they can destroy the estate? They'll take your life without a care. They'll murder you, and I...*

Tash returned the baby to Mayr. "I can't. I just can't." He ran out of the room before anyone could ask why.

Voices protested loudly as he fled across the corridor. Ignoring the pleas to return and the heavy footsteps chasing after him, Tash raced into his room and threw the door shut.

Instead of slamming, the door swung open, caught by Mayr as he stumbled into the room. He closed the door softly behind him.

"I can't talk about this now," Tash spat out, headed for the window. "I *won't* talk about this. I have to do things. I have to—"

"You don't have do a damn thing but talk to me," Mayr countered angrily. He hurried after Tash to cut in front of him, then gripped Tash's shoulder and pushed him back. "Here you are, throwing out the first moments with our daughter. So do it. Give up whatever's bothering you."

Tash growled, determined to escape. "How can I stay?" he shouted, clawing Mayr's wrist. "I'll get her killed! Her, Arieve, you—all of you dead like the priests. *I. Can't. Stay.*" He ripped Mayr's hand from his shoulder and shoved him away, yelling his frustration.

The next moment, Tash was on the floor, shaking violently, barely upright on his knees. Agony sliced his insides from heart to gut and tore his emotions apart, his body wracked with sobs that would not stop.

"I thought things could be different, but I'm still messing things up. I'm still hurting people." Tears flowed down Tash's cheeks and dripped to the floor. "I started over because it was better than staying. Ines left me before I could leave her. I left my parents and Ally because I knew they'd survive. Now..." He glanced up at Mayr. "Now I have everything and I don't want to give it up, but how can I stay?"

Tash pointed in the direction of the temple. "Look at what they did! *That's* them putting you and everyone we love in danger. We could die tonight for all we know. If I stay, I lose you all, because that's what I do. I break beautiful things," he whispered, avoiding Mayr's furious gaze.

Let his rage come. It doesn't make it any worse.

Instinct and habit waged a gruesome battle inside him, fighting the screeching voice that told him to stay. He was being torn asunder, ragged bits of his defiled self flung in every direction. Survival commanded he flee and start a new life where no one would come to harm, but sacrifice demanded he surrender to the Shar-denn and suffer their revenge.

They were nothing next to need, which entreated him to stay. Its silken voice was a loving whisper within the bitter chaos, asking him to be more, to do better and stand strong while the world collapsed.

Of all the possibilities, not one gave him a good enough answer.

But it's not about me, is it? That's how I ended up here—trying to save myself. It's always been about me, never truly about anyone else. And here comes fate, ready to collect the debt owed.

Tash pushed up from the floor. "I can't fix this the way everyone needs," he said, wiping tears on his sleeve, "but you all would've been better off if I'd never been here. You'd be safer without me. So maybe that's what I should make happen, because I can't stay, not like this."

If he had thought the fury in Mayr's eyes was bad before, it was nothing compared to right then. His gaze all but destroyed Tash where he stood, reducing him to ash before the flames even licked his skin.

"How *dare you*, you predictable, self-sacrificial bastard!" Mayr yelled. "You're *not* pulling that nonsense on me, not while I'm still here." He charged forward, one finger jabbed at Tash. "I know you. I know *exactly* what you'll do to *'fix'* this. *Not. This. Time.* You hear me? *Not* this time."

Closing the space between them, Mayr snatched Tash's robes in his uninjured fist and hauled Tash against him. "You're *not* leaving me or our girls," Mayr snarled. "You can't go dumping us because it's dangerous. You *promised* you'd stay. Running away won't do damn all— we'll be targeted whether you're here or not. Ress and Adren are targets, too, and Aeley's a pain in the Shar's ass. You're *not* the only one they want." His grip tightened. "If you think you'll push me away, you've got another thing coming. I'm not going anywhere and neither are *you*. You run, I'm tripping your ass and dragging you home. Stay and I'll fight this with you."

Mayr's lips crushed Tash's in a savage, bruising kiss. Brutal and punishing, the force drove a piercing ache through Tash's jaws. Fresh tears dripped down his cheeks, an unstoppable whimper ripped from his throat. When they parted, neither could manage more than a ragged breath.

"We'll do this together," Mayr insisted. "I

mean it. Let me protect you." He cupped the back of Tash's neck, strong and commanding. "You're overwhelmed and terrified, I get that. It's too much all at once. But there's no way you're losing me. I stand by every vow I made at our wedding. *No one* will take that away."

"How long can you put up with me? With this?" Tash held Mayr's face in both hands, searching his eyes for answers. "I'm a risk to everyone. It's going to be the same trouble over and over again. You can't possibly put up with it for the rest of our lives. You'll leave just to be free of it," he argued. "This isn't your burden, it's mine. I can't ask you to carry it for me."

Mayr snorted. "You're not asking. I'm taking it on, no matter *what* you say." He slid his arms around Tash. "You're not a burden—you're my fight. But you *know* I've got my faults, too. I pray you'll always humour me and tolerate my mistakes. I'm worried one day you'll realize you can't stand me or my moods. I won't leave you for being human." His lips trailed over Tash's cheek before he pressed their foreheads together, avoiding Tash's injury. "It's the leaving I can't deal with. Those bastards can't have this."

As Tash tried to protest, a pleading kiss silenced his effort.

"Please don't leave," Mayr whispered. "Raising our daughter, loving Arieve—I don't want to do them alone. I'd do anything for you, but I won't live without you."

With words alone, Mayr broke him.

Tash's heart burned, its deep ache slashing through his will as emotions flung themselves against his nerve. They had been in this position before, during the Uldana Trials when Tash believed Mayr could never be his. That time, he had ignored what their hearts told them and pursued the right answers in the wrong direction. By not listening to the messages love had screamed into their faces, he had nearly lost everything.

I decided wrong then, but I'm listening now.

There would be no other life. If he ran, he would die, either by his own hand or by someone else's. Survival meant nothing without those who made him feel alive.

Tash hugged Mayr tight. Even without the magical cuffs, he burned from the fire in Mayr's conviction and tasted the intensity of his fight. Mayr was the strength he lacked, the voice of wisdom he needed to hear, even when it broke him. Determined and honest, Mayr's intentions were fierce in their sincerity.

"I won't leave. I'll stay," Tash murmured into Mayr's shoulder. "I'll push back like I should've. I swear I won't abandon you. We'll go into this as one."

"Both of us go in, both of us come out," Mayr mumbled. "If Council even *thinks* about throwing you back at the Shar to settle things, I'll make them regret it. If they sacrifice you to save anyone or anything, no matter what it is, I'll choose you over Kattal so fast they won't know their own damn names." His embrace tightened, nearly crushing Tash. "I choose you, always."

In the silence, their steady breaths found a synced rhythm. The peace in their harmony hurt, reminding Tash of how long he had felt alone.

Not anymore.

People believed in him and needed him to fight. He would dust off his skills and protect them. He would get justice for them all.

Tash pressed his cheek to Mayr's. "You're so calm it's frightening."

"I'm not calm. I'm raging inside." Mayr drew away, the corners of his eyes tight. "But if I focus on it, I'll start shaking. Then I'll start hitting something, and if I start doing *that*, I won't stop. I need to focus on the baby. I'll skin the bastards from the Shar tomorrow, but tonight I'm hers and yours and Arieve's."

"Arieve…" Tash sighed. "We have to tell her about all of this, about my past. She deserves an explanation, but I don't know how."

"With me." Mayr lifted Tash's chin. "We'll tell her together. It took both of us to avoid telling her, so we'll take the fall together. Right now, you need to hold our daughter. She's the reason we weren't killed in the explosion. That *has* to mean something."

Tash stared at Mayr's lips, taking in his meaning. The very thought sent shivers through him.

"We need to make the world safer for her," Mayr said softly. "We'll secure her future, no matter what. *That's* what being a parent means. Tonight you hold her, you give her a name. Tonight you're Halataldris, flying above the pain and the grief and everything that scares us."

"And tomorrow?"

"Tomorrow we go hunting. Tomorrow we find out *exactly* who's responsible. We find homes for the priests. We start rebuilding the temple and send weapons masters to Araveena to keep their temple safe. We'll protect the other temples, too. We're finding a way to settle all of this, no matter what laws get in our way." Mayr cupped Tash's jaw. "You'd better invoke the name of every goddess, my love, because we're going on a rampage."

To put it mildly, Tash almost muttered. He recognized the look in Mayr's eyes. There would be no rest until Mayr's rage found resolution. The past would be nothing compared to what was coming. *Emeraliss, give us strength and compassion. Give us hope. We need every advantage we can get... and more than a little forgiveness.*

Chapter Seventeen

Mayr crossed the nursery with a bowl of warm water, yawning as he set the bowl on the table beside Arieve, out of their daughter's exploratory reach. Three months of little sleep since Aliss's birth was catching up to him. Arieve insisted she and Coye felt no better, though he suspected they had a slightly better time of it. Where they were kept awake by Aliss's feedings and desire to be held, he was plagued by work without the benefit of holding their playful infant.

At least that day was one he was excited for, sleepless night or no. The day Aliss was born had been a nightmare, but the morning of her blessing showed promise. Guests were already gathered in the yard behind the estate and enjoying the crisp autumn air. Pellon had ensured the guard remained tripled from the wedding the previous day, not one stranger allowed on the premises. From what Mayr had seen, everyone was in high spirits, including Tash.

Mayr handed Arieve a clean nappy and a vial of oil from the wicker basket at the centre of the table. "*Why* did we agree to have your wedding yesterday?" He wiped his eyes, careful not to soil his white shirt or his white long coat.

Coye snorted from where she stood on the other side of the table, also dressed in white with a thigh-length coat. "Something about making it so no one hiked across the republic twice—*your* idea, by the way."

"Rhetorical," Mayr sang.

"Sleep deprived," Coye sang back, pointing to her face.

"Ha! You're telling me." Mayr tickled Aliss's bare feet, smiling while she giggled and kicked and wiggled out of her dirty nappy with Arieve's help. "This little one decided her daddies didn't need any sleep *or* fun. So while her mommies enjoyed their wedding night blissfully alone, she kept us up, fussing and wailing just so we'd hold her." Aliss squealed as Mayr bent forward, his loose hair falling around her face like a curtain. She tugged on the black strands with small fists, her cheeks soft beneath his lips. Her fine, tawny hair smelled like honeyed berries, and the familiarity of her bright blue irises never failed to warm his heart.

Arieve snickered and swapped the soiled cloth for the clean, slipping it beneath Aliss. "You expected something different?"

"No." Mayr twisted his neck to peer up at Arieve. "I kind of hoped we'd get one good hmm-hmm-hmm in, though, while she was asleep. We were being *so* quiet, and I made sure her cradle was far enough away we wouldn't wake her." He turned back to Aliss, making a face as she gummed his chin. "I had daddy *right* where I wanted him, squeaky little half-pint. Then you went off, and he didn't, so I couldn't, and that was the end of that."

Coye laughed, deep and wicked, her green eyes gleaming. "Aw, poor you, all unresolved and turning blue."

"You have no idea," Mayr breathed, pulling back. "Last night was the first time he asked me to try something since… things happened." Destruction of the temple had left a lasting effect on everyone. Tash battled daily with painful emotions and sorrowful moods that sapped his energy and focus, a constant depression that left him with the desire for gentle intimacy without sexual gratification. Mayr accommodated Tash's every need and want with little question, thankful that Tash was there, alive, and not on his own. Even so, he feared he was not doing enough to help. He continued to seek Karane's advice on what else he could do for Tash, despite her assurances that he was doing everything he possibly could.

At least he still wants me around. He could just as easily tell me to back off. With a frown, Mayr gazed at the stained-glass window, its glowing panes a multitude of hues from creamy yellows and mossy greens to cheerful purples and icy blues. Cascades of purple and green curtains framed the window, pretty and light like spring. The colours were happy like he wished Tash could be. Only Arieve and Coye had achieved that joy, even with what they knew about the current situation and Tash's past. *Maybe one day we'll all feel the same.*

If he had any luck left, that day would come soon.

Depends on how today goes. Mayr poked Aliss's nose, sending her into another fit of squeals. The blessing ceremony and feast would occupy the rest of the morning and most of the afternoon. *What transpires at the meeting afterwards...*

They would pursue one thing a time, no different than the rebuilding of the temple. Costs were high, from materials and resources to managing people. Along with Kee and the Keepers of the Sacred Assembly, Lira had taken it upon herself to help everyone affected by the explosion, insisting that Aeley focus on being Tract Steward. The restoration had become Lira's personal project, burying her beneath paperwork, requests, and all manners of details.

Mayr and Tash helped however they could, though Tash did so from the safety of the estate. Adren had offered to fix the temple with magic and make it indestructible—a proposal Kee and Tash had adamantly refused to keep cir safe. Others, including Gorgan and the rest of the guard, invested time in building the temple itself, working with all of the priests, masons, carpenters, smiths, and architects who offered what they could to the project. If the months were kind, perhaps the temple would stand again in some form before Aliss toddled about.

The Sacred Assembly had also accepted help from the High Council to take protective measures in other temples, allowing specially trained spies to don the robes of priests and watch for visitors with malicious intent. The spies searched the temples multiple times a day for explosives and traps.

All the while, Mayr dealt with a surge of fifty new guards that needed to be trained up to his standards and eased onto the roster. According to his contacts in the republic's military, their number of recruits was equally on the rise—citizens wanted to fight back and keep the temples safe. Thankfully he had Pellon, Surie, Ralaern, and the rest of the senior guards, all of whom knew what needed to be done and took no guff from anyone. Without them and their determination to train the new guards in addition to their regular shifts, he had no idea how he would have handled the last three months. *Likely just crawled under my desk and cried for a week, to be honest...*

A sharp whistle caught Mayr by surprise. Coye snapped her fingers. "Don't tell me you're asleep," she chided.

"What? No." Mayr stuck out his tongue. "Just wondering how long it'll take until this place looks like a beast tore it up."

He gestured to the spacious nursery with a

weak wave. The walls were grey and red with splashes of colour from tapestries, flowers, and decorations Arieve had chosen. The simple table they stood at was in the middle of the room, half of its surface occupied by baskets of cloths and oils. Beneath the table sat a miniature bathtub and laundry baskets. Around the room, wooden chests spilled over with toys and blankets while clothes filled the two dark brown armoires. The wooden heaven's horse and ice-slider sat in separate corners, ready for when Aliss was old enough to rock on them. A brown cradle stood against the wall shared with Arieve and Coye's room. The cradle was a gift from Aeley, having been passed down in her family, along with the rocking chair by the window.

"It's all pretty now, but wait until baby starts walking. She'll do *dam-age*. Won't you, baby?" Mayr cooed and rubbed noses with Aliss. "You're going to be *so* much like your Aunt Aeley. Maybe she'll tell you where she used to stash my favourite sweets, hiding them like she was all clever."

"I remember *you* being oh-so-clever." Arieve smirked and toyed with Aliss's fingers. "Shall we recount all those times? Perhaps the night you hid in the cellar with Pell and Aeley, thinking you'd get a late-night snack when no one was looking, and you all got *locked in*?"

Mayr's face warmed. "Uh, no?" He leaned into Arieve to press his cheek to hers. "Not in front of our daughter," he whispered against her ear. "Wouldn't want to be a bad influence." Trailing a lazy kiss down her neck, he chuckled as she shivered.

"Clever." Arieve caught his lips as he drew back, the depth of her kiss filled with intent. Their romance was far from over, their desires bound tight. "Love you," she said.

"Love you, too."

"Me three?" Coye's features contorted, her lips twisted. "Does one love their wife's lovers?"

"If you want, or we could stick with respect," Mayr said gently. "You don't have to be in our bed to count. We can do this as friends. That's a love we could try."

Coye's lips parted in a quiet "Oh." A blush crept over her cheeks. "Thanks."

"Sure." Mayr offered Coye a smile, hoping she believed him. Since the explosion, he had reconsidered his behaviour towards her. There was no place for anger, not anymore. They would make things work.

"Thank you for being kind to each other." Arieve curled her arm around Mayr's waist and reached for Coye with her other hand. "It makes this even better. Happier."

"Anything for you," Mayr and Coye said in unison. They traded glances and shrugged.

"Now that we're all in the same mood, we should dress our tiny beast." Arieve fingered the blessing gown lying near Aliss. Soft and heavy enough to keep Aliss warm, the three layers of bright white dress shimmered with silver thread and delicate white embroidery. Clear glass beads and gleaming white pearls dotted the hems and cuffs in single rows, sewn in an alternating pattern. Arieve sighed as she undid the small, flat buttons down the back. "It's almost too beautiful to put on. I know how hard Tash worked on it."

"That *and* the little girl wearing it," Coye said, grinning.

Mayr laughed. "Maybe on the dress, yeah, but he didn't work *that* hard when it comes to Aliss. I was there when he was showing me how easy he and Arieve—" He snapped his mouth shut, glimpsing the way Aliss's big eyes stared at him. *Nope, not finishing that thought around her for another eighteen years. Or ever, actually…*

"Here, let me help," Mayr muttered, reaching for the gown. All Aliss needed to know was that she had enough family to spoil her with affection every day of her life, and her resemblance to Tash and Arieve made him happier than he could express. Much of Aliss was like Arieve: the curl of her hair, her infectious laugh, and her chin, nose, and ears. According to Tash's parents and sister, however, Aliss's tawny hair was the same as Tash's when he was an infant. If that was not convincing enough, her eyes said everything—an intense bright blue that brought Tash's mother to tears in recollection.

Together with Coye, Mayr and Arieve worked

Aliss into the dress, despite her attempts to wriggle and roll away. Once her arms were in the long sleeves and the gown pulled down, they attacked the six buttons. All but one slipped through their holes; the last refused to cooperate. Mayr tried, followed by Arieve, who gave up with a huff and surrendered to Coye.

By the time Tash entered the room, all three were biting back curses to the sound of Aliss sucking on her fist.

"Dare I ask?" Tash approached the table, laughing quietly. "Allow me. I've replaced that button three times. There's a trick." With deft hands and a twist, he forced the button through and flattened the dress. "There." Slow to back away, he rubbed his cheek along Aliss's, eliciting another of her giggles.

"Thank you." Arieve kissed Tash before tying a bonnet on Aliss and picking her up. Instantly, Aliss whimpered and craned her neck, letting loose a piercing wail. "You were fine!" Arieve rubbed Aliss's back, unable to stop the cries. "What's wrong, baby?"

"Here," Tash said. "I have a theory." He took Aliss from Arieve and laid her head on his shoulder, her cheek pressed to his beard. The fuss stopped as though it had never been. Both of them glittered in the sunlight, her gown radiant against his dark red robes. Making small, happy noises, Aliss tugged on his veil.

Coye snickered and held out the matching

blanket. "Clever boy."

"Oh, he knows," Mayr said. He wrapped the blanket around Aliss with Tash's help. "I swear these two plan things when we're not around."

"Hush, you. She knows what she likes, that's all. I'll go with it," Tash retorted, kissing Aliss's fingers. "I want her to know I'm here—that I'll never be far away."

Mayr smiled at the beauty in Tash's words. He was keeping his promise to stay, and each day proved he meant it. No matter the agony, he remained, bound to them.

Tash gazed at Mayr. "Now I know how you feel about Ili. Why you couldn't give her up. They wrap all your emotions around their tiny little hands and pull your soul into a dance before you realize you already know the steps."

"You're welcome," Mayr murmured, teasing Tash's lips with his. Their kiss blossomed quickly from chaste to an eagerness he missed.

"Boys, save that for later." Arieve smirked and drew on a lightweight cloak with lace capelet over her heavy dress, both of them bright white and tied with long white ribbons. "Let's get through the ceremony first, yes?"

"I suppose." Mayr sighed dramatically but winked and offered his arm to Arieve. "Shall we?"

Arieve shone with a smile as she hooked her arm around his. They passed through the bedroom and stepped into the hallway, joining Ralaern, Surie, Lisreft, and Gorgan. Dressed in white like all of the guests and guards, their escorts flashed wide smiles before they fell into step behind Tash and Coye. Since the explosion, Ralaern and Surie had served as Tash's primary escorts, while Lisreft and Gorgan looked after Arieve, Aliss, and Coye. They had Mayr's implicit trust, and he expected only the best from them.

The group descended the main staircase to the sunlit foyer. Ress and Adren waited at the bottom of the stairs with their four-guard contingent. Across the foyer, Nimae stood between two guards with another two behind him, his wrists cuffed by a set of manacles with a thick chain. He was the only one not in white, his crumpled clothes dark like the energy that emanated from him. His long hair was freshly washed, the spicy scent of soap wafting through the air, and someone had shaved his face as he requested every week.

Hostility pulled the air taut as Mayr stopped in the foyer. Adren flashed a strained smile, cir hand clasped around Ress's. Ress cleared his throat and glanced wearily at Nimae.

No one was comfortable when Nimae was nearby.

Holding Arieve close, Mayr kept her out of Nimae's reach. Once Tash stepped into the foyer, Mayr placed himself between Tash and Nimae, a decision that earned him Nimae's nasty glare.

He cared little for the intimidation attempt, challenging Nimae with a pointed stare. Nimae's current arrangements were compromises meant to soothe Tash and protect the rest of the family. They were not intended to coddle Nimae or make him feel better about his role in destroying the temple. Instead of being kept in a cell in the main house like an average prisoner, Nimae was confined to the Guard House on the lowest level, in the space meant for safety during an attack. All weapons caches had been stored elsewhere and the metal doors reinforced.

Mayr maintained that Nimae was far from all right. While Nimae's words and behaviour suggested he was a danger to himself more than others, Mayr put nothing past Nimae's desperation and internalized rage. He neither knew Nimae nor trusted him, and no one could vouch for him. To that end, Nimae was under surveillance at all times. Although he was allowed out each day to walk, eat, and partake in activities at Aeley and Mayr's discretion, Nimae was always accompanied by four or more guards. It was better than subjecting him to the limited mercy of High Council.

"Some fancy gathering you've got," Nimae said, eyeing Tash and Ress over Mayr's shoulder. "Can't think of a single reason why you're trotting me out—unless I'm the entertainment?"

"Never," Tash answered. He pushed past Mayr with Aliss in his arms. "I wanted to ask if you'd..." After a nervous glimpse at Mayr, Tash took a deep breath. "I was hoping you would attend Aliss's blessing."

Nimae snorted softly.

"Please, consider it," Tash pleaded. When he moved closer to Nimae, Mayr pressed his hand to Tash's back in warning, followed by a firm tug on his robes. "You're still family," Tash continued, obeying Mayr's silent command with one step backwards. "I want you there. My parents, Ally, Bremary, Cove—they're all here, asking to see you. They want to help. *Please*."

"Oh, sure, because this is *exactly* how I want them to see me." Nimae raised his hands, rattling the chain. "Nothing says family like patronizing the outcast."

"It's not like that," Tash argued. "They just want to talk."

"No, they don't, and you're fooling yourself." Nimae nodded towards the back of the estate. "Get the baby to her party. Don't keep them waiting."

Crestfallen, Tash glanced at Aliss. "Would you at least offer her your blessing?"

Silence fell in the hall, colder than Nimae's sinister glare. The air almost snapped from the brutal tension, unspoken words more threatening than violence.

"No." Nimae turned to his guards. "Take me back to my cell. Drag me out when the meeting's on."

At Mayr's nod, the guards led Nimae away. Tash stared after him and clutched Aliss tighter, his eyes glistening with tears.

"Hey." Mayr wrapped his arms around Tash. "This is Aliss's day. She's here, we're here. That's all we need." He nuzzled Tash's neck and brushed a kiss over his jaw. "I love you."

Arieve hugged Tash from the other side. "*We* love you, and it'll be all right. Maybe he'll come around one day. You've both been through a lifetime of hurt. He needs to heal in his own time." Caressing Tash's cheek, she turned his face to hers. "Nimae stopped running and came *here*. There's still hope."

Coye slipped around Arieve to tuck folds of blanket beneath Aliss's chin. "For now, we need to enjoy this little bundle of sunshine. We should go and be happy for a bit."

"For Aliss," Tash whispered.

"For Aliss," Arieve echoed, pulling him by the hand.

They glided through the halls to one of the back entrances, followed by Ress, Adren, and their escorts. The moment they stepped into the yard, they were greeted by cheers and whistles from excited guests. The yard was bright and shiny, overlooking the long length of grassy hill and expansive valley of harvested fields and autumn-coloured forest. Ribbons in at least a dozen colours were strung from tree to tree, twisted and braided and draped, trailing and catching on the cool breeze. Glass and metallic baubles hung from the branches, striking brilliant hues of gold, blue, and silver among the blood-red and bright orange leaves. Wood and wicker chairs sat against the back of the house, arranged in groups near tables with glass bowls of mulled ciders and warm biscuits. Strands of silver and crystal laced through the vines that clung to the back of the house, while chains of gleaming beads dangled from wood and wicker lattices.

An altar sat in the centre of the yard, readied with candles, white ribbons, flowery incense, a single glass goblet, and bowls of earth, water, and feathers. Next to the altar was a smaller table with a white wicker basket on top. Prepared by Kee and the priestesses with her, the altar area was modest, formed from simple tables covered by the best white tablecloths the estate had.

Kee had accepted it all with gracious thanks, similar to how she took to living at the estate with the dozen priests Aeley and Lira had taken in until the temple was restored, including Armamae, who Mayr had insisted they needed to take care of no matter what. Most days, Kee worked in the makeshift office Lira had arranged for her and spent time in the village, refusing to yield to the Shar-denn's threat.

To Mayr's relief, Armamae had recovered enough to work by Kee's side, even accepting Tash's continuous offer to help him rather than turning Tash away. Although Armamae could not move or speak as well as he had before the explosion, the healers were optimistic about his ability to partake in several activities. Fortunately, the blessing was one of those activities, even if he had to take it easy and rest more than wander. At least he was not alone: Mayr's mother was keeping him company. Both of them sat on a bench near the altar, wrapped in thick, colourful quilts.

Mayr glanced from face to face while he maneuvered through the crowd with Arieve, Tash, and Coye. Their families were the first to bombard them with hugs and playful nudges, followed by the onslaught of celebration from their friends.

Beyond the smiles and coos over Aliss, Mayr focused on the dozens of guards that patrolled the yard and guests who were not close acquaintances. Of them all, he was most anxious about those who were there for business: Councilmen Severn, Cota, and Lower; Tract Stewart Kayte Oaren of the Alosaa tract, his wife, Rosayra, and their guards; and the bounty hunters Rathen and Kirra, who looked out of place, their white clothes a contrast to their usual sleek, black attire. While they all were cordial and extended blessings to Aliss, most of them knew nothing about why they were there at all. Aeley had intentionally left the reason out of their invitations. To get around the spies of the Shardenn, they had kept the real reason secret from almost everyone.

At Kee's request, Mayr joined Tash, Arieve,

and Coye at the altar. The crowd formed circles around them except for the three priestesses standing behind Kee.

Kee beamed as she took Aliss. She crooned a blessing prayer before finally turning to the assembly. "Beloved family, friends, and servants of the divine, welcome to this joyful day," Kee greeted loudly. When Aliss poked at Kee's lips, she laughed and captured Aliss's fingers. Kee kissed Aliss's knuckles then clasped them to her chest. "Today we gather in spirit and love to bless this child with the best life has to offer. We come together as one, honoured with experience, wisdom, and the gifts that have been bestowed upon us. It is with the sacred graces of the Four that I present to you Aliss Varen, firstborn of Arieve, Coye, Halataldris, and Mayr. Blessed be the child."

As the assembly echoed her last words, Mayr watched Tash. For the first time in months, he looked happy, his cheeks coloured by a faint blush. A hint of sorrow teased his gaze, but joy pushed it back, allowing his pride to shine through.

Rightfully so, considering Aliss is named after Emeraliss. He can't give her that name without feeling good about it.

Mayr smirked. He turned his attention back to Kee as she invoked the names of legendary consorts and their sacred children, recounting lively tales of gifting and whimsical childhood adventures. Overwhelmed as he was to know the Goddesses were real, he was thankful someone was looking out for their family. Tash and he could have died just as easily as Arieve and Aliss. With a reverence he had rarely felt, Mayr supported Tash's suggestion for Aliss's name. Love would see them through anything, a belief that would cost Mayr his heart in the best of ways.

All the ways that matter. After everything, who knew we'd be here, doing this?

He would trade it for nothing.

But I'll do anything to keep it. This is me taking a knee to the Four and offering my soul up for whoever puts it to work.

Voices floated on the air around Aliss's tiny voice, singing the Merry Chant of Children while Kee laid Aliss in the basket of white silk pillows. Among the pillows was a garland of gold, auburn, and orange flowers with bell-shaped petals that hung over the edge of the basket. Kee grasped Arieve's hand and led her around the table, motioning for Mayr, Tash, and Coye to stand around the table with them.

Once the chant finished, Kee guided Arieve's flattened hand over Aliss. "In the presence of everyone here, the four of you may declare your commitment to Aliss Varen, a precious spirit that needs to be tended with great care. Hand on hand, may your promises be bound."

Mayr took Arieve's hand and squeezed,

returning her smile with a grin he felt all the way to his gut. Coye's hand slipped beneath Arieve's, while Tash rested his around them all.

Kee draped four long white ribbons across their hands. After she looped the ribbons around their wrists, Kee coiled and crossed the ribbons, tying their hands together. The beaded ends of the ribbons hung free, their strands of silver and white beads swaying above the basket. Aliss gurgled as she hit the beads back and forth.

Laughing softly, Mayr recited the vows of commitment with Tash, Arieve, and Coye. In that moment, they were more than lovers or spouses: they were parents safeguarding the power of a future.

I'll do right by you, he promised Aliss silently. *This is the dream I can't wake from. This is fate.*

Mayr glanced at Arieve and Tash, ecstatic at how they both seemed to glow with delight. The impossible had become possible. They were good together, not only as two or three but as four, with Coye tying the loose ends in Arieve's heart. Tash grounded Mayr, but Arieve anchored them all. Should they lose their balance, they could find a way to right each other.

Thank you for all of this, Emeraliss. Mayr caught Tash's gaze, only to fall once more for their stunning blue depths. Never had he felt so complete. There was nothing missing, nor was there space for anything to *be* missing.

I'll never leave you behind or give you up. You are

my light, my heart, my world. Wherever you fly, I'll follow, because you're the star guiding me home. Soulbound by fire and thread... Feels like eternity to me.

Epilogue

The blessing feast was over, but change was about to begin.

Mayr leaned against one of the tables in the centre of the well-lit room, surveying the doorway while guests entered. With Arieve and Aliss napping until dinner, his primary concern was the meeting with Aeley, Lira, and the people they trusted. Their plan required so much secrecy, they were meeting in a stuffy room in a back corridor two floors below the estate's main level, past the cells where prisoners were kept, in a suite of rooms usually reserved for when the estate was under attack.

The room's lack of windows concealed the oncoming darkness as evening descended. The hallway to the single entrance was heavily guarded, not only by Dahe guards, but by the guards with Tract Steward Oaren and the councilmen. Given the door was as thick as Mayr's hand was wide, few would hear what was said inside the room. Even fewer would get close enough to hear a muffled voice: Mayr and Pellon had chosen guards specifically for their discretion and the ability to keep unapproved parties at a distance.

The musty chamber filled quickly. Large enough to accommodate sixty people, the room was simple and unadorned. Two tables sat in the middle, pushed together and accompanied by twenty chairs. A dozen candles offered a bright glow in addition to the torches in the cradles on the walls. Goblets and decanters filled with various bitter alcohols waited on silver trays, surrounded by sliced rounds of nut bread, spiced cheese, and rolls of savoury meats.

Near the wall to Mayr's right stood a wood target painted with red, white, yellow, and black concentric circles. Set up by Ress, the wall behind the target was partially hidden by three stripped mattresses. A barrier of thick wood planks on weighted blocks stood between the target and the mattresses.

Curiosity toyed with Mayr, but he suspected the target had to do with the locked metal case in front of Ress. Waiting silently next to Adren, Ress sat on the other side of the table from Mayr, away from the door. The metal case never left Ress's reach; Adren's hand never left the knife strapped to cir thigh. Their critical gazes flitted from one face to another.

Their alert heightened as four guards led Nimae into the room and pushed him into the seat at the furthest end of the tables, his hands and feet chained. The door swung closed, the latches and heavy bolts thrown. Ralaern and

Surie stood with their backs to the door, hands clasped behind them, poised and observant.

From the end of the table closest to the door, Aeley and Lira greeted each guest. Pellon stood behind them, watching each hand and expression, his own features unreadable. Tash and Gorgan remained next to Mayr, both rigid and quiet. Everyone's guard was up. The nature of the people gathered was reason enough to question how long their tempers would cooperate.

"Please, sit, Councilmen," Lira said, motioning to the seats across from her and Aeley, her smile weary. She rested her hands on the two books before her. Both volumes were thick with worn pages and strips of ribbon sticking out. "We will keep this meeting as efficient as possible."

Severn, Cota, and Lower dipped their heads and sank into their seats.

"You neglected to mention brevity, Steward's Hand. I suppose we should settle in for the long haul?" Severn smirked at Mayr, her intent difficult to decipher. Amusement danced in her eyes, their usual cold, judgmental gaze tucked behind something that resembled civility. In a rare image of celebration, Severn had traded her usual dark attire for tight white pants laced down the sides, a simple white shirt with cowl, an elegant belt of white chain links, and white leather boots with silver buckles up to the knee. Instead of her customary dark red long coat, she wore a white leather long coat bearing the High

Council emblem on the back and spirals of vines around the arms, all sewn with silver thread. Her braided black hair was coiled at her neck and decorated with a spray of white flowers, silver leaves, and strands of tiny pearls.

Had Mayr not known better, he would have accused her of trying to look kind. As Councilman of Public Protection, Severn oversaw all matters of law enforcement, including Mayr's position. Along with Aeley and select members of the High Council, Severn had the power to force Mayr to resign. Thankfully, she had yet to do so, despite their disagreements. They served the same side of the law, but their attitudes tended to grate and clash until their anger was raw. By High Council standards, Severn was young but intensely committed to her duty, rumoured to be the product of too much family tragedy. Like Mayr, she came from humble origins and had nailed her obligation to the stake of responsibility. Perhaps their similarities were what made them chafe each other's nerves.

Though if the rumours were true, he figured Severn had the right to be bitter. Mayr still had both of his parents and siblings, all of them protected by Aeley. Severn was said to have no one, not one relative left to care. Crime had pillaged her family and left her to right the wrongs.

When Severn turned back to Aeley, Mayr sighed with relief. He got along better with Cota

Dalenvrae, the Councilman of Law and Justice and a senior member of High Council. Born to one of the oldest Grand Families in Kattal, Cota was tall and lean, but his stern, proud personality and carriage made him seem even larger. His pale green eyes contrasted his umber skin and short, dark brown hair, but the scar that marked the left side of his face hinted at a sinister past. The scar began at his temple, puckered down his cheek, and ended in a gentle curve around his jaw.

According to Aeley, Cota had been injured in a fight no one spoke about, a secret the Grand Families would take to Cota's deathbed. From what Aeley knew, Cota had been forced to duel a despicable foe in his youth—an enemy no one invoked the name of. Whether it had been a matter of family honour, personal vendetta, or something else altogether, Aeley did not know. Korre had refused to share details, insisting the past was dead. The only reminder was Cota's scar, a reward of success and a carving of loss.

Usually serious during High Council meetings, Cota was refreshingly jovial at social functions. He smiled often and joked with ease, his deep voice disappearing behind throaty laughter. Like Severn, Cota wore a white long coat with High Council emblems rather than his charcoal-grey coat. Everything about him was immaculate and polished: well-fitted pants beneath an elaborately embroidered, floor-length skirt without a front panel, short boots with fur trim, and a long-sleeved shirt with a high collar. Had Mayr not known Cota's position, he would have taken Cota for an oddly friendly aristocrat.

That would be Lower's place. Mayr glanced at the back of Lower's head. Shoulder-length red hair curled around the upturned collar of Lower's white long coat, its rich hue sharp against his bright white shirt, thigh-length vest, loose pants, and casually draped iridescent scarf. As Councilman of Tract Stewards and Republic Leadership, Lower was easy to tolerate. With playful blue eyes, youthful complexion, and a natural way with people, he was the councilman most likely to be bedded in an attempt to gain influence and the least likely to care that people erroneously assumed they could buy him that way. Aeley and Lower often conversed over casual meals, sharing jokes few would dare repeat around any councilman. In official meetings, he was appropriate and pleasant with all the irritation of his scholarly upbringing.

Outside of High Council, Lower was a complete rascal, determined to chase down the prettiest, foul-mouthed sailors he could find and scratch their nightly escapades into his bedposts.

Mayr's stare carried onto Kirra and Rathen, two of Severn's bounty hunters who stood together between Ress and Nimae. Although Kirra was the shortest there, she was difficult to miss. Her honey-coloured hair hung in tight curls with a faint glimmer of gold dust. Bright blue and pale purple powder coloured her eyelids, drawing attention to her golden eyes and glossy pink lips. Her bodice was little more than a shred of fabric held down by thick white straps and buckles, revealing glimpses of light tan skin. Her puffy white skirts and their gauzy top layer were a complete contradiction to the belt of knives around her waist, the silver chain wrapped around her punching arm from wrist to shoulder, and the glint of a weapon nestled between her breasts.

Rathen was no less prepared to take someone on. His white pants, shirts, and long coat did nothing to soften his appearance, especially given the knives strapped to both his thighs. With his short blond hair slicked back and dark gaze tamed of its sarcasm, Rathen almost blended into the group.

"Brief or not, we're all up and cozy in here," a husky feminine voice said near Mayr. "We'll be trading scandals and slurs before you know it. Nothing says 'welcome to the world' like getting sloshed and hanging ourselves out to dry come morning."

All attention turned towards Rosayra Oaren. Standing next to her husband, Rosayra was a short bundle of fire and red dawn, with cream-white skin and eyes that were an alluring pale blue-grey with thick amber rings. Vivid red hair with black and white tips tumbled down her back in airy curls and tight, twisted locks adorned with gold beads and crystalline charms. Instead of the customary blue leather of the Oaren guards, she wore a short white coat, vest, pants, and low-necked tunic. Even more notable were her multitude of weapons and the aroma of spice and salt that lingered around her, fragrant with a bite of the rocky seaside.

If Rosayra was fire and sky, Tract Steward Kayte Oaren was stone and flood, formidable and strong, never to be pushed or controlled. Taller than Rosayra by more than a foot and nearly twice her size, Kayte was never lost among a crowd. His dark brown skin was almost black, glistening with the hint of gold powder on his eyelids and a dozen thick gold hoops in each of his ears, curved around the shells from lobe to tip. He had bound his shoulder-length black-blond hair back with a gold clip encrusted with emeralds, vibrant like his green eyes. Dressed identically to his wife and considered as dangerous as a walking armoury, Kayte was the last person anyone in the room would fight.

"Sorry, too early?" Rosayra grinned. "Guess it's good I left out the other parts."

"Ros," Kayte muttered, leaning down to kiss her cheek. In subtle movements, he withdrew the jeweled knife from the sheath at her waist and held it behind his back. "Perhaps we should remove a weapon or two before you get *really* happy? You'll be the death of me, sea star."

Rosayra snatched his chin. "I'll be the death of

something if you don't give that back, blade witch. Seed giver, sight, or sound? You choose."

To the sound of muffled laughter and snickers that flitted about the room, Kayte rolled his eyes and yielded. "You're lucky I love you. Throw you back to the fishes, barbed tongue and all."

"Yeah, well, me and my seaweed keep your refined ass alive when you're too busy looking ahead." Rosayra shoved her knife back into place. "'Member your vows and I'll make sure you stay in one piece, you raggedy sea hag."

Lira snorted a laugh then clapped her hand over her mouth. "I apologize. I'll sit now," she mumbled. A blush coloured her cheeks. "Aeley… *Please*?"

Mayr chuckled despite feeling sorry for her. The longer Lira lived with him, Aeley, and their lot, the more she became like them, fitting in as though she had always been there.

"Yes, I agree." Aeley's dark eyes brightened with her grin. "As my wife *meant* to say: thanks for humouring us and showing up. This discussion couldn't be disclosed in a missive. Thanks to Councilmen Cota and Severn, we've been granted permission to proceed."

"Not permission. Strongly approved," Severn corrected. "Get this done and I'll grant you hero parades and bestow medals of honour on you *myself*."

"Isn't *that* an interesting image," Kayte breathed, crossing his arms. "Dahe, why is

Councilman Severn suddenly talking parades?"

"Because we have work to do, assuming you're willing." Aeley gazed over the room. "If you received an invitation to this, it's because I trust you. Kattal can't continue the way it has. Things have to change, and Council has expressed… concerns."

"*Concerns*," Rathen echoed, one blond brow arched. "How impossibly vague of you." Kirra swatted his ribs, and he scowled at her. "What?"

Cota smiled weakly. "We have finally accepted we cannot handle the Shar-denn matter alone." When sharp replies sounded, Cota raised his hand. "To date, Council has preferred tracts to operate on their own in a flexible partnership with us. You handle most criminals and we assist. Meanwhile, we've pursued our own agenda to round up major players and charge them with crimes against Kattal. This allows us to remove petty offenders *and* faction bosses simultaneously."

"But it's not going fast enough and they're breeding like pests," Severn said, her fingers interlaced on the table. "They're slipping through the cracks and getting comfortable. The attack on the temple proves that." Turning slightly, she glared at Tash. "They're changing the rules, upping the ante, and shoving it down our throats. We either play to them, run like fools, or hit them back twice as hard."

"Which leads to the problem this meeting aims

to solve," Cota said. "Our resources have limits. We are also bound by rules we cannot violate."

"Rules that don't necessarily apply to Stewards or their comrades," Severn added, "especially when Council can pardon those who save the republic from a disease that's rotting through Kattal. We tend to be… favourable with national heroes."

Kayte let out a slow breath. "So Council wants a puppet show with us up front?"

"No, better," Aeley replied with a smile. "We get to break things."

"Delightful," Rosayra purred. "Perhaps a little redecorating, too? Red is always in fashion."

"At this point, whatever it takes." Severn pressed her lips into a grim line. "Bust them till they bleed dry for all I care."

"*Severn*," Cota reprimanded harshly.

"Sorry," Severn sneered. "Bust them, cuff them, and drag them back to us for *justice*."

Cota scowled at Severn, followed by a stern look to Kayte. "You and Steward Dahe have plenty of connections that could be employed. You're also the best trained Stewards in terms of enforcement strategy, among other talents. We need your brightest, most creative means on how to end the Shar-denn, with both of you taking point."

"How about a task force, Oaren? They're only your favourite thing," Aeley said, tilting her head. "Maybe a brute squad with short tempers and long reach?"

Kayte lowered his chin, lips pursed. "Not saying yes, not saying no, but it'll take more than a diplomatic request. Give me a reason."

"We've got a realm's worth of new information you'll want." Aeley nodded towards the end of the table. "Nimae, repeat what you told us. Start with the temple."

"*Please*," Nimae muttered. He lifted his hands to the table, chains rattling as his metal cuffs scraped the wood. "I'm aware you expected an attack after the antics in Araveena. There was also a lull in criminal activity. The simple fact is this: there *was* no attack because the Shar figured pursuing new information was better than ripping Araveena apart for answers they might never get. They hunted for the priest seen with Ress and Adren, knowing he'd be their key." Nimae motioned to Tash. "Once they discovered this one, they devised a new plan. Since attacking Araveena *never* got his attention before, they figured they'd blow the temple."

Nimae leaned back and stretched his legs. "They wanted to make all of you complacent—your guard was up after Araveena, but you'd relax over time. You played right into it." He shrugged, focused on the wall opposite him. "Spies visited the temple, planning where to put the explosives. They hauled me in partway through, saying I needed to prove my loyalty. I told them not to blow it up, but they wouldn't listen. So I went in, set a couple things, and left everyone else to do what they wanted. Didn't have much of an agenda, except to die," he murmured, almost too soft to hear.

"And yet the estate's still standing." Rathen glared at Nimae. "Try pri-or-i-ties."

Nimae snorted. "Try not my problem." He cast Aeley an annoyed glance. "As I've already told you, the Shar won't take this place out. I don't know why. All I know is the bosses want the Dahe estate left alone—for now. You've got bigger problems, though." His attention swerved towards Kayte. "Gailarin's problems won't be contained for long. Changes here are spilling into the other tracts. The Shar can't afford any more snitches."

"Meaning what, exactly?" Rosayra asked.

"Shift in leadership." Nimae's expression darkened. "The Shar's doing more than hunting defectors: they're changing ranks, locations, strategies, and nearly everything they *can* change, save the bosses who won't give up their seats. There's a new mindset, too, a vicious change in generations. The young ones will do whatever to whomever. Lines the old bastards didn't cross are being crossed now—and that's just to start."

"Forcing us into twice the work," Kirra said.

"Essentially, yes." Nimae's manacles strained as he pointed to Tash and Ress. "Anyone who's lost contact with the Shar is being taken out, and anyone they've associated with is next. They'll come down hard, dirty. They've got new toys, new plans, and new morals—or a complete lack of them, anyway. However painful it's been, it'll get worse."

Nimae lowered his hands. A flicker of regret flashed across his face. "To be honest, the explosion wasn't solely to kill Taldris," he said quietly. "Killing him would've made their year, but punishing him—punishing the priests—is ten times better. They wanted to make sure *everyone* knows the score and who's in charge. This whole thing is a warning to everyone who thinks they can leave or gut them and take back control. They're sharpening their teeth on your humanity."

"Thus the Task Force," Severn interjected, "sanctioned by Cota and myself but *not* run by us. We've played on the nicer side of nasty for too long. There needs to be a concerted effort to do damage." She swept her gaze around the room. "Stewards, hunters, mercenaries, informants, families—we need to pull out everything."

Lower cleared his throat and raised his hand. "All well and good, but why are Gailarin and Alosaa the only tracts here? Lasael, Eruelme, and Riaes should be present—unless I'm missing something."

Mayr exchanged glances with Aeley. *That* was a delightful discussion for another day. The list of reasons was longer than they had time for.

"I would've invited them if I knew they'd join

and keep their mouths shut," Aeley replied, lips twisted with displeasure.

"A temporary measure," Lira added. "Steward Oaren was our first choice, given his family's experience in combat. Oaren ideals align with Dahe." Hands clasped on the books, she straightened, her chin raised. "Stewards Forey, Mahne, and Hewyth, respectively, are not as perfectly suited. Forey is a pacifist and would reject measures favoured by the Task Force. However well-meaning he is, Kattal has attempted peaceful resolution with the Shar-denn and failed." She lifted one leather-bound volume. "History supports this. Forey's preference for compassionate resolve is not viable."

Lira laid the book down. "Mahne and Hewyth are potential allies, except their interests are aligned more with commerce and economical ventures than anti-violence efforts. We anticipate their involvement will hinge on cost-benefit ratios than means alone." Lips pursed, she leaned back, fingers laced in her lap. "There's also the fact that Shar-denn activities generate funds from a hidden market—funds that end up in the most interesting of coffers. At this time, we'll err on the side of caution. Ideally, Stewards Mahne and Hewyth would be helpful should the Shar-denn enterprises be seized."

Kayte snorted. "Forget all that. There's one way to do this: hard, fast, painful. Though I'm curious how you expect to *make* it harder, Dahe.

I've been trying to run out the Shar vermin since before I was elected, carrying on my mother's work. I still haven't found all the tricks."

"I've got tricks of my own," Aeley said with a sly grin, "and people who'll bring all the hurt." She prompted Adren to stand. "You've all met Adren, but there are things many of you don't know. First, ce is the only child of Boss Rivane that isn't in prison. Second, ce can do things we can't. Adren?"

Half the room looked confused as Adren shifted cir feet. "Magic," Adren said, clearing cir throat. "The priests can tell you more, but I've got it. It's what I did for the Shar, making things disappear, changing them, getting in and out of situations no one else could. I can do it for you, too. Make raids tougher. Give you an edge, better weapons, sniff out leads."

"Wait, *what?*" Rosayra stared open-mouthed at Adren. "I'd call that an incredibly tall tale, but the councilmen look smug, so..." Her hands waved erratically. "How long have you been sitting on this nugget of ludicrous, Dahe?"

Aeley smirked. "Long enough, though Adren's been kind enough to offer cir help."

"Attacking priests is disgusting," Adren muttered. "They've gone too far in every direction and used me to do it. So fine, I'll tell them where to shove their pretty little explosives. You want it hard and painful? I'll get you bone-cracking and agonizing."

A dark smile crept across Kayte's lips. "Sounds like you and me need to talk."

"There's plenty of time to make friends," Severn drawled, "but save it for later. Are you in, Oaren?"

"Guess so." Kayte returned Severn's annoyed tone. "Can't let Dahe get into trouble alone."

"Please," Aeley said, snorting.

"And again, *save it for later*." Severn tapped the table. "We need everyone you can get, all the resources you can spare or repurpose. Pull in your guards, any and all tacticians from the Grand Families, and work out new strategies."

Rathen whistled and reached for Aeley. "Bring Gren in. He'd love a piece of this."

"You sure?" Aeley eyed Rathen, her uncertainty echoing Mayr's. While they liked Gren, his lack of loyalty to any one employer was questionable. In true mercenary fashion, Gren could be purchased with the right price—the same reason they had not invited him to the meeting. The Shar-denn could have already claimed him.

"Yeah, I'm sure." Rathen scowled. "He doesn't like the Shar any more than he does politicians. Gren's got bones to pick with them, trust me. Tell him he can settle his scores and he'll be your best friend. If that isn't enough, you tell Tracel and *she'll* remind him what side he's on."

"Very well, I'll think on it," Aeley conceded.

Lira let out an audible breath, her grey gaze

downcast. "It's like we're going to war."

"No, there is no 'like,'" Kayte said. "It *is* war, just not on a battlefield."

"Ha!" Rosayra spat out. "Kattal already fought to get free from one master. We'll win this rubbish, too."

"That's good, you'll need that," Nimae said, shifting with a grimace, "because if the Shar's willing to take down temples, they'll do a hundred other things you never saw coming." He nodded at the councilmen. "They've got lists of faces they'd love to carve up. Severn and Cota, you're on the must-die list, near the top. You might want to reconsider your security detail. Make sure you're still alive every morning."

Awkward silence fell through the room. A chill swept through Mayr, pushing his watchfulness to its peak. Tash had warned him of Nimae's brutal honesty. It was one thing to anticipate that honesty, but another thing to be in the same room with it.

Ress cleared his throat. "They're not the only ones with names. May I?"

"Absolutely," Aeley replied. "You said you had gifts."

"Two." Ress reached into his coat and pulled out a folded piece of parchment. "The first is a gift of knowledge." He inhaled deeply and fingered the parchment. After another nervous breath, he offered it to Aeley. "Four names. They're more than Shar sympathizers—they help keep it going."

Aeley scurried around Adren to snatch the parchment. As she read it over, her face darkened until it was blood-red. The paper crumpled in her paled fists.

"I'm going to shove that pacifism *so far* up his ass he won't have a head *left*," Aeley snarled, jerking her head up. She thrust the parchment towards Kayte, her fist shaking.

In a flash, Kayte was at the table, grabbing the list and reading it.

"*What in the Four's name is this?*" Kayte roared. More than one guard flinched. "One of your own assemblymen's on the inside!" He tossed the parchment at Cota. "No wonder you can't keep up. What have you fools been *doing*—raising *spies*?"

Shouts deafened Mayr from all sides. Bodies moved in a blur. High Council's guards charged Kayte, their swords drawn, while Kayte's guards responded in kind, forcing their way between him and the councilmen. Rosayra stayed at Kayte's side, knife brandished as she called for a stay of attack. Pellon yanked Lira from her chair and pulled her to Aeley's side, then pushed both back with one arm, allowing Dahe guards to fill the space where Aeley and Lira had been. On instinct, Mayr shoved Tash behind Gorgan and stepped in front of them both.

Mayr whistled shrilly until movement stopped. "Everyone get back to your own corners!" He motioned to make his point, snapping his fingers until the guards backed away. "Unless someone here's a traitor, no one's drawing blood. Put those things away, and Ress, explain this mess *now*."

From where he sat with Adren behind him, Ress regarded the guards with a wary expression. "I had access to *several* things the Shar shouldn't have let me near," he replied. "Pertinent members valued my skills. Others coveted my ability to traffic whatever they wanted, discreetly and for a decent price. Funny thing is, those people talk, and *their* people talk, particularly when they think no one's listening. I also figured out some things on my own. If anyone's a spy here, it's *me*."

Ress pointed at the wrinkled list in Cota's hands. "The first name is unfortunate. They all are. There's nothing I can do but tell you that Tract Steward Forey's name has appeared in my presence several times. He feeds the Shar information and harbours them. I've shipped goods to and from his tertiary estate, which doubles as a Shar cache house. Given how difficult it is to get through the rocky passes, flooded ravines and bogs, and poisonous creatures, I'm not surprised he'd lend it over."

"I'll kill him," Aeley seethed, golden eyes narrowed. "That bastard—"

"*Aeley*." Lira nudged Aeley's arm. "Let him finish."

"The second is Commerce Assemblyman

Graye Jesfret, as Steward Oaren noted," Ress continued. "I don't know her exact role, except to say she knows what money says and where it hides." He peered over his shoulder to Aeley. "I'm sorry it won't assuage your concerns about Stewards Mahne and Hewyth. I don't know if they have anything to do with it. I *do* know Jesfret likes her men beaten and drugged before they reach her doorstep. I also know her trade name is Jessice Blue. She likes dirty money that smells clean."

Lower looked a breath away from being sick. "This third one," he said, pointing at the list. "We can't do anything about it, not without starting a war."

Ress nodded grimly. "Emisay Dematahl, Lord Councilman of Arminloa, Kattal's favourite nation to despise. I'm sorry for that, too, because apprehending him would mean another full-out battle. He's all bite, waiting for Kattal to give him a reason. He's the secret head of their Restitution Coalition—he's just hiding behind the fop they have pretending to be their leader." Ress let out a long, frustrated sigh. "Dematahl calls the shots in Arminloa and at our borders. He's also buying up weapons, including ones we've outlawed and ones our military has never had. The list of his hidden transgressions against Kattal is long."

Curses fluttered through the room, harsh and mangled.

"The last name is one to worry over," Ress said

quietly. "The Colourless faction. It's one of the best kept secrets in the Shar. They don't use names or visible forms of identification—no gang colours, no obvious tattoos, no crests or insignias. Only the bosses of the other factions know who the Colourless's boss is. They're a ghost faction, but take them out, and it'll really deal the hurt."

"How?" Severn demanded.

Ress crossed his arms and leaned back. "Their faction relies on members of the Grand Families."

More curses filled the room, bouncing from one person to another. Aeley and Kayte growled, their visible rage a match to that on Cota and Severn's faces.

"They sink funds into the Shar," Ress continued, "manipulate Council, use other families, and feed the Shar from the top. Then it all trickles down, and well, you've seen the results."

"*Dammit*," Mayr swore under his breath. It was bad enough figures of authority worked for the Shar-denn, but some of the wealthiest and most influential families *willingly* supported them. What all did the Shar-denn know? How much danger were Aeley and Lira in? What about Dahena and all of Gailarin, especially if another Tract Steward had shared tract secrets?

What about Allon and his unsavoury lot? Are they in on it, using the Dahe name to get off on being so bloody clever? And what about Lira's whole damn family? Darkness reaches for darkness, and if they're part of it…

A quick glance at Aeley was enough to suggest the same possibilities turned over in her thoughts, as ugly as the look on her face.

Severn's nostrils flared. "Great. Filthy little liars are playing both sides. What other names have you been hiding?" she all but shouted at Ress. She clawed the table edge as though she wanted to shred his face. "All this time and you *never* said a word—"

"*Who cares?*" Kayte yelled. "We've got bigger things to worry about!"

Ress raised his hand, steadily meeting Severn's glare. "I didn't give the names because I knew there'd be a war if I did. Now war's upon us and the Shar deserves all the hurt to come." He lowered his hand, his expression sad. "There's one more name I can provide, one I didn't realize I had until several months ago. I'm truly sorry, because I don't want to say it, but I have to." Turning in his chair, he glanced up at Pellon. "Sorys Emeranth, your father."

All sound ceased. No one moved. Silence twisted a gnawing ache through Mayr's stilled heart.

Pellon looked as if he were dying, his last moments frozen between beats of time.

Aeley's arms were around Pellon's shoulders quicker than Mayr could force himself to breathe. Lira hugged Pellon around the waist, murmuring soothing words.

"I'm sorry, Pellon," Ress said softly. "You're a nice guy, and you've been good to me and Adren, but you need to put eyes on Sorys and Wynn."

"You're certain?" Aeley pulled Pellon closer. He remained speechless, motionless.

"Wouldn't say it if I weren't." Ress sighed heavily. "I've heard Sorys's name for years. He runs covert fighting leagues for the Shar, but I've also seen his name on records for goods. He's both a supplier *and* a buyer. I don't think he's in it alone, either: Wynn knows what's going on, considering all the freshly mined jewels and pretty metals that come through. Money, too, and the women, the men..." Ress peered at Pellon. "I'm sorry, really. They like their slaves, especially going through them. I don't know what they do to need so many, but I've heard stories. By the Four, I wish you weren't their kid."

Pellon's empty gaze fell on Ress. "Now I know where the servants come from. Where my mother..."

Mayr bit back the replies that came to mind. He knew Pellon's fears about his mother, a servant who had disappeared after his birth, never to be heard from again. Everything else Pellon knew was what Sorys and Wynn had bludgeoned into his head, fashioning him into what they wanted: an heir to both Sorys's sport fighting champion titles and Wynn's mining enterprise. Pellon loathed both legacies. He had no mind for business, and when he fought, he wanted to serve a larger purpose, not win status.

The more terrifying points of Pellon's past were in the details of his fathers' relationship. Wynn had the money and Sorys the gall. Pellon insisted his parents were married because Sorys loved to beat the life out of Wynn, accompanied by the threadbare illusion that Wynn was somehow in control. No doubt they kept slaves and went through them like they meant nothing: Pellon recalled overhearing things when he was a child, including Sorys's angry voice between loud slaps, cracking bones, and muffled screams for help, not all of them Wynn's. The violence only worsened when Wynn disappeared on business. To discover they were part of the Shar-denn was abominable but not a complete surprise.

Ress's breath was the loudest noise in the room. "If we're going to take down the Shar," he said, "we need to hit suppliers and buyers, too. Attack on multiple fronts."

Heads nodded. Murmurs collided, crafting a soft hum.

Ress's chair screeched across the floor, and the room fell quiet. "Since we're in agreement, here's my second gift," he said. Clicks sounded as he unlocked his metal case. "A new weapon, something I've been perfecting. Steward Oaren, you'll enjoy this."

More than curious, Mayr grabbed Tash by the hand and followed Kayte to the table. The case creaked as Ress opened the lid and withdrew a peculiar object: a smooth cylinder of charcoal-coloured metal streaked with dull black, attached to a handle crafted from the same metals and polished red wood that fit snugly in Ress's grasp. Jutting out from where the cylindrical piece met handle was a thick loop of metal big enough to slip at least one finger through and an angled switch.

"Fully functional," Ress said. He twisted his wrist to show both sides of the weapon. "Something the Shar's been working on for a while now. They're calling it a pistol after Pistoleyra, Maiden of the Mountain, because of her deadly darts that pierce armour and drill through bone. It's easy to carry, even easier to kill from a distance. If the Shar succeeds, they'll give these to members and sell them to allies. Swords and knives don't stop these unless you slice off the hand that holds it—just like Pistoleyra."

Mayr cursed vehemently. *That* was Ress's secret project. If the Shar-denn had such weapons, the number of victims would no doubt triple... or worse. A nightmare larger than even his dreams could encompass.

"The how of it is a complicated mess that's taken years to sort, and it's required more people than I can count, so I won't bother explaining. Here's what you need to know." Ress held out the pistol and pointed to different parts. "Barrel, grip, trigger, sight, and hammer for when you're ready to do the damage," he said, dragging his thumb over the switch.

Ress's fingers moved quickly over the grip. A metal chamber shot out from the bottom. He tipped the chamber forward to reveal a hollow compartment with small metal components. "Projectiles go in here. It'll take four just fine, but I'm working on one that allows more." From the case, he pulled out a handful of black metal pieces no larger than game tokens on a board, the rounded ends tipped with silver. "Put them in this way, replace—" Ress shoved the chamber back inside the grip with a loud click "—and it's ready. Aim with one arm like this, click back the hammer, sight it, then squeeze the trigger to send it off. It's got kick and takes effort at first, but once you get it, you *get it*."

"That's… unnerving," Lira said, wrapping her arms around herself. She backed away from the table. "Doing away with life just like that. No struggle, no fight."

"They'll do anything to seize control quickly and efficiently," Ress replied.

And make the world fall at their feet. Mayr stared at the pistol, unable to look away. The Shar-denn destroyed hundreds of lives with the weapons they already had. The lethal power granted by a collection of pistols was unfathomable. Although he never liked spilling blood, he would kill a thousand of the Shar-denn before allowing them to hurt his family or anyone else, even if it destroyed his soul. No mercy, no compassion, no apology. Nothing but hope.

"Want me to demonstrate?" Ress's voice slipped through Mayr's messy thoughts. "It's loud, so you'll have to cover your ears, but I can show it off… unless someone *else* wants to do it."

Mayr barely noticed the silence, transfixed until someone cleared their throat.

"What?" Mayr shook his head and glimpsed Aeley's smirk.

Ress held out the pistol. "Want a go?" He motioned to the target. "Everything's set up."

Under the heat of everyone's attention, Mayr nodded and accepted the pistol. Heavy like his boot, smooth like his knives, the pistol was a dangerous weight in anyone's hands. So much hurt contained in one cold form. "How loud?"

Ress studied Mayr, his dark gaze pensive. "Not enough to wake your girls."

"Good to know." Mayr pushed past the people in his way, the pistol lowered. He stepped into line with the target, facing it while he backed against the table.

"Everyone else, stand back here," Ress called. "Cover your ears."

No one hesitated to obey. They hurried to the wall furthest from the target.

"Mind the recoil," Ress added.

Mayr took a deep breath and clicked back the hammer, feeling the barest movements of the mechanisms inside. He straightened his back, pulled his body into form, and focused. The red circle in the middle of the target taunted him, waiting to be hit. With the pistol in his right hand, he lifted his arm and aimed, two fingers slipped around the trigger. The pistol wavered in his hand.

It was a life's worth of responsibility in one fist, a soul's name written on every projectile. It was a quick journey to the Realm of the Dead with an even quicker trip to the gates of guilt and lifelong regret.

But the Shar-denn was willing to take out temples and who knew what else to settle scores with Tash and anyone in their way. Nothing would stop them from blowing up homes or entire villages. Rules meant nothing. Guilt meant nothing. Suffering the death of an enemy was better than letting them take innocent lives.

No matter what High Council thought of him, rules would not stop Mayr from putting the gang in its place however he could. Whatever it took, he would protect his own. Cota had once warned him he would have to choose between loyalty to Kattal's laws or Tash. That choice was now, this meeting, this cause. *Generation after generation we've played by the rules, and look where it's gotten us—the muddy end of ass-crack nowhere.*

Playing nice was foolish, just as surrendering Tash, Adren, and Ress would be. *They won't stop their attacks, no matter who they get back. They want and want and want some more, and they'll blow more temples to get it all. If it isn't Tash, it'll be Rivane and other prisoners, or the heads of politicians and things they shouldn't have.*

To his relief, the High Council agreed. So far they had not uttered a word about giving up Tash, at least not to his face, but Mayr never knew how long he could trust them. The sooner they cleaned up the Shar-denn, the sooner Tash could enjoy true freedom with their family.

I can do this. I have to do this. For Aliss, Arieve, and him, Mayr promised. He cupped his other hand beneath the grip and sighted the target. *For Aeley, Lira, and everyone else, too.*

The pistol steadied. Breaths slow and even, he called on the shred of calm he needed, the same as he did whenever he threw knives. He focused on the centre...

A squeeze of the trigger sent thunder through the room, echoing as his shoulder slammed back.

Near the centre of the target, a hole was blown clear through, as wide as his finger. Mayr winced and lowered the pistol, his aching shoulder demanding Tash's gentle touch. His ears rang, muffling the sounds behind him, and his hands trembled. The target was cracked around the middle and bits of wood lay on the floor. One shot equaled the power of battle stuffed into a tiny metal cage. He could imagine how many holes the Task Force would put in the Shar-denn.

Enough to bring them to their knees. Mayr stared at the target, its darkness as empty as their lives would be if they lost the battle.

So we won't lose. There's no alternative but to win, whatever it takes.

Arms wrapped around him from the side, soft fabric sweeping over his skin as the scent of sweet incense wafted around him. Lips pressed to his cheek, murmuring words he could not hear but felt. Tash's hand clasped his, steadying his fingers and the pistol. His heart, his sanity, his partner in the fight…

The Shar-denn would never have Tash again, no matter what Mayr had to do.

We're stronger together, unified better than any Task Force. We're the bound souls that'll mess the Shar up. We're the nasty bit of Emeraliss that'll love those bastards straight into torture. Both go in, both come out, because there's only life, only love, only this.

Fin

Playlist for Soulbound

(Artists and songs are listed in alphabetical order)

Themes:
Dala — Butterfly to Wasp
Midnight Hour — Running Away
Sarah Brightman — Eden (Enigma Remix)
Secret Garden — Prayer
Secret Garden — Sleepsong
Tove Lo — Scars

Mayr & Tash themes:
Marianas Trench — One Love
Savage Garden — Truly, Madly, Deeply

Tash theme:
One Republic — Say (All I Need)

Rest of the Playlist!
A Great Big World — Say Something (feat. Christina Aguilera)

Bonnie Raitt — I Can't Make You Love Me
Bush X — Glycerine

Craig Armstrong — A Fool to Believe (from the film, "Moulin Rouge")

Darren Hayes — Insatiable

Ed Sheeran — Give Me Love
Enigma — Age of Loneliness
Enigma — Carly's Song (Remix)
Enigma — Return to Innocence

Evanescence — Anywhere
Evanescence — Before the Dawn
Evanescence — Forgive Me
Evanescence — Lost in Paradise
Evanescence — Missing
Evanescence — Understanding

Florence & the Machine — Over the Love

Halsey — Castle
Halsey — Haunting

Joseph Trapanese – Amity (from the film, "Insurgent")

Lindsey Stirling — Shatter Me (feat. Lzzy Hale)
Loreena McKennitt — Samain Night
Loreena McKennitt — The Old Ways

Marina & the Diamonds — Immortal
Marina & the Diamonds — Lies (Acoustic)

Mario Spinetti — When You Say My Name
Metric — Gold Guns Girls (Acoustic)

Placebo — Running Up That Hill

Radical Face — The Gilded Hand

The Weeknd — As You Are
The Weeknd — Love in the Sky
The Weeknd — Tears in the Rain
The Weeknd — What You Need (Remix)
The Weeknd — Where You Belong
Tom Odell — Another Love
Tori Amos — Caught A Lite Sneeze
Tori Amos — I Can't See New York

Within Temptation — Towards the End

The Republic will continue in
Rebel Call

If there's one thing Dawne Akene knows well, it's how life falls apart when he touches it. Years after the tragic loss of his family, work as a mason keeps his hands busy, but his head and heart are stuck on a past he can never get back—and the urge to stir a little trouble isn't helping.

When he attends a celebration known for being utterly seductive, however, one sensual night with Massy and Geyle offers more than just a warm bed.

Massy Kolhayn and Geyle Venerathe are no strangers to tragedy or the need to trade one lot in life for another. Geyle keeps his head down, his work a distraction from a past he has to forget, while Massy is a keeper of secrets, including the fact that ne feels things changing in the republic— a slow creep of darkness that could ruin lives.

The same darkness that intends to take Geyle down with a murder he didn't commit.

In a race to save Geyle from prison, their budding romance could completely fall apart. Though there's an even bigger problem: not only will they break the law, they'll have to violate a generations-old pact among their people—and destroy their lives completely.

Author's Note

Hi, and thanks for giving this a read! If you're new to this series, many welcomes, and if this isn't your first time around, welcome back! <3

This book was a surprise, and it just kept growing. I hadn't planned on revisiting Mayr and Tash's relationship in such a focused way—just little glimpses of them from other characters' perspectives. But a side novella made its way onto the To Write list while I was working on *Blood Borne*, and it's snowballed into another two books, bringing Mayr and Tash's story up to a three-book storyline: *Four*, *Soulbound*, and what's currently planned to be the final book in the series, *A Matter of Fate*.

In true Mayr style, they've hijacked the series. This isn't a short, happy novella to tie off loose ends: it's an entire turnabout for everyone in the series. Decisions made here have ramifications in the rest of the books, right up to the very end. Mayr and Tash are in the middle of things and privy to the war efforts that are now on the table. Things have changed for them as a couple—and the fight is just getting harder. More intense.

Their relationship is maturing, and they have even more to defend now that Arieve, Aliss, and Coye are involved. Hard decisions are coming, some that'll hurt more than others.

Like *Blood Borne*, this one was darker, particularly where Tash is concerned. How he presents outwardly and what he keeps to himself are very different things, and he struggles with mental health on a regular basis. The gang screwed him up—there's no way around that. He fell too far and now lives the consequences. Complex PTSD was already going to stay with him for a long time, but now there's entirely new trauma to deal with. For him, it's a matter of learning how to cope in a healthy way and turn to Mayr for help instead of handling it all alone. For all of Tash's fears and hurt, Mayr's desire to take care of him is a powerful force, righting them when things go wrong. There's a balance there: as soon as one starts struggling, the other steps in to keep them going.

But they also have a support system that can help, and as their found family continues to grow, Mayr and Tash will be taken right along with it. There are really tough times ahead but they won't be alone in the fight. And they still don't know the deepest secrets about their soulbinding... a truth that will come out eventually.

So here ends this trilogy inside the larger series. This book was such a long journey! It took over 1.5 years to write and edit, but it finally got out there. And for that, I have to thank several people.

First, such big thanks to Hudson and Victoria for beta reading this beast! Your thoughts on it really helped! (P.S. Victoria, you were *totally* the one who finally made me believe adding the map was a Most Necessary Thing. Thanks for that extra push!) And A.M. Valenza, thank you for the advice when I was freaking out over certain aspects—being able to talk it out calmed things down so much.

As always, thanks to Sam, Megan, Sasha, and Less Than Three Press for their unwavering support and for giving this book (and me) such a wonderful literary home. You've made all the difference. <3

Many, many thanks also go to my editor for the first edition, Constance Blye, for helping tighten this up originally; Nastasha Snow for the gorgeous cover that's *exactly* what I was hoping for (OMG, YOU MADE IT HAPPEN!!!); and Raelynn Marie, your map is everything I dreamed of! So right on I could cry.

And thank you—with all my heart, thank you—to

my partner for putting up with me and the authorly stuff! It's not easy but thank you for taking this journey with me. <3 xoxoxo

Finally, but certainly not least, thank you to you, readers! It's so humbling to have you all with me along the way. Thanks for being here and spending a bit of time. <3

So where does it all go from here?

Short answer: it's going to get a lot dirtier. The Shar-denn's started their version of an urban war, further complicated by a weapons race. It's not going to be an easy ride for anyone. Buckle up because here we go.

The long answer: the main story arc continues in book #5, *Rebel Call*, with brand new characters, Dawne, Massy, and Geyle. After that, books #6 and #7 (*Hunter* and *Light from Shadow*) focus on Rathen and Kirra. It's time the bounty hunters really get to work.

I do have plans to write book #4.5, however— Arieve and Coye's book, *Heartfastened*. I couldn't tell their story in this one because it's a novel on its own, so I separated it out instead of cramming it in. Don't know when it'll happen, but it's hanging around, waiting patiently!

But there are plenty of secrets coming and more about characters I haven't been able to reveal. That was one of the best things about writing this book, actually: getting to reveal details I hadn't been able to previously due to the POVs, mostly about Kee and Armamae who don't advertise or talk publicly about their personal lives. Very few characters know Kee is trans or that she's from an incredibly strict, cult-styled religion and has fought her way through life—she's a very private person. And most wouldn't realize what Armamae's survived or how much he actually knows. But both are important, and they have a soft spot for those in need, no different than certain other characters... but those are details to come.

For more about what's coming in the series or about my other projects, come by my website or find me on social media! My links are on the very last page. I love hearing from folks, so stop on by and say hi sometime!

Blessings and peace to you all,

Archer

Also by Archer Kay Leah

THE REPUBLIC SERIES
A Question of Counsel (The Republic, book 1)
Four (The Republic, book 2)
Blood Borne (The Republic, book 3)
Soulbound (The Republic, book 4)

NOVELS
For the Clan

NOVELLAS
Heart, Lace, and Soul
Of Kindred and Stardust

About The Republic Series

Welcome to *The Republic*, high fantasy romances for across the LGBTQA+ spectrum, where love, fight, and hope are at the very core, entwined with the lives of romantic partners, friends, and families… and maybe a few lifelong enemies, too. Come step into their world where games linger and foul play is afoot!

•••

Democracy. Family. Loyalty. Honour.
The perfect system.

Freedom. Belonging. Unity.
The perfect illusion.

With the right people and the right price, the Republic of Kattal can be brought to its knees.

Peace and security are never a guarantee when greed and lies threaten the balance. Fear and control know no bounds; and sacred tenets don't keep the monsters away. The right to choose can be a nightmare.

But for every line crossed, someone waits on the other side, ready to push back.

In justice, there is wisdom. In wisdom, there is protection. In it all, there is love. Maybe it means saving a village; maybe it means saving someone you can't live without. Sometimes it's just about doing the right thing and learning to love yourself.

Magic may lurk in the shadows.
Crime may never sleep.
But love doesn't back down.

THE REPUBLIC 3

BLOOD BORNE

ARCHER KAY LEAH

THE REPUBLIC 4

SOULBOUND

ARCHER KAY LEAH

About the Author

Archer Kay Leah was raised in Canada, growing up in a port town at a time when it was starting to become more diverse, both visibly and vocally. Combined with the variety of interests found in Archer's family and the never-ending need to be creative, this diversity inspired a love for toying with characters and their relationships, exploring new experiences and difficult situations.

Archer most enjoys writing speculative fiction and is engaged in a very particular love affair with fantasy, especially when it is dark and emotionally charged. When not reading and writing for work or play, Archer is a geek with too many hobbies and keeps busy with other creative endeavors, a music addiction, and whatever else comes along. Archer lives in London, Ontario with a non-binary partner who loves video games, composing music, and all things out there in the vast space of the universe.

Website: archerkayleah.wordpress.com
Goodreads: goodreads.com/ArcherKayLeah
Facebook: www.facebook.com/ArcherKayLeah
Twitter: twitter.com/archerkayleah

www.ingramcontent.com/pod-product-compliance
Lightning Source LLC
Chambersburg PA
CBHW030839030726
47495CB00005B/1298